GW01085618

THOSE WHO
LIVED BY THE
SWORD

BOOK TWO: THE SEEDS OF OUR DESTRUCTION

J. EDWARDS

EDITED BY MARIKO IRVING

Copyright © 2024 by Jonathan Edwards

All rights reserved. This book or any portion thereof may not be reproduced or used in any manner whatsoever without the express written permission of the publisher except for the use of brief quotations in a book review.

Printed in the United States of America

First Printing, 2024

ISBN-13: 979-8-9886040-8-2

EireneBros Publishing LLC
4414 82nd St, Ste 212, -318
Lubbock, TX 79424

www.eirenebrospublishing.com

To those who wish to see

THOSE WHO LIVED BY THE SWORD

BOOK TWO: THE SEEDS OF OUR DESTRUCTION

J. EDWARDS

EDITED BY MARIKO IRVING

Chapter 1

Home Sweet Home

The winds howled like a banshee in the night. He clutched onto his coat as his body shivered uncontrollably. Cain shivered as the ice-cold breeze sliced through his three layers of clothing easily. His socks were completely soaked, and his gloves were as effective as using a squirt gun to fight a forest fire. He was beginning to think that if the hypothermia did not kill him, the frostbite or gangrene would.

Wisps of snow blew through his hood, but he hardly noticed. His face was so numb from the cold that he could get punched in the nose and not feel a thing. With each step Cain took, he felt a growing sense of regret. Everything about this frigid climb up the mountain just seemed fundamentally wrong.

He pulled out an old wand and a large Firestone from his bag. The items he held seemed normal. The magic wand was made from a centuries-old redwood and covered in cobwebs. The only thing remarkable about the wand was that the head was shaped like a diamond with three ruby power stones embedded in it. No magical energy emanated from the jeweled stones, rendering them useless. The large Firestone in his right hand was equally unimpressive. There was absolutely no magic left in it. Usually, the rock would be a bright orange or red and feel warm. Instead of the bright and vibrant rock, the stone was cold and scorched from extensive use. Despite the seeming nature of the magical items in his hands that required him to risk his own life to steal, he knew his master must have bigger and better plans for these items.

The *Orias* sect of the Daimonia was notorious for finding new creative ways to cause pain and destruction. For the most part, Cain understood why their organization was the most violent and aggressive of the Daimonia factions. The *Orias* branch was considered "the bastards of the party," the black sheep of the demonic family. Their sect wasn't among the original twelve Daimonia organizations and was begrudgingly included as the thirteenth member. The *Orias* group was the most underfunded Daimonia group, which was why he was trudging up this godforsaken mountain. Unlike the other Daimonia groups with beautiful tropical island bases and offices in top-of-the-line skyscrapers, his sect set up shop in the northernmost mountain range in Aggeloi, called the *Devil's Corridor*. The mountain range was so named because it was home to the world's second-largest mountain in a virtually unlivable region.

The Daimonia chose the most desolate mound of dirt of them all, called *Mount Dirge*. This mountain was filled with rocks, caves, and giant insects. There was practically no vegetation, save for a few thorn bushes that just loved to entangle unfortunate travelers. No animals lived on this mountain; the birds and dragons avoided *Mount Dirge* like the plague. The cherry on top of this horrible hiking trail was that if you did not know which cave to enter, you could be eaten by one of the giant earthworms that made the interior of the Mountain Range their home.

He hated this place, and if he could turn back time, he would have never left Eiréné. Nothing good has come from his time in the Daimonia. He saw the world and discovered he had one full and two half-brothers. The Dark Prince, Drake, and Jason were the best brothers a boy could have...if that boy also wanted to become a murdering psychopath. But what else was he supposed to do? The only other home he had known was burned to the ground. Jayden and Sarah were better off without him. They didn't need a guy like him around, not with his past.

A blast of wind knocked him backward as he struggled up the mountain's west side. As Cain slid down the side of the mountain, he reached out for a protruding branch to stop his descent toward the edge of a cliff. He felt a sharp, burning sensation when his hand gripped a branch. Red droplets of blood stained the snowy ground. He took a moment to examine the bush that saved his life and realized that he had grabbed onto the thorns of a PoisonBerry Bush. *That is just great,* he thought. *My hand is bleeding, and now I will have a severe migraine from the poison.*

It took him a minute, but eventually, Cain regained his composure and got back on his feet. Then, he heard a voice shouting at him from further up the mountain. "You doing alright down there? You look a little lost. I can get a bandage for you."

The young man from Eiréné glanced up and noticed a warrior dressed in a dark cloak. Cain could see his blonde hair protruding from beneath the hood. He had a large bow across his back with a quiver full of arrows of every shape and color you could imagine. A long sword also hung on the lefthand side of his hip.

Cain grinned, "Well, if it isn't my half-brother Jason. Back from the war already."

Jason smiled, "My first name is Sergeant, and don't you forget it."

"That's hilarious. It's kinda hard to be a Sergeant without a real army. Did you even leave the army a two weeks notice? Or was helping to destroy a city a clear enough message for them?" Cain replied.

"Despite my pretenses for joining the army, I am proud of my work and was honored to serve. But this cause is bigger than any one army. Now let's get you inside; just a forewarning: the heater has malfunctioned." Jason said as he led his brother back up the mountain.

His brother guided him along a bend on the mountain's western side. The ground beneath their feet grew slicker the closer they got to the cave. The mouth of the cave was an unnaturally dark blue color from the ice and the magic crystals that decorated its frame. Sharpened icicles hung from the ceiling, giving the visual impression that they were walking into the jaws of an Ice Dragon.

Cain clutched onto his coat even tighter as he felt the temperature drop below 0. The negative energy expelled from the cave was overwhelming. With every breath, he inhaled the toxic and evil presence that filled his Arctic home. But he had no choice; it was too late to back out now. He had made his decision. Plus, he knew that the Fallen Wizard was here, and there was no way he would let him go.

His skin crawled at the soft sound of old sandals shuffling along the icy floor. A shadowy figure approached them slowly from deep within the cave. Cain struggled to embrace the familiar demonic orchestra of an old wooden cane gently tapping against the frosty floor and wheezing as their greeter drew closer. The old man was draped in a mossy green cloak that had faded over the years. His cheeks were sunken, and his orange eyes were as pale as a ghost.

The wizard struggled with every step, and he wheezed as he breathed. His arms and leg muscles were about as thin as a piece of paper. To most people, he would have appeared as threatening as a butterfly. There was an unwavering sense of determination about him, making the wizard so imposing. The old man had survived for thousands of years in this broken

10

state with a combination of wit and immeasurable magic power.

"My Dear Cain," the Fallen Wizard said in a hushed tone. "Were you able to acquire the items I asked for?"

He bowed respectfully to his master and removed the items beneath his cloak. "I retrieved them successfully, but I don't think these items will do any good."

The wizard reached out for the Firestone and examined its rigid surface. His pale eyes widened for a second and began to regain their normal orange color. Cain couldn't imagine the value the Fallen Wizard saw in that magic rock. The old man didn't even bother to examine the old wand. Cain thought this was just a setup to get him back.

His master stared at him as if he could peer directly into Cain's mind. With a toothy grin, the Fallen Wizard said, "Things are not always what they may seem, my young warrior. The magic in objects like this never truly goes away. In truth, these items will be just as important to us as *The Key* itself. Now, I want you to come with me down to the dungeon. There is someone I want you to meet.

Chapter 2

A Bird in a Cage

His footsteps made a hollow sound as he descended the concrete steps. Cain knew he could walk this path with his eyes closed because he knew this set of stairs better than most. He would spend the rest of his time slumming it in the dungeon when he wasn't conducting missions away from the base.

The prison itself was separated into three different pods. The first pod was where they kept prisoners of human or elven descent. Now, the second dorm was where they housed the dwarves. The third dormitory is where they keep any individuals with magical or enchanted abilities. Anti-magic technology imbued the prison bars and shackles in the third pod. Most members of the Daimonia were completely unaware that there was a fourth holding facility.

The fourth lockdown facility existed one flight below the third dormitory. For a staff member to gain access to it, the individual must be of a high rank and know precisely how to unlock the enchantments to where the door was hidden.

The fourth pod was relatively small. There were only four cells, with a maximum capacity of six individuals, housed in the dorm. This facility was designed for high-level targets that required the tightest security.

For Cain, this was a little unusual. In all of the times he's worked in the jail, there was never a prisoner kept in the fourth dorm for an extended period. The few he could recall were waiting to be executed or transferred to another location. Whoever they were going to see in custody was going nowhere fast. From what he remembered during his training; the Fallen Wizard installed at least half of the enchantments set up for this pod. There was only one way out and one way in.

Only a few Daimonia members were allowed to enter the fourth dormitory. The best-trained and most powerful members of the prison security force were the only staff members allowed to serve in this part of the facility. Since the security of the prison and the enchantments were second to none, it would make any attempt to escape the absolute definition of futility.

Once they reached the bottom of the staircase, Cain remembered why he hated coming down here. The dorm's ceiling and walls were painted in a pale green color. The longer you stared at the walls, the blander and more tedious the pod seemed to be. In this part of the jail, it was always eerily quiet. Cain never enjoyed coming to this part of the facility because it always felt like someone was watching him. He could easily see how a prisoner could go crazy in this pod.

Besides being creepy, the building was about as comfortable as a freezer. Even in the summers, the fourth dorm was extremely drafty. In reality, Cain didn't care who they would see; he wanted to leave this creepy place as soon as possible.

The head of dorm security beckoned for them to follow down a hall. They passed by two sets of empty cells and continued toward the back of the facility. The lights in the dorm were usually kept in great shape and were always shining bright. This time, however, the lightbulbs were flashing on and off sporadically. Even the lampshades were swinging back and forth from the ceiling.

As his eyes focused on the oddities in the room, out of nowhere, he felt a sudden intense pressure deep inside of his chest and found it tough to breathe. A sense of fear and dread grew with him the closer they got to the prisoner. Powerful magic was expelling from their captive's cell; it was almost too overwhelming. Cain was also beginning to understand how powerful the Fallen Wizard must be, even with his frail body and the magic in the air.

His master stopped in front of the cell and gave a respectful bow. Cain peered into the cell, and a middle-aged woman sat in the cold room. The prisoner lifted her head and gazed at them with an empty stare like she was looking through them. She had attractive brown eyes and a gentle smile, but there was no amount of joy in it. Her matted and unkempt hair was dark with traces of blue in it. Her body looked like she had been starving for months, and it was a terrible sight.

He noticed an odd material beneath her light blue prison gown. Cain tried to get a better look and realized that she had bandages across her chest, extending to both shoulders. She didn't appear to be in pain, but it was clear to him that she had barely survived her last fight. He glanced down and was shocked at the restraints on her wrists. They were the size of a large Bangle and made of an Elderian metal. Usually, there would be a solid green light that connected the restraints to both of her wrists. The light flashed bright red as the anti-magic handcuffs struggled to contain her magic. Cain had never seen the anti-magic bracelets this outmatched before. Who was this woman? And how could she be this strong?

A cruel smile creased her lips. "This wouldn't be Maverick's youngest son, would it?" She asked.

The Wizard wheezed and replied, "Yes, he is."

"The poor child," she sighed.

Cain glanced at her and then back at his master. "Who are you? And who is Maverick?"

She grinned at the Fallen Wizard, "So you still haven't told him? My name is Lady Coral of the Southern Convent and a former member of the Daimonia. And Lord Maverick is your father."

Cain shook his head, "How do you even know who I am? I don't even know who this Maverick is and if he really is my father. He can go to hell; he hasn't done a damn thing for me. I have done fine without him. Plus, aren't you the witch that Jayden went after? I thought he killed you."

Color began to return to her face as she prepared to answer. A large smile replaced her cruel grin, and she said, "Of course, I know who you are, Cain. I am Jayden's mother, after all. What kind of parent would I be if I didn't know his friends?"

For a second, Cain didn't know how to respond. It was complete BS; it had to be. He was there when Jayden's mother died. Cain remembered being at her funeral. There was no way this witch could be Jayden's mother.

Before he could reply, The Fallen Wizard said, "My lady, I'd prefer that you didn't get the boy all riled up. Now, I'm going to ask you this once. Does Elder's daughter have the map?"

Lady Coral nodded and replied. "She does but can't open the box. Lady Grace did not have the right key."

The Wizard laughed, "You were a fool to think you could plot against us, against me. You did not understand the power that you were trying to seek. The key you stole from that girl is the real one. You didn't have the blood of the Great Cryptologists flowing in your veins, but young Sarah does. But don't you fret, Miss. Corallina LoneOak, you still have a part to play in this."

Lady Coral gave him a smug look and rolled her eyes. "And what, Arthur, might this role be?"

The Fallen Wizard pulled the FireStone out from a pocket in his cloak. Lady Coral stared in disbelief and became fixated on the object cradled in his hand. He smirked, "I can tell by the look in your eyes that you understand what this is and what it requires to activate it. I will require your blood, the blood of a true fire magic user, to reactivate the magic in this stone. While I only need a few drops of your magic-filled blood, I will squeeze every ounce out of you. And if your pesky son gets in the way, I will drain the life out of him and maybe get two uses out of this."

Then he turned to Cain and said, "You will be the one to help me do it. There is already plenty of blood on your hands; it won't hurt to add another drop or two."

Cain felt like the walls of the dorm were closing in on him. The information flooding his mind from their conversation appeared too much for the warrior to process. He attempted to come across as composed and calm before his powerful audience. But he knew they could sense the struggle within him. Cain was a killer and executed people before; it was nothing new to him now. The last person he executed was the reason he left the Daimonia in the first place. Struggling with that dilemma nearly killed him, and now he was charged with killing Jayden's mother.

He quickly reached for his sword and tried to channel whatever willpower he had left to complete the deed. He felt a reassuring pat on his shoulder from his master. "Now, now, no need for that quite yet. Her hourglass still has a little bit of sand left in it. Let me educate you on souls who have become one with your craft. This information you have likely never heard. You would not get very far in defeating her by striking her down with that sword; a witch of her caliber can only be killed by magic. But don't worry, my young Cain, her time will come." The old man shifted his body and slowly began to shuffle away. When he reached the end of the corridor, he turned back to say, "And to think you thought that you could just come back here without a consequence, your arrogance knows no bounds. You truly are your father's son."

Chapter 3

Our Maiden Voyage

A cool breeze brushed against his skin, causing his body to stir. The gentle ocean spray was welcoming as he awoke from his dream. His dream looked so real and serene for a moment. He felt at peace. In his dream, all the horrors over the last few years were finally locked away, and he thought he could actually move on with his life. Unfortunately for him, in the end, it was all just an illusion, a trick of the imagination, a hopeful dream for a brighter future.

"Normally, you only smile like that when you see me," Sarah said as she sat on the bench across from him.

Jayden stretched as he sat up in the boat. He glanced up at the beautiful night sky. The full moon was shining with the radiance of the sun. A large Gray Hawk zoomed across the skies above, casting an imposing shadow against the moonlit backdrop. Seabass and black dolphins with fins that glowed in the dark jumped alongside their boat. The ocean's simplicity inspired him and reassured him that his dream of peace could come true.

Sarah kicked him in the shins for ignoring her. The sudden jolt of pain in his right leg and throbbing sensation caused him to sit up completely straight. "What the hell was that for?" He shouted.

"I said something nice to you, and you didn't even respond with your usual sarcasm. I was afraid that you didn't hear me." Sarah answered with a grin.

"O," Jayden replied as he sank back into his seat. "I did hear you; I just thought it would bug you more if I didn't respond."

After kicking his other shin, Sarah stood up and sat beside him. "So tell me, what were you smiling about?"

Jayden closed his eyes and said, "I had a dream we were all back in Eiréné. We even built Gracey a home of her own. It felt so real, like we were finally starting over. But it was just a dream."

"That would be amazing." Sarah beamed. "I'm sure Gracey would love you doing that for her."

"Probably not," said the princess from the deck below.

The floorboards creaked as Grace made her way up the steps. Once the princess reached the upper deck, dark clouds began to fill the sky, dampening the moon's light. Grace approached them, dressed in a black skirt, matching boots, and a T-shirt with some elven rock band that Jayden had never heard of. Even in the darkness of the night, he could make out that she was wearing latex gloves for some reason.

"So, how does it look?" She asked.

Sarah jumped up, filled with excitement. "It looks wonderful," she gleamed, with the biggest smile you could see in the dark.

Jayden glanced at both of them, feeling completely out of place. "Umm, how does what look?

"Are you blind, Jayden?" Sarah shouted loud enough for the dolphins to stop and take notice.

Jayden shrugged, feeling absolutely lost.

"She's talking about my hair. I changed it since you kept getting the two of us confused because her highlights are now red. And because the military and those pirates are still after us. So, do you like it?" Grace demanded.

"I can't tell it's too dark. I don't have magical see-in-the-dark eyes like Sarah." Jayden replied.

Then he snapped his fingers, and a white flickering light appeared above his thumb. Grace leaned in closer, and he examined her new look. Her hair was dyed a medium purple, with silver accents, and curled to complement the look. "You look amazing," he said.

Grace grinned, "Don't get any ideas. You can't afford me. Remember, I'm a princess."

"Whatever Gracey. I'm taking you on this fancy ocean cruise. What more do you want?" He replied.

They all laughed as Tony ran up the steps. His face showed concern, and he drew his weapon. He had channeled magic into his broadsword, making it glow light blue. He swung it over his head and shouted, "Heavy Fog!". Once those words left his lips, their visibility decreased. A thick and heavy fog gracefully moved throughout the ship. Within a few minutes, the gray mist billowed into the ocean and beyond the horizon.

Jayden lifted his hand, barely seeing it six inches from his face. The fog was thick enough for him to taste the moisture in the air. He reached for his .45 and pulled it out of his holster. Even though he couldn't see, he had to be ready for anything that might try to come on board.

From the moment they left Terracina, they were being pursued by the Eden military, Captain Rosso, and anybody else who didn't like them. Whenever a ship or boat got too close, Tony would summon a mighty storm to scare them away or help them escape. His magic made any situation extremely dangerous because once he started a storm, there was no telling when it would stop.

Thus far, they had been fortunate at getting away; they could even hide on a resort island for a few weeks. Every time they got close to the Eden mainland, their journey became more difficult. For the last two weeks, they had been traveling along the deep sea, trying to figure out how to reach his home country's West Coast. The worst part was that they were beginning to run low on fuel, and stopping off anywhere to get supplies was hazardous to their health.

He felt a hand reach out to him from within the fog. Sarah grabbed his forearm and led him to the main deck. Even though he couldn't see more than a foot in front of him, he could hear Tony pressing buttons on the ship's console. Somehow, his best friend could keep track of their surroundings while traveling in the fog; it must be an ability exclusive to storm magic users.

"We got a little out of their range," Tony said. "I'm unsure how long we can keep them off our tail."

"Great job with the fog spell!" Jayden said as he raised his hand to give his friend a high-five.

"Umm, you're facing the wrong direction. I'm over here." Tony replied, trying to fight a laugh as his friend kept turning around in a circle. "No, no, Jayden, I'm standing over here. There you go, now just a little to your left."

Jayden stopped, turned around, leaned forward, and bumped into something that felt solid. As he fumbled around to see where he was, it was at this point that he realized that his friend was a jackass. "Dude, were you trying to trick me into falling off the boat...again? One of these days, you will do your fog spell again, we'll get attacked, and I will be stuck in the ocean, unable to help. And you will be screwed."

Tony slapped him on the back, "I think we will be okay. Your specialty is fire, and we are surrounded by the water. How helpful would you be in a fight anyway?"

"Ouch. That was a good burn." Grace chuckled as she felt around in the fog and tripped over a bucket.

Jayden laughed, "Oo, look at that. I guess karma is a..."

Sarah put her hand over his mouth before he could finish his statement. "Now, Tony, as much as I'd love to see Jayden fall into the ocean again, we need a plan. Normally, you give us more of a heads-up before you do your magic. And that's the second time you've had to use that spell today. I know that's gotta be draining. What are we going to do?"

"The good thing is it's still pretty dark, and with the fog, we might able to shake 'em. But honestly, we're getting pretty low on fuel. We've gotta stop somewhere. Since I can see the best through the fog, I will stay up until it begins to fade away. There are a few islands nearby. Hopefully, they have what we will need. You all can get some rest for now," he replied.

Tony led them to their rooms. As soon as Jayden got to his, he crumbled on the bed. Usually, it wouldn't take him long to fall asleep, but the mattresses on this boat were tiny and uncomfortable. His legs hung over the side, and his living quarters were as spacious as a box of sardines. He didn't mind the boat swaying back and forth on the water; that made him feel most relaxed.

Jayden didn't like feeling trapped, and being below deck made him feel claustrophobic. So, he grabbed some bedding and proceeded toward the upper deck. Using the railing, he felt around until he reached his favorite bench. Once he placed his head on the pillow, he closed his eyes, and before he could count one sheep, he was out like a light.

His rest was peaceful; waking up was not. Jayden was dragged out of the world of dreams and happiness by receiving a pressurized blast of water up his nose. He flailed about from the pain as he tried not to fall over the side of the boat. He heard the insensitive sound of laughter and a happy roar.

"That was hilarious, Aiko." Grace beamed as she patted the small dragon resting on her shoulder.

Jayden wiped his face and tried to gain his composure. "God, I hate that stupid dragon," he said, deeply annoyed.

Sarah fed the dragon a salted biscuit. "Aww, Jade, you need to apologize. You know it hurts Aiko's feelings when you say mean things like that to her."

He blinked his eyes open and finally focused. Grace's beautiful face came into view, and resting on her shoulders was Aiko, the dragon. Aiko wasn't your typical blue Pygmy Dragon. Most of her scales were the standard aqua blue, except those on her wings. Her wings had dark blue scales with yellow spots shaped exactly like stars. Aiko also possessed the ability to conjure water breath attacks, but she could also send out yellow energy blasts. The most intriguing part about it all was that she wasn't real. After they left Terracina, Grace began to get back more and more of her memories.
One of those memories from her childhood was of a dragon named Aiko that she used to summon. Interestingly, Grace could resummon this same dragon repeatedly, and the animal could retain its memories of her.

Jayden had never heard of a conjurer being able to have a relationship with their summon. Even though the dragon drove him crazy, it was a blessing in disguise as Aiko liked helping the pirates at sea. However, the creature also gave Grace more significant opportunities to explore and use her abilities. If that meant that Jayden would be subject to getting sprayed by water from a dragon or being chased by it, it was worth it to see her happy.

He got up to pet the dragon when Sarah yelled, "Get down!"

As everyone dropped onto the deck, Sarah drew her twin blades and leaped into the air. While she ascended into the air, her body spun and rotated as bullets peppered the ship from just over the horizon. Her twin blades deflected the incoming bullets as she twisted in the air. When she touched back down, her swords glowed bright yellow. As she caught her breath, the next volley of bullets came. Sarah's body moved even faster, and when she deflected the shots back toward the enemy boats, the rounds exploded on contact.

Jayden crawled toward the boat's edge to better understand their situation. He peaked his head just slightly over the railing. Just beyond the horizon, 2 medium-sized speed boats approached them from the south. A third ship was coming from the east, and an even larger ship seemed content with hanging back.

"Sarah, keep deflecting those bullets. Grace, cover me so I can get my sword!" Jayden yelled as the rifle rounds whizzed by.

They nodded their heads, then Grace raised her arm, and Aiko took off to the skies. Grace shouted, "Grow!".

As Aiko flew skyward, her tiny body began to go through a transformation. Her small wings expanded until she had a twenty-foot wingspan. Aiko's three-foot-long body stretched until her frame was fourteen feet long from snout to tail. The dragon stopped her skyward climb when she reached the nearest cloud, and then she let out an earth-shattering roar that shook the boat. Aiko flew toward the first boat and fired blasts of energy that looked like stars at the approaching enemy. The blasts of energy exploded on the deck, launching the pirates into the sea. The second round of *StarBlasts* took out the engine, and the boat began to take on water. Then the dragon let out another eardrum-shattering roar and switched its focus to the approaching ship of pirates.

Jayden crawled down the steps to get to the cabin. He passed by Tony, who was frantically trying to keep control of the boat while avoiding the path of the gunfire. When he reached his room, he grabbed his bag and rummaged around for his Father's old sword. Once his index finger touched cold metal, he knew he found it.

Slowly, he pulled the sword out of his bag, and as he held the weapon, his muscles started to bulge all on their own. His anger grew, not enough to go into *Rage*, but just enough to increase his physical strength. Jayden rotated the blade and felt drawn to its power. There was something attractive to the energy it gave him.

As he held the weapon, Jayden remembered the last time his father used this sword. The blood his father shed to save people. Only to end up being left to die in the street all alone. Today, Jayden would redeem that loss and save his friends. He strapped the weapon to his hip and sprinted up the stairs. Returning to the deck, he switched his gaze toward the skies as Aiko's image shimmered in the sky. A few more rounds struck the dragon, and she faded away. Jayden quickly examined the boat she had been attacking and noticed it was still moving. He could tell it was moving much slower than before from the damage it took from Grace's pet.

"That's a good girl," He said.

"When she regenerates, I'll tell her you said that." Tony chimed in as he stepped away from the ship's console.

Jayden's brows furrowed as the three approaching vessels moved closer to their ship. Then he turned to his best friend and said, "Look, we don't have the firepower to take them out from here. I think I can get on one of their boats. If you have another storm spell left in you, I think we could probably stop them."

Tony appeared offended. "Of course. I can; I have more magic power than you. But to take them out, I must conjure a big spell. And I won't be able to control it once it starts. You might get hurt, which I'm okay with. Are you going to be able to deal with that?" Jayden nodded his head yes.

"Okay, here it goes." Tony drew his sword, glowing an aqua-blue color as he channeled his energy. The veins on his arms bulged as bolts of electricity surrounded him. He raised his sword, swinging it in the air. "Oceanic Thunderstorm!"

Instantly, powerful waves began to rock the boat. Dark, malicious clouds formed in the battle arena like a sign of impending doom. The wind picked up and seemed to accelerate with the force of a freight train. Thunder clapped so loud that it caused tidal waves. A powerful bolt of lightning slammed into the largest ship. For a moment, Jayden stood completely still as his mind wrestled with witnessing the raw power that storm magic could make. He greatly respected his fire magic because he knew it could do some incredible things. Still, even the weakest spells Tony could cast seemed strong enough to wipe out the earth.

Jayden grabbed onto the railing above and pulled himself onto the upper level. Then, he gave himself a running start and vaulted himself off the side of the boat. Orange flames swirled around him like a tornado. The intense heat and pressure launched him forward like a rocket as the fire grew more vigorous.

The Dragon Warrior summoned a gigantic fireball with an iron core in his hand. Then, he rotated his body in the air as he glided over the stormy water. His eyes zeroed in on the ship that Aiko had been attacking. Its hull was charred from the damage she had done to it. He only had one shot and had to make it count. Jayden cocked his arm back and then launched the *Meteor* at the pirate boat. The ball of fire and metal slammed into the motor, causing oil and gasoline to flood out of the vessel. Then, a lightning bolt struck the leaking fluids, generating a chain reaction that sent the boat skyward as the oil and gas exploded with intensity.

Such a showoff, Jayden thought. Tony was always trying to steal his thunder, no pun intended. He shrugged it off and refocused on his new target. The boat had nine sailors standing on the upper deck, firing a slew of bullets in his direction. He returned fire and protected himself from the lead storm using his father's gun and sword.

His pyrotechnic propulsion slowed down the closer he got to the pirate's ship. The fire swirling around him dissipated as he decreased his elevation. He had to land just right; if he were off by a fraction, he would end up in the ocean or land in front of the Pirate's machine gun. Jayden stretched his arms to slow his acceleration, then somersaulted forward in the air once he reached the speedboat. He jammed his sword into the boat's backside because he almost flew past it. His legs hung just a few inches above the motor, and he pulled himself up.

When he got his footing, he raised his Father's Sword above his head as his enemies approached. Instantly, his muscles bulged, and any ounce of fear he had dissipated. Jayden was ready to engage any pirates on this ship and anyone else. Before his first opponent moved, he knew he would win the day.

His training kicked in when the first pirate swung their cutlass at his neck. He ducked under the blade and then bonked the pirate on the head with the butt of his sword. As his enemy collapsed, he pointed his sword toward a pirate aiming a pistol at him. Then he shouted, "Flamethrower!". A stream of concentrated red flames expelled from his sword and slammed into the pirate, knocking him and the sailor standing next to him into the ocean.

Jayden grinned; there were only five left. Once they were out of the way, he felt he could take down their giant ship alone.

A gigantic seven-foot pirate rushed him, swinging two swords wildly. The Dragon Warrior blocked one sword strike and tried to sidestep his opponent to get around him. His adversary reacted quicker than he expected, and the pirate managed to whirl around and strike back at Jayden.

Instinctively, he dodged and deflected the onslaught of sword strikes. The pirate's attacks were so powerful that Jayden was on the verge of losing his sword. He had to end this fight quick, but there was no way he could overpower this pirate. His enemy's dual-wielding abilities were beyond what Jayden expected.

The pirate made a swipe with both swords across Jayden's chest. Jayden blocked the strike with his scimitar before the blades could slice him in half. The attack was so aggressive that it pushed him against the boat's edge. His right foot slid across the edge of the ship. If the pirate pressed any harder or Jayden lost his footing, he would either end up dead from a sword wound or be knocked into the vicious waves crashing against the ship.

The Dragon Warrior needed an out; he couldn't win fighting an enemy this big on a speeder boat. He was using too much energy and magic to enhance his strength that he couldn't muster a measly heat spell. Jayden shook his head and knew that he had gotten too cocky. The rain drenching them wasn't improving his chances; it was worsening. He closed his eyes for a moment and said a silent prayer.

He sensed extreme danger approaching him before he could finish his appeal for help. The need he felt to run away was not from the pirates; something more powerful was heading their way. Jayden channeled all the magical energy he could muster into his arms and legs. With all his strength, he pushed back against his enemies' blades just enough to get a little space. Then he jumped into the air as high as he could. Just as a large shell slammed into the ship. As he flipped in the air, he heard another projectile strike the boat, which exploded.

The explosive energy from the ship flung him backward as splinters of wood and smoke burst into the air. He felt a powerful cold chill permeate his body once he broke the water's surface. The salty taste of the ocean coated his tongue to the point that he never wanted to eat french fries again. A high-pitched noise was overwhelming his eardrums, and his head was spinning like he was on a roller coaster. Fear consumed his thoughts as he struggled to breathe while the powerful underwater current dragged him further away.

The swelling ocean water was so dark he almost couldn't tell which way was up. He felt hopeless momentarily as the weight of his weapons pulled him down deeper. He shook his head in frustration. *I can't give up now*, he told himself. He reached for his throat and adjusted the sword's strap, slowly choking him to death. Once the pressure on his neck was gone, he channeled all the magical energy into his legs and kicked his way toward the surface.

Jayden breathed a sigh of relief once he could taste the fresh air. Then he immediately regretted it, as he noticed a twenty-foot wave towering above him. Quickly, he dove back under, hoping to swim under the storm above. Once he returned to the surface again, he screamed out loud as he felt a stinging pain in his left shin. He glanced down, and there was a small Thorny Octopus with a tentacle wrapped around his leg, and six of its poisoned spines were lodged in his shin.

He whispered a heat spell under his breath, and slowly, the tentacled monster loosened its grip. The pain was excruciating. He went to scream, but suddenly, his mouth was filled with ocean water. While a mighty wave knocked him back down into the depths of the sea. The octopus still clung onto his leg as he descended. He conjured another heat spell and kicked his legs to release the creature. When the poisoned spines of the Thorny Octopus were dislodged from his leg, dark red blood began to ooze out.

Jayden stared with detached curiosity as the blood left his body. He wasn't concerned; it happened so often that it wasn't a big deal. He just needed to wrap it and let his slow automatic healing spell do the rest.

His cocky attitude quickly evaporated once he spotted a green angular tail fin out of the corner of his eyes. The approaching danger was not mistaken even in the dark and murky waters. The one thing that Jayden had forgotten was that the sea's apex predators could notice the scent of blood from miles away.

Unfortunately for him, the animals that caught his scent tended to travel in packs. The Emerald Shark is what they were called, a creature with a bite so powerful that even water dragons gave them their space. These creatures were covered in green scales that would reflect a beautiful green light when they were struck by the sun. This green light would sometimes shine so bright that it could temporarily blind their prey. Beyond their colorful appearance and life-stealing jaws, these enormous sharks grew up to 30 feet long. For a creature so large, they could swim with the speed and efficiency of a bullet. As if that wasn't enough, these Sharks were also blessed with magical abilities. Emerald Sharks could summon underwater vortexes that looked like small green tornadoes. The magical vortexes were used to draw in prey but could also blast an attacker further away. Once an Emerald Shark locks on a target, there is little chance of escape; Jayden LoneOak is completely screwed.

He channeled all of his magical energy and launched himself to the surface, barely escaping the bite of an advancing shark. Once he caught a breath of fresh air, his jaw dropped, not from the still-raging storm but from a green fin heading his way. He reached for his sword and dove into the sea's dark depths.

Even though the water was murky, he could sense a target approaching from below him. The young Dragon Warrior raised his sword, hoping to get a lucky swing. Before his weapon could make contact, the shark easily dodged his downward strike. He spun around to try again when he heard the sound of water surging below him. Jayden glanced down and saw what looked like a small green tornado. Before he could escape, the swirling vortex pulled him in with a strong force; he blacked out for a few seconds. When his eyes opened, he felt the sudden need to hurl. His body was spinning around like a top. He tried to fight it but was pulled down by the underwater tornado.

While the spinning was becoming too much to bear, he was launched forcefully out of the vortex. He rocketed through the surface of the ocean and flipped in the air. His stomach smacked against the water when he came back down, knocking the wind out of him. The pressure to breathe was intense, his mind filling with fear as he noticed the ten green fins closing in on him.

Jayden ducked back under the water and momentarily saw his adversaries as clear as day. His eyes were entranced by their emerald-colored skin and eyes as yellow as the sun. Their bodies sliced through the ocean depths effortlessly, with their powerful tail fins swinging back and forth softly. Each of these animals possessed rows of sharp teeth with jagged edges. The sharks would get very little sustenance from eating him; this was just a demonstration of their territorial dominance.

He had read a lot about these sharks when he was younger. After his mom died, he found solace in studying these amazing creatures; it was a blessing to finally see them in their natural habitat. They were powerful creatures to behold, and if they hadn't tried to eat him, Jayden would have tried to pet one or even ride it. It was unfortunate that he was at the top of the menu today.

The Dragon Warrior had to come up with something quick, or he would be fish food. He tried to think about his options. If he tried to swing his sword, he might get one shark and then be ripped to shreds by the rest. His gun might work, but he needed to find out if the bullets could pierce their hides. He knew he couldn't use fire magic; the icy sea had drained him of his magical energy. Jayden clenched his fists in frustration; *think, you idiot, think.* There had to be some way out of this mess that didn't end in death or dismemberment.

His eyes widened as a lightbulb went off in his head. There was one thing he could try, and if it worked, he might make it out alive. He was already bleeding a decent amount; this technique could worsen everything. With how close the sharks were now; he had no other choice.

Jayden closed his eyes and tried to concentrate. He breathed out slowly to release some of the pressure in his lungs. Then he mouthed *Yūrei* and immediately felt a tightening in his chest. The veins in his wrist bulged while the blood dripping from his leg increased. His body felt warm like he had just contracted a deadly fever. Jayden's muscles ached, his vision becoming blurry for a moment.

Then, a tiny light gray flame appeared in his right hand, and his senses heightened. His ears could pick up the barely audible sound of the sharks as their fins swayed back and forth like a rudder. Jayden's vision became even more acute, so much so that he could see the ocean clearly for miles in every direction. He could distinguish each shark's size and easily spot even the smallest scars on their emerald hides. His body felt strong, and his confidence was unmatched in the face of such danger. Even with the pain in his leg raging like the waves on the surface, on the inside, he felt invincible.

The small sprite in his right hand grew, and a second ball of fire appeared in his left hand. As the ghostly whisps danced in his palms, the Emerald Sharks slowed their approach. The powerful creatures sniffed the area around him as they circled, instantly becoming anxious. Their fearful yellow eyes shifted between him and the ancient magic that rested in his hands. At first, Jayden thought they might be confused because he could summon fire underwater. He shook his head; that can't be it. A pack of Emerald Sharks wouldn't be frightened by a simple spell. This fear in their eyes was different. The fear he could sense from them was primal.

To his left, a shark opened and shut its massive jaws. The water around the animal rippled from his mighty chomp. As if on cue, the smaller and elderly sharks began to leave, followed by the larger animals. Before too long, it was just Jayden and what might be considered the alpha shark. Then, the powerful creature's eyes darted between the lowly human and the gray fireballs floating in his hands. The fear in the shark's eyes was so intense it was unnerving. He couldn't imagine how a large and powerful animal could be so afraid of a lowly human.

Then, a thought popped into his head; he had witnessed this primal despair in an apex predator before. Jayden's mind flashed back to when he stood at the edge of a forest with a wall of fire enclosing a forest wolf. His ears could still make out that faint, helpless whimper that poor animal let out. The fear in the eyes of the Emerald Shark was the same, making Jayden feel a deep sense of guilt.

Jayden's body and mind relaxed when the alpha shark turned its tail and darted off to join the rest of the pack. The young man from Eiréné smiled because he figured this poor creature had to put on a brave face in front of his whole shark family, even though he was shaking in his nonexistent boots. His smirk became a face of concern as he stared at the minuscule flames jumping in his hand; there must be something terrible about this type of magic that two pitiful fireballs could make a pack of sharks absolutely terrified.

Jayden was starting to understand why this spell was forbidden. If his masters ever found out he knew it, let alone could conjure it, he would lose his title as a Dragon Warrior.

Yūrei, or the ghost flame, was Master Level skill. Most Dragon Warriors or Fire Magic users, in general, might not ever see it. Even the dark flame was more common. It was forbidden because it could be used without relying on any magic. Instead, it drew from the individual's life force, which was very risky. You could die in a fight from using the ghost flames. Any injuries a person already had would become more severe by tapping into the technique. One of the other reasons it was forbidden at the Dragon Temple was because you risked killing yourself. Another reason was that its only real purpose was to take lives. This technique was strong enough to amplify any spell he had. You could also combine it with a spell that drew from its magic. It was a powerful technique; the shark was right to be nervous. The animal knew that its death was near.

Jayden snapped his fingers, and the small sprites grew into fireballs the size of a beach ball. The intense heat made the water around him boil. The shark moved a foot forward and then quickly swam backward. As powerful as the animal was, it wasn't crazy.

The Dragon Warrior waved his hands, and the ghost flames disappeared. The shark let out a blast of bubbles and then sped off, leaving behind a blanket of foam. Before he ran out of air, Jayden kicked his legs and aimed toward the surface. His eyes darted back and forth as he looked for their boat amongst the crashing waves. The rain was still coming down in sheets, and the clouds were about as dark as the night sky. He glanced around methodically; it was more frantically, as his body was freezing and wanted to get dry. No matter where he looked, he could not find their boat in any direction.

Since his magical energy was still nonexistent and his body was aching from summoning that forbidden spell, he would have to do things the old-fashioned way. Jayden closed his eyes and tried remembering the sun's placement before jumping off their ship. When he jumped toward the pirate's speed boat, he was gliding in the sun's direction, which meant the boat was going north at the time. The current must have moved him further east, so he began swimming westward.

The waves and the powerful gusts of wind made swimming back just about as fun as going to the dentist.

Chapter 4

Area of Effect

He embraced the gentle sound of the waves tossing to and fro. His body felt completely relaxed as his skin welcomed the cool ocean spray. The beautiful stars above glittered in the night sky like a crystal-filled sea. Even the moon was courteous enough to share the spotlight with the nearby planets and a gorgeous teal-colored comet cruising across the sky.

Jayden sat up and scanned the area around him. While he greatly appreciated the ocean view at night, he needed to figure out where he was. In fact, he couldn't even remember how he got to this island. He closed his eyes, hoping to jog his memory. *Focus,* he told himself, *focus.*

The young Dragon Warrior scrunched his face hard as he tried to concentrate. Jayden was glad no one was walking by because they would have thought he was going to the bathroom on the beach. After a period of what was most likely a couple seconds, he realized he had absolutely no idea how he got onto this beach. The only thing he accomplished was looking like a complete idiot under the starlit sky.

He tried to get to stand but then crumbled back onto the ground. His leg was throbbing with pain. When he tried to stand again, he felt a stinging sensation. Jayden stared down at his leg; even in the dark, he could tell it was swollen. A dark purple liquid dripped from the wounds sustained by the octopus. When the poison hit the sand, it made a sizzling sound. Jayden watched, horrified, as it burned a small mound of dirt like acid.

Jayden grimaced at the thought of what this *octopoison* was doing to the inside of his body. He was already susceptible to poison, so he needed to get some medicine quick before he'd end up becoming the Legless Dragon Warrior. Jayden reached for his dad's old sword and used it to help him return to his feet. By using the scimitar as a crutch, he decided to make his way slowly and meticulously toward the shoreline before he passed out from the excruciating pain in his leg.

He lifted his sword, placing it firmly on the ground before him, moving his leg forward. Pain shot throughout his body while he moved at the speed of a turtle. Even his toes were irritated from the sand that was rubbing between them. He had no idea how much sand could get in his shoes.

Jayden looked down, "O, that is just great. The bottoms of my shoes are gone, and I'm stuck on this stupid island. Could it get any worse?"

After he finished shouting his frustrations, he planted his sword again to take another step. The weapon went too deep into the sand this time and got stuck. Unfortunately, he was already leaning forward, which caused him to faceplant into the ground. With the newly acquired pain on his face, he realized that he had spoken too soon; it could, in fact, get worse.

He glanced up momentarily. There was a small palm tree just a few feet away. Using whatever strength he had left, he dragged and pulled himself until he reached his destination.

Jayden sighed in relief as he relaxed under a palm frond and breathed in the cool ocean breeze.

As he began to fall asleep, he caught a peculiar scent in the air. His nostrils flared at the smell of a sweet, juicy bacon burger with BBQ sauce and a side of seasoned fries. Jayden's taste buds were watering as he began to feel in the dark around him. A smile creased his lips when his fingers brushed against a warm piece of glass. His fingers traced the object's sides, discovering it was circular. He placed his hand in the center of the plate, his fingers wrapping around a pile of fries. His heart jumped in his chest, stuffing his face like he was at a buffet.

The Dragon Warrior sunk his teeth into the juicy bacon burger. The saltiness of the bacon mixed perfectly with the sweet BBQ sauce. Every bite made the pain in his leg and the exhaustion he felt melt away. He couldn't believe how lucky he was to find this perfect meal beside him on the beach. Jayden had never been this lucky before but could get used to it. After taking his last bite, he felt like a beached whale and fell asleep.

***

His stomach churned. He wanted to vomit. He felt unbalanced as his body rocked back and forth uncomfortably. His back felt stiff, and he had a kink in his neck from sleeping on a flat surface. Jayden opened his brown eyes and immediately got a migraine from the sun.

All of a sudden, he felt overwhelmed as he realized that the reason his body was rocking back and forth was because he was being carried on a stretcher.

Four individuals carried him on a canvas stretcher with two wooden poles protruding on both sides. The two individuals on his left side were dressed in gray martial arts uniforms with red sashes similar to his own. On his right side was a similarly dressed group of individuals, and wrapped around their waists were white sashes.

As he "analyzed" the individuals carrying him further, he quickly noticed they were all women. The girls dressed in the red sashes all had long black hair, and one wore designer glasses. On his right, the girl in the front had short, spikey brown hair, and the other young lady had hair that was dyed gray. All of the women carrying him appeared to be athletic and had a poised demeanor.

"Ouch!" Jayden yelled as he felt a sharp pain in the back of his head from someone flicking him.

"Will you stop creeping on them, you weirdo? You're going to make them drop you." Grace said before she flicked him again.

Jayden rubbed his head. "Ouch, ouch, okay, okay. I'll stop. I was just checking my surroundings. It's not every day you get an awesome burger, fall asleep on the beach, and wake up being carried away on a stretcher. This is how most cannibal and human sacrifice movies start."

The Aggeloi Princess rolled her eyes. "You are such a loser. You do know that's not what really happened, right?" Jayden shook his head no. "Well, you did fall asleep on the beach; that part of your story is true. The part of you eating a burger, not so much. The poison from your leg injury made you hallucinate because what you actually ate was a beetle about the size of your hand."

When he heard the words beetle escape her lips, he felt queasy and leaned over to his left and began to purge every ounce of food he had eaten in the last year. The young woman standing closest to his left managed to move out of the way so quickly that it looked like she went invisible. Then, all of the women proceeded to drop him onto the ground.

"What the actual..."

Grace put her foot over his mouth before he could complete his statement." Jayden LoneOak, The First! No sir, we do not use that kind of language."

Jayden had never wanted to strangle Gracey until that moment. Before he could follow up with another retort, one of the girls in the red sashes flicked him in the back of the head, and he immediately fell back unconscious.

A devilish grin creased Grace's lips, "Why didn't you do that earlier, Priscilla?"

The young woman looked back at her with an expressionless face," I thought dropping him would do it. I'll just have to drop him harder next time.

***

A family of green parrots zoomed across their path. Nine-tailed monkeys were chattering as they jumped from tree to tree. She held out her hand so that a *NiJi* Ladybug could greet her. The bug was about the size of a bumblebee with wings that were rainbow color. From what she was told, they were always a sign of good luck.

The Aggeloi Princess smiled as the sweet bug flew away. She bowed as a young lady with a white sash ran up to her. The girl was carrying a wooden tray with fruits and crackers on it. There were slices of a blue apple, a starfish-shaped fruit, and a purple fruit that looked like a mango, with a side of peanut butter crackers.

"Is this for me?" She asked.

"Yes, ma'am. I hope you like it." The young lady replied.

Grace pointed at the fruits, "What are these called?"

The young martial artist beamed with pride. "Ms. Grace, this one is called a Navy Apple; this one is a StarFruit, and these purple ones are known as Violet Mangos. I learned in class that these mangos are very rare. I like them. They are very yummy."

The Aggeloi Princess reached out and grabbed one of the mangos. She felt nervous as she slowly tried to take a bite of the exotic fruit. When her teeth sliced into the mango's texture, her taste buds were enveloped entirely with unique and awe-inspiring flavors.

She took another giant bite of mango, which was just as amazing as the first. The Violet Mangoes tasted like a melding of a purple grape and mango. Its consistency provided just enough crunch to mix with the sour and sweet notes of the fruit.

"Do you like it?" The young lady asked.

Grace stared back at her, halfway through a gigantic bite of the mango. She managed to gulp it down in the most mannerless way possible.

"Yes, the fruit is amazing," she replied. "I have never had anything this good before."

The young lady bowed respectfully, "The honor was mine, princess."

Grace gave the girl a high five. Then, she grabbed a handful of peanut butter crackers. Before the young warrior was five feet away, Grace had already managed to scarf down crackers.

She quickly wiped the crumbs from her face and continued walking along the path. Her eyes could still not believe the immense beauty of the island. Tall palm trees and tropical plants surrounded the village. Her eyes were blessed with a canvas of multicolored birds gliding along the canopies. There were blue and red crabs scurrying across the sandy road. Everything on the island operated naturally, from the animals to the vegetation and the warriors. Everything worked in concert.

She passed by a row of huts. Her eyes landed on a hut that had a metal sign. The sign was a piece of metal shaped and painted to look like a mallet. Grace pushed past the beaded burgundy curtains used for the door.

The hut was a mecca for anything a warrior might need. There were swords, knives, and firearms displayed throughout the room. On the right side of the building was a large display table. The glass display case contained rows of magic crystals and magazines for semi-automatic weapons. She also noticed a row of gold and silver necklaces with magic charms attached to the lower shelf.

She glanced up just as the blacksmith stepped into the backroom. Sarah turned toward her and waved as she stood at the counter on the far side of the room. Her friend had her machine pistols laid across the counter.

"Is Ronny coming back?" Grace asked.

"Yep," Sarah beamed. "She left to finish fixing up my swords. I am super excited."

"That is awesome. I was hoping she could fix the dagger Jayden gave me."

A woman stepped through a beaded curtain in the back of the building. "Are you doubting my abilities?"

Grace's eyes lit up, "Ronny!"

She ran and wrapped her arms around the blacksmith. Her long brown hair brushed gently against her skin as they embraced. Ronalda smelled like a barbeque grill and a smelting factory. Her smock was covered in burn marks and metal shavings. She usually kept her brown hair up in the bun, only putting it down when her job was done.

The Aggeloi Princess's eyes lit up with joy. "Were you able to finish it?" She asked.

Ronny took a step back and gave a toothy grin. She pulled out a dagger from behind her back and held it out for her to see.

The pearly white blade shined like a star in the night sky. She managed to redesign the ivory handle. Ronny had removed the gold from the handles and remolded it to create unique lines and shapes along the handle. The part she loved most was that Ronalda had managed to engrave Grace's name in cursive letters made of gold.

"You don't have to tell me I did a good job," Ronny said with a toothy grin. "But you always can."

"You did an amazing job!" Grace cheered.

The blacksmith popped her nonexistent collar. "Tell me something I don't know. I even managed to increase the magical output of the weapon. Sometimes, I even impress myself. My hands are like that of a painter's. All they do is make art."

"Were you able to fix my swords too?" Sarah asked.

Ronny snapped her fingers, and two short swords appeared on the counter. "Not sure if you were listening to Sarah. But I am this island's most badass blacksmith/possibly stolen jewelry seller."

Sarah rolled her eyes, "You are so extra. A little birdy told me that you might be unable to fix Jayden's katana."

The 30-year-old blacksmith let out an exasperated sigh. "Did that good-for-nothing wannabe repairman, Stephen, make that statement?"

Sarah shrugged, "He may have hinted at it. But I ain't no snitch."

"And that attitude is why you are still single." Ronny retorted. "But to answer your question, Dragon Steel, in general, is easier to mold and make into a weapon than it is to repair. The way his weapon is now, there isn't a blacksmith in the world who can repair it as it is. That said, your friend has a habit of collecting unique weapons. That dagger is one of a kind. Did he come in with another edged weapon?"

"He's got a bunch of knives that he throws sometimes," Grace replied.

Sarah raised her hand, "I think she's asking about that sword that he got after his dad was killed. That black one."

Ronny nodded her head. "Yes, that one, the black scimitar. It's just like that dagger made of Elder steel; it is one of a kind. However, you need to be very careful whenever you are around that weapon. There is something very off about it."

"Should I be worried about Jayden too?" Sarah asked in a hushed tone.

"I would be very concerned if I were you."

***

He was dragged out of the world of dreams and unconsciousness. Once again, he awoke to the intense sensation of his head throbbing with pain. The source of his pain was the same as it has always been, his smartass mouth.

41

Miss Tonya would be richer than the king if she got a gold coin for every time he pissed someone off with the words he said.

The warm compress covering his forehead slid off as he sat up. The room he was in was pretty dark. He was lying on a mildly thick mattress with blue sheets and bedding. His head was slightly raised by the cylindrical pillow he rested on. The building itself was a moderately sized hut. Air mattresses were spread out along the walls. There was a small table in the center, with papers strewn across. Jayden was suspicious he wouldn't be the first person to trip on it in the dark.

In the back of the hut, there appeared to be a small shrine. A statue of a silver dragon with eyes made of obsidian rested on a gold table. Small candles were placed around the dragon. Their soft flames danced on their wicks, creating a beautiful stage for the dragon to shine.

The entrance to the hut was just a few feet away. The door was open, with a gentle glow coming from just outside. He leaned over to get a better look and saw what appeared to be a row of tiki torches that served as a cheesy red carpet for tourists to enter the hut.

A woman entered the hut and sat at the table in the middle of the room. She was adorned with sky-blue colored hair. The powerful woman wore a gray martial arts uniform with a black sash over her right hip. The wisdom that exuded from her made him guess that she was in her fifties or sixties. Physically speaking, she looked to be around Floriana's age.

She gestured for him to come sit across from him. Jayden was initially hesitant because even though she was hiding her true power, the magic energy he could sense from her was overwhelming. He shrugged, thinking *what's the worst that could happen.* So, he grabbed his pillow and placed it on the ground in front of her. He placed his knees on the pillow and bowed respectfully to her.

"Do you know where you are?" She asked in a soft tone.

Jayden scratched his chin briefly to give her the impression that he was in deep thought. Then he replied,

"Well, if I had to guess. I am either on a reality TV show where the losers get voted off the island, or I'm at an awesome resort that will sooner or later be taken over by cannibals or dinosaurs."

She stared back at him without a hint of emotion on her face. Jayden quickly sat straight in his seat and put on his serious face. "I mean, I have no idea where I am or how I got here."

"My name is Mariko, and you are at the Island of Dragons Monastery." Jayden shrugged his shoulders and had a confused look on his face. Mariko shook her head in disappointment, "now I see why you got a C in Dragon Warrior history. The Island of Dragons is a satellite school for the Dragon Monastery. We educate our students on using speed and oceanic-based water magic."

"Ooo," Jayden replied. "Now I remember. There used to be three satellite schools, but now there is only one. So how did I get here?"

She bowed respectfully, "You are correct, my young Dragon Warrior. Bringing you safely here took a great combination of power and skill from your friend Tony, our magic, and a cute little dragon named Aiko."

Jayden scoffed, "There is nothing cute about that winged lizard."

Mariko gave a sly grin, "As a pupil of Master Thai, you should respect all forms of dragons. No matter if they occur naturally, are conjured by a summoner, or even created by the mind of the Aggeloi Princess."

"Created?"

She nodded, "Yes, your precious Grace is no average summoner. She can actually create living things into being. Most people create cheap imitations, and others simply conjure entities that can only exist on this plane temporarily. She can create living, breathing creatures into existence. Not that she knows it yet, but eventually, she will gain an understanding of that power and responsibility. Speaking of power and responsibility, do you know what that tattoo on your arm is for?"

Jayden shrugged, "Honestly, I thought it was because Master Thai wanted us to look badass wherever we went. I mean, he wanted us to appear as well-respected ambassadors of the Dragon Monastery for all the world to see."

He didn't even see her shoulder move before he felt a slap to the back of the head. He also didn't see her shoulder move again when he felt a second slap to the back of the head. "Jayden LoneOak, I don't know how Master Thai dealt with your humor for so many years. God bless his soul. The real reason you have that tattoo is to limit how much magical power you can wield. Your tattoo is supposed to only allow you to use 40-50% of your power."

"Wait, what?" Jayden exclaimed as he rubbed the back of his head.

"Surely you have noticed in your battles that you can't use as much magical energy as you did at the temple. Unfortunately, as you also found, this limiter is not foolproof. You and Tony have exceeded the power the enchantment is supposed to grant you. For the most part, that has helped to keep you two alive. However, you still understand that the power you can wield has consequences."

Jayden felt rage building from within as he processed the information she had just given. "Why would you limit our power? What consequences are you talking about? Almost dying? Seeing my friends get hurt and lose their lives? What consequences are so damn important that we couldn't use our full power?"

The temperature of the room shifted. He felt a shiver as magical energy swirled around the Dragon Master. Her power was overwhelming and rivaled the fear imposed by Lady Coral. Even at his best, she could destroy him instantly.

"Do not forget your place, young Dragon Warrior," she commanded. "We, as Dragon Masters, have a duty to protect the world, that includes keeping them safe from the dangers that come from your abilities. Those power limiters help us watch how you use your powers. We have had to remove magical abilities from those who misused them. There is a reason why so few graduate from our programs. We train you to be servants and lights in this world. We are not in the business of turning you into gods. The consequences of using your power are that you can cause collateral damage you may not be aware of."

"Like what?"

"While you fought your battle at sea, a family not far away enjoyed a fishing trip. The storm Tony conjured was so powerful that it flipped their boat. One of the girls on the ship bumped her head really hard, and she fell into a coma. She will be fine, and she's being treated by one of our healers. The reality is that you were clear in your right to protect yourselves. Someone you couldn't have foreseen got hurt, and you are lucky that Tony had the wherewithal to answer their call for help."

Confusion and guilt washed over him like the waves at sea. When they were clashing back and forth, he never considered how their battles might affect other people on the water. He didn't quite know how to feel about the limiter on his arm; to a degree, it made sense. The amount of power that they both possessed was extreme. In fact, it made even more sense when he thought about his time at the Dragon Temple. Very few people their age started when they did and managed. Most just came for the martial arts and firearm training; the rest were kicked out.

She stood up as he sat in thought and began to make her way out of the hut. Mariko stopped just a few steps behind him and turned back. "Despite the hiccups you two have made, I can honestly say you have surpassed your Master's expectations. I know for a fact that he is extremely proud of you. Now get up and wash your hands; they smell like death."

***

Tony took a sip of the bitter drink in his hand. The beer was a red ale poured into a weird, orange-colored watermelon. Each sip brought in the sweet and sour taste of the watermelon mixed with the piney flavor of the beer. For all intents and purposes, it was a confusing experience for any flavor palette.

He took another gulp of the brew and stared out at the ocean. A white fin from an ivory shark breached the surface and began to lurk through the shallows. He hoped to push back the pain of guilt and sorrow with every sip. No matter how much he sipped, he couldn't block out the images of that capsized boat, of Sarah and Grace fighting to keep that little girl alive.

Tony knew that there was no way that he could know that his storm would hurt anybody outside of those damn pirates. He didn't think he had enough magical energy to conjure a powerful storm. Mariko said it wasn't his fault, but who was if he wasn't the one at fault?

He drained the last bit of his beer and picked up another watermelon. He took a sip and instantly felt a burning sensation as the liquid went down. This must be the rum that Mariko suggested. Judging by his sudden change in equilibrium, he could probably guess why she liked it so much.

Tree branches swayed, and the bushes rustled. Static energy filled the air, so anything he touched shocked him. Magic radiated amongst the foliage; whatever it was came closer.

He reached behind his back and realized he had left his pistol in the hut. Shit, he didn't bring his sword either because drinking and carrying weapons is always a bad idea. His storm magic wouldn't be as controlled without his sword, and he couldn't risk hurting someone again.

A bush rustled a few feet away from him and suddenly exploded. Smoke billowed, and a red-haired woman stepped out of the gray smoke. Her skin was pale white, and her eyes shone brilliant emerald green light. She was dressed in black shorts with a red tank top that said, "I went to Chaldea, and all I got was this shirt."

As she passed by him, a lightbulb went on in his head. For the first time, he realized what it must be like to be clueless like Jayden. The woman walking out toward the water was Sarah.

Intense magical energy swirled around her as she approached the crashing waves. She didn't acknowledge his presence, which was concerning. This must be the transformation that Jayden and the others told him about. Just being this close to her power, he understood why Jayden feared it. Even at Tony's best, he might be unable to take her down.

He jumped to his feet and yelled, "Sarah!" As expected, she continued her stride as she trudged through the rolling waves. Tony ran toward her. She turned and blasted him with a ball of explosive energy when he was within two feet of her. He was flung backward and hit the ground hard.

His shirt was singed, and he felt foolish. Tony returned to his feet and sent a small gray-colored gust of wind toward her. The water was now up to her waist, and without skipping a beat, she turned and placed her hand in the way of his oncoming spell. She snapped her fingers, and the gust stopped and started glowing bright orange. It exploded, and he was once again blasted into the air. He was ready for it this time and flipped in the air to control his fall, landing back on the beach like a badass.

Well, that didn't work, he thought. He needed to come up with something else quick because if she went any further, she would drown. Tony wasn't sure if she could swim in this form. He pointed his right index toward her and began to channel all of the magical energy he had. Tony took a deep breath, then shouted, "Storm Barrier!"

Dark clouds appeared above his childhood friend. Bolts of lightning flashed above her, and a wall of electricity surrounded her. Thunder cracked, and rain burst forth from within the barrier. Sarah stopped her progress as the barrier was completely enclosed around her. There was no expression or emotion in how she stared at her new cage. She stretched out her hand and was immediately shocked by a lightning bolt.

Her magical energy spiked as she raged within her magical form. She pushed against her enclosure despite the repeated strikes from the lightning bolts. The energy she was using on the cage began to cause it to expand. Tony quickly snapped his fingers, and blue lightning bolts were added to the cage. The power from the bolts slowed her down a little bit, but she was still pressing against the wall of electricity.

Tony couldn't keep the barrier up much longer; he poured all his magic into this spell. He had never used the *Azul Bolts* before. The fact that she was able to push back against them was frightening. He had two options left to keep her contained, well three, but he couldn't use that technique on a friend. Tony snapped his fingers, and the yellow bolts swirling around the cage became scarlet red in the blink of an eye. Streaks of red and blue bolts combined to strike Sarah in the chest. She was instantly knocked unconscious.

***

Her head was spinning, and she felt a burning sensation in every inch of her body. For a second, she thought she had become blind because her eyes were open, but she couldn't see anything. Then she realized it was nighttime, and she had a splitting headache.

She sprung up, "What the hell?"

Tony stepped out from behind a large palm tree. "It's not that serious. You are perfectly safe. I think."

Sarah tilted her head to the side, "When I went to bed, I was inside of my… Wait a second." Her face instantly turned green, then she turned to her left and vomited out everything she had eaten in the last year.

He pat her on the back. "I'm sorry about that. My storm magic spells can sometimes have the added effect of making someone super sick. It is pretty random when it happens. You should feel better once you get more sleep and food."

She held up her right index to his face. "Please don't mention food again. Anyway, how did I get out here? All I remember was going to sleep in my hut, and now I'm here. My clothes are wet, my body hurts, and apparently, you hit me with a magic spell."

He moved to sit down next to her. "Well, you were in a trance and had transformed into that thing."

"Tony, I really expected more from you. I can understand Jayden saying I transformed into that thing. But you are better than that," she replied. "I like to consider it my Super Sarah form or my Jayden is Super Afraid of Me Form."

Tony squinted and shook his head. "I don't think you should use any of those names for that form. This was the first time I saw that form. Does it happen often? Do you think you will ever be able to control it?"

"Grace has told me that sometimes, when I'm asleep, it happens. She told me it's usually just me sitting up or walking to the door and standing there. This was the longest time I have spent in that form. I don't know if I can control it or ever be able to." Sarah wiped a tear from her eyes. "I don't want to be a burden to any of you. I'm so afraid that I may hurt someone and not even know it. That reality scares me to death."

He put his arm around her. "I don't know how it will all pan out. I am going to tell you something that I haven't told Jayden. While you two fled the Water Temple, I managed to go into a Rage during that battle. I was consumed by the Red Eye, just like Jayden had been. Until then, I thought I had full control of myself, my temper, and my actions. I used to think Jayden was the only one still fighting those demons. Then I learned I am no better. I am still just as broken as he is."

She glanced up at him, "But we are all broken. How can we ever expect to be normal or function like the average person?"

"You are not wrong. That's what I realized when I lost control of myself. This anger is a part of me; this sadness and loneliness are all parts of my soul. We can lose control when we forget and ignore those less important parts of ourselves. I realized the best thing for me to do forward is learn how to live with those broken parts of me. I chose to learn to use my brokenness. One day, you will learn to use that power within you. It may not be perfect, and it might not be easy to do, but it is a part of who you are, even if it isn't pleasant."

Chapter 5

Whispers of War

Jayden ducked beneath her swipe at his neck and was quickly knocked back by a blast of salt water. She made a slashing V motion with her wooden blades, and waves of water slammed into him. This was originally supposed to be a magic-free bout, but apparently, Mariko forgot about that.

The Dragon Master was so quick that he couldn't land a hit if he wanted to. He might have a shot if he could use his magic, but he didn't want to do that. He wanted to prove that he could win without it.

He sprinted toward her while holding his sword loosely behind him. She flipped over him, sending a blast of water raining down on him. A shield made of fire appeared just above his head to intercept her spell. There was a hissing sound as the flames turned the water into hot steam.

Mariko landed a few feet away from him and dropped her wooden blades onto the ground. "I was under the impression that you were not going to use magic as we sparred."

"I lied, and apparently, you did too," He said with a smug grin.

She smiled back ever so sweetly, "I guess I did. I'm impressed that you can activate your Auto-Shield without thinking about it."

"Yeah, I had no plan to use that spell. It just happened on its own, which is pretty awesome on my part."

Mariko shook her head, "I still don't get how Master Thai dealt with you for all those years."

A yellow circle appeared in the air right next to her. She reached her hand into the circle and pulled two Jian-styled swords from another dimension. The blades were three feet long and made of white dragon steel. The handles were painted black, with a golden hilt and red tassels that hung from the bottom.

"Tony!" She shouted. He appeared to ignore her call because he was "distracted" by a group of girls working out within his line of sight.

"Tony!" She shouted again.

He looked up momentarily, feeling completely annoyed, and said, "What?"

Seeing her eyes narrow, he realized the mistake and potential consequences he might reap. Then he cleared his throat and said, "How can I help you, Master Mariko?"

"Come down here and join us. I want the two of you to get your weapons and come at me with all that you've got. Do not hold back."

Jayden grinned. This should be fun. Tony joined him by his side, but he still seemed a little distracted by Priscilla and the other girls who were training. Jayden couldn't blame him; they were all beautiful and strong. Unfortunately for Jayden, whenever he watches the girls train, Priscilla threatens to kill him. Considering how strong she was, he believed her.

He switched his focus back to the task at hand. He grasped the black handle and drew the curved scimitar from his scabbard. Just holding the weapon caused his muscles to bulge and his eyes to narrow on his target. He felt no fear, just the desire to defeat his opponent.

Without warning, he lunged toward her with his sword held to the side with his right hand. When he was within just a few feet of her, he pulled a knife out of his left sleeve and let it fly. She deflected it with one of her swords as he made a slash across her chest. Mariko blocked it and held him in position with her swords. Jayden pressed against her, then jumped high into the air just as Tony launched a blast of lightning at the Dragon Master.

She redirected the blast and sent it skyward toward Jayden. He didn't have time to react. The bolt struck him hard in the chest, and he crumbled to the ground.

Tony summoned a gust of wind under his feet to propel himself forward. He pushed a button on the handle of his sword as he flew through the air. The handle on his weapon began to lengthen a few more inches as the hilt shrank. Suddenly, a second blade began to protrude from the base of his sword handle. Before the second blade could finish extending, Mariko was right in his face with her weapons out.

He never even saw her move from her spot, meaning she used that invisibility speed technique. As their blades clashed, he became aware of the gap between his training and hers. She was a practitioner of speed magic, and he could sense and anticipate her movements. The honest-to-God reality was that if she increased her speed by even one percent, he would get diced up like an onion.

She disappeared before his eyes, and instinctively, he blocked her strike from behind. He backflipped over her and sliced at her from left to right with his blades. She avoided his strikes and blasted him backward with a water spell. When he stopped his momentum, she sped toward him.

Jayden was now back to his feet, noticing them entangled with their swords pressed against each other. Then

Tony pushed Mariko back a few feet. Jayden channeled his magical energy, pointing his sword toward the young Master, shouting, "Wall of Fire!"

A pillar of raging orange and yellow flames surrounded Mariko. Jayden snapped his finger, and the fire wall closed on her. He thought he had her for a second until she came bursting through the top of the wall, riding on her column of water.

While she was still in the air, just above his wall of flames. He put his hands together and shouted, "FireBlast!"

A stream of fiery energy shot out of his hands and darted toward Mariko. The Dragon Master didn't have enough time to dodge it. So she used her swords to protect herself as the blast launched her backward. Then Tony slammed his sword into the ground and cried, "Thunderbolt." A yellow lightning bolt came down from the sky above and slammed into their instructor while she was still fending off Jayden's attack.

The air around Mariko exploded as both spells connected. She fell to the ground and didn't move. Jayden wanted to jump up and see if she was okay, but he also wanted to cheer because they won.

He lifted his sword above his head, "We did it! We won! Did you see that, Priscilla?"

Priscilla shook her head as she stared at them from the stands. He waved at her and Sarah while glowing with pride. Then he felt a sharp pain in his left side and ended up on the ground, unable to move his legs. Jayden glanced up long enough to see Tony get disarmed and flipped on the ground.

Tony grimaced as he turned toward his friend with a pained look. "You frickin idiot."

Standing next to him was Mariko. Her hair was staticky, and her eyes were glowing ocean blue. She didn't acknowledge her lip bleeding or the bruise on her arm. The young Master just stood there, with magical energy surging through every vein and cell in her body. At that moment, he realized how wide the gap was between him and her. She was like a lion, and he was barely a house cat.

Mariko picked up her sword and walked off without a word.

***

Tony was sitting at a table on the far side of the bar. Jayden joined him and passed around a red ale poured into an ice-cold mug. They clinked their glasses and tried to relax after their 2-on-1 match with Mariko.

Jayden's side ached, and his pride and dignity were basically nonexistent. Not because losing to a girl was such a big deal. It was the fact that even at arguably their best, after having trained for weeks now, they weren't even close to beating her. However, they got her to the point where she had to try, so I guess that's some sort of moral victory.

Tony took a sip of the cold brew. "So, do you want to be on Sarah watch for today?"

"Heck no, last time she transformed. I had to swim about a mile out to bring her back. I love her, but not that much."

"Yeah, you do. Plus, she likes it when you look out for her."

Jayden shook his head as he took another swig of his Red Ale. The cool, refreshing taste of the beer made him feel relaxed. Just the thought of looking after Sarah in that form was terrifying. Her power in it was amazing, but she couldn't control it. She didn't try and leave every night. When she would sleepwalk in that form, it seemed to happen randomly. Every time she walked out with her hair blood red, she always went in the same direction northeast. Whatever was northeast of here must be very important.

Grace, Sarah, and Priscilla approached them from the other side of the bar. The girls were carrying a locally made rum drink poured into a pineapple. Sarah sat down across from him and took a sip of her tropical drink. "So, boys, how does it feel to have been beaten by a girl? That should teach you not to spy on women while they are training."

Jayden went to speak but was quickly stifled by Grace, who put her hand over his mouth. "Now, Jayden, think before you speak. Remember we talked about you working on that?"

He smiled, "Gracey, you look so pretty today, it's unbelievable. Sarah, we appreciate your support and weren't spying on you ladies. I just wanted to make sure that Priscilla was teaching you proper technique; you are welcome for that."

Sarah rolled her eyes, "you know she can kill you, right?"

"Still worth it," he replied.

Tony looked up from his drink. "I think we need to head north."

Sarah's eyes widened at his statement. "Look, I know I have made things difficult for you, but it's not yours or Jayden's responsibility to help me with this curse. Wherever this thing leads me, I can tell you it's nothing good. You three can finish the journey home; I've caused enough trouble already."

"Sarah, we aren't going to let you go on your own." Jayden said, a little louder than he intended.

"Jayden, just stop. You didn't want me coming on this trip in the first place. I'm going to do what I've gotta do, okay. And that's final!" She got up and stormed out of the bar.

Priscilla stood and grinned, "I see you are very good at communicating with women, Jayden. You impress me."

"She's being sarcastic, you know," Grace said with a stone face. "Now you know we can't let her go..." She began to trail off as a Breaking News Alert appeared on the television.

A military figure approached the microphone to begin their speech. This man was dressed in a blue commander's uniform for Eden Air Corp. His hair was black and cut short. A cutlass with a small handle and a black scabbard was on his right side. He had lightly tanned skin and brown eyes. He stared out into the waiting crowd.

"As of 0900 today, King Aelius has been removed from his position as commander and chief of this country. After a thorough investigation conducted by Internal Affairs, it became clear that our beloved King colluded with a terrorist group living amongst the Aggeloi. He used this group to gain further power, leading to the destruction of Eiréné. All parties involved with this attack against our populous are being rounded up as we speak. They will be held accountable and prosecuted to the fullest extent of the law. Before I continue, are there any questions?"

A gray-haired reporter raised their hand. "How is the Aggeloi leadership responding to this group? They should finally be held accountable for their citizens."

A roar of agreement arose from amongst the crowd. Some demanded war, others wanted the King to be strung up from the tallest trees, and a small minority suggested peaceful actions to avoid further conflict.

Commander Drake held out his hands to calm the crowd. Once they had quieted down, he approached the mic again. "Not too long ago, that group resurfaced again in Terracina. They attacked the residents of that town, killed members of the Southern Convent, and, worst of all, they attacked our soldiers who were stationed there. As of today, the Aggeloi have yet to bring any of those individuals forward. The dead deserve peace, and their government does not seem to want justice to prevail. Therefore, to the governing bodies of the Aggeloi heed this warning. Quiet is the sleeping giant, but pain and sorrow will surely follow if you ever cause it to stir. You have 24 hours; the clock has started."

Grace turned toward Jayden with a look of pure terror in her eyes, "What just happened?"

Jayden was too shocked to respond and just stared at the news feed.

"I think traveling north just became even more difficult." Tony said.

Priscilla stood up, "Tony, it's time. Let's go see Kayla. I must also inform Mi Lady about this development in the news."

***

Her curly blonde hair and relaxed expression on her face gave him the impression that this young woman was completely at peace. Her lungs expanded and compressed as she breathed gently. She possessed a silent spirit that appeared content with remaining in the world of dreams. Even though he knew better, he was still afraid that he might disturb her slumber.

They had given her a customized hospital gown adorned with pictures of her favorite cartoons. Even the blanket and quilts that covered her were dark pink, her favorite color.

The room was filled with cards signed by everyone on the island. Vases with sunflowers were placed on her nightstand and end tables. Kayla's parents were asleep on the pull-out bed. Besides their gentle breathing and the medical machines, the hospital room was deathly quiet.

Tony sat next to the twelve-year-old girl and held her hand. She was such a tough kid. Memories from that day filled his mind to the brim. Their fishing boat had capsized, and the waves battered her parents. Somehow, she managed to get on top of the boat and flagged him down. Even though she had a bump and a gash on her head, she didn't stop helping. It wasn't until that night, when they went to sleep, that she fell into a coma.

Her Father wasn't mad at him for what happened, nor was her mother. They just wanted their girl back if he had it in his power. In all honesty, he was lucky that Sarah had training in healing magic, or else she would not have made it to the Island of Dragons.

Tony looked up. Kayla's eyes were still closed. He would honestly give anything to see those hazel eyes again. It wasn't fair that her family should suffer because of the journey they were on. It wasn't fair that Floriana and many others were gone because of them. It almost seemed like the destruction of Eiréné placed a permanent curse on him.

His heartbeat jumped when he felt a squeezing sensation in his hand. Hope jumped into his mind once he heard a soft cough. He didn't want to look; he didn't want to get his hopes up. Tony turned anyway, and that's when he felt a second squeeze. This time, it felt stronger and more intentional.

He glanced up, and two hazel eyes stared back at him. A gentle smile creased her lips as she squeezed even harder. Tony reached for a glass of water and gestured for her to take a sip. Kayla held onto his hands as she placed it to her lips and managed to take a few sips down. Color returned to her face, and the guilt he held started to wash away.

"Thank you," She whispered.

Tears brimmed in his eyes as her parents woke up and realized what was happening. They swarmed around Kayla and held onto her without letting go. Tony wanted to leave, but she wouldn't let go.

While Kayla held on to his wrist, he began to get a glimpse of the bigger picture. As twisted as their situation had come about, he realized why they needed to keep fighting. The people seeking *The Key* and the power it provides won't hesitate to hurt families like this. Just like they destroyed his hometown and Terracina, no amount of life lost would stop them. If they didn't take action, more innocent lives would be lost. It sucks that on their way to help others, people like Kayla end up getting hurt in the process.

He stood as the young girl released his hand to fully embrace her family. The tears flowed, and a hint of joy began to fill the room. A family was finally reunited, but should they have been divided in the first place? Could he honestly have done anything different?

Kayla's mother, Serenity, glanced in his direction. Her graying blonde hair and the dark circles under her eyes made it clear to him the toll the last few weeks had brought on her. Serenity's lightly tanned skin had become pale over the last few weeks, and she had hardly eaten. In some ways, she looked worse off than her child.

Serenity cleared her throat and used a tissue to wipe the tears from her eyes. "I can't express how much it meant to see you come here daily. You didn't have to, and your friends surely didn't either. It does my heart good to see young people like yourself willing to go the extra mile to help people they don't know. You were already fighting for your lives and came to save ours anyway. Don't feel guilty for what happened to my little girl; don't let this bring you down. This experience has brought us closer together and has shown me a world I didn't know existed. I am extremely grateful, and we will never forget you, Tony Santos. Now go and get back to making the world a better place.

Chapter 6

To the Land of Emeralds

Mariko had her dad's old sword resting on the table in the center of the hut. Tony was already sitting across from her at the table. Jayden joined them quietly and bowed respectfully once he was fully seated.

The Dragon Master met their gaze and examined them. Jayden felt she could read his thoughts like words on a page. Mariko was a vastly different instructor than what he was used to. She possessed a level of warmth that his Masters did not. From what he had experienced over the last few weeks, she managed to push him harder. Master Mariko made him feel more unbalanced than ever on the battlefield. He learned quickly that he wasn't as fast as he thought and that fighting water magic users put him at a great disadvantage. Jayden knew he was stronger now than before they got here, which shows how amazing of a teacher she was.

Mariko used a levitation spell to lift the blade into the air, and it began to spin slowly in the air. She smiled gently and asked, "Jayden, who did you acquire this from?"

"It belonged to my dad," he replied.

"Who else has touched this weapon?"

Tony looked up at her, "I have Master. I helped maintain that sword over the years and gave it to Jayden before we left the monastery."

She grinned, "that young man is an impressive feat. You see, this weapon is a *Chaos Blade.* Now, you two are familiar with *Chaos Magic*, as you are practitioners of it. In a weapon like this, *Chaos Magic* can be even more destructive. You see, this weapon, if you are not worthy of it, will drain every drop of energy you have in your body and leave you to die. So, the fact that neither of you has dropped dead from touching it is quite a surprise."

The boys stared at each other like they had just seen a ghost. To think that they had been carrying around something that destructive without an ounce of concern. It was a miracle that none of them had died from handling it. Now they understood why not even the Daimonia tried to take the sword with them.

Mariko took a sip of green tea and returned her mug to the table. She rotated the weapon in the air so the blade hovered between them. "I want you to understand your uniqueness and responsibility regarding this scimitar. You see, this weapon is made from Elder Steel and obsidian. So, unlike your Dragon Swords, this weapon will not increase or amplify your magic. Instead, this sword can affect the battlefield without your awareness. In the core of this sword is the soul of a monster called a Berserker. They are foul and aggressive beasts. As Jayden has probably already experienced, this weapon caused you to fight more aggressively and even affected how you two worked together. Your random fighting was fluid, quick, and aggressive, which isn't always bad. However, this sword casts not only a light version of the Berserker spell on you, but it does it for all parties within close proximity of that sword. The Berserker spell is not as destructive as Rage but can be as difficult to manage. My question to the both of you is, can you manage a power like this?"

They both nodded yes.

"I asked that question because I have been talking with Master Thai about what to do with you two. I know you two have used master-level magic in your fights that you were not taught to do. I also know that you have tapped into the *forbidden*." She stared at the both of them with a glare that could pierce through steel. "So, we were left with very few options, not because you are abusing your powers, but simply due to the abilities you can use. We are responsible for protecting the world, and you must not forget that. Your friends have fully explained why you have used your powers in extreme ways. Considering the noble task thrust upon you, I would like to make you two Dragon Knights."

"A what?" They shouted in unison.

For shouting out of turn, she flicked droplets of salt water into their eyes.

"We want to bestow upon both of you a new rank based on your abilities, experiences, and growth. We do not give this title often because it comes with a big burden. Consider it one of the levels between a Dragon Warrior and a Master. Your role as a Knight would symbolize hope and strength for the world. You can access more of your magic, but it will come at a higher consequence should you misuse it. Are you willing to accept that responsibility?"

"We agree." They replied in unison.

The young Dragon Master grinned from ear to ear. "It is an honor to give you both this new title. You will find that you can access more powers you were allowed to use while training at the Monastery. But that is a double-edged sword. While it can be useful, those powers are also very destructive and dangerous. You also need to remember that both of you are stronger than before. That can make it even more tempting to misuse your gifts intentionally or accidentally. So, do you both still agree to take on this responsibility?"

They glanced at each other nervously, "We think so."

She gave them a devilish grin and then snapped her fingers. Instantly, both shouted in pain. Jayden reached for his chest and felt it burning. It was like having a scorching, hot, jagged knife digging through his left pec.

He winced as he struggled to lift his shirt to take a look. His jaw dropped as dark lines appeared on his chest. The pain increased as the dark ink began to elongate and form into the ancient symbol for fire 火.

Tony lifted his shirt, and on his left pec was a different image, a pale blue wave tattooed on his chest. A few millimeters above his wave tattoo was the ancient word for storm 嵐.

His best friend grinned as he examined his new ink. "Master Mariko, this tattoo looks awesome. It hurts like hell, but will this tattoo limit our magic even more than our original ones?"

She smiled back, "No. In fact, this symbol will nullify the original limiters we gave. The new markings you both received will allow you to use up to 80% of your original power and 80% of any power you gain moving forward. However, as I said, this is a tremendous responsibility not to be taken lightly or misused. Also, we can always remove this tattoo if you cannot live up to the expectations of being a Dragon Knight. You can be officially demoted back to a Dragon Warrior. You should never view yourself as your new title implies. I want you to view yourselves always as Dragon Warriors. Young men who are always willing to serve and learn. Always willing to push yourselves, not for personal gain but because you want to simply better yourself. Let your Knighthood be your rank, and let the spirit of a Dragon Warrior be your heart."

"Master, what will happen if we misuse it?" Jayden asked.

"We will kill you," She replied with a straight face.

His heart jumped into his throat as those words left her lips. He felt a mixture of fear and guilt. He hadn't thought about how they used their abilities until now. Yes, he normally did restrain himself, but he had never considered whether he should be using his powers at all. He needed to be more careful with them. Kayla ending up in a coma was a wake-up call for him, too.

Jayden met her gaze and said, "Mariko, if you and the other Masters are so concerned about protecting the world, why don't you go out and fight these battles?"

She handed him his father's sword. "That's why we sent you."

***

The ocean's hue painted the horizon in every direction. Seagulls and ospreys cruised through the sky above. The salty smell of the ocean consumed his senses. Powerful waves pummeled the beaches below as the sheer majesty of nature greeted them with an unforgettable roar.

He peaked over the side of the cliff and was enamored by the beautiful tropical forest below. The palm fronds stretched tall and proud, like the children of Mother Nature herself. Even from such a great height, he could still see the juicy and plump fruits hanging from the branches below. They stood only a hundred feet above the tallest tree, but he still felt at ease. The last thing he wanted to do was to slip on a conveniently placed rock and fall to his untimely death.

Sarah appeared next to him and leaned against him. "You know you don't have to do this. It's not your fault I keep having these dreams and sleepwalking at night. You have already risked enough."

Jayden put his arm around her, "I know. The Daimonia and the Dark Prince will soon follow wherever that curse leads you. When they do, I will be more than ready for them. Plus, we are family; you've been there for me when I've almost died a thousand times. It's time for me to return the favor." He adjusted the wings on his glider and looked back at the rest of the group. "I just don't get why she's going."

He didn't have to wait for the bruises to form on his rib cage to know Priscilla took offense to his statement. Nor did he have to look at Sarah to know she was staring daggers into his eyes. All in all, he thought the joke was worth it.

Sarah lifted his arm off her and gave him the prettiest smile in the world. Then she said, "I think it's funny that you should mention her. I will fly on her glider, and Grace will go with you." She patted him on the shoulder and quickly dashed over to Priscilla, who had a large and obnoxious grin on her face.

Jayden turned to his best friend, "I guess that means you'll be riding solo," Tony responded to his friend by giving him a hand gesture that would have gotten his fingers taped together if they were still in school.

He noticed that Gracey was now sitting under a small palm tree. She seemed to be avoiding eye contact and hoped nobody would notice. Jokes on her; you can't hide on a cliff.

Jayden reached out to help her to her feet. She brushed his hand aside and looked away from him. The Dragon Warrior grinned and quickly moved behind her. He gave her a bear hug and lifted her onto her feet.

She pushed him away, "I'm just going to stay here. You guys can go."

"Why are you being so difficult?" He asked.

Grace peered over the ledge, "You know I'm afraid of heights. I think it will be safer for everyone if I stay here."

Jayden cocked his head to the side. "After all we have been through, you don't trust me to keep you safe on this trip?"

She shook her head, "Last time I trusted you, I almost fell down a crevice!"

"She's not wrong!" Sarah shouted as she strapped into the tandem glider with Priscilla.

"You're not helping," Jayden shouted back. "Look, I'm not going to let you fall. I promise that I will keep you safe, weirdo."

Grace nervously bit her lip, "Fine, I'll do it, but you better not fly fast."

Jayden adjusted the metallic bag on his back. Then he pressed a green button on the left strap, lengthening the bag. A second set of back straps appeared once the bag had lengthened enough for a second person. Grace stuck her arms through the straps and took a deep breath.

The Aggeloi Princess turned to him, "If we die on this ride. I will haunt you."

Jayden brushed her newly purple and silver hair out of her eyes and kissed her forehead. "I'm counting on it."

Before she could elbow him in the side, he pressed a blue button on his right strap. Then he heard a whirring sound as mechanisms in the bag started to move. Silver and white metallic wings started to protrude from their bag's left and right sides. Miniature rocket engines were connected to the base of each wing.

Once the wings had finished expanding, he gave Gracey a quick nudge. She cracked her neck and ran begrudgingly beside him toward the cliff's edge. Then, together, they jumped over the side and plummeted toward the palm trees below.

The sea of green objects below seemed to stretch out their palm fronds to impale them as they fell. As they picked up speed, Grace's screams became slightly muted by the roaring wind blowing in his ear. He adjusted the angle of the rockets and the wings in the nick of time. With the adjustments made, the Princess yelled in his ear even louder as they were launched skyward. Truthfully, he could have adjusted the rockets sooner; he just wanted to mess with Grace.

***

The word bliss, or even the truest sense of freedom, could barely describe the feeling consuming him as they soared through the beautiful sky. Like a caged bird released from its prison, he felt freer with every cloud they passed through. Jayden felt he could conquer the world as they sped over the blue ocean.

He sniffled, and tears appeared as he watched a family of ospreys flying below them. They were large and powerful creatures simply moving forward in life. Their beautiful white and black feathers made them appear so regal and saintly. They seemed so content and at peace with their lot in life. He was beginning to wonder when he would find his. Would he ever find peace at the end of their journey?

Grace turned toward him, "How are you able to control this? Where did you learn to fly a glider?"

"Normally, you would use joy sticks or some control arm. I use my magic to control it. I can even use my magic to make us go faster. When I was at the Dragon Monastery learning to do our *Glide* spells, they had us practice using these. It helped and hurt a lot."

"That's cool, but if you try to go super fast, I will summon Aiko to eat you."

Jayden smirked as he stared out across the ocean, trying to think about where this road was going to lead them. Unlike before, this time, they were traveling without any idea where they were going. Their only guide came from a sleepwalking Sarah. For most people, following a guide like that would be a no-go. He hoped it would be worthwhile and Sarah could finally get some peace.

"Jayden, I'm scared," She whispered.

"I know you are afraid of heights, but we have gone too far to turn back."

Grace shook her head, tears glistening in her eyes. "No, that's not what I'm talking about. I'm scared of going home. I haven't been there since that awful day. I can remember some things about my past, but there is a lot I don't remember. There is no one there for me; it's like we're going to a place that used to be important. But the only thing I can remember are the nightmares."

"I get that. I still remember when Tony and I arrived in Eiréné after so many years. It was so weird because it was like walking into a ghost town. The weeds and overgrown trees had actually taken back most of the town. It was hard to believe that we grew up in the same place. Going back, you'll feel weird, but I think this might be good for you, even if we are only briefly there."

She looked him in the eyes, "Do you think any of them will be glad that I'm alive?"

"Ehh, probably not," he replied.

Grace quickly elbowed him in the side, which created a large amount of pain for him in the ribs.

"I'm kidding, I'm kidding. Well, I am sure some people would like to know the truth about you. In all honesty, I'm glad you're alive. Without you, I wouldn't have a backup if things with Priscilla or Sarah don't work out."

Grace rolled her eyes, "I am literally a princess. If anything, they should be the backups. For one, I am literally too punk rock for you. I change my hair color constantly; you can't keep up. Plus, you would also have to be a prince. The whole small-town guy marrying the long-lost princess only happens in the movies. I'm sorry, Jayden, it just won't happen."

Based on her response, Jayden felt the sudden urge to push her eject button. So, instead of sending the princess plummeting to her death, he returned to oohing and ahhing at the beautiful ocean below.

***

His copilot began reminiscing as they drew closer to the Aggeloi coastline. Grace mentioned that when she was a young girl, her parents used to take her to this part of the country for vacation. The seaside town they were flying to filled her with pleasant memories. From learning to swim to catching a shark and even getting her toes squished by a crab. The truth was that it was almost too overwhelming for her memories to come flooding to the surface, but she was glad they did. From his point of view, this trip would be a great reintroduction for her to a land she once called home.

There, nestled along the southwestern Aggeloi coast, was a small shipping port called Lechaion, originally used by the military. From what Grace could recall, Lechaion was one of the oldest cities in the country, and the waters near the port were said to be the most dazzling in the world. She mentioned that the waves would shimmer a bright green from the many magic crystals that filled the ocean below.

Their view from the skies as they flew in from the south was a far cry from a welcoming party. In fact, the images that were slowly coming into view were a sight he had become all too familiar with.

Wisps of gray smoke drifted into the skies. The thunderclouds and the fiery smoke coiled together like a python. Even though they were still miles away, the stench of death made his stomach turn. He wanted to escape. He wanted to do anything but continue moving forward. Nothing good would come from them continuing in this direction.

If his heart pounding in his chest wasn't uncomfortable enough, the dead silence echoing across the sea was warning enough. There were no cries for help, no service crews or sirens blaring across the streets of Lechaion. The only sound he could make out was the barely audible melody of waves breaking against the lonely beach.

He didn't need to hear the sniffles or see the stunned look on Grace's face to know her world had been turned upside down once again. There were no words he could say to fix what stood before them. She had already experienced so much from just traveling with them. Now, the curse of death and destruction seemed hellbent on paving a path of sorrow for them.

He went to console her but then felt a twist in his stomach. Instinctively, he constricted the wings of a glider and went into a barrel roll. His ears popped at the sound of bullets whistling just inches from his face.

A black shape appeared in the clouds above them. Metallic wings and talons pierced through the gray clouds. A gloved hand gripped the silenced machine guns attached to the shoulder straps of the glider. Armor-piercing rounds and explosive-tipped bullets whizzed past them like a swarm of bees from the pits of hell.

His jaw just about hit the nonexistent floor as dark wings unfurled in the clouds above them. They descended upon them like angels of darkness, coming to judge the earth. Their weapons extended out from demonic wings as if they were birds of prey, revealing their talons to make a kill. They flew like a pride of lionesses with their trap sprung and ambush set. Their bloodlust and deadly efficiency were on full display.

Jayden focused his mind and channeled his magical energy into the glider as he dove. He used his abilities to avoid the volley of bullets being rained down upon them. As good as he was, he knew his own limitations. There was a time limit for how long he could avoid their rapid fire. Sooner or later, his magic would run out, and they would be royally screwed.

He felt a twinge in his stomach and quickly glanced downward. His face was filled with horror as an enemy glider appeared below them. Jayden closed his eyes and prepared to meet his maker. A flash of lightning peeled across the sky, slamming into the soldier below. After that, a hail of explosive rounds were launched from Sarah's machine pistols.

The soldiers above them scattered as Sarah's rounds created an explosive light show in the sky. Grace turned toward him with a look that chilled him to the bone. "Are those the assholes who destroyed this town and killed so many innocent people?"

"Most likely," he replied.

"Great," she said in the coldest tone he had ever heard.

Grace grabbed onto his hand, and their fingers became entangled. He could feel his magical energy flowing into the space between his fingertips and hers. Their magical power began to swirl together as her anger was brimming to the surface.

Her magical energy radiated with a sense of cruelty, becoming consumed with a desire to destroy. He could never have imagined that such darkness like this could exist in the sweet and damaged soul of the Aggeloi Princess. The power swirling between them was built to serve one purpose: rain down terror.

The powerful Princess of the Aggeloi commanded the glider to roll over onto its back so they could attack the soldiers gliding through the clouds. Grace brimmed with magical power and shouted into the sky, "Aiko! Dragon of The Red Flame! Rise and destroy these murderers!"

***

A shockwave of energy shouted out across the deep. The waves churned, and steam rose from the waters below them. Intense heat filled the air, and a blood-curdling roar pierced through the sounds of shouts and gunfire. Magical energy rose from the depths below, and for a second, Jayden wondered what hell Grace was about to rain down upon them.

Horns made of iron slowly breached the surface of the deep. Red and black scales and wings thirty feet long appeared below them. Razor sharp claws and fangs as sharp as daggers became visible as the monster's body moved closer to the surface. Droplets of liquified metal and puffs of smoke spewed from the dragon's jaws. Words like power and strength failed to describe the bringer of death that was now ascending into the sky.

Aiko's normally smooth and relaxed scales are now rough and jagged like the side of a rock. The gusts of wind kicked up by her powerful wings were even more tense in her scarlet-colored form. Her teeth were now filled with jagged and pointy grooves. The dragon's pupils were as crimson as a few of his strongest spells. It was as if two fire spirits were dancing in their reptilian friend's eyes.

The sweet Pigmy Dragon that used to play pranks on him was gone. She might as well be a distant memory at this point. The form flying above them now differed from that blue dragon, as the night was from the day. Instead of a silent joy and prankster spirit, this version of Aiko possessed no warmth in her eyes. Her soul was consumed with a lust for blood and vengeance. He still couldn't quite process that the monster staring back at them was full of rage and determination.

A squadron of gliders sped downward toward the red dragon. The airmen opened fire upon her, showering the dragon with machine gunfire and anti-magic rockets. The bullets bounced off her armored hide. Aiko darted to the side with tremendous speed to avoid the next volley of rockets. As the rockets sped past her, she flapped her wings and climbed through the clouds effortlessly. She turned her head and stared down ferociously at her prey.

Aiko opened her powerful jaws, and molten lava oozed from her mouth. Then the wind in the battle arena became scalding hot as her mouth sucked in the air. Her eyes glowed bright red and let out a deafening roar, with a blast of fire and molten rock destroying the gliders below.

Without warning, red and blue sparks of light exploded off the dragon's back. Her form shimmered in the skies above as if she was beginning to phase away.

Just as Aiko fought to maintain her form, a volley of anti-magic rockets were launched in her direction. The dragon countered their assault by summoning a series of fireballs she sent toward the wall of rockets heading her way. Before her spell could contact the incoming missiles, an unfortunate glider had flown in too close to the dragon and was quickly run through by her claws.

She let out an earth-shattering roar as her enemies rained lead down upon her. The machine gun fire and anti-magic rockets were taking their toll on the poor creature. Despite the pain and strain the attacks 0 on her, she seemed to try and persevere. The Red Drago Aiko chose to stand her ground and let out a second roar brimming with the power of defiance. Her crimson eyes were filled with rage and determination despite the odds significantly stacked against her.

With a look of determination on her face, she quickly darted to her right to avoid another onslaught of bullets. Then she flicked her tail, and orange flames began to encircle her like a tornado. The dragon flicked her tail a second time, and the flames became blood red. Lava oozed from the rows of her razor-sharp teeth as her enemies continued shooting fire and lead. However, her armor of dancing flames melted and destroyed their feeble attempts at hitting her. At this moment, the tables were turned against them. The scales would now tip in favor of Grace's beloved friend.

Aiko snarled, her eyes narrowing on the column of soldiers descending upon her. The Crimson Dragon flapped her mighty wings and rocketed through the clouds. She moved like a blur, striking down any soul that made the mistake of getting in her way. Aiko had blood dripping from her fangs and claws. The gliders were no match for the sheer tenacity and power of a monster consumed with rage.

***

Jayden was so entranced by the battle above that he had completely lost track of the glider pilots pursuing them. The sound of metal slamming into metal and sparks bursting from their glider brought his mind back toward the real battle. He glanced behind them, his eyes zeroing in on two pilots zooming their way. The Dragon Warrior channeled his magic into their damaged vehicle, forcing the engines forward.

Gasoline and fluids spurted out of their wings. They were in big trouble and needed to solve it fast. Jayden guided their glider to the right, so they flew parallel along the coast.

There was a hill that rose up along the sandy beach. At the top of the hill was a forested area extending for miles. If they could reach the forest, they would have some cover.

Unfortunately, their glider would either get shot down before they got there, or they would blow up in the air.

"Grace, do you see those trees over there? That's where we need to go."

"Can we even make it that far?" She asked.

"Probably not. Do you know how to do a pencil dive?" Grace nodded her head yes. "Perfect, now do it."

Before she could respond, he pressed the release button on her strap. Immediately, she plummeted toward the ocean below. He couldn't make out exactly what she screamed at him, but he got some enjoyment when he heard her splash into the water.

He made the glider accelerate as he flew parallel to the beach. Jayden summoned a barrier made of fire to protect himself from the bullets whizzing by. As the rounds became vaporized by his fire shield, he waited until the gliders were within range. Then he rotated his body so the wings were under him, staring right at the enemy.

Jayden spread his arms and brought them back together, shouting, "FireWave!" As the words escaped his lips, a wave of red and yellow flames flew toward his two attackers. Before the glider pilots could react, the flames engulfed them completely, falling into the waters below.

The Dragon Warrior clicked a button on his harness and was released just in time. As he fell, the glider exploded overhead. Jayden absorbed the flames and the heat from it. Then he channeled his gliding spell, with white and orange flames surrounding him. Once the magic spell was set, he flew toward the beach. Within a few seconds, he reached the tree line and landed safely on the ground.

When his feet hit the ground, he looked up in just enough time to see Aiko's form begin to shimmer. Her final blasts of plasma and fire completely decimated the remaining gliders in the sky. Thanks to that Dragon, they might make it out of there alive.

Tony and the girls descended on the cliff just a few feet from him. From what he could tell, they were all okay.

Priscilla's glider had a few bullet holes, but not enough to keep her out of the skies. Once Priscilla detached Sarah from her harness, she ran into Jayden's arms.

"That was a nightmare," She said between sobs. "Those poor people were just slaughtered. How many more times will we have to go through this?"

"I agree. This whole, being unable to save everyone, is getting old," Jayden replied.

Sarah wiped her tears as he released her. "What happened to Grace? Is she okay?"

Jayden smiled awkwardly and said, "I think she's okay."

As those words escaped his mouth, he felt a sudden increase of pain in his face. His body was now falling to the ground from the shoe that was rocketed at him. While reeling from the pain, he looked up at the completely soaked Aggeloian Princess, who did not look amused.

Grace gave him the death stare. "The next time you ask me if I can swim, I will kill you."

Sarah glanced at both of them, feeling really confused. "Did I miss something?"

"He pressed the release button on my harness and dropped me in the ocean," Grace replied.

"Jayden LoneOak!" Sarah shouted.

Jayden got up and put the most apologetic look on his face. "Look, it was the best idea I had at the time. We were getting shot at, and I didn't want her to die. So, I dropped her in the ocean, and it worked. She's here with no bullet wounds. You are welcome."

Grace stepped into him, "You son of a..."

Tony clasped his hand over her mouth, "We can't stay here. We have to get moving now."

"I agree," Priscilla said as she sharpened her sword.

"Why?" Sarah asked. "We should be safe under these trees."

Priscilla sniffed the air, "Because we are not alone."

Chapter 7

The Enemy of My Enemy

A gentle breeze blew through her scarlet hair. Goosebumps formed on her arms as a film of frost covered her swords. Her body shivered uncontrollably from the freezing cold. She clutched onto her jacket for warmth, but she might as well not be wearing it; it was so cold.

Intense magical energy flowed through every fiber of her body like an endless river. The power brimming from deep inside was nothing compared to the energy from the ice wall in front of her. She had never felt a magical presence like this before. To say it was overwhelming would be an understatement.

The wall was so cold it was like standing inside a walk-in freezer. Sarah placed her hand against it and felt a sudden sharp pain coursing through her veins. She winced from the pain. Her soft skin felt as if there was a jagged, serrated blade being pressed through her hand and up into her wrist.

Sarah stared in horror as blood began to trickle down from above. Streams of crimson flowed over her pale skin. The liquid chilled her to the bone, soaking the goosebumps covering her arms.

She felt a sense of cruelty and sorrow as her hand pressed against the ice wall. In her mind, she could hear painful screams and cries for help. The raw emotion consuming her body and mind was overwhelming. Sarah wanted to run. She wanted to escape from this freezing Hell.

Come to me. Come to me. A demonic voice demanded. *Come and fulfill your destiny. Bring the two together!*

"Sarah! Sarah!" Grace shouted as she shook her awake.

"What? What?" Sarah croaked, "Why is my throat sore."

"Well, your hair turned red again, and you've been screaming in my ear for the last twenty minutes. I wanted to choke you to death, but I didn't because I like you. Also, why is your body cold and clammy? Did you have another one of those dreams?"

Sarah sat up and stared back at her royal friend. "Well, that explains a lot. I did have another frightening dream."

She proceeded to share the details of her dream with Grace. The Aggeloi Princess nodded her head as she processed the story. Then she grimaced, "Ugh, I hope this doesn't sound too princessy. I'm tired of dealing with snow and cold. Can we just send the boys instead?"

Sarah grinned, "I like that idea. By the way, where is Jayden?"

Grace pointed toward a nearby tree just a few feet away. "So I've been screaming this whole time, and he hasn't come down once to check on me? Let's go ring his neck!"

Together, they climbed the humongous Sequoia tree. Sarah and Grace were not the biggest fans of climbing trees, but they had to ruin Jayden's morning. As she grabbed another branch, she cursed under her breath. Not because the climb was difficult, but she could not, for the life of her, understand why Jayden had to be at the top of the tree.

He was resting against the tree while staring at the rising sun. A smile creased his lips as the sky filled with a yellowish-pink hue. There was a level of peace in his eyes that was inspiring. To be honest, Sarah wished she could borrow some of that peace. Between her nightmares and sleepwalking, she felt she was slowly going crazy and that she might be dragging the others down with her.

Jayden glared at the two girls as they pulled themselves onto his branch. "Thanks for waking up the forest."

"I'm sorry I had another freaking nightmare. It's not like you even give a crap!" Sarah snapped.

"It is too early for you to act like a jackass. Why do you need us to be quiet anyway? We are miles away from the city." Grace said.

"Because," said a voice from further up in the tree.

The branches near the canopy jostled back and forth as a shadow came down from the treetop. Tony landed on the branch right in front of them. "The group that attacked that city is a special military strike force known as the Ravens."

"The who?" Grace asked.

"The Ravens are a special military group designed to strike quickly to destabilize their enemy. They are the same buttholes that attacked the Water Temple. The last thing they would want is for survivors to walk away from that city."

Grace's eyes flashed red with fear and anger. "Then why did they attack them in the first place? They didn't even wait for the twenty-four hours they promised! They just killed those people like it was nothing."

"I think they did it for two reasons: to create fear and to get access to some of the magic crystals. The Eden military isn't as big or as advanced as the Aggeloi. So, I figure they did this attack to make themselves seem more ferocious than they are. And with the magic crystals, they could power more of their weapons. It doesn't make it right. It proves that Eden's government isn't better now than before."

Jayden stood up and patted his best friend on the shoulder. "I agree with you. Plus, they had to have planned and set up those attacks for months. There is no way they could have taken it down so quickly without time and preparation. Which is why we need to be even more careful moving forward. This war is already out of hand and has barely even started."

Sarah rolled her eyes, "Be careful he says. This coming from the same guy who's been in and out of the hospital since we started this journey."

"I know", Grace interjected. "He's the clumsiest moron in the world."

At that moment, Jayden was tempted to strangle the both of them. He didn't, mainly because he feared he would accidentally fall out of the tree.

***

They gathered their things and decided it was time to move on. Together, they made their way down the tree. Once they reached the bottom, they moved toward a small dusty trail that led them out of the forest. Exiting the vast arena of trees, they found themselves at the edge of a large plain with a series of grassy hills bounding off in the distance.

The air smelled of a combination of sweet spearmint and berries. They were greeted that morning by bluejays and orange cardinals chirping as they searched for their early morning meal. Amongst the weeds and flowers of the plain, he spotted groups of green wasps with curved stingers buzzing as they flew from flower to flower.

Smoke billowed from the chimneys of a nearby town. The houses and buildings were all painted in light pastel colors. Golden retrievers and Aggeloian Shepherd dogs greeted them as they reached the town entrance.

Everything about this small city seemed pleasant, except for the soldiers running around dressed in their military blues. Steel-toed boots bounded against the ground as they marched in their units. Rifles and sabers rattled, ready for war. It was clear to them that, at this point, the destruction of Lechaion had not gone unnoticed.

Jayden hesitated momentarily as they walked toward a small wooden gate set up by the soldiers. He knew that they didn't have any I.D.s on them. Also, considering that it was his country that had attacked, they were totally screwed. However, it would be even worse if the soldiers found out he was traveling with the long-lost princess of the Aggeloi.

A large soldier dressed in military blues with a matching helmet stood outside the gate. He waved for them to come talk to him. He blew out a cloud of water vapor from his electromagic cigarette. He scratched his scraggly beard and said, "I am Johansson. I am one of the commanders of Azul Centurions. We are among the most badass fighting forces you will ever see on Aggeloi soil. I tell you all that because I can tell that you are not from around here."

"My name is Jayden." He reached out his hand for the centurion to shake. The commander of the centurions eyed him suspiciously before taking his hand. The man's grip was as tight as a boa constrictor, and his hand was as rough as sandpaper.

The commanding officer grinned, "I've been in the military for many years. One of the things I learned during that time was you can tell a lot about a man by how he shakes your hand and the look in his eyes. There is a deep sadness behind your eyes; you have seen horrors that few could only imagine. Your hands have been stained with blood from battles, one of which was quite recent." Before they could react, they were surrounded by soldiers dressed in blue. "I know you came from Lechaion, and you were there when the bullets started flying. Now, you and your group of heavily armed miscreants will have to answer this long list of questions I have for you. Understand that I have been granted the power to hold prisoners indefinitely due to the current situation."

The soldiers raised their rifles as he finished his speech. They were forced on their knees and hands placed behind their backs. The commander of the Azul Centurions began to encircle them like a jungle cat. His orange eyes seemed to analyze and scrutinize their very existence. He was a man of honor, but his bosses wanted results quickly. If he could make an example out of them, his superior officers would shower him with blessings.

Johansson stopped his pacing when he reached Gracey. His eyes peered into her avoidant gaze. If they didn't come up with a way to get out of this situation, they were going to be completely screwed. There was no way that he couldn't figure out who she was. Hell, she was spunky and difficult enough that she might just tell him who she was and tell them to shove it.

A man in his forties stepped out of an office just a few yards from the gate. He wore a blue suit with a gold watch and suede shoes. His eyes were bright silver, and his brown hair was gelled and slicked back. From Sarah's jaw drop, Jayden guessed she might have found him at least mildly attractive. As far as Jayden was concerned, this was just another rich toolbag coming to laugh at their predicament.

The gentleman ran his fingers through his hair as he approached the commander without reservation. "Commander Johansson, God bless your soul. You have found my wandering band of misfits. They were out researching some insurance claims for me when that dreadful attack occurred. I feared the absolute worst. If you could follow me back to my office, I would love to see your reports."

Commander Johansson took a hit from his vape and blew it in the man's face. "James, you understand that I have the authority to detain anyone who appears to be a threat to Aggeloi people at this time, right?"

James grinned his pearly whites, "I am quite aware of your bloated and overreaching powers. I would also like to remind you that I will be having a conference call with your superiors tonight about how you are handling this situation. I would love to give Rolando a glowing report about your progress."

Johansson chuckled to himself, "If I didn't know any better. I'd swear that I was talking to the devil himself. You may have to take your squad back to your coveted office. However, I expect a detailed report of their activities and a conversation with your team within the next 48 hours. If not, I will have you arrested quicker than you can deny an insurance claim."

James grinned and bowed respectfully, then signaled for them to follow him. He directed them toward a peach-colored building with two floors. A wooden sign on the building read, "Atlas Insurance."

He pushed the door open, stepping onto a wood floor. Their footsteps sounded hollow as they made their way up the stairs. In the center of the stairway lay a cream-colored carpet made of wool that extended to the top of the landing. James was their guide, directing them past rows of luxurious offices until they reached his. A plaque made of gold hung in front of his door with the words *Executive Office* inscribed on it.

The insurance broker pressed the letter O on the plaque, and the door faded into nothingness. Once they crossed the threshold, the door reappeared behind them just as normal.

The room was way more spacious than it had appeared from the outside. A large mahogany desk took up the center of the room. A black computer and stacks of paperwork covered the beautiful wood finish. In the back of the room was a treadmill and some free weights.

From what Jayden could tell, the room was designed for James to spend as much time here as possible with no chance of a social life. There was even a large couch on the side and a bean bag chair the size of a car. If that wasn't enough, large flat-screen televisions hung from the walls. The only thing missing from this office was a popcorn machine and snacks.

James gestured for them to sit in these turquoise-colored, egg-shaped chairs. Tony and Jayden were not the biggest fans of this alternative chair design. So, they decided to plop on the couch. Gracey thought it would be helpful to sit between them.

Priscilla stared daggers into his eyes, "Who are you really?"

Her tone didn't seem to faze him in the slightest. James seemed to be amused by her directness. Judging by the power he must wield in this office, he probably wasn't used to this level of confrontation.

James leaned back in his chair like all evil geniuses do. He grinned toothily and said, "Well, as you can see, I'm just a mild-mannered insurance agent."

"Bullshit!" Tony shouted from the couch.

"You might be right," James replied.

Grace sat up in her seat, "Why did you help us? Do you know us somehow?"

The insurance agent waited to respond, and, for a moment, he stared at her with silent intrigue. "In a way, I could say I know of you."

Jayden tuned out their conversation for a moment when he became interested in the tattoo ink he noticed through a slit in James' shirt. From what he could tell, the image had sharp and frightening edges. Something about the design made the hair on his neck stand up.

He looked up at the insurance agent and said, "I don't mean to be rude, but are you a member of a group of jerks called the Daimonia?"

James grinned as he rolled back his sleeve, revealing a demon tattoo. The monster had sharp teeth stained in blood and razor-sharp claws. As he rotated his wrist, the image became an ancient god carrying the world on its shoulders.

At the sight of a Daimonia member, Jayden would normally reach for one of his weapons. Instead, he practiced restraint, just as Mariko had taught him. Honestly, he felt a greater sense of curiosity than he did vengeance. There was something different about him compared to any of the other Daimonia members he had met. Normally, he could sense dark energy coming from them. Besides the fact he worked at an insurance agency, he couldn't say there was anything nefarious about him.

"You aren't like the rest of them, are you?" Jayden asked. "I can't sense any magical or dark energy coming from you."

James grinned, "I can tell that you are quite the observer. You are just like your Father in that regard. You can't sense my energy because of the enchantment placed on this tattoo. It allows me to conceal my identity and abilities. I could be a complete weakling or the strongest magician ever. With this enchantment, you or anyone else would be none the wiser."

"If you are a member of the Daimonia, why did you try to help us back there? Or is this some elaborate plot to trap us like Jason did?"

The insurance agent leaned back in his chair, "Despite your experience with us, not all of us in the Daimonia organization are like the *Orias* group. You are safe with me for now. The reason I helped you was strictly business. You owe our automobile rental company money. You failed to file the proper paperwork with our insurance office, stating the vehicles were taken from you."

Jayden's light caramel skin started to turn red from embarrassment. He completely forgot about the car and the motorcycles they rented and just left on the side of the road. He shook his head and tried to put on a bold, professional face.

"I did submit that paperwork," he lied. "I gave it to Tony to pass to one of your offices. It must have just gotten lost."

Tony nodded in agreement, "I agree. I remember giving it to a lady named Sandra. She said everything would be fine."

James scanned their faces momentarily, not because he believed their lies but because he couldn't decide how to respond to this ridiculousness. Before he could respond, Priscilla cleared her throat, "What is the *Orias* group? How are they different from you?"

"I guess you all haven't been told much about us. I will share what I can. The Daimonia were originally made up of twelve organizations. Those twelve organizations joined "The

Witnesses" at one point or another sometime after the Great War. When the twelve leaders decided that "The Witnesses" would never achieve their goal through indirect methods, they left and created The Daimonia. A thirteenth member created their own off-shoot organization, later joining the Daimonia. The Orias group is that thirteenth member; they are the individuals that feel the need to be violent and aggressive to the point that it shows up on the news. The rest of the Daimonia organization believed that to follow our bylaws and achieve our goals, we needed to operate in the shadows by controlling the systems everyone needed. This included governments, insurance companies, and even currency. The *Orias* group sees things differently. Hell, even the twelfth group shares a vastly different philosophy. Lord knows what those devil worshippers are up to now. I, however, am from the Atlas group, the oldest group within the Daimonia. Now that I've shared a bit about myself, I'd like to ask you a favor. If you complete this favor, all debts will be paid. I promise this isn't a secret trap or anything."

Jayden turned toward his best friend, who gave a simple shrug. Neither of them particularly liked the idea of doing a favor for the Daimonia or the Atlas group. However, they couldn't afford to shell out a ton of money. Plus, they honestly had no idea where they were going, so it might not be such a bad detour, at least for now.

"We will do it, "Jayden replied.

James smiled from ear to ear, "Perfect."

Chapter 8

Truth and Lies

He felt a chill down his spine as he entered the fourth dorm. A light hovered over the cells. The lampshades swung back and forth like he was in a horror flick. Lightbulbs flickered on and off as he approached her cell. Fear and dread filled his soul as he approached her.

Cain hated having to guard her every day. For one, it was a waste of time. She could not get out, even if the witch wanted to. Secondly, even if she did get out, she wouldn't get far. He only had to guard her because the Fallen Wizard wanted to remind him that he would have to kill Jayden's mother. Not that he believed she was in the slightest. No witch like her could be a mother to anyone.

The worst thing about the fourth dorm wasn't even the eerie setting but simply being in the presence of Lady Coral. Staring into her eyes was like staring into the eyes of a tiger.

She had nothing to lose, and when she stared at you, she ensured you knew it. The violent intensity in her eyes was only surpassed by the darkness that emanated from her. The dark energy surrounding her could only be matched by the Fallen Wizard. It was almost too overwhelming to behold.

Cain placed his folding chair a couple of feet in front of her cell. He fixed his gaze on her, and she stared back at him. Her head was tilted to the side in the creepiest way possible. She didn't say a word; he almost couldn't tell if she was breathing. The look in her eyes was wild, untamed, and the pure definition of danger. As much as he feared his brothers and the Fallen Wizard, something about her frightened him in a way they never could.

Lady Coral had said very few words since the day he met her. Even when she did talk, she seemed to be talking to herself, the walls, and even a cockroach once. He couldn't tell if she was just putting on an act just to scare him or if she was legitimately crazy. Cain did recall one night when he could hear her screaming in terror. Those cries at night he knew were genuine; they were different than her normal theatrics. Whatever the Fallen Wizard did to her must have caused her insurmountable pain. He still didn't feel that bad about it if everything the Fallen Wizard said about her was true. She was just as much of a monster as he was.

She gave him a quick, condescending smirk as he stared into her eyes. He hated it when she did that, not simply because it was a jerk move, but because it meant she knew things about him. She obviously knew about his father, and that alone was a subject he didn't like thinking about. Whenever he dared to ask her about his past, she stared back at him like he was an idiot.

The footsteps on the stairs diverted his attention from the crazed witch. He placed his hand on the hilt of his sword because there shouldn't be anyone coming into the dormitory. Gray pant legs and a green shirt attached to a dwarf named Fear appeared in the doorway. He was carrying a shotgun with a blue tip on the end of the barrel. Normally, they weren't allowed to carry lethal firearms into the dorms. For Fear to bring a lethal weapon with anti-magic shells meant something major was going down.

Fear approached him and gave him a handshake. The callouses on the dwarf's hands were almost older than time itself. His red eyes glared right back at him. Normally, someone glaring at you would be bad, but Fear glared at everybody. Although rumor has it, he was quitting his habit of smoking a pack of cigarettes a day. So, he might have been mad at the whole world.

"It's good that you're here, Cain. I brought you a lovely present. The Master said that you and your new girlfriend were getting bored down here. I hope you enjoy it."

"A present?" Cain replied.

Fear grinned as a group of guards began to descend the staircase. The sound of metal jingling and feet shuffling against the concrete floor meant the dorm was getting a new guest. She must be significantly powerful from the number of guards surrounding her. Even Lady Coral seemed to be mildly interested in the morning ruckus.

She was dressed in a light blue prison gown. Her face was covered by a black hood. A braided ponytail protruded from the bottom of the hood. She had brunette hair with blonde highlights. Her anti-magic restraints had a green light running across them, which meant she wasn't that magically strong. This all seemed like overkill to him. They didn't need this many guards for someone like her.

When the guards got close to the witch's cell, they stopped. He watched as they ripped her covering away, and immediately, his jaw dropped. The room instantly felt colder, and magical energy filled the air as the black hoodie dropped to the floor. Her beautiful golden eyes slowly turned from him to the witch in the cage.

She flicked an ice crystal at Lady Coral that moved with the speed of a bullet. A shield made of green flames appeared in front of the witch and intercepted the projectile. The light on General Floriana's restraints turned bright purple as she slammed the back of her head into the face of the guard behind her. She stepped on their foot just as she swung her arms into the throat of the guard on her left. As the guard reeled backward, she snatched his revolver and quickly let off 5 of the 6 rounds into the guards that surrounded her. Then she fired off the last round at the witch. Lady Coral yawned as she redirected the bullet into a wall behind her.

Fear raised his shotgun at Floriana as she rushed toward him. Just as he was about to squeeze the trigger, she jumped and did an aerial in the air. The anti-magic pellets slammed into the connecting piece for her restraints, and with a gentle tug, her hands were free. When she landed, she summoned her rapier, and before she could strike, Cain called forth a wall of black flames that swirled around her like a tornado.

Floriana glared at him through the wall of fire, and through gritted teeth, she whispered, "Traitor."

***

A deep silence washed over the prison after Floriana's glorious arrival. Lockdown protocol was put into effect for all dormitories. It would normally take about an hour to complete all the facility's checks. Alas, the Fallen Wizard wanted to be involved in the whole process this time. Since he was quite a slow walker, this would take all day.

Besides calling him a traitor, Floriana had not made a sound. He was still shocked to see her. This whole time, he thought she was dead. Even his brother Jason thought she had been killed during the battle, but here she was just as scrappy as ever. He couldn't understand why they would bring her here.

He jumped when he heard a popping sound just to his right. Smoke began to dissipate in the area where he heard the sound. A shadowy figure hidden by a dark green robe appeared in the room. The Fallen Wizard had arrived, and instantly, malicious energy filled the room. His wand hung from his belt, and his orange eyes darted between the two women locked in their cells.

He shuffled his way forward, "I am grateful for you two being here. My goal could not be achieved without your participation."

Lady Coral bowed respectfully, "Arthur, I have not been formally introduced to my roommate. I was wondering if you could provide an introduction of sorts."

The Fallen Wizard laughed, "I'm surprised you haven't done it yourself, Mrs. LoneOak. This young lady next to you is the Great General Floriana Alba. Her uncle, you might remember, was also a great General, so great that he gave his job to her when he retired."

The witch smirked, "I see, so she is Robert's niece. Now, what purpose does she serve for you? I can't imagine that an amateur ice wizard would be of any worth to the Fallen Wizard."

"Your sweet words of flattery are always coupled with condescension," he replied. "To answer your question, I need the blood of an ice mage. As there are so few these days, I was fortunate to have one come to our doorstep. No one has come close to finding our little slice of heaven. But she...." The Fallen Wizard snarled, "came a little too close."

With the snap of his finger, Floriana doubled over in pain from an invisible spell. She didn't scream; her pride as a warrior was too great for that. He snapped his finger again, and she reeled back in pain. Her face turned a scarlet red with sweat dripping from her brow. The Fallen Wizard snapped his finger again, and the pain stopped.

"While I appreciate your willingness to be involved in the success of my projects, I hope that in the coming weeks, you will tell me how you tracked us here." The Fallen Wizard turned toward Cain, "I know that a coward like you wouldn't dare help her. Understand this, Cain, the longer she goes without sharing her secret. The more blood I will make you drain from her veins."

Before he could respond, Arthur disappeared in a cloud of smoke. Now that he was gone, Cain was again in a room with women who wanted nothing to do with him. So, he reached into his pocket and pulled out a flask of whiskey.

Cain raised his drink to give a toast, "To your youth."

***

Floriana chewed on a stale piece of bread. The dry wheat loaf was just as tasty as a piece of drywall. Between the nasty bread and whatever purple mystery meat they gave her, she felt like she was having the breakfast of champions. If that championship was centered around having the most depressing meal ever.

The only solace she found was in the bottle of wine they gave her every morning. Even though it was clearly made in someone's dirty sink, it beat the hell out of drinking just water. On top of that, the jail was relatively quiet, except for Cain's questions, which she ignored, and Lady Coral's night terrors.

She had completed at least part of the task Raiden had given her. Floriana could track the Daimonia to the Devil's Corridor Mountain range. It was her own rotten luck that she was spotted in one of the nearby mountain towns by ten Daimonia members. Instead of fighting back, she thought it would be better to go quietly. Since they blindfolded her and cast a confusion spell on her, she had no idea which mountain their base was on. If she could only get out of jail, she might be able to get an idea of where she was.

Floriana sipped her wine and almost gagged. It was so gross. She looked up at Cain, who avoided her gaze. He was a snake, but he might have some good information. If she had to guilt him into giving it, oh well. She bit down on the inside of her lip just enough to make it bleed. Then, she pretended she needed to throw up and coughed up the blood onto the floor. It wasn't much, but dramatic enough to get Cain to look her way again.

He clapped his hands and shouted, "Bravo, bravo! That was a great performance."

"Easy for you to say," Floriana replied, spitting more blood on the floor. "You aren't having to eat food and drink wine that has been clearly poisoned."

"Look, Floriana, you didn't have to come here. You put yourself in this position and must live with the consequences." Cain looked away from her momentarily, and in a softer tone, he said, "We all do."

She spit more blood on the ground and stared daggers at him, "I have honor and a duty, just like you. Only I can sleep at night knowing I tried to do the right thing. You are a coward for betraying Jayden and Sarah. How long were you secretly talking to the Daimonia when he found you?"

"I imagine for quite some time," Lady Coral interjected. "This one comes from a long line of undesirables. Your father makes even the devil look like a saint."

Cain laughed, "Wise words coming from a lunatic who supposedly tried to kill her own son."

The witch shrugged off his response and turned toward Floriana. "You must be quite special for Arthur to bring you here. Your magic is quite powerful; color me impressed."

"Are you really Jayden's mother?" Floriana asked.

"No, I am not. His mother died many years ago."

Cain took a swig of his whiskey, "Figures as much. I was at her funeral, and I remember Cindy LoneOak. She was the sweetest woman in the world. It broke Jayden when she passed. It is an insult for you and The Fallen Wizard to think you had anything to do with the LoneOak family."

Lady Coral curled in a ball on the floor and closed her eyes. In a hushed voice, she said, "Cindy was a great mother, something I could never be."

They sat silently for a moment as the witch went to sleep. Floriana stared at her exhausted and wounded body. Her health seemed to be going downhill. She hardly ever ate, and this was the most she had ever heard the witch speak before. Despite her bad health, it was clear that she was holding on to some dark truths. Even though she carried on this whole crazy lady vibe, she could tell there was some real sorrow behind her crooked smile.

"So, what does the Daimonia want from me?" Floriana asked.

Cain stood up and walked toward her cell, "I don't know, but I would suggest you find a way out of here. Whatever he is planning is happening soon.

Chapter 9

A New Flame

His stomach was in knots as they hiked up the trail. He wanted to turn back, but if he did, they would be screwed. Jayden couldn't believe they were doing a mission for a member of the Daimonia. But what other choice did they have?

The mission wasn't the only thing that concerned him; it was the conditions James had set. They could bring weapons, but Grace had to stay behind. When he made that stipulation, Jayden knew that James was fully aware that she was the long-lost Princess of the Aggeloi. Luckily for them, James agreed to allow Tony to stay with her. Jayden could only imagine what horrible plans the insurance agent had for Grace.

Besides having to help out a Daimonia member, he was worried about what they might actually be up against. James didn't tell him much other than he had hired three mercenaries to find an object. According to him, they decided to keep it once they acquired it and were on their way back. So, he sent some of his men to track them down, and every person he has sent so far either ended up dead or walking home in just their underwear. For Jayden, if the Daimonia needed his help, whoever they were going after would be a pain in the neck.

The forest they were passing through smelled like the inside of an old taxi. Pine trees and pine needles were everywhere. Cute squirrels and yellow rabbits chased each other across their path. Multicolored Finches and red quails darted between the trees. The forest was full of life. It was a beautiful sight to see, which concerned him. Why would mercenaries pick this cheesy forest scene as their hideout?

He stopped when his eyes recognized the all too familiar shade of black fabric mixed in with the forest greenery. Peering through the trees, he spotted a group of hooded figures. They were armed to the teeth and the source of his nightmares. He could even see the varied tattoos of demons on their necks and arms. Even Sarah was hesitant to get any closer; she knew helping the Daimonia was fifty shades of a bad idea.

They made their way toward the cave where the Daimonia were gathered. The dark warriors looked up at them without an ounce of welcome in their eyes. This was the Daimonia they were used to, not smooth-talking James. Behind each of their scars and tattoos were the minds of a killer. Even though this group wasn't directly involved with his Dad's death, part of him wanted to strike each and every one of them down.

The largest member approached them. He had yellow eyes and a scar that ran down his cheek. A broad sword hung from his belt, and an assault rifle was slung over his back. His muscles bulged from beneath his black robe. In all reality, he was the last guy in the world Jayden wanted to talk to.

"James is an idiot for sending you chumps. It's insulting that he would think you could do better than us. I doubt you'll last three minutes in that cave. Good luck." He stretched out his hand to shake, but when Jayden tried to do the same. The

Daimonia warrior pulled his hand back and spit on the ground in front of him. "Chumps, I hope you come back in pieces."

Well, that was very kind of him to say, Jayden thought. Honestly, he was surprised that neither of the girls slapped him for being a complete tool. If Jayden had said that same thing, Sarah and Priscilla would have beaten him half to death.

The hooded warriors made room for them to pass and snickered as they entered the cave. Once they crossed the threshold, they were bathed in a green light. Crystals filled with magical energy lit up the cave.

Moss and four-leaf clovers littered the cave floor. Black lizards with green spikes skirted along the walls of the cave. Moving from daisy to daisy were strange ladybugs as big as your hand, with bright red wings.

Magic filled every inch of the cave. His body and his magic reserves seemed to relish in it. Normally, his magical energy would drain significantly in a damp cave like this, with water dripping from the ceiling. Instead, he felt powerful and ready to take on anything.

Sarah nudged him, "I can see why the Daimonia might not want to pursue those mercenaries here. It is too nice and pleasant here."

Jayden laughed, "I think you are right. They would have a heart attack from looking at one of these nice ladybugs."

"Yep, this is easily the nicest cave we've been in. This is like the first cave we've been to where we haven't had something try to kill us."

They took a few steps forward but stopped when they heard the sound of metal tapping against the rock. Jayden took a few more steps forward as they reached a bend in the cave. Then he heard it again; the metallic tapping against the rock sounded almost rhythmic.

Sarah shrieked as the source of that rhythmic sound appeared in view. Golden lights were bouncing along the walls as their metallic bodies moved forward. Large pincers clicked back and forth as they opened and closed. Green liquid dripped from their gigantic stinger. The monster's fangs were as sharp as a razor. Intense heat radiated off their bodies; it was uncomfortable even for Jayden. Everything about the two creatures approaching them filled him with fear.

Sarah grabbed onto his arm and squeezed way harder than she needed to. "Ja..Jayden, what in the world is that?"

Jayden gulped down a heavy dose of fear, "I learned about them then in school. I believe they are called Sasori. They are a tarantula and scorpion hybrid." Both Priscilla and Sarah dropped their jaws in surprise at his answer. "Jade, is there anything else you might remember?" Sarah asked.

He beamed from ear to ear and replied, "Nope, I was too distracted by your pretty eyes. Didn't you take notes all the time? Shouldn't you know what they are?"

His childhood friend groaned and punched him in the side. "You are such an idiot."

The Sasoris were much quicker than he had anticipated. Before he could even react, one of the creatures had closed the gap between them in a flash. Within a second of him realizing what was happening, the creature grabbed his left leg and squeezed.

Jayden quickly pushed Sarah to the side and pulled his leg back just as its fangs tried to take a bite out of him. He used his knife to block a downward strike from its stinger. Green liquid dripped onto his hand as he struggled to keep the stinger from cutting him open. The Sasori grew frustrated, grabbing his right leg with its other pincer. Then, it threw him against a wall of rock.

Pain spread throughout his body as he bounced off the cave wall. His legs were in searing pain, which was unusual because heat magic didn't usually affect him. The wind was knocked out of him. He couldn't move just as the Sasori slowly approached him.

***

Sarah awoke from her initial shock and fired one of her machine pistols at the monster going after Jayden. The bullets bounced off the creature's body and ricocheted off the cave walls. Both she and Priscilla quickly ducked as the air became filled with lead.

A Sasori rushed toward Sarah with blazing speed. As the blur of metallic gold drew closer, she channeled her magic and jumped over the creature as its pincers reached for her. While in the air, she made a crossing swipe with her swords and slashed at its stinger. She did three backflips when she hit the ground to distance herself from the monster. Blue blood burst forth from the stinger, but it was still attached. It seemed as if her blades could not go deep enough.

Sarah glanced over toward Priscilla as she faced off with the larger Sasori. The Dragon Warrior summoned a Jian-styled sword out of another dimension. The blade was a greenish-blue color and shimmered like the crystal sea. A cool ocean breeze filled the room as she swung her sword over her head. The magical energy radiating from her, and her weapon was inspiring. At that moment, Sarah understood why Jayden was afraid of Priscilla.

Priscilla swung her sword across her body and shouted, "Crashing Wave!"

A wall of water appeared in front of her and slammed into the metallic creature. The Sasori rolled around like a beach ball as it became submerged. Trails of steam came off of the water as the creature was pressed against the rocky wall.

The Sasori lay flat on its side against the wall. The monster's legs and underbelly were exposed as the waters receded. A pink, pulsing layer of skin was visible near the creature's fifth leg. She noticed it briefly, but it appeared that might be the monster's only weakness.

Sarah dove to the side without thinking to avoid an incoming stinger. The Sasori she had been fighting ferociously rushed at her. With every stinger she blocked and pincer she avoided, the creature backed her further and further away from the others. Jayden still wasn't back on his feet, so she had come up with something to defeat it.

Her twin blades began to glow light blue as she channeled her magical energy. Then she shouted, "Ensnare!"

Blue cords of magical energy began to envelop and coil around the creature's body. Then she snapped her fingers, and the cords started to tighten. The monster tried to struggle against her magical power, and within a few seconds, the creature couldn't move.

Sarah channeled another spell and launched a blue ball of energy at the creature. The monster was struck so hard that it flipped and landed on its back. She had to move quickly while she had an opening. Sarah launched herself toward the creature and charged her swords with explosive energy. She jumped, jamming both weapons into the Sasori's skin. Sarah quickly flipped backward as her swords began to glow, and the creature exploded.

Priscilla watched in awe as the metal plates from the giant bug burst into the air. With her brief reprieve from fighting, she could see what she needed to do to defeat her opponent. She sidestepped a grab from her opponent's pincers. Then she ducked as the creature swung its stinger in a circle.

She jabbed her sword into the ground and shouted, "Geyser!"

A hole appeared beneath the monster, and bursts of hot water came rushing out. The Sasori screeched as it was pressed into the ceiling by the surging water. Priscilla jumped into the air with her sword aimed skyward. Her blade sliced through the creature's soft skin like it was butter.

Her upward motion stopped when her sword pierced so deeply that it struck a rock. Priscilla pulled her blade out from the monster and the ceiling. Once she landed on the cave floor, the monster's body disintegrated, showering her in gold dust.

Sarah ran over to her, "Priscilla, that was amazing! You are a certified badass!"

The young Dragon Warrior grinned, "It was nothing. I am more ashamed of my fellow warrior who dropped like a sack of potatoes five seconds into the fight."

Sarah laughed as she turned toward Jayden, who was barely starting to sit up. She walked over to him and sat next to him.

He leaned against her and said, "I think you did a wonderful job out there."

She smiled and kissed his forehead. "See, why can't you be that sweet all the time. What happened to you anyway? I've seen you take hits way tougher than that before."

Jayden took a deep breath and showed her a small cut on his chest. "I'm unsure how it happened, but the monster's stinger got me slightly. I could hardly move when I hit the ground, and my magic felt completely drained. I'm glad you two were here, or it could have been terrible."

Priscilla stood over him, saying, "Lady Grace was right; you would be lost without a woman to save you."

***

The light guiding them into the cave was now so faint that they could hardly see where they were walking. Tripping over rocks and landing face-first was becoming the norm for all the clumsy group members. Normally, he would summon a fire spell to help them see, but his magical energy was still too low. The pincers and the poison from the Sasori must have drained him more than he thought.

Even if they could see, it wouldn't help much because they had no idea where to go. He could not sense any magic from anywhere else in the cave. This meant that the mercenaries were exceptionally good at hiding their magical energy or didn't have any. He was pretty sure they did because there was no way they could put this much fear in the Daimonia unless they were extremely powerful.

"I smell peaches," Priscilla said out of nowhere.

"Okay, thanks for sharing that with the group," Jayden replied with as much sarcasm as his voice could muster.

She turned toward him, and he instantly regretted the way he responded. Partly because she was a no-nonsense kind of gal. Also, she stared back at him with dark green eyes that glowed in the dark.

"Let me apologize for my transgression and say I love peaches. They are amazing fruits, and they smell nice while walking through a musty cave." Then it hit him; it shouldn't smell like peaches. In fact, he couldn't smell any peaches. "It shouldn't smell like peaches in a cave. How are you able to sense that. And why are your eyes so green?"

"I'm doing a Dual-Cast, which, as you know, involves using two spells simultaneously. One of those spells is *Dragon Sense,* which increases my senses of smell and hearing. The other is *Dragon Sight*, which you are more familiar with. When you train with that spell long enough, you gain the ability to see in the dark. You focus too much on training for fighting that you neglect your other skills. Anyway, I can smell peaches coming from over there."

Jayden pretended to look at where she was pointing because he had no idea where she was pointing. He couldn't understand how any aspect of this cave would smell like peaches. Maybe a giant peach monster was waiting to eat them.

Priscilla led them through a tight spot in the cave. Sharp rocks jabbed him in the back, as he had to suck in his stomach to get through. Centipedes and what he assumed were either salamanders or snakes crawled across his arms as he tried to push himself along the wall. He wasn't opposed to creepy crawlies but would appreciate it if they would respect personal space.

After getting scratched and bruised from climbing through the tightest spot on God's green earth. Their path opened up to a larger room. The air in this part of the cave felt wet and cold. He could hear the faint sound of water trickling down the walls surrounding them. Fish splashed in a nearby pond that was as black as night.

Jayden sniffed the air, "I can kinda make out the smell of peaches. I still can't tell where it would be coming from."

Sarah took a deep breath and said, "I think it's perfume. I believe it's called *Peachy.*"

102

"*Peachy*? That was the best name they could come up with?" Jayden shook his head, "It's kind of lame."

"No, it's not!" shouted a voice from the ceiling.

Jayden was startled by the disembodied voice. He glanced up in enough time to watch a magenta-colored fireball speeding their way. Jayden stretched out his hand and absorbed the spell.

As he absorbed the spell, his body started to feel warm, his wounds began to heal, and his magical energy returned. All of which was to be expected; still, there was something odd about this magic. His head felt dizzy as his body continued to absorb the fire spell, and his stomach felt sick.

A small shield of fire appeared just a few inches from his face. Hot pieces of metal showered the floor near his feet. Jayden bent over to see what the metal pieces were. Fear seized him as he realized his spell intercepted a bullet. This meant two things: another attacker in the dark cave and the fire spell he absorbed kept his body from reacting; thank God for his Auto-Shield.

Jayden's head was spinning like a top when he heard the sound of shoes tapping rapidly on the cave floor. He doubled over from his stomach churning so bad that he wanted to die. Through his blurred vision, he saw a black sword with silver painted along the blade, being held by a man dressed in designer jeans rushing toward him.

The blade glowed bright red as it swung toward him. Jayden knew he couldn't move to dodge it, so he did his best to defend himself. He raised his dagger, now covered in orange flames, to block the attack. Once the blades touched, Jayden's weapon went flying out of his hand, and his body was knocked backward into a wall.

His attacker sprinted toward him so quickly that his body looked like a blur. Jayden closed his eyes and waited for the final blow. When Sarah let loose a burst of gunfire at the swordsman. His attacker ducked and deflected her bullets. Priscilla launched a blast of water, which pressed his enemy up against the cave wall and knocked him unconscious.

A figure came bursting out from the shadows. As the young woman came into view, he could tell they were about the same age as him. She had beautiful blonde hair that was held up in pigtails. Her smile was beautiful, and there was something unique about her eyes. Her irises appeared to have a small flame dancing within them. Watching the small flames flicker back and forth in her eyes was entrancing.

He could sense powerful fire magic within her when she got closer. She held a ninjato sword in her left hand that looked similar to his now broken katana. There was something about her weapon that concerned him. There was a trigger just below the hilt and a black metal plate at the base of the blade. This meant that her weapon wasn't a normal sword but a gunblade.

Jayden stared anxiously as Sarah approached her. She drew her twin blades, and a smile creased her lips. Jayden knew that his childhood friend used her guns more often than her swords. Most people didn't know she secretly liked going blade to blade with an enemy. With that in mind, he was still nervous because he was pretty sure she had never fought someone with a gunblade.

The girl threw a magenta-colored fireball at Sarah. Then Sarah made an X with her twin blades. Once the fireball reached within an inch of her, it stopped mid-air and bounced back toward its caster. The young woman stuck her hand out and absorbed her own spell. She gave her a quick smirk and rushed Sarah.

Sarah slid forward and slashed with both swords. Her opponent flipped over her and slashed with her sword. Sarah blocked her strikes with the sword in her left and tried to stab with her right. Her enemy pulled back to avoid the thrust and clicked a button on her sword. In one motion, she spun the sword toward herself, and as it spun, the weapon began to fold into the shape of a pump-rifle. She squeezed the trigger, and instinctively, Sarah blocked it. Her sword glowed bright orange as the bullet slammed into steel. The air between them exploded, knocking them backward.

"Watch out!" Jayden shouted. "That's not a normal sword; it's a gunblade!"

Sarah slowly got back to her feet and dusted herself. "No shit. Why didn't you tell me that earlier, Jayden? Let me guess, you were too busy being entranced by her to help me. I see how it is."

Her attacker turned toward him. "Well, is it true? Were you really distracted by me? I remember just a few minutes ago, you thought my perfume sucked. You can't find me entrancing and hate my perfume."

Jayden was shocked that they had completely stopped their fight to chastise him. He took a moment to think of a response that wouldn't get him killed by either one of their swords. Once, he had come up with a good comeback. He stood and said, "Sarah Lynn, I was distracted by how good you two ladies fight. And I didn't say your perfume sucked. I just think that peach might not be an ideal scent for a cave."

"Wow, I spent two gold coins on this perfume; everyone likes it." The violent girl replied. She turned toward his childhood friend. "Are you from Eiréné?"

"Yes, we both are. But how did you know that?"

The violent girl ran toward Sarah and wrapped her arms around her. Tears streamed down her face, and a smile of pure joy creased her lips. "Of all the caves you could have stumbled upon, I am so glad you came to this one. I thought I'd never see you again."

"Okay...." Sarah replied, glancing at Jayden and awkwardly patting her on the back.

She released her and wiped tears from her eyes. "I spent so many nights hoping and praying to see you again. I thank God that I got to see you again."

Jayden stepped between them, "Excuse me, ladies, but this is not how an epic fight is supposed to go."

"Jayden! "She squeaked as she ran and wrapped her arms around him now.

Sarah rolled her eyes," I thought you said you weren't entranced with her. Apparently, you two are on a first-name basis."

Jayden's jaw dropped, "what the hell. I just met her." He stepped back as she held on tight to him. "How did you know my name?"

The violent girl frowned momentarily, "You don't remember me? I'm Macy!"

Jayden shrugged, "Nope, can't say I do."

Sarah pushed him out of the way like he was a paperweight and wrapped her arms around Macy. Tears streamed from his childhood friend's face like a wave of sorrow bursting from her soul. Years of sadness passed between the two as they warmly embraced.

Jayden didn't know what to think as he watched them hold on to each other. At one moment, they were fighting to the death, and now they were locked in a never-ending embrace. To think Sarah still felt such pain from their past was heartbreaking, but he was glad she found someone else in this dark cave who could understand such sorrow.

Macy turned her head toward Priscilla, standing over a young man's body. "Bryce...look, it's Sarah, and she's alive."

Priscilla looked back at them as pressurized water pounded against her opponent. She snapped her fingers, and the gushing water ceased. Her opponent stood and ran his fingers through his dark, curly hair with highlights. His silver eyes landed on Sarah, and he gave her a gentle grin.

Immediately, her face turned bright red.

Chapter 10

War and Regret

A bright light blinded him momentarily as he rotated the amulet in his hand. The frame of the object was made of gold. The item was crafted with a pointed snout and teeth made of diamonds. The image of a jackal was engraved into the solid gold amulet. A platinum chain dangled off the side of the jackal. The Anubis necklace was every bit of class and sophistication.

According to Macy, the Anubis necklace was supposed to increase a person's luck. She said the Atlas group would use the necklace when making large insurance and money deals. Apparently, they could make larger sums of cash whenever they wore it. Magical energy radiated from the amulet, but he couldn't tell how a shiny piece of metal could make someone lucky. Jayden didn't feel any luckier as he held it in his hand. In fact, he had tripped and fallen on the ground while holding it three separate times. Maybe it was an unlucky amulet, he thought.

Jayden expected to be greeted by warriors dressed in black when they exited the cave. Instead, the morning welcomed them with the beauty of nature. The Daimonia was gone, and any malicious energy surrounding them must have dissipated. Jayden figured they would try to rob and kill them when they stepped out with the amulet. The fact they had left concerned him.

On top of that, his mind was swirling with thoughts. For the longest time, he had thought that only a few people had survived the destruction of Eiréné. Seeing Bryce and Macy alive made him wonder if more people could survive that night in Hell. Although he wasn't the biggest fan of Bryce wanting to join their group, truth be told, he couldn't remember much about the guy. The memories he could were not the most pleasant. The guy was a jerk and full of himself.

He glanced up as they stepped out of the forest and saw the old wooden sign, *Back to Civilization.* Jayden chuckled to himself. Even though the walk back was only a few miles, he appreciated the Aggeloi's sense of humor. He nudged his childhood friend.

"Why are you so quiet?"

She stared in the distance, "I've got a bad feeling."

Jayden shrugged, "Because Bryce is still alive?"

Sarah rolled her eyes, "I knew you would get jealous, but no, that's not what I'm worried about. I'm just afraid our plan won't work."

He shook his head, "I'm not jealous at all. Plus, Grace reassured me she could make an exact copy of it. She even said it would be able to make a little luck. This won't blow up in our faces if we are lucky."

"You're a moron, you know that? You know how our luck is; chances are this will blow up in our faces, and you'll end up almost dead."

"I love your confidence in me, Sarah."

Priscilla stopped in her tracks and pointed toward town. "What is going on over there?"

Jayden followed her gaze toward a crowd forming outside the checkpoint. Members of the town were sprinkled throughout the crowd. The majority of individuals in the mob were Aggeloi Army Soldiers. He could spot blue uniforms mixed in with the green military garb, which meant the Azul Centurions were amongst them.

In the center of the group were six of what he assumed were prisoners. The poor souls were adorned with tan sackcloth covering them from their heads down to their elbows. They wore black work pants with anti-magic shackles wrapped around their wrists and ankles. Their feet were bare, and their arms were covered in bruises from being beaten.

Tony sprinted away from the crowd toward him. He gestured for them to look at a spot in the center of the crowd. Lying down on the ground was a prisoner whose sackcloth was stained red from blood. Soldiers stomped on him while others whipped the prisoners who had stopped walking in a circle.

An army soldier dressed in green knelt over the prisoner with a gun in his hand. He stared down at his captive as a devilish grin creased his lips.

"Are you getting tired of this?" The soldier asked.

The prisoner stretched out his hand for support. Gunsmoke exited from the soldier's barrel as his captive slumped to the ground. Jayden didn't hear the gunshot, but the crowd of town folk ran away screaming. He got the feeling that things were only going to get worse. What they were watching was illegal; there were laws that protected prisoners.

His stomach churned as he tried to rationalize why he didn't try and stop it. The tears rolling down Sarah's face and the stern look on Tony's didn't help. They were supposed to be heroes, right? Then why were they just standing by doing nothing?

An Azul Centurion cocked back his fist and slugged a prisoner that was walking next to him. Blonde hair dangled from beneath the captive's sackcloth cover. Other Centurions joined in, kicking the prisoner on the ground. The poor woman screamed out in pain, crying out for them to stop.

The Centurion raised up his hand to gesture for them to stop. "It's okay, boys, we can let this bitch up."

She reached out her hand for him to grab it. As she stretched her arm, her sackcloth cover slowly slid off her face. Her beautiful blonde hair was matted, and black and blue bruises were on her face. A small cut below her right eye dribbled blood down her cheek. He also noticed a barely visible tattoo of a raven on her neck and the look of pure fear in her eyes.

The Azul Centurion lifted her back on her feet. She gave a weak smile and thanked him softly. He smiled from ear to ear as she joined her fellow prisoners in a circle. Once her back was turned, Sarah squeezed Jayden's arms.

"Please..." she whimpered, "Do something."

Once those words left her lips, the female prisoner was struck with a whip across the back of her neck. Then another soldier punched her in the mouth so hard she was knocked back to the ground. The remaining soldiers proceeded to spit on her, kick her, and hurl insults at her and her compatriots.

"Jayden, please.....help her," Sarah cried.

He shook his head, "We can't."

"Please, Jayden, do something. You can't let them do this."

Jayden tried to pry his arm out of her tight grip. "I just can't...we can't."

Sarah turned his body toward her so he could see the tears rolling down her face. She lifted his wrist so he could see the bracelet on his wrist. The white and blue beads looked just as beautiful as the day he made it.

"I know you wear this bracelet for her. I know this bracelet reminds you of everyone we lost that day. How we were all hunted down like animals. I don't care what that girl and her people have done. This just isn't right. You couldn't backtrack then, but you have the power now to help people. If you don't use it to save them, I won't talk to you ever again.

And if you don't help her, you live with this nightmare forever."

Jayden nodded, "Fine."

Slowly, he pulled his dad's gun out and chambered a round. Tony gave Jayden an item as he began to channel his magical energy. The Dragon Warrior pointed his pistol toward the ground just behind one of the soldiers. Then he squeezed the trigger.

The soldiers wheeled around at the sound of his gun. A wall of fire surrounded the mob of soldiers. Then he snapped his fingers and a meteor the size of a car appeared above the crowd.

Tony's body morphed into a yellow bolt of lightning, speeding toward the wall of flames. He reappeared next to the young girl they had been beating. Sparks of electricity danced along the blade of his broad sword that he pointed toward the sky. Then he shouted, "Storm Barrier!"

A cage of white electricity surrounded each soldier. The fear and despair that resided in the prisoners of war were now reflected in the hearts of the men dressed in military garb.

Tony quickly turned to look at the prisoners dressed in sackcloth. He looked into their eyes and said, "I know they have done terrible things to you all. I also know that you have done some terrible things to their people. We will protect you for now, but you will still reap what you have sown."

Sergeant Johansson appeared off in the distance. He sprinted toward them with his pistol and two military police officers at his side.

His face turned bright red with anger as he shouted, "What the hell are you doing?"

Jayden pointed his sword toward the soldiers who were begging to be freed and said, "Your soldiers are the worst possible human beings imaginable. There are laws protecting POWs, and your men spit all over those principles. I hold you responsible as their commanding officer."

"Screw you, I will have all of you arrested!"

The Military police, running at his side, raised their rifles and pointed them in his direction. Priscilla snapped her fingers and disappeared from his side. Then she reappeared in front of Sergeant with her blade pressed against his neck.

"Your men have lost their honor," she said. "Would you like to lose yours too?"

The Sergeant shook his head frantically, "I didn't order my men to do this. You have to believe me!"

James appeared amongst the crowd. He was dressed in a blue suit with a matching pocket square. The insurance agent clapped his hands with a smug look on his face.

"My Dear Sergeant, now what do we have here? It appears your men have violated International Law for the Protection of Prisoners of War. I hope to God you did not commission this torrid affair. I believe your CO will be very displeased with this blemish on the army's name. Now, I will take young Jayden and his pals to my office and discuss these dreadful things you are doing with your boss in full public view."

***

His fingers brushed against the curves of the amulet. The image of a jackal was engraved on the magical item. Platinum glittered from the necklace as he lifted it over his head. Once the item was in place, the jackal began to glow, and a cruel smile creased the lips of the insurance agent.

"Excellent, the amulet looks absolutely perfect. I'll have you know this pendant has been worth its weight in gold," he glanced up at Jayden and gave him a toothy grin. "Now, what happened to the degenerates that took this from me?"

Jayden met his gaze and replied, "We killed both of them in the cave. There was a small lake in the cave, and they attacked us without warning. We had no choice."

The insurance agent raised his eyebrow, "What do you mean by both? Don't you mean three?"

112

The young Dragon Warrior shook his head, "No, we only saw two people. We only saw this girl and boy."

James smirked, "That is very interesting. Now that you have completed half of the bargain, all debts are paid. Do not hesitate to ask if you require any help down the line. You can pick up my business card at the front desk."

"Why would we still need your help?" Grace asked.

The insurance agent grinned as he looked into her eyes, "Because, my young princess, the war has just begun. If you want to make it through, you will need all the help you can get.

***

Once they made their way back out onto the street, they began to travel northeast. Macy told them of a small town called Koinonia that was friendly to foreigners. She said it was just on the other side of the Grandees River, and they would be waiting for them at the inn.

The rolling hills were filled with green trees and apple orchards. Orange and yellow parrots flew from branch to branch. It was a pleasant scene that contrasted with the droves of navy-blue airships flying overhead.

Considering the rumors they heard about how powerful the Aggeloi military was, Jayden understood why his home country drew first blood. With the magical energy he sensed from the Azul Centurions and the show of aerial might in the sky, he could imagine what horrors lay in wait for his countrymen. As the old saying goes, War is hell, and he had a feeling the Daimonia were playing a big part in making it happen.

Their path split into three directions. According to the map Priscilla had "borrowed" from the insurance company, they needed to follow the trail to the far right. The sign pointing northwest read Grandees Bridge Crossing. Their map must have been old because it didn't indicate where the bridge was.

Jayden started walking along the path leading to the Grandees Bridge with Tony while the girls started on the path that went right. He looked across the way and realized they were determined to go the other way.

"Hey, where do you think are going? Did you not read the sign? It says bridge this way!"

Grace replied, "We don't want to go that way. This way is quicker."

"Ya, but how are we going get across the river?" Tony asked.

The princess shrugged, "I don't know. Sarah told me your new girlfriend Macy said it wasn't that big of a river, and we could just walk across."

Jayden shook his head, "She's not my new girlfriend. If anything, Priscilla is, but that's not the point. We need to take the longer route to get to the bridge."

Priscilla sighed, "It's never gonna happen."

"Jayden LoneOak, you and Tony need to get your butts over here, or did you forget the war just started. I guarantee you that the bridge will have troops stationed near there. We can't afford to get caught, especially if they figure out who Grace really is."

He shrugged and followed Tony to join them. At this point in his life, he realized that arguing with the girls was a waste of his time. Even if there was a chance, they could be wrong, his life was less painful when he kept his mouth shut.

They continued along the trail for a few miles. Their path quickly became encroached by large oak trees and evergreen shrubs. Geckos and three-tailed iguanas scurried along the thick branches. The smell of spearmint and lilac filled their nostrils as they entered the forest of the Grandees.

According to their map, this forest was one of the largest on the continent. It was home to the Mossy Bear, which looked like a combination of a teddy bear, a swamp creature, and a werewolf. Luckily for them, the bears tended to live on the far eastern side of the forest.

Jayden was actually excited to be going into this forest. When he was younger, he remembered learning in school about a creature native to this forest called the Draco Python. From what he could remember, they were large snakes with razor-sharp teeth and red scales. They could breathe fire, and like the Mossy Bears, this was one of the few places in the world where they could be found.

Priscilla took them off the dirt road they were on and led them to hike through dense brush. Thick moss covered the trees as they struggled to move forward. The forest floor was damp and muddy. Jayden's white socks were getting soaked and began developing a brown tinge.

He thought it was stupid for them not to follow the sign leading to the bridge. He even thought it was even dumber for them to have left the trail they were just on. Somehow, he found comfort in knowing that Priscilla seemed to know what she was doing. Not once did she have to look at the map; she seemed to be able to sense exactly how to get to the river.

"Shit!" Grace screamed.

Jayden wheeled around, "What happened?"

"I think, I think something is crawling up my back. Can you check it?"

"I'll do it," Tony grunted.

He pushed past a pair of green thorn bushes to get to her. Tony turned her around so Jayden could see what caused the disturbance. Jayden tried to cover his mouth but failed to stifle his laughter.

Grace's face turned bright red as she looked back frantically, "Well, what is it? And why are you laughing?"

Tony patted her back, "I would love to, correction, we would love to. Unfortunately, the Verde Frog on your back is extremely poisonous. I would die if I tried to touch it."

Jayden grinned, "He is absolutely right. We will surely die if we try to take the frog off you. It is best to let it crawl off on its own."

"That's not true," Priscilla said.

115

Sarah crossed her arms and cocked her head to the side, "Jayden, that doesn't even make sense." She walked over to the Aggeloi Princess, quickly grabbed the frog off her back, and placed it on a nearby tree. "See, Gracey, it wasn't that serious. I think the boys were just trying to be jerks."

"O, were they now," she growled.

Grace's eyes flashed red, and she snapped her fingers. A popping sound echoed throughout the forest. The sweet smell of blueberries filled the air. Jayden heard a tiny squeak that was soft and quiet, like a mouse. Blue wings and a tail appeared in his peripheral vision.

He whimpered at the sight of yellow eyes staring back at them and yellow star-shaped balls of energy launched at them. At this point, Jayden and Tony realize they have made a critical error.

They spun on their heels and ran, as the energy attacks from Aiko exploded as they hit the ground around them. While they sprinted toward safety from the wrath of Grace's pet dragon, Jayden "accidentally" tripped his friend running beside him. Tony immediately face-planted into a mound of dirt and shouted some words that would have made a sailor blush.

Jayden glanced back at his childhood friend and laughed. Then he felt his body surge forward as his right foot slipped on some loose gravel. His right cheek slammed into a pile of small rocks and sand. Pain surged throughout his body as humiliation and karma began to set in.

Grace stood over him and grinned, "Well, would you look at that! You found the river."

Jayden lifted his head and said, "I found the what?"

Immediately, he felt a rush of warm, pressured water against his face. He felt searing pain as the water filled his nose. Jayden felt like he was drowning from the water that was now filling his lungs.

Sarah laughed, "I think he's learned his lesson."

Grace shrugged, "I guess we're even now." She snapped her finger, and the blue dragon from Hell disappeared.

Jayden stood up and dusted himself off. His gums had a salty and metallic taste to them. He ran his finger along the rim of his mouth and found blood.

Tony slapped him in the back of the head. "Karma's a B now, isn't it?"

He shrugged, "I guess you're right. So how are we going to get across the river?"

"That is a good question, "Priscilla replied.

She walked toward the water's edge and placed her index finger in the cool river. Her eyes turned blue momentarily as a pale white light flashed across the waves.

Priscilla frowned briefly, "I think swimming across will be quite difficult. This river is quite deep, and there are rapids sprinkled throughout it. I can get across pretty easily, but how will you all accomplish it?"

Jayden scratched his chin as he pondered how they could do it safely. He looked up in time to see Grace summon Aiko in her medium-sized form. Then, the Aggeloi Princess and Sarah climbed on the creature's back and were carried to the other side of the river. Once they had landed, Aiko quickly returned back to her smaller form. Priscilla snapped her fingers, her black shoes turning an aqua-blue color. With her new shoes, she sprinted across the river. Her toes dipped in the water as she moved across the rapids, but her feet never sunk below the waves.

Tony shook his head, "I guess a perk of training on an island is that you can walk on water."

"I know, it's not fair," Jayden replied.

"Well, I guess we will have to try and glide across the river. You think you can do it?"

Jayden nodded, "We are not going to let Priscilla show us up."

Tony looked at his old friend and said, "I worry about you sometimes, Jayden."

Together, they climbed up to the top of the nearest tree. Tony had decided to go first. So he channeled storm magic and summoned a gray-colored wind to circle around him. Then he jumped in the air, and the wind launched him forward with blazing speed. Once he was almost to the other side of the river, he snapped his finger, and the wind around him dissipated. He flipped forward as he descended and landed on the soft ground. Tony turned to look across the river and gave his friend the go-ahead sign.

Jayden channeled his magical energy and felt a warm tingle from his back down to the bottoms of his feet. He began to push off from the tree limb while summoning his fire magic to launch himself forward. Just as he was about to leap from the tree, the branch beneath his feet snapped. At this point, he realized he would be in a world of hurt.

His body lurched forward from the flames he had summoned. He flipped uncontrollably as he flew toward the water below. Jayden slammed into a flat rock so hard that he bounced off it and landed in the rushing river.

The icy river filled his lungs with water and drained his magical energy like holes in a sinking ship. The rapids pushed against his body with the force of a tsunami. His body seized with pain as he struggled to keep his head above the waves.

Fear in its purest form filled his soul. The thought of drowning or falling to his death and being skewered by sharp rocks made his heart pound in his chest. Each breath he took made his insides churn from pain. It felt like a butcher's knife was being jabbed into his side with every attempt he made to pull himself toward the surface.

Desperation was all that drove him to fight against the crashing waves. He had to fight or die because he was clumsy. Jayden could only imagine the jokes Tony would give at his funeral. Only he could be so clumsy to die like this.

Still, he had to find a way to make it through. Despite the pain that consumed his body, it was nothing compared to the sorrow his friends had already known. He wouldn't want to add to their pain. Sarah and Tony were strong but losing him would create a new wound for them that might never heal.

He blinked and realized the world around him was starting to go dark as water filled his lungs. The glimmer of hope he had was slowly drifting away. He didn't know what he could do to prevent his impending doom. This wouldn't be like before, when someone would come along and save him. He was too far away for them to save him. Jayden must do something, but what?

A light bulb popped in his head. He realized he did have one more option. However, in his current physical state, it might kill him quicker than the water would. But he had no other choice; it was this or drown to death.

Jayden forced his body up to the surface and took a deep breath. The sound of the water rushing down the fall he was heading toward filled him with fear. He had one shot and had to make it count.

The Dragon Warrior ducked back under the waves and closed his eyes. As he concentrated, he felt a warm sensation through every limb. The pain he felt began to lessen. Blood started to drip profusely from the gash on his forehead and his lip, as wisps of smoke were being expelled from his fingertips.

Jayden mouthed a quick prayer and hoped for the best. Then, he stretched out his right palm toward the southern shore. He channeled all his energy into a blast of smokey, gray flames. In an instant, the rushing waves to his right side were completely evaporated. The force of the blast was so powerful it propelled him into the shallows on the other side of the river.

His body slammed into a flat rock, and once again, the sensation of intense pain consumed him. He grabbed the rock and pulled himself on top of it. Jayden stared at the sun and felt entirely at ease as green vines covered in thorns began to wrap around him and slowly rock him to sleep.

Chapter 11

The Evil Within

She felt the cool wind brushing against her as they flew through the clouds. Fields of green and white roses covered the expanse beneath her. Flocks of seagulls flew alongside her with the same goal of embracing the moment.

Sarah noticed a brown-colored object just a few miles ahead. She dipped below the clouds to get a better view. Brown bricks covered the frame and base of the structure. Red-colored shingles covered the roof of the tiny house. The door frame was a mustard yellow, with an engraving of an angel near the top of the door.

From what she could tell, the building was pretty old. It was also clear to her that no one had been there for many years. Rusted toys, tractors, and even a small pink bike were almost entirely hidden by the large, overgrown weeds.

She angled her body downward to get closer to the tiny house. However, her body was instantly yanked higher into the sky. Sarah tried to dive again, but her body snapped upright in the sky. She tried to turn, but she could not change her course. Something was forcing her to keep moving north.

Her crimson hair blew into her face as she picked up speed. Within a few seconds, she had passed the house and was now staring at the ocean below. It was absolutely breathtaking to watch as dolphins skipped across the ocean.

Sarah smiled as she heard the squeaks and moans of whales swimming below. She always loved going to the beach with her family. She could still remember when her Dad took her whale watching, and he got too close to the edge of the boat and fell in.

Those were some of the best moments of her life. As she flew over the deep blue sea, she felt a hint of sorrow as those moments in time were now just a memory. She still wasn't sure what happened to her parents. As much as she would love to see them again, she hoped they were happy. Wherever they were.

An invisible force pushed her body downwards. Her hair blew in her face as she sped toward the blue sea. She tried to fight against it, but it was a waste of time. No matter what she tried, she could not fight it. Sarah knew this must be some type of magic but had never heard of body or mind control magic that could make her move like this.

She closed her eyes as her body slammed into the ocean. A tingling sensation spread throughout her body from the force of the impact. Goosebumps formed along her arms as she sped through frigid waters.

Her body was moving so fast that it did not take long to reach the bottom of the ocean. Just below her appeared to be a long tunnel-shaped object. From what she could tell, it connects from the tip of Aggeloi to the Northern Continent of Shinobi. The tunnel was covered in barnacles and underwater plants. Schools of fish and pods of pigmy whales swam alongside the snake-like object.

Centuries of rocks and plants covered the tunnel. Maybe it was even older than that? She had never heard of a tunnel like this before. Why was it here, and who made it?

Sarah tried to control her descent again, but her body still moved on its own. She found herself gliding just a few inches above the tunnel. The underwater creatures seemed to avoid her as she invaded their territory. Even the sharks were keeping their distance. There was something odd about her, and the animals could tell.

One of the things she found interesting about this manmade object was that it was still standing. With the weight of centuries or even thousands of years lying on top of it, she expected to see at least some cracks in the tunnel. But every inch of it was pristine; there were no depressions in the structure or even a cave in. There was no way something this old could still exist in this condition.

Unless it was made by aliens? She chuckled at the thought of green men from space building an underwater tunnel just to confuse the humans living above. The only alternative she could think of was that some kind of magic was used to maintain the structure. However, she could not sense any magic from the object, nor had she ever heard of any magic that could be used to keep this tunnel around for so long.

Sarah grinned as she thought of the scores of magic spells and enchantments, she had read about from the books that Miss. Tonya had given her. They were a wonderful escape from the sadness she felt at the time. Still, from all she read, there was not any spell that could make something like this. Not even a magic crystal could last this long. So, whatever had built this was still probably the aliens.

She felt her body tense up and accelerate at a blazing speed. Sarah glanced up just in time to realize what was happening. Whatever power was controlling her was directing her to crash right into the side of an underwater mountain.

Sarah winced as she expected to be flattened like a pancake or at least very badly bruised. Instead, she found herself standing in what she assumed was a cave.

Stalactites hung down from the ceiling. Droplets of saltwater dripped down from the minerals, landing on her tongue. A cold breeze sliced through her clothing, causing goosebumps on her arms.

As she moved deeper into the cave, it was quite unnerving. For one, her body was still moving on some twisted autopilot. Also, it was deathly quiet. The only sound that stood out to her was the tapping noise being produced by her shoes. Even the cool draft of wind was as silent as the grave. It was eerie, to say the least.

Sarah reached a fork in the road, her body forcing her to take the right turn. She felt very uneasy when she crossed the threshold into the next tunnel. Goosebumps formed on her arms, and the hair on the back of her neck stood on end. She wanted to turn back, but her body refused to listen.

The temperature of the room dropped like a hammer. She could see her breath in the frigid cold. Sarah felt like she was walking through a freezer. Even the water dripping down from the ceiling would turn into ice before it shattered against the ground.

Her lungs felt like they were on fire from the icy cave. The air was so thick with frost, to the point that it was difficult to breathe. She tried to bundle up the best she could, but dressing in jeans and a T-shirt wouldn't help much. Sarah tried to summon a thermal grenade to see if that would help, but the freezing wind would snuff it out as soon as the ball of energy started to form.

She got a glimpse of blue light bouncing off the tunnel's walls. This illumination source seemed to come from something just around the bend. Sarah tried to hurry to see what the source of the light was.

Her body moved rigidly as the power controlling her led her closer to that brilliant blue light. Once she moved into an open room, she had to blink because her mind was completely shocked at what lay before her. Her jaw about hit the floor as she tried to breathe in the immense beauty.

A gigantic wall of light blue ice and magic crystals blocked her path. As light bounced off the wall of ice, it shimmered like the ocean. Glowing white fish swam up and down from within the wall. It was the craziest thing she had ever seen.

She crept in front of the oceanic wall and placed her palm against it. Pain shot through every nerve in her right arm the moment her skin made contact with the wall. Sarah winced as it felt like someone was driving a knife of ice through the center of her hand.

Take the knife...

Sarah screamed when she heard a voice coming out of nowhere. Unfortunately, as far as she knew, no one else was in the cave, which was exceptionally creepy.

She bumped against an object with her shoe, skidded across the rocky floor, and bounced off the wall of ice and crystal. The metallic object she accidentally kicked was a knife with a curved blade and a white handle. She reached to pick up the knife to look at it.

At this point, Sarah was familiar enough with bladed weaponry to know that this knife was unique. Based on the weight and some of the etchings in the handle, it was clear that this blade must have been quite immaculate at one time. Even though the steel used for the blade was of high quality, it still was decently sharp. Unfortunately, the knife was left in such terrible conditions. The blade was blanketed with dirt and ash. When she touched the tip of the knife, it was just as cold as the wall in front of her.

She rotated the weapon in her hand as she pondered how the knife ended up in this tunnel in the first place. A tool like a hammer or a chisel would have made more sense, but a ceremonial knife? She brushed her finger against the blade's edge. While parts of it still held a sharp edge, other parts of the knife were as dull as a butter knife.

Sarah felt a light pressure on her left shin as she examined the ceremonial knife. At first, she shrugged it off but then felt a cold pressure on her leg, like an ice pack on a wound. The sensation seemed to expand and wrap around her leg. Her leg was then jerked backward, and she faceplanted onto the ground.

Blood dripped from her nose as she tried to get up. Her head was in a daze just as she tried to see who had attacked her. Fear seized her as dark brown eyes stared back at her. Her brunette hair drooped over her pale blue skin. Her bones protruded out of her body as they pressed against her skin. Every bone in the creature's body cracked as she reached for Sarah.

Sarah felt a tug on her right ankle. She turned her head just in time to see another creature coming for her. This one had dark black hair with streaks of blue in it. She had sharp yellow teeth and skin as pale as a ghost.

Fear seized her as the zombie-like creatures slowly dragged themselves closer. Sarah didn't know what to do; she had no weapons, and her magical energy was less than zero.

Her eyes scanned the area around her, stopping on a piece of metal just a few feet away. She stretched out her arm to grab the knife, but her body jerked backward. The creatures tugging her were oddly strong. To combat their combined strength, she tried to trudge forward using both her arms to move.

Searing pain shocked her body, stopping her progress. She glanced back and let out a scream as both creatures bit her leg. Blood dripped from their jaws as horror and pain seized her.

She bit down on her lip to distract herself from the pain in her legs. Sarah forced herself to move a few inches forward and stretched her arm to the point that her shoulder popped. Once her fingers touched the surface of the weapon, she gripped it tightly and swung her arm with the blade out. She jammed the weapon into the head of the zombie biting her left leg. Then Sarah rolled onto her back, loosening the grip of her remaining attacker. She grabbed the zombie by its hair and then, with one swipe, slit the creature's throat.

Sarah chuckled as blood dripped from the blade. She jumped back to her feet. Her clothes were now completely stained in the blood of her attackers. Like a ballet dancer, she spun on her toes, feeling completely elated. Her smile grew wider as she smeared the blood on the wall of ice and crystal.

Tears of joy streamed down her cheeks as rocks from the ceiling came crashing beside her. The blood on the wall of ice began to boil. The ice wall splintered, and cracks spread across its light blue surface.

Sarah continued to laugh as the cave around her continued to crumble. A cruel smile creased her lips.

"It's time to let the world burn," she whispered.

Chapter 12

My Dear Friends

A small halo hovered gracefully over the glowing I.V. bag hanging just a few inches away from his bed. A dark blue solution dripped down from the I.V. bag into his veins. He could not tell what was in it exactly, but it seemed like it was working. He did not feel much pain. The only sensations he noticed were tightness around his chest and the sharp pains in his ribs.

He tried to adjust his seating but stopped when he felt a stinging pain in his ribs. Jayden slumped back down and turned to look at his friend. Her hair had just transformed from its crimson state back to her predominantly black hair. The magical energy radiating from her was now back to its normal levels.

Her head was now resting on his right shin. Part of him wanted to reach over and flick her nose, but he had a sense she might actually murder him if he tried. So, he decided to go with the safest option. Jayden pretended to yawn, causing his ribs to hurt and his leg to kick.

Immediately, Sarah sat up straight, wheeling her head back and forth like a crazy person. "What the hell was that?"

Jayden smiled innocently, "I have no idea. I think you must've had another bad dream."

Her eyes widened, "How'd you know I had a bad dream?"

He looked away momentarily, "Oh, I don't know. You did your whole red hair thing for a bit and then returned to normal."

"But that's all you saw?" Her friend nodded his head yes. Then Sarah's face turned bright red as she felt completely embarrassed. "Jade, can I tell you something?"

Jayden raised an eyebrow, "You're not going to propose, are you?"

Sarah gave him the deepest eye roll imaginable. She began to tell him everything that happened in her dream. At first, she wanted to hide the crazier details, but she figured he could handle the truth. Even if he could not, he already loved her and probably wouldn't run off.

Jayden scratched his chin as he tried to process what she had just said. It was more apparent to him now that the map was revealing itself in her dreams and when she transformed. It also seemed as if the closer they got to whatever the map led them to, the more vivid Sarah's dreams became. Her story's darker and more violent part did not worry him because he knew she wasn't twisted like Lady Coral. However, she could hurt someone in her red hair form and not even know it. Backing out now or trying to return to Eiréné seemed impossible.

The Dragon Warrior cleared his throat, "I want to say this to you, and I don't want you to be offended. But don't tell Bryce or even Macy about your dream. I know they want to help us, but I think the less they know, the better."

Sarah held his hand and went to say something when there was a knock at the door. She got up and reached for the door handle. Before she turned the doorknob, she glanced back at Jayden, "Thank you for listening to me, and one more thing…I know it was you that woke me up. Understand that payback is coming."

His childhood friend winked at him and flung the door open. A gray blur sped past her.

"What the heck is that?" Jayden shouted.

"Jayden Federico LoneOak! No sir, we do not talk to people like that!" Sarah scolded with her index pointed at him for emphasis.

"I told you we should have left him at the river," the stranger added. He stretched out his furry gray paw to shake. "My name is Shane. I'm a team leader for the organization you know as the Witnesses."

Jayden stared at his furry paw for what seemed like a lifetime. His eyes seemed to have been playing tricks on him. There was no way the talking figure standing next to him was real.

The Dragon Warrior went to shake his paw but quickly yanked his arm back. His brain was still struggling to process what he was seeing. The figure beside him had a long snout, with canine teeth protruding from his lips. His eyes were green, and he was dressed in a dark trench coat, reminding him of the old gunslingers from the movies his dad used to watch. Shane had two large revolvers hanging from both hips and a belt filled with bullets of every shape and color imaginable. His tail was about three feet long, with a white stripe down the center that wagged back and forth as he stood.

Jayden finally took Shane's paw and shook it. It was the weirdest feeling in the world, he thought.

"Who? I mean, what are you? Why are you here? When'd you get here?"

"Idiot, I'm a werefox, can't you tell?" Shane replied, shaking his head. "I saved your ass back there."

Jayden was taken aback for a second, "From what? Last I remember, I was in the shallows, chillin' on the rocks."

The werefox shook his head, "No, you moron. Don't you remember vines wrapping around you? That was from a Mossy Bear; they can use plant magic to trap their prey. Your dumbass is lucky that I never miss a shot."

"Ohhh," Jayden replied. "Well, how did you know where I was? There was no one out there but us."

Shane pulled out one of his pistols and placed it on the bed. "As dense as you are, you probably didn't notice, but this is the gun that shot at you when you were all in the cave."

"Wait, what? You were with Bryce and Macy, too?"

The werefox pat Jayden on the top of his head. "You are something else. I hope you know that. But yes, as their team leader, I felt it was important to observe you. Plus, from the moment you stepped out. I realized I knew who you were. That bullet I fired was non-lethal."

"Oh, okay, that makes sense," Jayden replied. "But why couldn't I sense you in the cave? I can't even sense any magic from you right now."

Shane gave him a toothy grin, "Because, young man, I specialize in defensive magic." He raised his furry hand and snapped his fingers. Instantly, a light green shield appeared in front of him. "This is an anti-magic shield spell. It allows me to resist damage from most spells. A byproduct of this spell is that it makes people unable to sense my magical power. It works great for hiding from morons like you."

Jayden nodded his head as he ignored Shane's insult and his unique power. Something like that would be a game-changer in a battle. Jayden felt the werefox hid other skills that made him a great fighter.

He tried to sit up and felt a sudden onset of paint so great he almost passed out. The young Dragon Warrior slumped back down in the bed. He lifted his blanket and finally noticed that his ribs were wrapped with some type of linen with a yellow glow.

Shane cackled, "You are so dumb. You broke two ribs and bruised the rest. Take two of these now, but read the instructions, okay? If you take these pain pills too many times, they won't work. You only have so many."

The Dragon Warrior took the pill box the werefox handed him. On the side of the container was a disclaimer label with instructions. They read the medication was a hybrid pill that used a combination of magic and opioids. He could take the pills twice a day without any problems.

Jayden twisted the top and emptied two pills into his hands. They were covered in a dark red coating and had a chalky feel. Outside of their color, they didn't look magical at all. Of course, Jayden had no idea what magical pills would look like.

He shrugged and said to himself, *here goes nothing*. Jayden popped the pills that tasted like cinnamon-flavored gum. A warm sensation spread across his body. The pain in his ribs dropped considerably, and he felt the muscles around them begin to lose their tension.

This medication was like nothing he'd ever taken before. It was as powerful as morphine but without any of the drawbacks. He could even feel his magical energy being restored by the medication. He felt ready to get out of bed and back on their journey.

Shane placed his paw on Jayden's shoulder. "I know you're thinking you can just run off with us, but you gotta wait until the doctor comes to release you, okay? You also need to get used to the medicine and how it affects your body. Don't forget to run by the pharmacy to get more of that medication; it's called Yakkyoku."

***

Sarah stepped out of Jayden's room and strode along a tan carpet toward the exit. She passed by nurses and hospital staff decked out in various colors of scrubs. Art and photos made by the staff and former patients were displayed along the walls and next to patient rooms.

The building's interior was designed like a log cabin and an inn. Many of the doors were made with a stained redwood or oak finish. The floors were carpeted in some areas, and others had handmade rugs. Each room was furnished with top-of-the-line beds and couches for guests. Normally, a place like this would cost an arm and a leg to get treatment, but each medical physician in the building was also trained in magic. Their medical expertise, coupled with healing magic, allowed them to cut costs where they were needed. Seeing a doctor rush into a patient's room with a needle in one hand and a wand in the other wasn't unusual.

For Sarah, this environment was completely new to her. The hospital where she had worked before was just like your average hospital. They didn't have magic users treating patients. All they had were your typical everyday white coats. But this place was special, where you could feel at home and heal. For her and her friends, that was all they wanted.

The atmosphere of the building was simply peaceful. She could feel the stress leaving her body with every breath she took. Even as she passed by a room filled with a family holding on to a loved one, she could still feel some ounce of hope for a better day. That hope was very much needed. Since the war between her homeland and the Aggeloi started, the realities of war were all too clear, as some of the hospital beds were filled with Aggeloi soldiers and even a few POWs. This hospital was not intended for military service. In times of war and desperation, all medical facilities in the country were commissioned to help the soldiers.

She pressed a silver button and pushed open the white exit door. Her eyes were momentarily blinded by the bright morning sun. She blinked and was amazed at the beautiful green and yellow scenery surrounding her. Corn stalks and 6-foot-tall, emerald-colored arborvitae bushes surrounded the complex. The road was paved with dark brown dirt that was soft to walk on yet compacted enough for ambulances and cars to drive on without any issues.

The great Carmel Mountain loomed in the distance, casting a shadow over the town. This towering behemoth was one of the largest mountains; today, it is dressed in a light dusting of snow. Sarah couldn't take her eyes off it and even stumbled when she reached the road.

Bryce, Macy, and Grace were waiting for her at the Carmel Cafe. They sat on the patio with their drinks and a plate of scones. Macy jumped up and gave her a big hug. After they embraced, Sarah took her seat. Then Bryce handed her a white coffee mug on a plate.

"What is this?" She asked.

Bryce snorted. "Don't worry about it. Just try it."

Sarah shrugged and took a sip. Her tastebuds were enveloped with the creamy taste of vanilla and chocolate. The cool vanilla ice cream in the drink mixed with the hot chocolate was almost indescribable. She was impressed that he remembered that hot chocolate ice cream floats were one of her favorite drinks as a kid. He even tried to hide it in a simple coffee mug.

She grinned from ear to ear, "Thank you for this. I'm glad you remembered."

Bryce grinned his pearly whites as he leaned back in his chair. "It's been years since I last saw you, but I haven't forgotten what you like."

Macy rolled her eyes, "Oh, please don't start this crap again. I hated dealing with your off-and-on elementary and middle school relationship."

Bryce pat Macy on the back, "Don't worry about it, Mace. We technically never broke up, so we are technically still together."

Sarah stared directly into his eyes and gently touched his knee. "Now, Bryce, I'd hate to tell you this, but we will have to break up. I found a new man, and her name is Macy."

They all laughed to the point that Grace fell backward in her chair. Together, they continued to laugh and catch up with each other. Bryce ordered a plate of cinnamon rolls, which made the girls very happy because, let's face it, who would turn down a free cinnamon roll?

Bryce "accidentally" scooted his chair closer to Sarah. "So, Sarah, let me get this straight: you all have found the box that *The Key* opens, but you haven't found *The Key* itself yet?"

"Duh," Grace interjected before Sarah could respond.

"Okay," Bryce replied. "And you plan on going further north because you think it's somewhere in this country?"

The Aggeloi Princess gave him an annoyed stare. "Shouldn't you already know about their mission? Since our parents were part of the Witnesses."

Bryce shook, "Your parents weren't part of the real Witnesses; they were Rogues."

Sarah and Grace glanced at each other with confused looks on their faces.

Macy squeezed Sarah's hand, "Let me explain that a little bit since Bryce's answer was a little douchey. Your parents and a few others made a subgroup that broke off from The Witnesses. They are called Rogues or Rogue Witnesses. They broke off from what I understood because they felt like we weren't doing enough. Since that split, our organization has been mostly in the dark about what the Rogues were up to. We only knew about *The Key* incident because Jayden's father had passed some information on to us to steal it. When the upper brass decided not to go after it, your parents and Eiréné paid the price."

Sarah yanked her hand back, "Are you saying my parents are why our town was destroyed?"

Bryce signaled for them to chill out. "Whoa, whoa, that's not what we mean at all. It's just that the Rogues tend to do their own thing, and the Daimonia chose to destroy Eiréné. That's not even the issue; what I want to know is if you're trying to keep the Daimonia from hurting more people, why not just destroy the box that *The Key* opens?"

Grace and Sarah quickly glanced at each other. They didn't want Bryce to know the truth about *The Key* and the Map.

"Umm," Grace replied, between bites of her cinnamon roll, "Well... you see, that was the plan we had at the time. It was mostly Jayden's idea, so if it sounds stupid, you can blame him."

Bryce shook his head, "Jayden....you know he's going to get y'all killed, right? That kid is still weak after all these years. How he and Priscilla are both Dragon Warriors makes no sense to me. He's still just as pathetic now as he was back then."

Grace jumped to her feet, "Don't talk about him like that! Sarah, aren't you going to say anything?"

Sarah's words were trapped in her throat. She didn't know what to say and knew Bryce was wrong for what he said. But the way Jayden's been fighting recently has gotten him hurt. Considering the dangers ahead, he must return to his old self.

"Figures," Grace said as she walked away fuming.

"I think Jayden is plenty strong," Macy chirped. "I think you're still mad that she liked Jayden more than you when we were kids. You two have always had this silly rivalry since we were kids. You do know that it might be possible that he's a lot stronger than you think. And with that, I will leave you two love birds to gossip." Her childhood friend got up and followed Grace's directions.

Bryce shook his head, "Wow, after all these years later, she still has a thing for him."

Sarah raised an eyebrow, "She does?"

He nodded yes.

She sipped her drink and said, "Oh well, good for her. Back to what you said about Jayden. I want you to know that he's stronger than you think. He has done so much for Grace and me that I could never thank him enough."

Bryce snickered, "I hope you're right because that guy is one mistake away from losing it all."

135

***

Sarah knocked on Jayden's door. No one answered. She knocked three more times, but still, there was no answer. Sarah turned to walk away, but then she heard laughter from the other side of the door. *That bastard*, she thought. She turned around and opened the door.

"Jayden!" She exclaimed. "Why didn't you answer the door?"

"Because I knew you were gonna barge in anyway. Why miss out on a chance to make you angry? Am I right?" Jayden said, turning to Tony and giving him a big five.

"You two are freaking idiots," Sarah replied.

She sat in the chair to the right of his bed. Macy had somehow managed to squeeze in next to Jayden on the hospital bed and was drawing henna on his hand. Grace was on the other side of the room, painting Tony's nails for some odd reason. Neither of the girls seemed to have acknowledged her presence. They were probably still mad about earlier and had the right to be. She should have stood up to Bryce earlier but had never had much luck doing that before. Why would it be any different now that they are adults?

"What are you all doing?" She asked.

Jayden grinned, "Well, we were playing a game of UNO, and I hit Macy with basically two back-to-back Draw 4s, and Tony kept skipping Gracey. So, they both got mad, and Macy burned the cards, and to add to our humiliation, I'm getting hennaed, and Tony's getting his nails painted."

"Wow, that's crazy! Way to go, girls!" Sarah exclaimed. Neither of them reacted to her support. Oh well, they will get over it eventually.

"Anyway," she continued, "is it okay to talk with you and Tony."

"I think you two can have a lovely conversation, but as you can see, I'm stuck sitting here with Jayden. I guess I will just have to tag along for your discussion. Wouldn't you also like to stay, Gracey?" Macy interjected.

Grace shook her head, "Jayden, why did you have her call me that? But yeah, sure, I'll stay. I still need to finish Tony's nails."

"I don't know what's up with you ladies, but sure, we can talk." Jayden said.

Sarah cleared her throat as all eyes in the room were now focused on her. Normally, this wouldn't be an issue, but Macy and Grace were in a catty mood. The last thing she would want is to have to duke it out with her two friends in a small hospital room.

"Well, I've noticed this more with Jayden than Tony, but you both seem to be holding back more. I know for you, Tony, that Kayla getting hurt made things difficult for you. And with you, Jayden, I just don't know what happened. Normally, you run headfirst into battle, and that's why you end up in a hospital bed. Now you're holding back and in a hospital bed. I want to know what's going on because we could be in some real danger depending on what happens next. I think Jayden's injury will make moving forward even more difficult.

Tony sat up in his chair and met her eyes. "Hurting Kayla and endangering her family taught me something. It taught me that while trying to do good, sometimes we risk hurting people we don't even know are there. In fact, the whole reason I chose to study storm magic wasn't because I couldn't summon fire," Tony snapped his fingers. A dark blue fireball with a yellow core appeared in his hand. "I chose this path because, after everything that happened in Eiréné, I never wanted to be weak again. Storm magic has given me the power to easily destroy almost anything and anyone. I never imagined that power would hurt someone like her."

Before she could respond to Tony, Jayden chose to chime in. "I'm in a similar boat with Tony. I chose my path because my dad studied storm magic, which didn't save him. So, I chose a different one. I've made some mistakes because of it. When we were given our new ranks as Dragon Knights, they gave us more power to use, but it came with a bigger consequence. If I misuse my powers again, not only do I risk hurting other people, but they will kill me. And I just want to learn to solve problems without always blowing things up. That is something my dad tried to do."

Grace leaned forward in her seat. "Jayden, you promised to protect me and be there for me. How can you do that if you keep getting hurt? And Tony, it's not your fault Kayla got hurt. There was no way we could have prepared for that. And she's better now, so stop beating yourself up about it."

Macy tilted her head toward Jayden and said, "I thought all three of you were dead for a long time. I felt so alone. The thought of you two holding back for whatever reason seems crazy. Don't come back into my life only to just leave it. We all have powers that come with some level of danger, but that does not mean we stop using them; that just means you need to know when and where to use them."

"Well, I didn't know we would have an intervention today," Jayden muttered.

"I know your heart is in the right place most of the time, but sometimes you two forget that both of your lives have value," Sarah added. "If you two keep doing things as you have been, how will we save anyone, let alone ourselves?"

Tony stood up with his freshly painted and polished fingernails and walked toward the door. He turned to the group and stared directly at Jayden. "Look, I greatly appreciate what all of you have said. You might even be right, and I speak for myself when I say this. Both of us have a path to walk and will do the best we can. The power we can access now is even more destructive than we thought possible, to the point it is almost frightening to control. I hope you all can appreciate that. I will do better. We will do better; just don't expect perfection."

Tony's words hung in the air like smoke from a cigarette. To say the issue was resolved was an understatement. Jayden was indifferent, and Tony refused to let go. Nothing was accomplished besides the other girls sharing their opinions about the subject. *Men can be so stubborn,* she thought.

Chapter 13

The Beautiful Countryside

A green blob bounced up and down before him, with its purple eyes staring back at him and its stupid smile. The slime seemed to mock him with its seeming lack of enmity and ability to kill it.

For the 30th time, Jayden attempted to stab the stupid slime. Why? Because the slime and its gang of other slimes attacked them and ate their roast beef sandwiches. Now, to the average person playing a video game, slimes are supposed to be the easiest to kill. Not so in real life, because stabbing or cutting a slime does two things: if you cut the slime in half, the one slime you were fighting now becomes two, and the other issue is that when you stab them, it does nothing, not a darn thing. It's like stabbing Jello, only this is the Jello you can't eat.

Jayden slashed his sword down the middle of the slime. The two halves of the slime lay on the ground, lifeless. He thought he had finally beaten it; he felt proud of himself until two heads formed and bubbled up from the pool of slime, followed by a popping sound. The split halves were turned into two slimes, slightly smaller than the first.

I'm going to need a different strategy, he thought. Jayden grabbed his .45 and fired off two rounds at the slimes. The green blobs were knocked backward, splattering across the grass.

"That oughta do it," he said as he holstered his gun. "Shit!"

The blobs of slime started to shimmer and then jumped back onto their nonexistent feet. He pouted for a moment because he was all out of ideas. He felt a tap on his shoulder and turned to see another stupid face. He was standing face-to-face with Bryce.

"Don't worry, Jayden, I'll help you. I'm sure you can't beat these level-two slimes because of your broken ribs".

Jayden had a confused look on his face. "What do you mean by level?"

Bryce shook his head, "Why am I not surprised you don't know. One of the things they teach you when you become a real member of *The Witnesses* is how to measure up an opponent. They teach you to account for their strength, skills with a weapon, and magical energy. All of those factors combined determine what they call a level. The higher the level, the stronger we assume the target is. Level two creatures are pretty weak, but don't worry, I'll fix this for you."

He lifted his black sword with a coating of silver lining the edge. The blade glowed, swinging it horizontally. His sword cut through the slimes like they were butter. Their bodies burst and turned into sparks of light that rained on the ground. He sheathed his sword and walked away like a badass.

Tony ran up to him, breathing heavily. "Jade," he said while trying to catch his breath, "How many of those slimes did you beat? I'm at six. Priscilla has dropped seven."

141

Jayden looked down in shame and replied, "You know, I'm not quite sure. There were so many attacking me. I just sorta lost count."

His best friend laughed and shook his head. "Dude, you are freaking hopeless. Watch this!"

Tony grinned as he turned toward the three giant slimes hopping their way. The slimes that were approaching them were known as Acidic Slimes. These slimes were notorious for being a nuisance for travelers because anything touched by their gelatinous bodies would be at risk of being burned by their acid. They also have a second ability, which allows the slimes to absorb other creatures or objects smaller than themselves. Once their targets have been absorbed, their physical size can increase in a matter of seconds. Tony pointed his broadsword at the slimes and launched a flurry of white lightning bolts that blasted the three slimes into smithereens.

"It's just that easy," he said. "Just swallow your pride and do it. This is what Sarah wanted us to work on."

"Fine," Jayden replied.

Jayden looked up toward a large group of red slimes chasing Macy and Grace. Chasing is a loose term because the girls were just having fun outrunning an army of jello.

He snapped his fingers, and a red fireball with a yellow flame core appeared in his hands. He snapped his fingers again, and red lightning bolts flashed on and off around the ball of flame.

Jayden turned his right palm up and aimed toward the red slimes. Then he shouted, "Fire and lightning, I beseech you to come forth. Flamebolt!"

A blast of fire, encircled by red lightning, slammed into the mob of slimes. Upon contact, the monsters and the ground beneath them exploded. The grass beneath Jayden's feet shook like an earthquake from the impact of the blast. Static lightning sizzled over the pool-sized crater that he made.

Macy and Grace stared daggers back at him while they stood just inches from the smoking crater.

"You idiot!" They shouted in unison. "Were you trying to kill us, too?"

"Maybe..." Jayden muttered under his breath.

Sarah bumped against him flirtatiously. "That was pretty awesome. I didn't know you could do Storm Magic like Tony."

"I can usually only do lightning magic combined with fire magic. I was surprised the spell worked; I've only done it once before." He replied.

"It was reckless, is what it was," Shane growled as he approached him from the side. "You could have burned the grasslands or even killed somebody. That spell was overkill, and you know it."

Jayden ignored him and stared blankly at the crater he made.

The werefox continued his speech. "Now, if that's all the slimes, we have only an hour to make it to the Carmel train station. Let's get going."

The Dragon Warrior stood by the crater. He had never made one from his magic outside of training at the Dragon Temple. Making a crater this size was pretty easy for him, but it scared him. Before Mariko took off their limiters, doing a spell like this would have been very difficult. In this case, it required minimal effort; it was almost like breathing. Shane was right. It may have been overkill, but what Sarah and the girls had talked about the other day made holding back even tougher.

Bryce strolled beside him and said, "Those slimes were barely level 4 creatures. Don't get too full of yourself yet."

While Bryce walked away, Jayden was tempted to try that spell again on his childhood nemesis. He chuckled to himself and could only imagine what sort of Hell Sarah would rain down on him for vaporizing her ex. Granted, they stopped dating after Eiréné was destroyed, so maybe she wouldn't be that upset.

One of the things he always hated when he was training was hiking up hills. Shane suggested that they take a train if they wanted to travel north. He picked this out-of-the-way train station about halfway up the Valley. Shane called it the Carmel Valley train station, but considering it was off the beaten path, it would be more like a ghost town.

Macy ran up to him with her pigtails flailing along beside her. She had the biggest grin, which was usually a bad sign.

"Why are you walking so slow? Didn't they teach you to walk faster at the Dragon Monastery?"

Jayden puffed out his chest, "I'll have you know I once got first place in a contest running up a mountain before."

Tony bumped him, "Yeah, that's true. Of course, there were only two other people in that race. One of them was fighting a fever from strep throat, and the other tripped and was knocked out by a tree."

Jayden grinned and replied, "It still counts as a win."

Macy put her arms around her two childhood friends. "I think we should race to the train station."

He crossed his arms, "I don't think that will be fair because he can turn into lightning."

Tony shrugged, "Fine, I won't do that; plus, I can't travel that far in that form anyway."

Jayden pulled out a platinum coin from his pocket and tossed it in the air. As the shiny metal flipped in the air, he caught it with his right hand. "I will bet this coin I will make it to the train station before you."

Priscilla snatched the coin from his hand and said, "I think I will have to take you up on that offer."

"Let's go!" Jayden shouted.

Macy jumped high into the air. Wings with red feathers began to sprout from her shoulders. Magenta-colored flames swirled around her body and wings. Then she launched her body up the valley like a rocket.

Light blue lightning bolts coiled around Tony's legs. He jolted forward with the increase in speed from his spell. Priscilla channeled her speed magic into her legs to dash up the valley. She used the Invisibility Speed technique, which involved moving so quickly it looked as if she had disappeared and reappeared in a different location. This was interesting for him to watch because the technique was designed for short distances. She seemed to be able to time it so she wouldn't run out of energy quickly. Jayden could not help but admit she was a badass.

The young Dragon Warrior pulled out his bottle of pain pills. He knew he shouldn't take another one, but the battle with the slimes made his ribs tender. Jayden popped open the top, grabbed a red pill from the bottle, popped it in his mouth, and swallowed.

Instantly, he was showered in a green light, like sparks from a firecracker. The sharp pain in his ribs was gone, and he felt his magical power doubled from the medicine. He put his arms at his sides as he channeled his magical power. Orange-colored flames swirled around him like a tornado. Nearby, plants and shrubs combusted from the heat his body was expelling. Every muscle in his body bulged as he channeled his Fire Armor spell. Then he directed his palms behind him and leaned forward like a skater.

Flames appeared in his palms as he shouted, "Fireblast!"

For a moment, he felt absolutely weightless. A powerful breeze kissed his skin as the world around him blurred. His vision was obscured by flashes of red and orange flames that wrapped around him like a tornado. To any bystanders who were observing him, he probably resembled a meteor.

The bright, orange-colored energy bursting from his hands made him feel powerful. Animals and birds scurried across his path, hoping to avoid the ball of fire charging their way. He found it to be absolutely exhilarating to be able to move like this. Deep within his soul, he wished he could always move like this. Maybe Sarah was on to something. Maybe he really should use his powers more freely.

He could feel intense heat and tremors in his hands. The powerful blast of energy he had been releasing ran dry. Even

145

though his spell's power had phased away, he continued to run up the valley with blazing speed. He knew if he kept at this pace, he could win. Jayden took a deep breath and channeled more magical energy into his Fire Armor spell. With an extra boost in speed, he jumped from rock to rock up the hill.

A large tree with fading leaves stood just a few yards ahead. He knew that landmark meant that he was almost to the station. He remembered that if he passed the tree, it would dip down to a small hill and flatten out for the train tracks. He would win easily if he could jump past this tree once he got close enough.

Jayden channeled more energy into his legs and jumped further up the hill. He blasted more energy behind himself with his palms. He used too much power as he flew completely over the grassy hill. His body twisted out of control, his head spinning like a rollercoaster.

Once a wooden platform appeared, he knew he was in trouble. He grit his teeth as he slammed into the train platform. The flames swirling around him completely disappeared as he continued to roll forward. Luckily, a pair of hands grabbed him in enough time before he could roll off on the train tracks below.

Jayden opened his eyes and stared at the two blonde pigtails dangling just inches from his face. Her beautiful eyes, with their flickering flames, stared back into his. At that moment, he remembered how sweetly Macy treated him when they were kids. He pulled her toward him and kissed her forehead.

She quickly pulled back as her lightly tanned face turned bright red. "Hey, don't you be doing that when Sarah's around!"

Jayden laughed, "You know you love it."

Macy grinned, "Whatever, get up, loser."

The Dragon Warrior stood up gingerly. The magical medication he took was struggling to fight back the wave of pain in his ribs. Crashing into a train platform was a dumb idea, perhaps even his dumbest, and that's saying something.

***

Sarah sipped on her margarita, staring at the beauty outside her window. Water as blue as the sky shimmered as the train wrapped around the countryside. Humongous trees with green palms created a breathtaking canopy the sunlight struggled to pierce through. Blue butterflies and purple parrots flew amongst the dense foliage.

She had always wanted to ride a train through the countryside. Who knew that country would be Aggeloi? On top of that, they got bumped up to 1st class. Apparently, the war created a major damper on traveling by train, partly because they were a big target for airships to drop bombs on. But also because most people traveling on them were either government officials or soldiers and their families. There were very few tourists or wayward travelers onboard.

Macy sat across from her, and Bryce gestured for Sarah to scoot over. Begrudgingly, she moved over for her former boyfriend. Macy gave a toast to their reunion. She sipped that sweet liquor and felt more relaxed as the train sped along the tracks.

"Where's Jayden?" Bryce asked in a snarky tone. "I figured he'd love to sit with you two beautiful ladies."

Both of the girls gave the biggest eye roll in the world. "I think he's hanging out in the medical wing. He said his ribs were bugging him, and then he saw that pretty blonde doctor and got lost." Macy replied.

He laughed, "I'm surprised that doofus didn't try and sit with you. I saw him trying to make a move on you."

Macy's face turned a shade of deep red. "I have no idea what you are talking about. He only has eyes for Sarah."

Sarah smirked, "You are absolutely right. Jayden LoneOak only has eyes for me when there's no one else in the room."

Bryce huffed, "You two are both blind; he's had a thing for you since we were kids. Only now he has the cojones to

147

actually talk to girls, albeit in the most awkward and inept way possible."

"He's not wrong," said a voice across the aisle. Sarah scanned across the car and spotted Tony sitting with Priscilla, playing chess.

"What do you mean?" She asked.

"Well, do you remember back in the fifth grade when they did that event where you could write an anonymous love note to your crush?" The girls shared an amusing look and nodded. "I kinda dared Jayden to write separate love notes to both of you since he couldn't decide which one of you he wanted to marry."

Sarah's eyes flashed red with rage, "That bastard. I freaking loved that note. I always wondered who wrote it."

Macy shrugged, "It makes sense because the handwriting on both of our letters was oddly similar. Hey, at least the letters didn't come from Steven."

"Steven?" Bryce asked. "Wasn't he that loser that sat in the back of class drooling with his rusty braces?"

Sarah glared at them, "That loser you two are talking about lives in some fancy apartment on the Eastside of Mirage. I'd be ten times richer if he had written me a love note."

"On second thought," Macy said with a smile, "Maybe I should give Steven another chance."

Tony shook his head, "You two are such gold diggers." Then the Dragon Warrior moved his Knight into position and shouted, "Checkmate!"

Without saying a word, Priscilla stood and grabbed the chessboard. She threw it out of their open window and walked toward the back of the train.

"Don't you think that was overreacting a little?" Tony shouted.

***

Smoke billowed from a hole in the seat in front of him. He never heard a sound, but the fear was all too familiar. A figure dressed in all black stood in the doorway at the front of their car. His extended barrel pistol was pointed directly at him and Grace. Jayden tried to jump up but sank back into his seat from the sharp pain in his ribs.

"Shit," He whimpered. "Get down!"

He tried to cover up Grace's body as their attacker let off a volley of gunfire. Another smoking hole appeared in the spot where his chest had been only seconds before. His eyes widened as a red stain appeared on the seat in front of him. The blood stain expanded from the center of a smoking bullet hole that was meant for him. Tears brimmed in his eyes as he did not hear a sound from the person sitting in front of him, which meant only one thing, another innocent soul took a bullet that belonged to him.

Grace pulled out from her ankle holster a .44 Magnum Pistol. She leaned into the aisle and let the bullets fly. The man in the dark clothing was slammed backward against the door and then dropped like a sack of potatoes.

She jumped up and scanned the other people in their train car. Many of the other passengers were still ducking in case more bullets were to come. A young lady was sitting behind Jayden, nursing a bullet wound that grazed the inside of her left arm. The person sitting in front of Jayden was slumped to the side in a row all by themselves. Blood dripped from their left pectoral, staining their seat and the carpet below.

Grace shouted for people to board the doors so no one else could enter. She instructed a group of strong men to move the bodies to one side of the car and cover them. Then she reached under her seat, grabbed her bag, slung it over her shoulders, and strapped her dagger to her right hip. Jayden found it hard to believe that this girl dressed in a band T-shirt with a matching black shirt and shoes and purple and silver hair had become such a brave warrior and leader.

She turned to him, "Are you done checking me out already? This is not the time nor place."

Jayden felt accosted and replied, "I was so not checking you out, Gracey. I was just trying to make sure you weren't hurt."

The other passengers echoed Grace's sentiment that he was being creepy. Even some implied that Jayden was clearly not good enough for her. None of their comments seemed appropriate, considering they had all just been shot at and should worry about something else besides Jayden's awkwardness.

She reached for his hand and asked, "Can you move?"

"Yea," he replied as he rummaged through his bag for his pills.

"Don't take them. You've already had enough!"

Jayden popped the pills before she could stop him. He also knew she was probably right, but they would be sitting ducks on this train if he couldn't fight. Then he quickly brushed past her before he could hear her complain about his medication use.

The Dragon Warrior walked toward a bronze-plated ladder. He climbed to the top and released the lever. He pushed up gently on the hatch, and the incoming sunlight blinded him for a second. His eyes locked on the ten or so warriors dressed in black robes spread out amongst the train cars. There was no telling how many more were walking around inside the train. He knew they had to be the Daimonia; those jerks would do anything to get what they wanted.

He jumped from the ladder and quickly scanned the scared faces staring back at him. He had to protect them, but he also had to find the others. The First-Class seats were near the front of the train, and there was no telling how many enemies they would see trying to get there.

Jayden gulped down his fears and addressed the crowd. "I don't know why all of this is happening, and I'm sorry if us being here puts you in danger. But I have a plan to keep you all safe. We will disconnect your car from the rest of the train, and you can all call for help."

He didn't wait to hear their responses; Jayden grabbed Grace and whispered his plan to her.

She climbed up the ladder, and he followed. Once she got to the top, she crawled toward the edge of the car and jumped down. While she worked on disconnecting them from the rest of the train, he had to do his part.

He reached into his enchanted backpack and pulled out his sniper rifle. His body moved into a prone position on the moving train. He locked his sights on the farthest target, seven cars away. Jayden took a deep breath and gently squeezed the trigger. His bullet slammed into his target with the force of a freight train. Jayden waited to see if he killed him. Then he bolted a new round and fired at the next target that was closest to them. He was able to drop a third target before they returned fire.

Instinctively, he rolled to his right to avoid a volley of lead. Their destructive rounds slammed into his rifle, knocking it off the train. As he rolled to the right, he switched to his pistol and quickly let off six rounds.

The train lurched backward as the car was disconnected. Jayden's legs were beginning to slide off the side of the train car while it continued to move backward. Before he could fall off the side, he pulled out a glowing knife and jammed it into the side of the vehicle at the last moment.

His shins bounced off the side of the caboose as he dangled over the side. He quickly pulled himself up and rolled over until he was back on top of the train car. Jayden pulled his sword out of his bag and glanced at the train moving steadily ahead. He took a few steps, sprinted forward, and jumped into the air. Orange and red colored flames wrapped around him like a coat. Then, he was launched forward like a rocket.

He feared he would overshoot the next car or land on the train tracks below. Gracey seemed to have the same idea as he did. The Aggeloi Princess summoned Aiko, who flew just above him. The blue dragon kicked Jayden downward, and he landed face-first onto the train car. Blood trickled down his face, but at least he was alive and back on the train.

Grace beamed as she looked at her friend. "I believe the word you are looking for is thank you." She said with a smile brighter than the sun and just as smug as a trial lawyer.

Jayden wiped the blood from his face and replied, "I don't think so. I could have made it on my own."

Grace shrugged, "You can never be too careful. Now, let's go find the others!"

They darted forward and then jumped across to the next cart. Aiko swooped down and knocked off the enemies in their way. The hooded warriors on the next train car fired off a series of anti-magic and full metal jacket bullets at Jayden and the blue dragon.

The Dragon Warrior deflected back their bullets, but Aiko wasn't so lucky. She was riddled with anti-magic bullets and began to fade away. While her fading away wasn't a rare sight, it always seemed to royally piss Gracey off.

Grace let her again fuel her power. She pulled out the Elven Dagger and channeled her magical energy. She used the invisibility speed technique to disappear and reappear behind one of the cloaked warriors. Grace bumped him slightly with her hips, and he went sailing over the side. Before the other three could react, she summoned a swarm of Twin-Stinger Wasps and directed the bugs toward them. Before the wasps could sting them to death, two of the cloaked warriors jumped over the side with the cloud of insects sprinting after them.

Grace used her speed to cut down the final Daimonia warrior in the blink of an eye. His body hung over the side, with his blood dripping into the wind. The Aggeloi Princess stared out at the gorge below. Her purple and silver-streaked hair blew gently across her face. Her commanding presence at that moment reminded him of the Great Floriana. The poise and confidence she was displaying was remarkable to behold. In some ways, it was hard to believe that this was once a shy and rebellious daughter of the King. Now, she was a full-blown warrior. She was able to unlock the speed magic from the dagger he had received at the Water Temple in a way he never could. For the most part, Grace had gained greater control of her summons.

As he watched her standing boldly like a conquering king, he felt a twinge of guilt. When they had first met, she was something like a tortured soul reaching out for any semblance of hope. Now, she stood like a champion for good with a blood-crusted blade. In his mind, he had seen that same look before, which turned him into a killer. His greatest worry was that she was now following completely in his footsteps, that has left behind a trail of violence and blood.

"Wow, that is quite impressive…"

Jayden wheeled around, his jaw nearly hitting the floor. Ten warriors in black garb stood facing them from the train car behind them. A platinum hilt was clearly visible on the belt of a soldier standing in the center of the group. Resting across his arms was the unconscious body of his childhood friend Sarah. To his right was a young man with caramel skin and dark curly hair with highlights. His silver-colored eyes stared back at them coldly. He brushed his hand against the hilt of his sword, which rested gently against his overly-priced jeans.

Jayden did not wait for them to say a word. He raised his pistol and dumped off every bullet in the magazine. Bryce managed to deflect each round except one that managed to slice along the bicep on his right arm and slammed into the Daimonia warrior behind him, who was unfortunately knocked off the train by the bullet's force.

"You Bastard! You are going to die just like your piece of shit Father!" Bryce screamed as he clutched his bleeding arm.

A glowing blade appeared beneath Bryce's throat. The platinum hilt attached to the sword glinted brilliantly in the afternoon sun. A gust of wind blew gently against his hoodie, revealing his spiked blonde hair and pale-complected figure. As he held on to Sarah over his left shoulder, The Dark Prince locked his eyes on his compatriot like a lion prowling around looking for a soul to devour.

"You will not dishonor his father." He demanded.

153

"Yes, sir," Bryce replied.

With his blade still pressed against his neck, The Dark Prince turned to look at Jayden. His eyes briefly shifted to the right as two of Jayden's friends appeared on the train car behind them. Then he redirected his focus back onto Jayden and said, "I see your masters have removed one of your seals; maybe there is hope for you yet."

Metallic wings sprouted from the backs of the Daimonia warriors. Rocket boosters roared to life as they ascended. Bryce was the last remaining fighter on the train. He grinned as his glider slowly lifted him into the air.

Then Jayden grabbed Grace and shouted, "Jump!

Chapter 14

As We Fall From Grace

The world around them was saturated in clouds of dust and flames. Shards of metal rained down upon them with the force of a hurricane. Droplets of blood stained his shirt as shards of glass and metal pierced Grace's shoulder.

His ears were ringing from the sound of the explosions. Metal pressed against metal as the bridge collapsed beneath the train above. Before they hit the water, Jayden heard the faint sound of people screaming out in the distance as they fell to their deaths.

A sharp pain shot up his leg once they hit the surface. Ice-cold water filled his lungs as they descended into the deep. At some point, he had let go of Grace and had no idea where she had gone.

His body was freezing as he continued to descend. The water was dark, and he could not see his hand in front of him.

He had no idea where his friends were or even how badly he was injured. His ribs were screaming with pain, which made any movement unbearable.

Before his fear and pain consumed him, he took a moment to focus his mind. Then Jayden kicked his feet and made his way toward the surface. Freshwater waves slammed his face as more pieces from the bridge and train plummeted into the gorge.

He spotted a small sandy beach running parallel to the river. He begrudgingly swam toward it and slowly climbed out of the water. Jayden kicked his shoes off and sat on a gray rock. He curled his toes as he clawed at the soft, brown sand.

During his time at the Dragon Temple, he read that rubbing your toes against the sand on the beach was beneficial; the term they used in the book was grounding. According to what he read; it helped him deal with stressful situations beyond his control. Since the world seemed to be crashing around him, he figured a little grounding wouldn't hurt.

A smile creased his lips as Grace emerged from the water. Streams of blood dripped from a hole in her shirt just below the collarbone. Pieces of metal and glass had managed to break her skin when they fell from the bridge. Jayden felt bad for her because his Auto-Shield spell managed to burn up 99% of the shrapnel that came their way. Several metal pieces jammed into her upper body when he ran out of magic.

She crumpled into his arms the very moment that she could. He reached into his bag and began to apply ointment to her wound. Next, he pulled out a square bandage and placed it on the wound. She winced as the bandage made contact with her skin.

Grace held on to him tighter as she shivered. Her arms and hands were like clutching onto an iceberg. He placed his hand on her forehead and summoned a heat spell. She sighed as her body started to feel warm again. Her clothes were instantly dry, and her sarcastic smile returned.

"So, you waited until they blew up a train and a bridge to try and touch my chest. I am very disappointed in you, Jayden. I thought you had more respect for me than that."

Jayden let out the loudest groan in the world. "You are the absolute worst. Whoa, whoa, I did not try to make a move on you at all. All I did was touch your collarbone area; that's not even trying to make it to second base. It is more like first base and a half."

"You are such an..." Grace stopped midsentence at the sound of movement. She jumped out of his lap and drew her Magnum pistol. Her eyes darted toward the rapid sound of water splashing. The look on her face was not the same as the calculating and deadly warrior he had seen on the train. No, he was staring into a face filled with fear and desperation driven by adrenaline.

Jayden pointed his gun toward a small grove of nearby trees that jetted into the river. He flicked the safety off his pistol when he saw water splashing intensely in that direction.

For better or worse, his Father's old gun was all he had left of him to use. His ribs were filling his body with such intense pain that he wanted to pass out. He didn't have the strength to swing his sword, and the river drained almost all his magical power. In short, he hoped the 3 bullets he had left would be enough.

Strands of blonde hair appeared amongst the thick greenery. A young woman with pigtails stepped out from the nearby grove of trees. Tears streamed down her face as she rushed toward them. Laying across her arms was a young man with a gash on his forehead. Blood stained her pale forearms as she laid him on the ground in front of them.

Jayden rummaged through his bag and pulled out gauze pads and bandages for his childhood friend. He attempted to jump to his feet but was immediately dragged down by the sharp pain in his ribs. Grace reached under his arm and helped him to his feet.

Tears streamed from Macy's eyes as she applied the gauze. Her dripping mascara added a dark tint to her pale face.

The strained look on her face and her desperate attempts to save his friend gave Jayden some perspective. He could now see what it must have looked like for Sarah and the others when they had to save him. The panged look in Macy's eyes would forever haunt him. At this moment, he vowed never to make them feel that way again, and he would begin that vow by saving his best friend.

Macy looked at Jayden as she frantically applied the gauze to Tony's gash. "He needs serious help if he's going to make it. If I could use my magic, I'd be able to help him out a lot more. But the water drained most of it. Can you do anything?"

Jayden shook his head, "No, I don't have any healing spells like that. I have one, but it works slowly, and I don't have enough magic to transfer it. But we gotta do something! Please don't let my friend die!"

"Well, I don't what else to do! I'm doing the best I can!"

Jayden felt a cold chill on his right arm that made him jump. He turned to see Grace holding on to him and Macy. The Aggeloi Princess closed her eyes, their arms glowing. His body tingled, and he felt his strength returning. Grace had managed to transfer her own magic to them. He didn't even know that was possible.

"Spirit Flame," Macy whispered.

A light blue crown made of fire appeared above Tony's head. The light blue flames swirled as the crown rotated in a circle. His gash and the blood that covered his face slowly receded. Even Tony's fingers twitched as his body responded to her healing magic.

For a moment, it seemed like her spell was working. However, as the minutes dragged on, the healing seemed to slow down. He also noticed that more blood was starting to seep from Tony's wound. Jayden tried to help by transferring his Auto-Healing spell to his friend, but that did not work.

Macy's face was turning a dark crimson as she grew more frustrated. So, she snapped her fingers, and the blue crown expanded above Tony's head. The light blue flames became denser, and the crown rotated faster.

Still, the progress was slow. His friend was barely breathing, and his heart was beating a little bit, but it wasn't enough. Jayden knew his friend needed a boost somehow to make it through this.

Tony's skin looked paler as Macy fought to save his life. Jayden sensed that both girls were starting to run low on magical energy. He was grateful Grace could transfer enough magic to Macy to keep his friend alive. Jayden also knew they couldn't keep this up forever. One thing that would help is Tony's own Auto-Healing ability, but from what he could tell, it wasn't working. Normally, it would start working when he got hurt, but it seemed to have stopped. If he could find a way to turn it back on, then Tony would be able to heal naturally.

Jayden put his hand on Macy's shoulder and said, "I need you two to step back. I've got an idea."

Grace raised an eyebrow, "What kind of idea?"

He shook his head in frustration and shouted, "Just frickin move already!"

Grace shrugged and scooted over to the side. Once Macy was far from Tony, Jayden took a deep breath and tried to concentrate. He raised his right palm and pointed it at his best friend. The young Dragon Warrior channeled all the magical energy he had left.

Beads of sweat dripped from Macy's brow as his power increased. Water in the nearby river began to boil while the air around him was enveloped in intense heat. His muscles bulged, and his eyes became laser-focused on Tony.

Then he shouted, "Scarlet Bolt!"

A blood-red bolt of lightning launched out from the middle of his palm. The bolt of electricity made a crackling sound as it slammed into his best friend. The Scarlet Bolt snaked around Tony's body, causing him to convulse and shake. The spell exploded once his best friend was completely covered in the blanket of scarlet electricity. Whisps of light gray smoke were expelled from his chest. The ends of Tony's shirt were as black as charcoal.

Grace could not believe her eyes as she stared at the steam and smoke coming off of Tony's body. Macy turned and grabbed Jayden by the collar.

"What the hell were you thinking? That was your brilliant idea? Well, congrats, you just killed your best friend?"

"I, I," Jayden stuttered. "I thought it worked."

Macy slumped back onto the ground, tears streaming from her eyes. "Well, I guess it doesn't matter now. Goodbye Tony, it was nice to see you again."

Grace stepped to console Macy, but she crumbled to the ground from exhaustion before she could reach her. She tried to reach for Gracey, but her eyes rolled back, and she fell unconscious. A dark cloud appeared overhead as Jayden moved toward the girl. He turned back toward his best friend and grinned.

"I guess my lightning bolts are strong enough to wake the dead. Master Thai was right. I am the greatest Dragon Warrior ever."

"Only in your dreams," Tony whispered.

***

The adrenaline coursing through his veins now seemed like a distant memory. His high energy was now being replaced by doubt and sorrow. The events that had transpired were now as real to him as the sweat on his brow. Thoughts of betrayal and guilt filled his mind to the brim.

He wished his eyes would shed tears of pain and frustration, but no ounce of release would be granted. His heart was swimming in the very depths of defeat. The soul-crushing truth is that his decisions since becoming a Dragon Warrior have led to lost and stolen lives. His best friend was taken away, and the innocent people on the train were lost because of his arrogance.

Why in hell did he think he could be a hero? What made him think he had any right to try and save the world? There must be better people out there than him. If there were not any, then the world was absolutely screwed.

Jayden was not remotely surprised when a small close-combat airship appeared in the sky above them. He was even less shocked when the soldiers dressed in black slid down on ropes from the aircraft. Truthfully, he felt completely numb when they were placed in anti-magic restraints to be shipped off to the capital. If he was honest with himself, they deserved it. There was nothing innocent about them; the blood was on their hands, too.

Chapter 15

A Happy Reunion

Once Sarah could open her eyes again, she turned to the unfortunate soul on her left and puked her guts out.

"Sorry," she croaked.

The poor soul's face turned a sour green as he shouted, "That is disgusting! I just got this robe dry-cleaned! I hate you Witness scum!"

Sarah shrugged; she didn't feel too bad for him. I mean, they did kidnap her and drug her. They decided she should fly hundreds of miles on a glider. It's basically their fault his robe got covered in her last meal. Hopefully, the Dark Prince can refund his dry-cleaning cost?

She felt a deathly cold breeze against her skin and instantly felt woozy. Sarah turned to the unfortunate soul on her right and puked her guts out again.

"What the hell is your problem? You could have easily given me a warning. This my best robe; I wore it just for Him."

Sarah glanced up and saw the young woman's face turn bright red.

"You're a girl?"

The young Daimonia Warrior rolled her eyes, "Obviously I am. What, you don't think women can be a part of the Daimonia?"

Sarah lifted her chin, "Of course, I think women can be in the Daimonia. I never knew there were any. Let's be honest; it's kind of tough to tell you all apart with the whole black robe thing. What's your name, by the way?"

"You are so ignorant," she replied. "You can call me Kelly. Not that it will matter; your destiny has been sealed."

"What do you mean?"

Kelly didn't answer as they approached an old wooden door. The young Daimonia Warrior pressed her hand against a wall. The wall shook, and a digital pad appeared. Kelly pushed a combination of buttons that was impossible to track. Her hand and finger movements looked like a complete blur.

The old wooden door creaked open when she had finished pressing the buttons. Sarah was led down a spiraling staircase made of stone. When they reached the landing, they stepped into a small dorm. The walls were covered in pale green paint and were starting to chip. Her body tensed up as a bone-chilling draft snaked through the cracks in the walls.

There were four prison cells in the dormitory. They looked dreadfully small, like the cages they put animals in. The dorm was eerily quiet, save for what sounded like someone muttering to themselves.

She noticed someone sitting in the back of the dorm. There was a man dressed in a black robe relaxing on a chair. Sarah assumed he was a guard, although he appeared blatantly unprofessional. The guard had a bottle of liquor resting at his feet and a silver flask in his right hand. The way he was leaning in the chair, she could not tell if he had simply passed out or if he was dead.

Kelly reached into her robe and pulled out a small bag. To the untrained eye, it looked like a simple bag of chips. It was a small bag of firecrackers that could be set off with just a little magic. She turned to Sarah, gave her a mischievous grin, and mouthed, "Watch this."

"Wake up, you idiot!" Kelly shouted as she tossed the firecrackers at his feet.

The orange firecrackers exploded, and he did not react for a second. Kelly let out an exasperated sigh. Then she tossed a second volley. Once the gunpowder exploded, sparks landed on his black robe. As his robes started to burn, he began to stir. Once his eyes opened, he briefly glanced down at his clothing. Unfortunately, he was still pretty intoxicated, and he leaned a little too far forward and fell off his chair. He frantically began to stop, drop, and roll.

After rolling around like a drunken idiot, the flames coating his outfit had subsided. Then he dusted himself off and took a swig of what was left in his flask. He reached down, picked up his liquor bottle, and drained its contents.

Kelly rolled her eyes, "Have you had enough for the day? We get it; you're the whole tortured soul type. Will you get up and do your damn job? Sarah is here."

"Sa, Sarah?" He muttered.

Sarah shrugged, "Should I know you?"

"You should; he betrayed all of you, it seems…"

He turned to the cell closest to him, "I'm not the only one with skeletons in my closet, Mrs. LoneOak. Isn't that right, Samantha Kelly?"

Kelly drew a pistol from her robe, and in one motion, she hit Sarah in the back of the head and fired a lightning bullet at Cain before he could react.

"You will hold your tongue."

***

She was nauseated and dizzy when she came to. If it were not for the fact that her stomach was completely empty, she probably would have vomited again. The back of her head was throbbing, and the red stains on the green floor told her that she was really hurt.

Sarah moved her hand to the back of her head. She felt a painful electric shock in the middle of her palm.

"Ouch!"

She tried it again and found the back of her head was wet and sticky. Her hand was stained with blood. Sarah wasn't sure how bad she was bleeding, but in this prison cell, she wasn't sure what she could use to stop it.

"Are you okay?"

Sarah turned her head in the direction of a familiar voice. Her eyes widened and began to fill with tears as the face staring back at her was one that she had missed for what seemed like an eternity. Sarah's arms wrapped around her dear friend. Her tears soaked Floriana's blonde and brunette-colored hair.

The former General wiped tears from her eyes. "I'm sure Jayden would just love seeing us bawling like this."

Sarah sniffled, "I'm sure he would use it as an opportunity to hit on us, or worse, try and cheer us up."

"You're right, so give me an update? Why isn't he here with you?"

Sarah went to reply but then remembered that they were not alone. She placed her hand on Floriana's wrist. Then she channeled whatever magical energy she could muster, which wasn't much. She wasn't sure if the Mental Text technique would work with her.

For a brief moment, Floriana's eyes widened and then became deadly focused. She appeared to concentrate and take mental notes as Sarah transferred her thoughts and experiences.

The General cleared her throat and said, "I'm sorry to make you worry. I lost the coin they gave me at the Water Temple. It's just that this is a lot to process, and I'm not sure what that means for us being stuck in this hell."

"Keeping secrets, are we? I can sense some Bond Magic being used. Tsk, Tsk, Arthur will not be pleased," hissed the prisoner in the cell beside them.

Sarah's irises narrowed, and her heart pounded like a drum. The hairs on the back of her neck began to stand on end. She hoped the voice she just heard was all in her head. That dreadful witch could not possibly be in the tiny cell next to her. Out of all the evils she had seen in the world, why in God's name was the worst evil just a couple feet away.

"Your silence tells me all I need to know."

Sarah covered her ears as she tried to block out the sound of Lady Coral's voice. She still had nightmares about the way the witch had treated her. The evil in her voice and the hate in her heart were unimaginable. The torture she was capable of, her power to manipulate people without a second thought, made her quiver. She never thought her life would be graced by Lady Coral ever again.

General Floriana gently touched Sarah's shoulders and gave her a little smirk. "If it makes you feel any better, Sarah, I've already tried to kill The Witch."

Sarah shook her head and said softly, "It doesn't."

"Plus," the General continued her desperate attempt at cheering up her friend. "Karma for Lady Coral has been the quite the bitch. There is not a night that goes by where she is not screaming into the night from one of her many night terrors, which I believe is a fitting punishment for all of the pain that she has caused."

"My young General," Lady Coral hissed. "I am shocked you would echo a sentiment of such arrogance. I can only imagine that a Goddess like yourself could only do so from such a lofty moral high ground. My mind must be going in my old age when, on many nights, I recall hearing you pace back and forth in your cell. The fear of closing your eyes seems ever your adversary. Might that be from all of your years of military service? Could it be a result of a young girl becoming a warrior to serve the great King of Eden? I must say, the blood on your hands looks just as red as the blood on mine."

"Go to Hell."
"I look forward to seeing you there."

***

The hours dragged on with the intensity and speed of drying paint. During that time, Sarah and Floriana spent most of their time discussing ways to escape. They weren't too afraid to talk about it openly because Lady Coral was busy mumbling to herself too much to care. Cain spent most of his time going on "breaks," leaving them with very little parental supervision.

Sarah was impressed because their discussions were quite fruitful. If by fruitful, you mean a complete waste of time. Between the anti-magic prison cells and the pressure-sensitive tiles outside their cells that would set off an alarm when touched. They also had to contend with an army of soldiers and the drunkard sitting 20 feet away. For Sarah, it had become painfully obvious that escaping their current predicament was just about as likely to happen as Lady Coral giving up the witch life to join a country band. In short, they were absolutely screwed.

She could not help but feel nervous about their current predicament. Only God knew what their hooded nemesis had in store for them. She did not like the hints about their future, that God was leaving them. Although she felt uncomfortable about their situation, Floriana shared with her that the Daimonia needed them to help with whatever they had planned. This meant that she had a little more time to write her last will and testament.

Sarah yawned, "If you look at it twistedly, this whole situation is kind of funny. Who would have imagined you would somehow come back from the dead? It's like a twist from one of Jayden's movies. Or that our new next-door neighbor would be the most precious angel to grace our planet. Or the people we have been trying to avoid, slash kill, are now our landlords."

Floriana picked a straw of hay and chewed it like an old farmer. "You know what, Sarah, you just might be right. In a messed-up way, our plans have blown up in our faces. Which makes me a terrible General. I guess Lady Coral was right. I only got the job because my Uncle was in charge. In fact, me not dying was more a matter of luck and less skill."

"Ignore her; you are a great General. We would have died long ago if it weren't for you," Sarah said as she leaned back against a pile of hay in their cell. "By the way, you never told me how you survived. Tammy said she saw a grenade blow up right by you. The only thing we had left to remember you by was your sword."

The General leaned back as her mind went back to that fateful day. "As you know, transformative magic is one of my abilities. That ability is a rare one to have within my family, and I was lucky enough to get it. One of the aspects of that ability I had to learn to control was my fear. The downside of that ability is that if I get scared or am in significant danger. It will automatically make me transform into something to protect me."

"But you never get scared."

Floriana laughed, "I've gotten pretty good at pretending I am not. When I was first recruited to spy for the Eden Army at thirteen, I was often in tough and scary situations. During some of the most nerve-racking times, my body would transform all on its own when the bullets started flying, and often, my fellow soldiers would be left high and dry. I hated myself whenever that would happen, but eventually, I learned how to control it better. So that day, when I saw that grenade heading my way. My body automatically transformed into an Armored Burrower in the blink of an eye. Before I knew it, I had dug down so far and so quick that the grenade didn't affect me. But the elves from the Water Temple fighting alongside me weren't so lucky. You see, I'm a fraud and coward."

Before Sarah could respond, a dark shadow appeared just outside the bars of their cell. The pungent smell of regret and alcohol bleeding through the bars of their cell made it clear that their unwanted guest was Cain. He knelt down, and his pale face came into view.

He took a swig from his flask and stumbled for a second. Cain met their eyes and said, "I don't think you are a fraud. Not even close. The things I've done to the people I cared for and trusted me should never be forgiven. I could never earn back an ounce of grace from anyone. You two are doing your best; don't be so hard on yourselves. You aren't in the same boat as me and this witch."

Lady Coral cackled in her cell, "Young man, you chose your path. For most of my life, that right was stolen from me. My hands are covered in the blood of souls that I had no intention of harming. On the other hand, you were given a chance at a better life and squandered it. It's hard to believe that Jayden's father and many others fought so hard to save you when you were just a baby, only to have you fall back into the hands of the Daimonia as a teenager. Such a disgrace you have become."

Sarah raised her eyebrows and said, "How do you know anything about Cain? Or even Jaydem's father, for that matter? I've never fully understood that part."

Cain grinned from ear to ear, "Well, if the rumors are to be believed, she is actually Jayden's mother.

Chapter 16

Chained to the Past

Innocence was in the eye of the beholder; the judge had said before he slammed the gavel. One of the guards had said that guilt was a matter of perspective. Either way, their trip to the gallows was all but guaranteed at this point. Even though all of the evidence pointed toward their innocence. They even had witnesses from the train car they had saved stating their innocence. The political engine needed scapegoats for the war effort, and the two boys and a girl from Eden were the perfect candidates.

According to the news reports, they were known as the Eden Three. They had been dubbed as mass murderers hell-bent on the destruction of the Aggeloi people. Another broadcaster mentioned they had warped the minds of the people they had saved. One of the reporters for a trendy news outlet had even stated that Macy's outfit was so last year, which, according to her, was crossing the line slightly. Apparently, her outfit being despised by the public was a greater offense to her than being sentenced to death.

Their trial went by quicker than any he had heard of. Tony expected Jayden to raise hell before the judge, but instead, he was reticent. Macy did her best, but it seemed they were screwed either way.

They had three more days left before they were to be executed on live television. The broadcast would be viewed not only by Aggeloi but also by his countrymen.

Tony still wasn't sure how they were going to be executed. All he knew was they were told to "be prepared" for the worst. Considering all they have gone through thus far, he wasn't too worried about it.

He jumped when he heard a loud bang against his door. Tony stood up and stared through a small glass window. Standing on the other side of the door was one of the HVT Guards. The HVT Guards specialized in transporting and dealing with highly valued prisoners. They were the only guards allowed to carry retractable swords that looked like small poles on the sides of their hips. Once activated, the blades would extend out from the tip of the hilt. The HVT Guards could also use magic, or so they claimed. Tony couldn't sense much magical energy coming off them, so that fact might be slightly exaggerated.

"Place your hands against the door!" He barked.

Tony pressed his palms against the steel door. The cold metal beneath his hands seemed to melt, feeling his body lurch forward. His face smacked against the door as his hands sunk deeper into the metal.

"Hurry up!" The guard shouted.

"Screw you," Tony replied.

Tony gritted his teeth and yanked his arms back. He felt a popping sensation in his elbows once his arms dislodged from the door. His wrists, which had been bare, were now wrapped in a tan metal that was made from the door. This metal that the doors were made of possessed an enchantment with anti-magic properties.

The Dragon Warrior presented his now restrained wrists to the HVT guard. His cell door began to swing open with the speed of a turtle. In fact, Tony had enough time to close his eyes and start daydreaming. His daydream about hanging out with pretty ladies and eating a bacon burger was completely ruined by the guard smacking him across the hand with his metal button.

"Ouch, you douchebag, that wasn't necessary!" Tony shouted.

"You can sleep when you're dead," he growled.

The guard grabbed Tony by the collar and dragged him forward. He was led out of the solitary confinement dorm and down a brightly lit hall.

Tony had to blink his eyes to get them to adjust to the light. Having spent almost every waking minute in the last week stuck in his dark cell, he was almost blinded by the fluorescent lights. He didn't appreciate the stares as they moved within the facility. Since he was dressed in a trendy pale green jumpsuit covered in dirt, he stood out amongst the crowd. Most of the residents in the facility wore orange or blue outfits. In contrast, the staff wore either black combat uniforms or suits.

A few of the jerks he walked by spit on the ground as he moved through the hall. He even noticed some of the other inmates in the facility look down on him. One inmate felt bold enough to give him the finger as he passed. Tony took note of what the elf looked like because he was going to kick his ass if they ever staged a prison break.

His uniformed escort led him to the right, entering an even narrower hall. The carpet was light blue, and he could feel a gentle breeze from the air conditioner. Offices were on each side of him. He chuckled as he noticed a group of nosy employees peaking their heads out from their cubicles. Tony assumed they could not resist getting a glimpse of their local terrorist. They must have felt the need to continue the narrative that he was pure scum.

He was directed toward a small office at the end of the hall. In the center of the room was a silver table with two chairs on one side and one on the other. Cameras hanging from each corner of the room would adjust their angle based on his every movement.

The guard forced him into his seat and then shackled his legs to the chair. Then, he placed a glass of ice water on the table for Tony. Tony reached for the glass and stopped when he sensed magical energy emanating from the clear liquid. He wasn't sure what it was, but he always remembered his grandmother telling him to not talk to strangers; he assumed not taking cups of water from them was also a good idea.

The guard got up to close the door but was stopped by another man who met him in the hall. They exchanged a few words, and the guard moved aside to let the other man in. A soldier in a blue camo uniform stepped into the room and sat just across from him.

"Hello, Mr. Santos. How has your stay been in our illustrious hotel?"

Tony shook his head, "Sergeant Johannsen? What the hell are you doing here? Don't you got a war to fight?"

The Azul Centurion laughed as he pressed his index finger against the table. A red circular light appeared beneath his finger, and immediately, Tony was hit with volts of electricity. The jolts launched his chair backward, and he slammed into the wall.

The guard moved to help him sit back up straight.

"The next time you say something smart. I'm going to hit this little button again. Do we have an understanding?"

Tony nodded his head, "Yes, sir!"

The Sergeant pressed the red button, and Tony was shocked again. "That tongue will get you into trouble, boy. I was hoping that you would be more useful than your compatriots. I can see that you are equally as useless."

"You, you interviewed my friends?" Tony asked.

He grinned, "Well, of course. The boy ended up getting shocked the most. He hardly said a word. And Macy, well, her answers were damn near useless. I didn't shock her as much; I learned my lesson from our last encounter."

Tony, seething with anger, said, "Fine, I will help you. What do you need from me?"

"I knew you would see things my way," the Sergeant replied. "Now, tell me where the other girl you traveled with went?"

Tony shrugged, "I'm not sure. I'm assuming wherever you put her in this building."

The Sergeant grinned, "That's cute. I'm going to ask you one more time. Where is the girl that you were traveling with?"

"I don't know. Did you guys lose here?" He replied.

The guard picked Tony's chair up and tossed him against the wall. Then, he proceeded to kick him repeatedly in the stomach. The red button on the table glowed brightly as the Sergeant jammed his index finger into it. The volts were so strong that Tony's chair bounced in the air for a second.

Tony spit out blood as he lay on his side. "Sergeant, can you help me back up? I might be able to provide some useful information."

"I will allow it," The Sergeant replied. "However, you will need to not only know where she is. I want you to tell me exactly who she is and how long you have known her."

The guard moved and set Tony's chair back upright. Tony leaned to his left and spit out some more blood.

He cleared his throat, "Help me to see if I got this straight. From what I've gathered, she might have escaped somehow after we got here? Is that correct". Sergeant Johannsen nodded yes. "Well, my guess as to where she might be now is probably at your mother's house. I heard she's been baking cookies all day."

The Sergeants face turned bright red, "You stupid son of a bitch!"

A black button appeared beneath the Sergeants left hand. With eyes filled with rage, the Seargent slammed his fist down on the button. Scarlet bolts of electricity wrapped around Tony like a python. The sparks of light singed the walls in the room.

The Sergeant whimpered, "Wha, what are you?"

Tony smiled as the bolts of electricity continued to encircle his body. He snapped his fingers, and his body absorbed the rest of the electricity in the room. He pointed toward the guard and launched his own bolts of red lightning. The bolts slammed into the guard so hard he bounced off the wall behind him and was killed instantly.

"How can you still use magic with the restraints on?"

The Dragon Warrior released a burst of energy that shattered his restraints. He stood up and made his way to the door.

"To give you the short answer, you should know your opponent before confronting them. Since you hurt my friends, I will leave you with this warning. If I ever see you again, if you ever get near anyone I care about again. I will make your death so painful you will still feel it in the underworld."

***

Macy wiped blood from her lip. Her body was covered in bruises, and her hair was something else. She felt sick from the mystery meat and mildly poisonous soup she'd been eating for the last week.

According to the tack marks she made on the wall, tomorrow was the day they were to be executed. She still didn't know how they were going to do it. All she knew was that it was supposed to be recorded live for the whole world to see. To a degree, she was hoping they would let her take a shower and clean up beforehand. I mean, who really wants to die looking like the crazy lady shopping at a grocery store late at night?

She leaned back and spoke into the darkness.

"Jayden?" She shouted. No response. "Jayden don't make this awkward. Can you please say something?"

There was still no response. She jumped up and banged on the wall behind her like a crazy person. Still no response. Then she stepped back, channeled all her energy into her legs, and kicked the wall with her bare heel.

"Ouch!" She cried as she hopped on one leg. "Are you just going to let me make a fool of myself?"

"Sounds like he is," said an older female voice from a nearby cell.

"Shut up, Rhonda! He is going to talk to me."

Rhonda chuckled to herself. "Sounds to me like he's just not that into you. I've got a young nephew you could try."

Macy rolled her eyes, "Rhonda, I am sick of your sass! Whatever happened to strong women supporting other women."

"When you find one, I'll support them," she replied.

"Wow, that hurts. He actually likes me, you know."

Rhonda sneezed, "Sorry, I'm allergic to BS. You are living in denial, Macy dearest."

"Jayden this embarrassing," she whimpered." Would you please just talk to me?"

"Why?" He replied.

Macy grinned and shouted, "See Rhonda, I told you he liked me!"

"Oh wow, he said one word to you; that must mean he loves you, and hell has frozen over. "Rhonda replied. "Now hurry up and have your little conversation so I can get on with the rest of my life."

"What do you want Macy?" He asked.

"I'm worried about you." She said with a struggle. "Ever since we arrived, you've hardly even said a word. You've sat in that room quietly while the guards came into my room and beat me. You didn't give a shit when I was interrogated and electrocuted over and over again. And from everything that Sarah's told me about the person you are today, that's not like you to sit back and do nothing."

Jayden yawned loudly, "Look, we both know you have enough hidden power that if you wanted to fight back, you could. The anti-magic walls and restraints aren't holding you back as much as you think."

Macy got up and pressed her forehead against the wall that separated their rooms. "You don't know that, and even if it was true, it doesn't change anything. We are supposed to be executed ten hours from now, and all you care about is yourself right now. You don't care about your friends and what they are going through. What happened to you? Is this because of what happened on the train? That was tough on all of us, not just you!"

He sighed, "I know; I'm just sick and tired of people dying and getting hurt because of us."

"So you're saying the people you saved on the train don't matter? You can't control what the Daimonia or anyone else does. Sarah even told me about how you saved people on that ship. Does that not matter to you?"

Jayden replied, "All those people would have been safer without us being around. Sarah would be safe living with Miss Tonya, and Floriana would still be alive. Even my dad would still be breathing if we hadn't asked him to save Miss Mara. All I do is put other people in danger, and for what? Is the world any better? No!"

Tears streamed down her face, "You know damn well your dad was going to lay his life down for other people regardless. That's something I know he's passed on to you. Has it been perfect or easy? No, it never is. I mean, look at my situation. I was betrayed by my own teammate. All of the people who lost their lives on that train were killed because of me. I didn't know Bryce would double-cross us; I didn't know he was a part of the Daimonia, and I should have. So, if you're going to mope and feel guilty, understand that you aren't the only one with that right."

Jayden stood and began to pace around in his room. "But that's the thing. You didn't know, and that's not the first time. I've been told of other people who were part of The Witnesses that were secretly part of the Daimonia at the same time. If we can't tell who is a friend and who is an enemy, then we will get people hurt. I'm just tired. I'm tired of fighting and seeing people get hurt. I don't want to try anymore. I've decided to give up. I deserve whatever happens tomorrow. I am at peace with it."

Macy stared at the bruises that covered her arms and her legs. "If that's true, I will give you your reason to fight again tomorrow."

Chapter 17

The Hangman's Noose

There was a rough and tingly sensation between her toes. Sweat dripped down from her brow, drenching her black hood. Her hands trembled uncontrollably as their cruel reality slithered into her mind.

The nerves in her skin were inflamed by waves of heat bombarding her. Macy's ears perked up at the sound of people cheering and booing. Beneath the roar of the crowds, she could make out sounds of animals growling and baying. A pungent smell caused her nostrils to flare. She wanted to puke. From what she could sense, it smelled like a combination of rotting flesh, smoke, and manure with a hint of barbequed chicken.

The only reason she wasn't puking her guts out at this moment was because she didn't want the whole world to see her blow chunks. Plus, she could also sense Jayden was right next to her. She figured that if she threw up, then he would lose it, and it would turn into a whole thing. Macy wanted to die with some dignity, dammit.

She quickly covered her ears at the uncomfortable sound of high-pitched feedback from a microphone.

"Is this this thing on? Is it on? Oh, that's what the green light means; well, l that makes sense." The announcer whispered very loudly into the microphone. "What? The whole audience can hear me now? Well, this is embarrassing."

The announcer cleared his throat loudly into the microphone. "Ahem, are you ready for an execution!!!"

The crowd roared in response.

"That's what I like to hear!" he shouted. "Today, on this wonderfully warm afternoon, we have an amazing show for you all. Right now, our armed forces are out there kicking the military of Eden's ass. Can I get a hell yeah?"

"Hell, yeah!" The crowd shouted in unison.

"For your viewing pleasure, we have the legendary members of the Red Baron Squad!" He screamed as the crowd replied with cries of adoration. "These legendary warriors will execute a slew of POWs, monsters, and drumroll please? We have for you three of the worst, most evil, and most violent human beings to ever walk the earth. Wait what? We only have two of them? I mean, we have two of the worst pieces of crap to ever walk the earth. I present to you all the Eden TWO!!!!!!"

Between the boos and what she assumed were copious amounts of cabbage being tossed at them, she came to the conclusion they were not well-liked. Macy figured everyone would be gunning for them, and thanks to the mountain of cabbage next to them, they would be the easiest people to find.

"Before we begin, I want to remind our viewers of the rules. This is going to be a modified version of a free-for-all. Our Red Baron Team of Executioners will be tasked with wiping out all our unlucky contestants. If, by the grace of God, a lucky soul manages to be the last person alive, and the Red Baron Team is defeated, that individual will be allowed to walk out of here alive…probably. Now fighters, start your engines!"

The announcer burst out laughing at his joke. "Let the carnage begin!"

Monsters roared as they sprinted across the field, searching for their victims. Blades clashed against each other, sending sparks in the air. Gunshots echoed throughout the battlefield, sending both monsters and humans to their graves.

In a word, she was reliving her worst nightmare. She was once again frozen in fear as people died around her. Only this time, instead of her parents being by her side. Who, from what she could tell, was feeling the same way she did. His hand was trembling and dripping with sweat, which normally she wouldn't mind holding hands with him. The middle of a battlefield was not an ideal time to do so.

Macy had no what to do. They were at a serious disadvantage with the black hoods over their heads. On the one hand, she could sense two people were walking toward them. She also couldn't tell if they had guns or swords or could use magic. Macy hoped they were wearing dark hoods and was just as blind as she was.

"Look what we got here. A little loser, and he's holding hands with his little girlfriend. Brad, do you think they will let us out if we bag these two?"

Brad laughed, "We can only hope. I still have a bone to pick with that crappy lawyer. Now, Steven, which one do you want to cut down first."

"You know what? Normally, I would say, ' Let's kill the guy first. But in these modern times, I think we have to be fair and occasionally cut down the girl first." He replied. "It's a shame, really, to have to ruin such a lovely face."

Macy felt a rough hand on her left shoulder. She grinned; what an idiot. Then she took a deep breath and grabbed his wrist with her right hand. With blazing speed, she moved her left palm and pressed it against his elbow until it snapped. Then she struck him in the throat with the edge of her hand before he could howl in pain. He crumbled to the ground, gasping for air, and she stomped her heel into his face.

She felt a dull pain in her right cheek and lost her balance. Blood trickled from her nose as she was struck again. Macy fell backward as she tripped by Brad. When she hit the ground, he proceeded to kick her in the stomach.

"You like that bitch?" He shouted. "I'm a make you pay for hurting my friend."

Macy curled her body and sucked in her stomach before his next move. She squinted her eyes, fearing the additional pain from his powerful kicks. Then she screamed as an overwhelming bright light enveloped her.

Her eyes blinked uncontrollably as she adjusted to the sunlight. She glanced up and saw her old childhood friend staring back at her. His expression was cold and empty. It was unsettling to see him this way. She was so used to his infectious smile and awkward conversations.

"You know you could have taken your hood off, right?" He said in a flat tone.

"Oh," she giggled. "Now I feel like I took that butt-kicking for no reason."

Macy almost threw up when she noticed what lay at her feet. She was struggling to process the battered face of her attacker, who, just moments ago, had been yelling at her. His dark brown hair was matted and covered in dirt. What frightened her was that Brad's neck was bent and twisted awkwardly.

"Did you, did you kill him?" She asked as she struggled to think that Jayden could do that to a person.

He took her by the hand and helped her to her feet. "Yes, I did. It's all that I'm good for."

She stared him dead in the eyes. "I know you are more than that. You did what you had to do to save me. Now give me a chance to save you. I won't let you carry this burden alone, okay? And that's final."

Jayden put his hands up in surrender." Fine, convince me."

"I will," she replied.

Macy put her arms around him and held him close. He didn't hug her back, but she just wanted him to know she was there for him. Normally, it would have been Sarah or Tony doing this, but this was her time.

She opened her eyes, and he was staring at her. For a second, she thought he would try to kiss her since they might not make it out of there alive. The thought of him locking lips with her gave her butterflies, partially because she liked him a little bit, and she was nervous about the wrath Sarah would rain down after the fact. The Daimonia would pale in comparison to her insurmountable rage.

Jayden's eyes squinted as he pulled back, "Why are you looking so weird? Are you going to pick up your gunblade or what?"

Macy pushed him back. "What do you mean I look weird? This is my normal face. You got caught off guard because you're used to gawking at Grace and Sarah. Typical man."

Jayden shook his head, "You give me heart palpitations."

She watched as he turned around to pick something up from the ground. Then he placed her weapon in her hand. She gawked at the blade that seemed to appear out of nowhere.

"How did you get this?"

He shrugged, "They've been here the whole time. You didn't know because you kept your hood on the whole time."

Her face turned bright red out of embarrassment. She couldn't believe she took a beating for no reason. Macy shook her head; *get in the game*, she told herself.

She glanced to her right and noticed a few items lying amongst the gray dirt and crabgrass. A black scimitar with a red sash wrapped around the handle was sitting right next to it, and a black pistol rested gently against the sharp blade.

Macy asked Jayden, "Why didn't you grab your weapons?"

He shrugged, refusing to provide her with an answer.

Her eyes shot daggers into his. "Look, if you won't use them to defend yourself. Then I will use them to protect you, whether you like it or not!"

He placed his hand on her shoulder as she turned on her heels to grab the weapons. He turned her back around.

"Don't you ever touch them," he said with a firm tone. "They are cursed, and I don't want you to get…"

He stopped mid-sentence, and his eyes narrowed on a nearby grassy hill. The mound of dirt and grass was too steep to see over it. Then, she began to scan the area around them. Outside of a few clods of dirt and crabgrass, they were mostly surrounded by a wooded area. The wall of trees was immensely thick, and it was virtually impossible to see anything within them. This made it clear to her that they were only dropped off in this spot so that they could be easily ambushed by anyone.

Macy could tell that her tank of magical energy was close to empty, and it would be quite a while before it was fully restored. Fighting would be quite difficult due to her lack of magical energy and her injuries. She would also have to use her magic sparingly, which was not fun.

Macy put her index finger up to her lips and signaled Jayden to be quiet. Then she channeled some magical energy into her legs and sprinted toward the grass mound. Once she had reached the base of the hill, she jumped as high in the air as she could.

While her body gained altitude, she felt like she was sailing above the hill. Her eyes locked in on her target. The creature was adorned with black and red scales and sprinted toward Jayden at a speed most cars would struggle to reach. Macy rotated her body as she continued to fly in the air. Then she hit a button on the hilt of her weapon, and the blade began to fold against itself. Her sword's metal backing extended forward as the blade completed its folding motion. Then, a barrel became visible at the end of the metal piece, and a set of iron sights popped up.

Macy took a deep breath, which was tough while flying. She fired off a round, striking the creature in the neck. It dropped like a sack of potatoes and skidded to a stop at Jayden's feet. Before she touched the ground, she managed to fire off a second shot that took out another creature rushing from Jayden's right side.

Once her feet hit the ground atop the hill, she pointed her left palm toward a creature approaching Jayden from his blindside. She shouted out loud, "Confusion Flame!"

A magenta-colored ball of fire was expelled from her hand and slammed into the creature. The fire spell struck the monster so hard that it bounced off a nearby tree. A magenta-colored halo appeared over the creature's head when it got back up. The animal yelped at Jayden and sprinted off to attack another unlucky soul.

Macy sprinted toward Jayden and jumped into his arms. Upon reflection, she probably could have given him a heads-up because he was not remotely prepared to catch her, and her hug turned into more of a tackle.

"Whoops," she laughed. "I'm sorry. I didn't mean to tackle you, but are you okay? Those mean old monsters didn't scare you, did they?"

Jayden coughed as he struggled to breathe with her full weight on his stomach. "Well, I was okay until you saved me. Those Tiger Stripped Raputās were rather pleasant and not crushing my ribs."

"I am not overweight!" Macy shouted. "Now, let's go."

With her arm stretched out, she helped him back to his feet. She almost tripped over the first Raputā she shot when she turned around. Her eyes couldn't believe what she was seeing. The creature was at least six feet long, from head to tail. Their gray scales were adorned with red and orange stripes. The monster's eyes were bright orange slits like that of an alligator. On its feet were three claws about two inches long, and a fourth claw was higher on its ankle. This fourth claw was about 4 inches long and was much thicker than the others. She guessed the creature would use the larger claw to slash and wound its prey or Jayden.

"Are these dinosaur-type monsters?" She asked.

Jayden looked up at her and replied, "Yes, they are. I read somewhere that a scratch from their claws does like a heat spell and can damage a person's skin or clothing. It's kind of crazy. By the way, that confusion spell you cast on the last one. How did you know it was going to work? I thought spells that affected the brain only worked on normal people."

Macy grinned from ear to ear, "I'm not going to lie; it was a gamble. I've never tried that spell on a monster before today. So, you are welcome. I did have one more question, what would you have done if I hadn't stopped them?"

Jayden turned his gaze away from her and began walking into the woods

***

A light blue dome covered the battlefield. The viewers looked on from the stands, with the safety of that light blue shield of protection. Pictures of humans, monsters, and elves appeared on the large screens. Some of the images were of those who were still alive, but the majority were of those who had been killed. This was a very calloused way to treat people. What was even more depressing was the cruel reality of the joy that violence and suffering can bestow on a paying crowd.

Macy found all of the spectacle and glam to be absolutely heart-wrenching. She didn't know why the other contestants were in the same predicament, but they didn't deserve to be treated like animals. Even the animals and monsters forced to fight deserved better. In a twisted way, the executioners weren't much different than the Daimonia.

The scariest part about it all was that even though she was afraid, Jayden was too. As they stood in the epicenter of this well of violence, they honestly felt at home amongst the carnage. The destruction of their hometown allowed them to adapt rather quickly to immense bloodshed and hatred. This is probably why she felt comfortable joining The Witnesses because, in a sick way, the chaos brought her some level of comfort. She wondered if she could ever return to the person she was before. If she could ever go back to being normal, whatever that was. In her heart, she hoped Jayden could find that solution, for all of their sakes.

Macy tapped Jayden on his shoulder. "Help me to understand something, okay? I want you to know a little more about me before I ask. I wanted you to know that I chose to become a part of The Witnesses because that is what my parents did. You kind of stumbled into this role. I've been wondering, what is your end goal? "She asked.

"Well, honestly, all I wanted was vengeance," he replied, stepping over a branch. "As things went on, I dreamed of moving home with everyone. It was amazing. But now, I realize that it was truly just that, a dream. I don't see things getting any better anytime soon."

"Jayden, I'm going to tell you this now. The whole brooding, no upside to life persuasion you have right now. It is not a good look on you. That type of thinking belongs to punk rockers and guys who hate their dads. You aren't in a band, and I know you liked your dad. So, get your head out of your ass!" Macy exclaimed before she gave him a gentle push into some nearby bushes.

"Well screw youuuuuuu…" His voice trailed off as he stumbled backward and slid down a muddy hill conveniently hidden behind the bushes he had been pushed into. Jayden managed to zig and zag down the muddy hill with the skill and grace of a skier who had never gone skiing before.

Macy giggled, then fell down laughing, watching her childhood friend scream for his life. She thought it was hilarious when he hit the bottom of the hill and launched his body into the air. Her lungs felt like they were on fire from laughing so hard when her friend crashed hard onto the ground. Since she didn't hear any bones crunching or see an ominous puddle of blood, she felt that her gentle push was well worth it.

Fifteen minutes had passed by, and she was still laughing at Jayden. Until she remembered he had hurt his ribs not too long ago, and that might be the reason he still hasn't moved from the spot where he face-planted. Macy did have the sinking suspicion that he might be overexaggerating things and playing dead until she came down the hill. Once he began to stir and grabbed his ribs, she realized she could have quite possibly been a little too rough on her friend.

Without warning, her vision became laser-focused on a clearing a couple yards away from where Jayden had fallen. The clearing was filled with trees with light green leaves and bushes with less-than-appealing flowers. She could see low-cut grass through a few empty spaces between the foliage but not much else. Macy knew something was wrong; her eyes only narrowed on their own when there was danger.

She caught glimpses of scarlet threads moving amongst the lush green backdrop. The red spots seemed to disappear and then reappear as they drew closer to where Jayden was curled up on the ground. She put her gunblade into sword mode and channeled her magical energy.

Her heart pounded like a drum, as a nervous sweat began dripping down her palms. The hairs on her neck stood up from sensing the powerful magical energy signatures approaching her childhood friend. Normally, she could handle whatever was coming. However, her energy was still pretty low, and she didn't have many bullets left. She had promised to give Jayden a reason to keep going, which would be her opportunity. Her life was important to him; she couldn't afford to die now. The only option left was to be a badass bitch and show the whole world the power of the Phoenix Monastery

Chapter 18

Fire and Smoke

Magenta-colored flames encircled her body like a tornado. The blade on her Ninjato was bathed in an orange light. Smoke billowed from the plants that happened to be too close to the young woman from Eiréné. An unbearable heat spread throughout the woods, emanating from every pore within her body.

Anger fueled the energy bursting from within. She stepped back, sprinted toward the edge of the hill, and jumped toward the foliage below. Her body launched forward with the speed of a bullet from the flames she conjured. She sent off two fireballs below her as she flew over Jayden to completely obliterate the two warriors approaching him.

Macy spun her sword over her head as she slowed her approach. Then she adjusted her momentum and directed her body into a dive once she reached a small clearing. Her orange blade pierced the ground like it was butter. Macy released a shockwave of intense heat from the impact of her touching down. Her enemies standing too close to her explosive magic were eviscerated by her overwhelming power.

A poor, unfortunate soul made his way toward her. He was carrying a large mace in his left hand, swinging it over his head as he sprinted toward her. His plated chest armor was painted a crimson red, matching his boots and hoop earrings.

From head to toe, his body was covered in bulging muscles trained to absolutely decimate any opponent. Unfortunately for him, they were going to be of no use.

Macy stabbed her sword into the ground again, and a geyser made of melted rock, dirt, and fire appeared beneath her target. His body launched skyward as the pillar of heated dirt and flame exploded beneath him. She flipped her sword into gun mode and fired off a round. Blood spurted from her opponent's neck as he crashed onto the ground. Without missing a beat, she ducked instinctively, avoiding a blade that was aimed at her neck. She swung the barrel of her gun beneath her left arm and squeezed off two rounds. The coward that tried to attack her from behind dropped like a sack of potatoes.

She looked down at her opponent as he took his final breaths. His eyes were filled with rage and contained a hint of fear. The black gloves he wore were stained red as he tried to cover his fatal wounds. He was dressed in a similar garb as her previous adversary. His pants were a red camo, matching his crimson body armor, which apparently was ineffective against rifle rounds.

When he closed his eyes and took his final breaths, she felt a twinge of guilt. While she was fighting for her life, she knew becoming a killer was what Jayden was afraid of. As she examined her attacker, she could see how easily a person could fall prey to that type of thinking. Even though this wasn't her first rodeo, she needed to keep her head clear and remember this was just about survival, nothing more.

She went blind momentarily as her body was lifted in the air. Her ribs were filled with sharp, unbearable pain to the point she wanted to cry. The blue Gi she wore was sticking to her skin like glue from being soaked by high-pressure water.

The blast of water knocked her over twenty feet away before crashing hard into the ground. Macy felt the wind get knocked out of her as pain spread through every molecule of her being. Droplets of blood trickled down her chin from biting her lip as she fell.

Her lungs were on fire as she gasped for air. The only thought her mind could produce as she struggled to move was how she could have been so careless. To be more accurate, she was a sitting duck at this point, well, a collapsed and utterly useless duck.

While she lay on the ground in disgrace, she had an epiphany; her friend was still in danger. The sound of boots crunching on dry grass nearby made her body tense. Macy had to move, or she was a goner. If she didn't find the strength to move, then they would kill Jayden. He was her childhood friend, and she had promised him that she would keep.

Macy jumped to her feet and nearly fell back down on the ground. Not because she was super clumsy, but her equilibrium was completely thrown off, and her vision blurred. She felt like she was in the middle of those Spinney Cup rides at the fair.

Even though her head was bobbing back and forth from being absolutely dizzy, she tried to focus her eyes on three blurry figures decked out in red. Macy swung her blade across her body with a wave of magenta-colored flames slamming into her approaching targets. She couldn't tell what happened; all she knew was that the blurry figures were there for a moment, and after her spell, they were gone, which hopefully meant that she didn't miss.

Her right hand spasmed and jerked, and her gunblade dropped out of her hand. Then, she felt a sharp pain like a dagger being pressed into the center of her palm. Tears brimmed in her eyes as blood flowed down her hand and her arm.

Macy felt her body become weightless, staining the green grass crimson from her blood. She shrieked, realizing she was floating a few feet off the ground. Red slashes appeared across her forearms and shins from thin blades made of water. Every nerve in her body was screaming with pain when she dropped onto the grass.

"Seems like someone got a little too confident in her abilities."

Macy blinked her eyes open as a blurred figure dressed in scarlet garb. "Who are you? What did you do to me?"

"My name is Michael, and I guess you could say you've met your match." He laughed in the most pompous way.

Macy scoffed, "That wasn't exactly helpful jackass. Why is my vision screwed up? Did you drug me, you sicko?"

Michael felt accosted, "I would never do such a thing to a lady. All I did was use some magic to incapacitate you."

She rolled her eyes, "That's not much different, you perv."

He shook his head, "You are literally the worst. All I did was use a little bit of water magic to put out your flames."

"I've been hit by water spells before, and none have made me feel like this. I feel like I'm on a crazy rollercoaster and forgot my glasses simultaneously." Macy replied.

Michael chuckled to himself. "Well, you took out plenty of my men. The Red Barons are known throughout Aggeloi as the best executioners, and my squad is among the organization's best. You have made a mockery of us. To address your blurry vision, I used my variation of water magic. Most use salt water or your average lake water in their spells. On most fire users, that can be enough to stop them. However, it isn't always enough for a lady of your caliber. Instead, I use bog and swamp water with my spells. The bacteria in those bodies of water add toxins and poisons to my most basic water spells."

"Well, that's absolutely revul…" Before she could finish her retort, Macy turned to her left and began to throw up every ounce of prison food she had consumed.

He snapped his fingers, and a translucent water blade appeared in his hands. Then he whispered into her ears, "I made this sword just for your neck."

***

Jayden's eyes narrowed on the buff gentleman strolling his way. He had a thick beard with a matching mustache. His shirt was blood red, which complemented his black pants and boots. He carried a long machete with a golden hilt in his right hand. The weapon was iron but looked as sharp as a razor blade. Based on the way the man was staring at Jayden, he safely assumed that his intentions would be extremely violent.

The Dragon Warrior tried to move, but his ribs were still throbbing. He glanced up at his enemy approaching him and was tempted to let the guy win. What was the point of trying anymore?

His ears perked up at the sound of someone crying out in pain. He quickly glanced in the direction Macy went. His eyes widened as he saw her slumped on the ground, surrounded by members of the Red Baron execution squad. Something inside him stirred, and he wanted to save her. Witnessing her body covered in blood and the fear in her eyes broke him.

She was risking her life for him, just like his Dad had. He vowed in that moment that he would not let it end the same way. He grabbed a handful of rocks and tossed him at his enemy because he still didn't have enough energy to move.

His adversary laughed at the feeble attempt as he sliced through the incoming projectiles like butter. "From what I could see on the big screen, you looked like a stone-cold killer. Now, I think even my 3-year-old niece could pummel you into oblivion".

"Can you blame a guy for trying," Jayden replied with a grin.

The Dragon Warrior made a second attempt at throwing rocks at his approaching enemy. The man scoffed at the insult and started swinging at the incoming pebbles. While distracted by the rocks, Jayden pulled out his Father's old pistol and fired three rounds. His opponent managed to deflect two of the bullets but was unlucky when the third struck him in the right shoulder. The force of the round knocked him to the ground.

Jayden managed to get back on his feet with the grace and sophistication of a zombie. He walked over and stared down at his attacker. "The only reason I am letting you live is because I appreciate your humor. "Jayden snapped his finger, and his opponent's sword began to melt like ice cream in the sun. "Now, if you follow me after this confrontation, I will have no choice but to end you. I would hate for your niece to hear of your passing."

The man lying in front of him was taken aback by his statement. He was even more surprised when Jayden cut off strips from his sleeves so the man could cover his wounds. The Dragon Warrior's eyes switched from his wounded enemy to the small mob surrounding his childhood friend.

A crowd of seven men and women dressed in various combat uniforms surrounded his friend. Standing beside her was an eighth soldier Jayden assumed to be their leader. The jerk paraded around the center of the mob with the boisterous and charismatic attitude of a lion tamer.

Normally, Jayden would love to slap the crap out of a cocky prick like him, but he didn't have much magical energy left to use. Whatever magic he did have available was being used to temper the extreme pain in his ribs. He had one other option, and he winced at the painful thought, but it was the only chance he had to save her. So, he would have to be quick.

The young Dragon Warrior took a deep breath, and as he exhaled, he felt his muscles bulging. Whisps of a smokey-colored flame snacked around him like a python. Droplets of blood were secreted from the freshly healed cuts on his arms. The process was in full swing, so he would have to make every second count.

Jayden slammed his sword into the ground, and instantly, a cylindrical tower of fire surrounded Macy. The blast from the heat knocked the closest executioners to the ground. Mass confusion disseminated throughout the crimson mob, who could no longer torture their prey. Jayden realized they still had no idea who had summoned the spell.

He sprinted toward them with his pistol raised and fired six rounds before they even knew he was coming. He managed to drop five out of the eight executioners, who were now exceptionally pissed at him.

He swung his sword over his head and shouted, "Bring forth fire from the depths of hell! Rise and come forth now! I Summon the great Seraph!"

The clearing became draped in intense heat as the ground beneath his approaching enemies rumbled. Small flame sprites appeared between Jayden and his attackers. The sprites grew in numbers and coalesced and formed a gigantic snake. Horns made of red flames sprouted from the creature's forehead. Razor-sharp teeth formed beneath its upper jaw, dripping pools of lava onto the grass. The serpent's eyes were blood red, narrowing as it found its prey.

In the blink of an eye, the Seraph slithered so quickly that it absorbed the two unfortunate souls that had gotten too close to Jayden. Next, it sped toward their leader. He managed to dive to the side and roll away from the slithering creature from hell. The Seraph turned around and sent forth a blast of orange venomous flames. He summoned a shield made of water that quickly extinguished the flames. The executioner sent a blast of water at the flaming snake, instantly turning the creature into a puddle on the ground.

The executioner turned toward Jayden as he chuckled, "My name is Michael. I am the leader of this team of executioners. You are quite talented; your only flaw is that you are a complete idiot. You fire users are nothing but predictable when it comes to your magic. You rely on it so much that you ignore its fundamental weaknesses made by the God of nature himself. I hope you enjoyed your brief rally to save your friend because your five minutes of fame have just ended. I have a reputation to protect."

Michael directed his right palm toward the young Dragon Knight and sent forth a high-pressure blast of water. A gray shield made of fire intercepted the spell, and the gushing water instantly turned into steam. Jayden smiled as the executioner's face turned bright red.

His enemy sent another blast of water. This time around, his attacker used both hands to summon the spell. The force of the water speeding toward Jayden made him wince at the thought of the pain. Instead of his ribs cracking and a hole blasting through his chest, he was greeted by the gentle hissing sound of steam.

Jayden widened his gaze, standing there in complete shock. The smokey flames orbiting his frame had turned the approaching flood of water into a spa.

Michael's light-colored complexion turned even redder. "How in the hell were you able to stop that?"

Jayden shrugged, "I don't know. Maybe you missed?"

The executioner was fuming and sent another blast of water, which instantly evaporated. "How can you turn my spells into steam? No fire magic user has ever countered my water spells. Plus, I can't sense any magical energy coming from you. How are you able to do any of this?"

"This might sound really stupid, but no rule says your magical power must come from your reserves. Power like this comes from deep within, requiring you…"

Before he could finish his response, Jayden fell into a coughing fit. Streams of blood dripped down from his lips, and a crimson stain appeared on the green grass. His hands were covered in blood from trying to cover his mouth.

The executioner laughed, "I can see that power comes at a cost. I hope it was worth….." Michael's eyes widened as a blade pierced through the center of his chest, and he fell to his knees.

Jayden grinned, "It was worth it. You see, I was just stalling for time. I used all of my real magical energy in one spell. That great wall of fire you ignored was used to restore my friend's energy. Since then, the spells I've been using have been used to waste time. I couldn't hold this form much longer, I've sustained too many injuries, and you are too powerful."

Michael spit out blood as his vision blurred. "I appreciate your respect for my abilities. However, don't think for one second that you have won. While you have been fighting for survival, the Eden military has descended upon the surrounding area. This means everyone watching has been escorted to safety bunkers, and no one is left to see you reach your victory. It also means you are stranded here. Not even God himself could crack through this shield."

Chapter 19

Exceptional Luck

A dark shadow loomed over the dome. Magical energy radiated from the dark presence floating above the stadium. The pitch-black image appeared to expand in the sky, like a bat unfurling its wings.

The image of the monster was imposing and filled Macy with fear. She couldn't tell what it was, but it made her cower in fear. Normally, they couldn't see anything through the blue dome, so the fact this creature cast such a large shadow was downright scary.

A bright light appeared near the top of the black mass. Then, the light slammed into the shield. Her body rocked back and forth as the stadium shook violently. Macy held on to Jayden tightly as the light slammed into the shield again.

"Are you going to let me breathe?" He asked.

She squeezed him tighter. "Shut up. Something bad is happening, and we are probably going to die."

"Something's trying to kill us again? I am super shocked by that. I might need to take another nap just to be safe." Jayden yawned and closed his eyes again.

Macy tightly held on to him as the bright light slammed into the dome again. Cracks splintered across the dome like a spider web. Electrical and magical energy collided in the skies above as the shield's integrity was fighting for survival.

A lightning bolt pierced through the shield and struck the ground below. An overwhelming heat filled the stadium from the flaming crater that was made. Sparks of electricity rained down on the stadium as the shield shattered.

"Ja, Jayden.." she whispered. "What is that?'

Jayden opened his eyes and immediately sat up, completely alert. He gulped down a heavy dose of fear. His eyes shifted toward his childhood friend, and he said, "That, my dear, is a Storm Dragon."

The monster cast a dark shadow that made every creature and human still alive in the stadium shudder in fear. Blue and black scales covered every inch of the dragon's structure. Lightning bolts splintered across the sky, and thunder roared with every flap of the creature's wings.

A slender rope dropped from above and landed just a few feet away from the tree they were hiding in. Her ears perked up at metal grinding against the rope as someone slid down from the top.

When their invader hit the ground, her eyes locked on someone in a dark trench coat. Silver metal flashed in the darkness of the night, and she could tell that he was armed with a pistol. Once he stepped into the light, she noticed his gray tail swinging back and forth.

She leaped down and sprinted toward him. Her arms swung around him, and tears streamed down her face. His warm fur and comforting tone made her feel safe for the first time in quite some time.

"I'm sorry we didn't get here sooner," he whispered. "Where's your idiot friend?"

"Oh, that's a good question. The last time I saw him, his head was in my lap, and then I..." Macy wheeled back around and cringed when she saw Jayden sitting at the base of the tree, with his head spinning like a tabletop.

"He had his head where?" Shane growled. He spun his pistol and fired two rounds.

Jayden's eyes widened when he noticed the smoking bullet holes on each side of his head. He quickly swung his hands up in defeat. "It was nothing like that, I promise!"

Macy ran to his side and gave Shane a stern look. "No, sir, we do not shoot at our friends. He did nothing weird; I promise. We got chased up this tree yesterday by a big old monster. Jayden was just taking a nap, I promise."

Shane spun his pistol and fired another round that landed in the tree an inch above Jayden's head. "That was for being a chicken; you should never get chased up in a tree. What are you, a cat? Now let's go!"

***

Jayden pulled himself up and grinned as he stood on the back of the dragon. A cool breeze blew gently against his skin as they cruised through the skies. He took a step forward, almost losing his balance. He dropped down and began to crawl up the neck of the powerful beast.

As he cruised atop the dragon, it reminded him of being on a boat. The way the creature bopped up and down from the force of its powerful wings felt like the gentle up-and-down push from a wave. This was going to be a moment he would never forget. The feeling of true freedom was indescribable, even if the moment would be gone in a flash.

He leaned to the left as a volley of bullets whizzed by. Clouds of smoke and fire appeared sporadically around them. The sound of the explosions from the shells and the flack cannons was deafening. A normal functioning person would be disturbed by intense violence heading their way, but for him, it was expected. God forbid he asks for a normal day.

According to Shane, his home country had been bombing the Aggeloi capital for a week now. It had started on the day they were to be executed, which was too hard to believe because it seemed like it was just yesterday they got placed in that colosseum.

Based on the explosions surrounding them, it would appear the Eden military was winning. Shane informed him that wasn't the case. What he learned was during the previous war between the two countries, the Aggeloi placed bombs and magical spells throughout his home country. Once the new war popped off, they set off all those weapons to explode it, crippling the Eden economy. This meant that the battle they witnessed in the skies and below was a last-ditch effort from his home country.

He crawled a few more feet forward while keeping his head down. Lightning bolts swirled around Tony and Grace as they stood on the top of Aiko's head. Their eyes were glowing brightly, to the point that they looked possessed. Grace held Tony's arm with her left hand while her right hand gripped one of the dragon's horns. Their combined magical energy allowed Aiko to maintain her Storm Dragon form. It was frightening to witness how much power they could produce.

Jayden got back on his feet and tried to balance on the flying dragon. The remaining magical energy he had left was used to deflect gunfire aimed at the dragon's neck. He cocked back his pistol and fired off five rounds at a glider team attacking them from the rear. They managed to avoid his volley of gunfire and let off some machine gun rounds in response.

A humongous iron shield appeared in front of him and intercepted the bullets. Shane appeared beside him with a smug look on his face. The werefox moved with blazing speed and fired two rounds from his pistols. Shane had moved so fast that Jayden couldn't tell what happened until he witnessed the glider pilots falling toward the city below.

Shane reached into his trench coat and presented him with a glass bottle filled with a blue liquid. "Drink this because you are useless without your magic."

Jayden shrugged and downed the liquid in one go. The potion tasted a little bitter and sweet, like blueberry lemonade. A warm and relaxed feeling disseminated through every nerve in his body as he digested the liquid. His muscles became less tense, and bruises seemed to fade away. Jayden's vision became more focused as his magical energy was almost fully restored from that blueberry-flavored liquid.

He grinned as a pair of magic-tipped rockets appeared on the horizon. Jayden drew his sword, pointed it toward them, and shouted, "Wall of Fire!"

A wall of orange and yellow flames appeared between them and the rockets. Sparks of red metal exploded, and shards of ice shattered when the rockets made contact with his spell. An armored glider pilot pushed through his wall of fire. The soldier's dark-colored armor radiated with the intense heat from his spell. The pilot pointed his wrist at Jayden and fired five mini rockets from his gauntlet.

The Dragon Warrior smiled, pointed his swords at the rockets, and let loose a volley of fireballs. He sprinted toward the dragon's tail as the rockets exploded from his spell. He then pulled his gun from his holster and fired three rounds at the glider pilot. His nemesis drew a massive sword and deflected the bullets with ease.

Jayden channeled his magical energy and jumped high in the air. He let loose orange and yellow flames coiled around his legs and propelled him forward in a glide. The Dragon Warrior raised his sword and slashed at the armored warrior. His enemy deflected the strikes and pushed Jayden back with minimal effort. Then Jayden flipped backward, channeled his glide, and sprung forward again.

A large blade appeared in his peripheral as the glider went on the attack. Jayden pulled out his knife and blocked the attack. His knife blade glided along the side of his enemy's weapon as Jayden closed the gap. Then, in one motion, Jayden shoved his scimitar into the side of his adversary. Once the hilt was pressed against his opponent's armor, he yanked his sword back out and pushed off with his legs against the pilot to gain separation.

Jayden turned back toward the dragon and channeled his magical energy into his legs. While his body went into a glide, he pointed his sword toward the falling glider pilot. He summoned a meteor that slammed into his chest as he fell toward the ground. Flames burst from his legs and launched him forward, speeding toward Aiko like a rocket.

Once his feet landed on a row of dark scales, his balance was completely thrown off, and he began to fall backward. His body stopped descending when a furry paw clasped his wrist and pulled him back.

"Was that a Magi-Knight?" Shane snarled.

"I think it was. I thought they were just a myth in school," Jayden replied.

Shane growled. "They are very real; the Eden and Aggeloi have a few. A few of the other governments are rumored to have one. Even though they are relics of The Great War, they are almost unbeatable with modern technology added to them."

The ground beneath them shook violently, and by the ground, I mean the Storm Dragon. Aiko let out a roar filled with pain and anguish. Jayden looked over the side and noticed that parts of her legs and underbelly were starting to disintegrate. He knew they'd only have a few minutes before they fell to the ground like characters in a cartoon. Without thinking, he sprinted up toward Gracey. Her eyes were no longer glowing, and she had a confused look on her face as he ran toward her. He wrapped his arms around her and dove off the side of the dragon.

***

In his mind, the whole glide off the dragon, save the damsel in distress thing was a great idea. Some might even consider it a baller move. However, trying to be the hero in one's mind tends to run much smoother than in real life. The mildly annoying heroic challenge he faced as he plummeted to the street below was not one he took into account. The challenge he was struggling to manage as he sped toward the concrete was holding onto his passenger in front of him, who was slightly heavier than he had predicted (No, I am not calling her fat). So, as they descended, he was a little off balance and managed to crash land into the second-story window of a furniture store.

"Jayden…." She said, sounding exceptionally perturbed. "I greatly appreciate your desire to save me, but next time, let me fall to my death; it will hurt less."

He grinned and replied, "I am glad to spend time with you, Gracey. I've been in jail for the past week, and I was beaten almost to death while you managed to escape. So, I guess that makes us even, yeah?

She shrugged, "I guess that's fair. Now, let's hurry up and get out of the city."

They sprinted down the stairs, tripping over furniture and equipment on their way to the exit. Once they reached the sidewalk, Tony and the others were huddled on the other side of a large shipping truck. The storage container and the cabin of the truck were riddled with bullet holes.

Jayden and Grace approached the truck and slid in next to Tony. The truck rattled from a fresh set of rifle rounds sent their way. Shane loaded three orange-colored bullets into one of his pistols. The rounds were engraved with the image of a tiger, wrapped around the length of the casing.

"Cover your ears," he whispered.

Shane leaned to his left just enough to look around the truck. He took a deep breath and fired off three rounds. The bullets slammed into a row of cars where their attackers were shooting from. Upon contact, the cars exploded, sending a giant fireball.

Jayden knew it must have worked because the street became deathly quiet. In fact, their section of the city was now as silent as the grave. Going from ducking bullets to complete silence disturbed the young Dragon Warrior.

Grace stood up and said, "I want us to go north."

"Why?" Shane growled.

"I, I don't know," she replied. Grace pulled her necklace from under her shirt and showed it to him. "I know this thing wants me to go there."

Shane scoffed at the thought. "I'm sorry, Princess, but that seems like a terrible idea. We need to get The Key to The Witnesses' main base of operations. If we do what you suggest, it's going to fall into the hands of the Daimonia or some other asshole.'

"I remember Sarah mentioning that we needed to head north. So why do you still think that we need to go north?" Jayden asked.

"Well, you remember how Sarah was having weird dreams?" she replied as she paced back and forth, rotating *The Key* between her fingers." I have similar dreams whenever I wear this necklace to sleep. They aren't as crazy as hers, but I've seen some of the same landmarks. And I feel like if I don't do what this thing wants, it will kill..."

Grace stopped midsentence and crumbled to the ground beside him. Blood streamed down her right arm. Jayden grabbed her and pulled her back behind the truck. Macy and Shane huddled around her and began chanting healing spells. Jayden ripped off his sleeves and wrapped them around her bullet wounds. Tony jumped to his feet and summoned a cylindrical cone of lightning to block the gunfire from the cross street.

His heart was pounding in his chest as he stared at his friend, crying out in pain. Her blood stained the asphalt beneath them. There was nothing he could do. Every part of him wanted to blow them away for causing her pain. All of the vengeance he held inside, he wanted to rain down upon them if it would change the fact she might die right in front of him. Life was too cruel. After all the suffering Grace had experienced in her life, fate deemed it necessary to bring her back to her home country just to die on the street like a stray dog.

Shane slapped Jayden in the back of the head with his bloodstained paw, "Don't you dare make this about you. We will save her; now, you and your spiky-haired friend need to do what you are trained to do: make a big distraction so we can patch her up with no problem. You got it?"

Jayden replied coldly, "Say no more."

Shane beamed. "Good, now raise some hell! Show me you two have surpassed your fathers!"

He got up and drew his sword. Orange and yellow flames encircled him like a tornado as he stepped through the barrier of lightning. Bullets melted in the air as they sped by, and metal shards coated the ground around him. Tony stepped beside him and pointed his broadsword toward the unit of soldiers approaching them from the cross street. In unison, the Dragon Warriors from Eiréné shouted, "Firestorm!"

Dark storm clouds began to form in the night sky. Thunder roared like a lion consumed with rage. Gusts of scorching wind made their enemies shudder and tremble. Bolts of crimson light and balls of fire descended upon the city. To a nearby observer, the spell wrought upon the Aggeloi army would be described with one word: Armageddon.

Chapter 20

A Spoil of War

He was jolted awake at the sound of a gunshot. Before he had even opened his eyes, his pistol was already raised to eye level with a round in the chamber. His tummy rumbled as he scanned the rooftop of the warehouse.

His ears rang just as another round pierced through the silent streets of the Aggeloi capital. Jayden adjusted his head to glance over the side of the building to get a better view of the street. There were no military units, local militia, or even a crazy gun owner roaming the streets. Save for the two gunshots he heard; this part of the city was even quieter than most cemeteries.

He scooted toward a corner of the building that ran parallel to the alley. Jayden glances over the side. The alley was covered in dust, with a perimeter fence that connected the warehouse to the building next to them. There were two pink

-colored dumpsters in the center of the alley. His best friend sat in a car that had been parked in the alley and was attempting to get it working.

Tony turned the ignition with a screwdriver, and the car roared to life. It backfired, and the vehicle shut off as quickly as it had started.

The sound of the car backfiring made his heart pound like a drum. Even though he now knew the sound of gunfire he heard was just coming from the car, he still felt anxious. Flashbacks from the last couple of nights from Grace crumbling to the ground covered in blood, to intense combat with both members of the Aggeloi military and his own countrymen, to even getting attacked by a local militia and a street gang. Images of these conflicts flooded his mind with every attempt Tony made at starting that car, which invariably backfired.

By the grace of God, they managed to escape their many pursuers and hid in the city's industrial district. As far as he understood, the capital city was known by two names. His country called the Aggeloi capital the Shimmering City; other nations called it the Emerald City. The residents of the city called it the capital. The idea was that there was no other city like it.

The capital gained the moniker of both the Emerald and Shimmering City because of its immense beauty. If a first-time visitor were to come to the capital within their first couple steps onto the concrete, their eyes would be treated to a spectacular array of light and dark green colored buildings littering the city's center. The emerald-colored glass of their skyscrapers shimmered in the morning light, casting a light green shadow of hope. Many old capital buildings were shaped like diamonds cut straight from a mountain.

However, the industrial side of town was objectively less attractive. Their buildings were adorned with dull colors of faded brown and primer. Jayden concluded that it must have been their paint color of choice. Above the industrial sector, the sky had a permanent light brown tint from the smog collected over the years. A rich smell of sulfur and burning metal filled his nostrils from the oil fields and machine shops.

For the most part, this industrial district was rather peaceful, save for the few factories allowed to stay open to support the war effort; the streets were basically empty. It was unfortunate for the businesses that had to close down throughout the city due to the fighting. Jayden couldn't imagine what sort of hardships were falling on the poor labor workers and the business owners who were now experiencing a loss in wages.

He jumped to his feet when the car backfired again. Instead of sputtering into nothingness, the car roared to life this time. Jayden glanced at his right hand and noticed how tightly it gripped his pistol. The scariest part was that he didn't remember picking it back up again.

Jayden climbed down the ladder that led down into the alley. His friend was sitting in the primer and rust-colored car. The seats were covered in a faded red, almost pink-colored fabric. A cheap silver paint covered the plastic spinning hub caps on the car, and a pair of pink dice hung from the mirror.

When he slid into the seat, his nostrils flared at the musty scent of old cigarettes. The stitching on his seat was torn, and he could feel the uncomfortable stinging pain from a spring poking through the seams. Dark smoke bellowed from the exhaust behind them, creating a small black cloud. The car's engine roared powerfully and then sputtered as the power fluctuated up and down.

Tony popped the car into first gear, and they jetted toward the gated fence. Metal screeched, and sparks flew as they crashed through the fence. A homeless man shouted at them and gave them the finger, as Tony almost hit him when they made it onto the street.

The engine roared as they sped down the empty streets of the Industrial District. Normally, Jayden would have been yelling at his friend to slow down because they couldn't afford the ticket, but they were wanted men. However, the military and the local police were focused on other parts of the city where the fighting was much more intense, so they didn't have to worry too much about getting stopped. Their true challenge will come when they go through a checkpoint.

"So, do you know where we are going? I know we are supposed to go north, but how will we find the others?" Jayden asked.

Tony turned to his friend as the traffic light turned green. "I don't know. I've never been here before."

Jayden almost fell out of his seat at his best friend's response. "Then what the hell, man? You kept saying we could catch up with them while we were getting shot at. You even said it would be a piece of cake."

His friend rolled his eyes, "Bro, you are so annoying; me not knowing where we are going has nothing to do with my ability to track them. Don't worry about it, I got them on the CLOUD."

The Dragon Warrior raised a suspicious eyebrow. "The CLOUD? What kind of nonsense is that?"

Tony jabbed his best friend in the ribs. "See, this is the crap I'm talking about. You never pay attention. If you had been paying attention during our General Studies classes at the Monastery, you would have remembered that Storm Magic users are adept at using tracking magic. How do you think I was able to track you when you were lost at sea? I'm doing basically the same thing with them."

Jayden nodded his head as if he understood what his buddy meant. "Ahh, yes, The CLOUD, I was just checking to see if you remembered how to use it. Of course, I was paying attention during our General Studies class taught by Master Takashi."

Tony chuckled, "Now I know you're lying. Our General Studies teacher was Master Tanaka. How did you even get your sash? They must have rounded up all your grades to a C." The Dragon Warriors laughed as they continued their cruise through the capital's mean streets.

As quiet and empty as the streets of the Industrial District were, the sidewalks and alleys were not. A healthy combination of factory workers and homeless teens wandered the streets. He even spotted groups of refugees huddled in the alleyways and abandoned buildings. For Jayden, it was a terrible sight to see. It broke his heart to see children with bloated bellies from a lack of food or labor workers stressed to the max to complete deadlines for the war effort. The reality he witnessed was of a country that cared about its function more than its most vulnerable citizens.

Jayden felt a twinge in his stomach as Tony turned down an empty street. This road led them toward downtown, which was hard to believe because the street was emptier than his list of dating prospects ☹ . Shopping malls and shoe stores lined the sidewalks they sped by. No shoppers spent their hard-earned tax return checks on items they didn't need. Instead, they had an open road that was suspiciously quiet.

The twinge in his stomach grew stronger, and he felt like he would be sick. At the same time, he felt his heart pounding. His eyes looked in every direction as they cruised down the street. His right hand gripped his .45 with a round already racked in the slide. He didn't remember picking up his gun, but when his heart started pounding in his chest, and his stomach started making him feel sick, that meant danger was coming.

He plugged his ears as he heard a screeching sound on the radio. Jayden turned the dial so the sound was completely off. Then he heard it again, and he kicked the black radio. Still, the sound persisted.

A scratchy voice pierced through the clearly terrible speakers. The voice said, "Please identify yourself?"

Jayden turned to his best friend and shrugged.

The radio made a high-pitched sound, and a voice appeared on the frequency again. "Please identify yourself! This is your second warning. Please advise."

Jayden turned to his best friend and said, "Well, aren't you going to say anything."

Tony made a quick left and replied, "How? This is a normal radio that you can get in any car. How do they expect me to reply? Should I stick my head out the window and shout at them?"

Jayden shrugged. "You aren't wrong; this isn't a CB radio or anything. Their people must be using the wrong frequency. This is supposed to be a rap station."

Tony shook his head, feeling completely annoyed, and put his foot down on the pedal. The engine roared like a lion. Still, Jayden felt that twinge in his stomach again, and his heart began to race. He felt anxious because he wasn't sure who was trying to get a hold of them or even why. Plus, there was no way to respond to their unwanted guests.

The radio crackled again, and a gruff voice burst through their speakers. "We repeat, please identify yourself now! Please acknowledge this transmission!"

Tony made a left at the next light as he sped toward a ramp that led down to a motorway. This part of the freeway went under the city through a series of tunnels that spread throughout the city like a web. Normally, this would be an amazing way for someone to travel within a large city, especially in the capital. The only issue was that their driver needed to be able to keep his eyes on the sky to track his CLOUD, which would be quite difficult to do underground.

The bright morning sun bounced its brilliant light across the gray motorway pavement. No other cars or city buses joined them as they crossed the threshold into the tunnel. Once they descended the ramp, their eyes reflected the bright green and yellow bioluminescent lights illuminating the pitch-black tunnels. Digital traffic signs hung from the ceiling as they sped through the tunnel. Orange-colored texts provided instructions about traffic safety, distances to the nearest exits, and tunnel intersections. There were even large billboards illuminated by magical crystals to advertise the various restaurants throughout the city; he even spotted an advertisement for the new attraction of purple koalas at the zoo.

Tony did not deem it necessary to stop and see the purple koalas. He didn't seem to find it important to stop for anything. They hadn't eaten much in the last few days. The few truck stops they had passed had smoke clouds billowing from their chimneys, bringing the smell of savory and highly unhealthy fried food to his nostrils. His mouth salivated at the thought of biting into a drumstick, a fried burrito, sushi, basically anything better than hearing his stomach growl louder than the car engine.

Jayden sighed, "Dude, I want to get a bite to eat."

"Dude, we can't stop, and you know that. Stop being stupid," Tony replied.

"What do you mean? You don't even know where you are going!"

Tony shook his head and ignored him as he pressed on the gas.

Jayden was annoyed that his best friend had no interest in stopping. All of a sudden, he realized why his friend called him stupid. His best friend was trying to avoid whoever had been following them. The people trying to contact them through the radio stopped once they entered the tunnel. His friend was choosing to drive around cluelessly to avoid another fight but also didn't want to lead them to where Grace and the others were.

He wheezed as his seatbelt pressed against his neck, and his head bounced off the glove compartment. Blood trickled down from his forehead. He felt a deep desire to strangle his friend for slamming on the brakes. Before he could reach across the car, he caught a tiny glimpse of a series of reflectors they would have crashed into. As his eyes pierced through the tunnel's darkness, he could see that the reflectors were attached to thin traffic cones. A series of silver-colored cylinders about the size of a small keg formed a line.

Green lights flashed on and off from the top of the cylinders. His ears twitched at the faint sound of a beep from the metallic objects. He wanted to leave the car to look closer but couldn't convince his body to move. The massive energy signature from the cylinders kept him frozen in his seat.

He turned to his friend and asked, "Are those what I think they are?"

Tony nodded, "C5s, a whole shit ton of C5s."

Jayden replied, "Good, I am thrilled you slammed on the brakes because I was going to pop you for this blood on my forehead."

Tony ignored him and began turning the car around. Jayden scratched his chin as thoughts began to swirl around in his head. Why was there a blockade of traffic cones and C5s? Blocking a freeway tunnel with something so destructive hidden in the darkness didn't make sense. C5s, from what he remembered during their training, were a type of modified plastic explosive that could be amplified in power with a spell that would activate once the canister exploded or if they happened to be powered by magic crystals. They were difficult to make correctly and had to be monitored constantly because the spell or magic inside the canister could become unstable and activate the explosive. So, leaving them unattended was always a risk because if they went off, even a small one could destroy a city block. And the ones that they almost drove into were the largest C5s he had ever seen.

"Why do you think let left those C5s out like that?"

Tony shook his head, "I don't know. For one, they could be using them to demolish that part of the tunnel for construction, which I doubt because you wouldn't need that much explosive to do that. They didn't leave any warning signs, and if you remember from school, which I know you don't, it is challenging to control the explosion of C5 because, sometimes, the spells attached to the explosive can be overpowering. I think they were placed there for the Eden forces that might be fighting above, like they set a trap or something. Or, there is something vital at the end of that tunnel section. I just hope there aren't any more that we might stumble across. We got lucky this last time.

"So, I guess the danger now isn't just where the next blockade is but what will happen when we pop back up on the surface. Will we appear in the middle of a warzone, or will we get lucky, and there will be a parade of nice people waiting on us?"

Tony shrugged as he turned the car and sped up a ramp. Bright sunlight pierced through the windshield. They were reintroduced to the daytime as the tunnel exited onto a street. Their eyes were mesmerized by a sea of large skyscrapers draped in emerald paint and adorned with precious gems and metals. As they cruised through the city, he was impressed by the carriages drawn by bicycles with liquor bars attached to them, filled with patrons as they passed. One of the most shocking scenery changes he noticed was the city buses and taxis with machine guns mounted to their hoods. These tactical forms of public transportation were driven by your everyday taxicab driver and hospitality workers guiding tourists to their destinations. He also noticed the city had ceased using stoplights to dictate traffic, instead using police officers and military officials to control traffic.

The epicenter of business and commerce of the capital was oddly active. The citizens stopping by ice cream stands and buying corndogs seemed perfectly content with living their best lives despite the battles being fought in the distance. Jayden was completely flabbergasted when he noticed a row of breakdancing street performers next to a coffee shop. Despite the heavy police presence, it seemed like what he assumed was a typical day in Aggeloi. The only thing that seemed out of place was them. They were driving around in one of the few personal vehicles; all other forms of transportation seemed public.

Tony pulled up behind a bus at the nearest intersection. A police officer waved for the cross traffic to move. Horns blared, and the turbos from the buses squeaked as they moved across the street. Both of their hearts began to pound in their chests when the cross traffic died down, and the officer set their sights on them.

The bus driver placed his vehicle in gear and turned to the left after being coaxed by the policemen. Tony crept the car into the intersection, and the officer waved them on to follow after the bus without a second glance. They both let out a sigh of relief. There was no way they could fight off the city and military officials conducting the traffic.

***

Tony managed to get them to the east side of the city. The CLOUD they needed to follow was still moving north of their position. His best friend said he wasn't following it because he wasn't sure if people were following them and a bunch of other nonsense. Jayden believed his buddy was just making excuses for not knowing where he was going. You can only take so many wrong turns before admitting you have no idea what you are doing.

The eastern side of the capital was a sprawling suburban area. The houses were nicer than any place he had ever lived. Their gigantic lawns were a mixture of dark green and blue blades of grass. Each house was painted a creamy white color with peach accents. The larger houses had a three-car garage and a port for a boat. He couldn't tell what their backyards were like, but Jayden guessed they probably all had pools and maybe an outdoor BBQ pit. Crimson magic crystals imbued with fire and heat magic orbited just inches above the chimney tops. As nice as the houses were, they seemed to be designed the same. There was no originality to the cookie-cutter homes, which told him a lot about the richer people living in the capital.

A high-pitched sound screamed through the speakers. Jayden covered his ears, and Tony swerved and bumped gracefully into a parked car. Their bodies swung forward and backward from the force of the crash. Tony jumped out of the car to examine the damage between both vehicles. The steel body of their slightly borrowed car had a few scratches along the grill. The gold sedan they drove into was in much worse shape. The sedan's brake lights had popped out of their sockets, their trunk looked like it had been crushed like a soda can, and their license plate hung on for dear life.

Tony jumped back in the car, and before he could turn it back on, Jayden handed him a piece of paper and a pen. "I think you are supposed to leave a note when you get into an accident."

His best friend gave him a look of disdain. "And what do you think it should say? Sorry, I accidentally drove into your parked car with a stolen car. I will probably be on the local news in the WANTED section if you want to contact me."

Jayden scratched his chin, "I like it. Make sure you put hearts over your eyes and sign it XOXOXO just like Hayley from school used to do."

Tony grinned, "You are so dumb. I miss when she made Valentine's Day cards for everyone in third grade. Man, she was something else."

For a moment, the two boys reminisced on one of their shared childhood crushes. Then Tony jumped up and placed the note on the car when they both realized she was simply nice to everyone, and they never stood a chance.

The radio crackled as they drove around a winding curve. Tony slowed down to listen for a voice or something coming through the speaker, but there was nothing. He shook his head and pressed the gas, and the car lurched forward.

A low-flying cloud, as white as snow, drifted just northwest of them. Tony wanted them to drive parallel to the cloud. He didn't want them to follow right under it because their luck was somewhere between nonexistent and downright awful.

Jayden felt a twinge in his stomach as the radio crackled again. He felt his palms getting sweaty and his heart beginning to pound his chest. The car backfired again, and his vision narrowed, darting up and down the suburban streets, looking for an enemy. Jayden reached into the backseat and grabbed a semiautomatic rifle that came with the car. He dropped the magazine and found that it had 10 rifle rounds, which wasn't much for a warzone, but what's life without a little challenge.

His stomach continued to churn to the point that he thought he was going to get sick. Jayden wanted to stick his gun out of the window and just start shooting, but at what? As far as he could tell, they were the only idiots weaving in and out of these suburban neighborhoods. Still, his finger wanted to squeeze that trigger.

Glass shattered, and Jayden felt a burning sensation on his left cheek. His ears were ringing with a high-pitched sound. The car's trunk rattled like it was being hit by a hail shower. Droplets of crimson blood dripped onto his left shoulder, staining his shirt. His body shifted back and forth with incredible force as his friend steered the car left and right.

Tony hit the E-Brake and drifted the car onto the lawn of a 3-story house. He gunned it as they drove through a wooden gate into their backyard. His best friend swerved the car around a swing set and drove straight through a plastic slide. Blades of grass were blasted into the air from the rounds slamming into the yard.

They jetted through the yard and knocked down the fence for the next-door neighbor's house adjacent to them. Mud and dirt painted their windshield as their tire marks destroyed the emerald-colored grass. The car bounced as they drove through the back of the fence and onto the street.

Tony grunted, and the car swerved as they sped up the street. Blood trickled down his right arm, and he tried to cover it with his other hand. Jayden tore his sleeve off and wrapped it around his buddy's arm. Tony cursed when the fabric pressed on his wound.

Jayden leaned back in his seat and glanced at his side mirror. From the reflection in the mirror, he saw a flat metal sheet in the sky behind them. Flashes of red and yellow light explode from the object's center. While he couldn't tell exactly what it was, the sound of small pieces of metal tagging the car and the blood dripping down from his friend's arm told him all he needed to know.

The young Dragon Warrior racked a round and took a deep breath. He didn't quite know what to do or how he could shoot back. The car was moving so erratically to dodge the bullets that he would probably fall out of the car before he got a shot off. If he tried to crawl to the back, he might have a better angle, but of course, he might catch four bullets in the face in the process. He and Tony were still drained of any magic, so the only options he had to fight back with were the rifle and his pistol.

Jayden locked eyes with his best friend and nodded. Tony grinned as he feigned they were going left, then he hit the E-Brake and drifted the car to the right sideways. For about half a second, Jayden had a perfect view of the three gliders approaching from the rear as the car drifted. He quickly fired off six shots from his pistol in quick succession before the car whipped back around, making a 360 spin.

He dropped his pistol, grabbed the rifle, and crawled toward the backseat. Jayden placed the gun barrel on top of the backseat and took aim. The glider units had regrouped after his initial volley and were now flying in a V-Formation. He took a deep breath while he aimed as the car bounced like a rollercoaster. Jayden squeezed the trigger and fired off five rounds at the attackers.

Smoke and sparks burst from the wing of a glider flying on his left side. His aircraft began to spin out of control. Then, the pilot pulled a green object out of his vest that looked like a grenade and threw it toward the ground below. The pilot pressed a button on his strap and was released from his spinning death trap. Once his green grenade hit the ground, it bounced like a ball and cracked open like an egg. Gigantic orbs of liquid and foam came bursting out of the container. Once the pilot landed on the wave of foam and bubbles, the liquid orbs gently carried him down onto the ground; it was like watching an angel landing on a cloud.

Jayden was flabbergasted by what he saw and bumped Tony on the arm. "Dude, did you just see that? "he exclaimed.

"Dude," Tony replied, sounding perturbed as he winced in pain. "I literally was grazed by a bullet not too long ago, and you just had to hit the exact spot where I got hit! And, of course, I saw that. I had never seen any magical orb like that. By the way, how did you hit that guy? I know you're a great shot, but that was something else."

Jayden beamed from ear to ear. "I have no idea. I was actually aiming for the guy on the right."

Chapter 21

A Little Grace

"Wake up, silly head!"

Her body remained still and motionless. Her father gave a toothy grin. "Ahh, I see you are still infatuated by sleep. Don't worry, young lady, we can quickly remedy that."

The King of the Aggeloi reached into his pocket and pulled out a red stink bomb. He placed the object gently behind her head. Once the item was in a comedically appropriate position, he stepped back toward the door to her bedroom. He put three fingers together, and before he could snap, he heard a pleasant voice coming from down the hall.

"If you set off another stink bomb in this cabin, I will literally murder you."

"Mercy, that's technically a terroristic threat to the king of a country. I'm pretty sure there are laws against that," he shouted.

The Queen of the Aggeloi scoffed, "I don't care; it's not like you know the law anyway. In fact, a normal king would have brought his security to deal with threats like that, especially since we are in the middle of nowhere."

"Fine, you win," the King said, feeling utterly defeated.

He glanced up and stared into the beautiful eyes of his 8-year-old daughter. Her hair was disheveled, and the stare of complete derision she gave him made it clear she heard his shouting match with his wife. She did not seem amused at the hilariously placed stink bomb on her pillow.

As her eyes shot darts back at him, the Aggeloi Princess gave him her patented grin. "Daddy, you are just so sweet. I can't wait till they put you in a home like Grandpa."

"That joke might be a little dark for a seventeen-year-old," he replied.

She laughed, "Good thing I'm eight."

Her dad kissed her forehead, "Hurry up and get ready, my little rockstar. We have a little adventure to go on, remember? Don't forget to put on normal kid clothes."

She yawned, "Whatever, get out of my room."

The King jumped back up, "So feisty, you're just like your mother."

"I heard that!" his wife shouted.

***

Grace jumped out of the shower and sifted through her closet. She reached in and pulled out a black T-shirt with the name of a band emblazoned in glitter. Then she grabbed a pair of black jeans with matching combat boots. The princess placed her dark hair with neon blue tips in a ponytail and was ready to go.

Her father swung open her door like a madman. She almost jumped out of her shoes and gave him a scowl. He smiled his pearly whites and ran his fingers through his slicked back, black and graying hair. The King was dressed in a gray T-shirt from his college fraternity $\Delta\alpha\Delta$. He matched the shirt with tan-colored cargo shorts and the most "basic dad" looking running shoes. Slung along his back was a custom crystal white lever-action rifle with a bayonet attached. In short, he was the purest definition of a King who had no idea what he was doing.

Grace's mother appeared beside him and kissed him with her peach-colored lipstick. Her bleached blonde hair, which she claims to not be dyeing, was placed up in a bun. Her tan skin was covered by a pair of blue jeans and low-top sneakers with a matching long black T-shirt of a metal band her mom listened to when she wasn't hosting parties for dignitaries or putting in her votes with the nation's Parliament.

She held her husband close and whispered loudly into his ear. "Now, Damon, you take good care of her while you go on your hike. You can do that, right? You know, be a caring and responsible adult?"

The King shrugged, "I will do my best, but if she doesn't make it back, then she doesn't make it back. It's the risk you take when you go hiking with me."

"I'm going to pretend that you didn't say that," her mother replied as she walked back toward the kitchen.

The King of the Aggeloi led his daughter out of their vacation cabin. They were instantly greeted by the light of the warm morning sun nestled in the bright blue sky. Her pale skin was caressed by the cool ocean breeze as it gently brushed the blades of grass. The teal-colored seagulls of the North Sea squawked as they cruised through the sky without a care. Grace loved their vacation home; she never felt comfortable in the capital, so witnessing a morning like this was breathtaking.

Their vacation cabin was built in the northwestern part of the country. The lush Emerald Hills surrounded them with rows of rose bushes and magenta maple trees. Her family had owned this cabin long before being brought into the royal line. The building was made of white oak and redwood. Their cabin was a simple single-story building with a brick chimney and a modern air conditioning unit that was installed due to her mother despising dry heat.

Her black combat boots demolished the soft grass beneath her feet. Despite her small frame, she was a rebel, a trait she got from both parents. Grace was born to be a rocker. She grew up with a guitar beside her bed, headphones, and an attitude. While she could rage with the best of them, she could also appreciate simpler things in life.

Grace began to tear up once they reached the top of a grassy hill, her eyes enveloped by a view no words could describe. The horizon was painted with a brush that was coated with a mixture of light and dark blue paint. Accents of white were sprinkled across her view from the waves as they broke. The King took a panoramic picture of the beautiful ocean as seals barked and sea dragons roared. Their beautiful grassy hill ended with a sheer drop to the ocean below. Gigantic rocks with an edge as sharp as the edge of a spear protruded through the tops of the waves. The seas roared like a dragon, soaring over her domain. Her grandfather used to say that the point where the cliffs and the ocean meet created a power that was both ancient and beyond anything that man or magic could conjure.

Her father walked along the side of the cliff, which led up a small gradient. The King indicated that their hike would go just a little further. He pointed toward a small wooden building next to a lush weeping willow.

When they got closer, she raised an eyebrow and looked at her father like he was crazy. Standing before them was an old wooden building that looked like an outhouse used 200 years ago. A hallowed out crescent moon had been engraved at the top of the door. The door had a bronze handle tilted to the side like it had been broken off at least a century ago when outhouses were still used.

The King turned to her, "So, are you ready?"

"To go potty? No, Dad, I could have done that at the cabin. Why did you take me to see an old bathroom?" She replied.

Her dad tilted his head to the side while giving the outhouse a once-over. "You know what, I see how you could get that impression. But this isn't a bathroom by any means. Now give me that key, and we can go inside."

Grace cocked her head back, "What key? I don't have any keys."

The King's facial structure began to morph. His gentle eyes became filled with rage, and his nostrils flared. "I said give me *The Key!*"

"I don't have it!" She cried.

Damon reached for her throat. She curled up in a ball and screamed. Then she felt a soft hand on her shoulder, and she jerked away. A second hand tried to grip her other arm, and she screamed again.

Gracey, it's okay.....Gracey, it's okay.

She struggled as she felt the sensation of fingertips on her shoulders. Her body curled up even tighter, waiting for her father's hands to seize her throat. Grace winced as a sharp and burning sensation ran through her arm. She let out a scream of agony, and her eyes burst open.

Her vision was blurry. The first thing she could recognize was the burnt orange light of an old lantern. She could feel two hands on her shoulder, but she couldn't quite make out the face of the person holding her. His skin was about as dark as a mocha latte. The hold he had her in did not seem aggressive; it was almost like he was trying to comfort her.

Grace's ears perked up at the sound of voices just a couple feet away. There were three blurred figures at the other end of the room. It looked like two people were on each side, with one in the middle. The two on the outside appeared to be trying to murder or help the person in the middle; either way, with her vision being so blurry, it looked confusing.

She felt a cold sensation; her mind envisioned icy claws wrapping around both sides of her neck. Grace recoiled, thinking it was her father. What she felt was much different. Instead of the feeling of fingers on her neck, it seemed like they were the talons of an eagle. A stream of ice-cold water appeared above her and slammed into the person attempting to console her. Their body slammed into the blurred images of the other group of people. They didn't seem extremely happy about the sudden change in events.

Grace curled her fingers around the being that had placed its claws on her neck. The skin was mostly smooth and cold, like a snake with a few rough edges. She took a soothing breath and felt a wave of calm crash over her. The soul protecting her was Aiko. Aiko? What's Aiko doing here? She blinked her eyes and forced them to adjust.

Once her vision became clearer, Grace breathed a gentle sigh of relief. She wasn't at her parents' old cabin; it must have been a nightmare. Pain seized her soul, and tears brimmed in her eyes as she processed the idea of getting to see her parents again. Since the power of the brainwashing the witches had done to her was so intense, many of the memories of her parents were too vague to recall. Even though the dream was twisted, seeing them and hearing their voices again was nice.

Jayden crawled back to sit next to her very cautiously. Aiko moved to a perch just above her, but the dragon's eyes were fixed on her friend. She stared into his eyes and felt a twinge of guilt. In the last few days, really, since he met her, he has risked his life for her. The paranoia and bags under his eyes were due to her. Bruises on his cheeks and the specks of blood on his arms and clothes were all earned from a nightmare he would never forget. Yet here he was, still trying to protect her.

Grace shifted her eyes to the three individuals in the back. Macy was sitting on the left; her blonde hair was in a bun, and her hands were glowing sky blue. On the far right was Shane; he was using a needle and string to suture the arm of an unfortunate soul. In between them was Tony; he was lying on his left side. From what she could tell, at least one bullet had nicked the side of his arm, and it had gone deeper than he initially thought. She made this conclusion based on the blood-soaked rags strewn beside him. It was also possible that the bullets that hit him were unique and more destructive than the average round.

Jayden's eyes looked like he had not slept well in quite some time. He stared at her with a look of concern that made her feel both loved and creeped out because Jayden only does that for Sarah.

"You okay?" He asked.

"Yeah. I'm alright. It was just a dream," she replied. "When did you get here?"

He placed his arms around her again and held her close. "About twenty minutes ago. Macy told me you've been in and out of consciousness. I'm glad you're alright."

Her eyes brimmed with tears as the memories from the last time she saw him came flooding back. Grace pulled him in close and kissed his forehead. "Thank you," she whispered.

He kissed her cheek. "I told you I would always be there for you."

The Aggeloi Princess smiled, "But you still left me."

Jayden raised his voice, feeling completely accosted. "I literally left you to save you. What more do I gotta do to make you happy? Most ladies would feel happy that I came to save the day. They would fall in my arms, asking me to marry them."

Grace rolled her eyes. "First off, I am still a princess; you have to be a prince for me to marry you. Second of all, you shouldn't have let me get shot in the first place. A good wannabe prince would have taken the bullets for me. Lastly, we both know you just want me to be your side chick. I told you before I am either one or none, and right now, you have like thirty girlfriends and a Tony."

Jayden began to place a blanket over her face to smother her when Macy stopped him. The Aggeloi Princes grinned, "Not today, Dragon Warrior. How dare you try to assassinate the princess!"

His face looked exasperated by her sass. "I hope you get shot again. And Macy, one of these days, I will feed you a phoenix and tell you it's chicken."

Macy grabbed his hand and smacked the top of it. "Jayden LoneOak! No sir! We do not talk to ladies like that. Now go run security; you're annoying the Princess.

Jayden looked into her eyes. "But Macy, I can't stand spending a moment away from you."

She blushed, "I know you don't mean that. Now go!"

Grace's eyes widened, "Actually, I needed to talk to him.'

Macy looked over her arm, "How does it feel?'

"It still hurts from time to time," Grace replied. "I think it's a lot better than it's been. You and Shane did a great job fixing me up. Without you two, I'd probably be dead."

Her friend shrugged, "I don't know, you are pretty tough yourself. Just keep an eye on it. My magic is great at healing, and Shane's shield magic can fight the spread of an infection. But our magic is no substitute for time and rest, okay?"

She nodded, and Macy helped her back onto her feet. Grace took a few steps and got woozy. She took a deep breath and a few more steps, and the dizziness returned with a vengeance. Her body would take some time to get used to being upright for any length of time. Unfortunately, they had little time; they couldn't hide in this abandoned school forever.

Grace strolled down the main hallway of the school. From what Macy told her, it was a high school. She never got to go to high school, which, when she considered the group she was traveling with, was actually not unusual. The only person she could think of that it might have been was Sarah, and even then, she wasn't quite sure if she got to have the whole high school experience.

As she strolled through the halls, the Aggeloi Princess passed by countless rows of lockers. About halfway down the hallway was a set of double doors that led to the gym. She tried to peer through the glass, but it was quite difficult to see what they had in the gym since the only lighting in the school was coming from the room where they were operating on Tony. Grace missed out on gym class growing up and always wondered what it might be like. Sure, she hated running and being around many people, but still, she was curious about what a normal life for a kid might be like.

Her footsteps echoed down the hall as she approached a set of stairs. The stairs resided near the end of the hall and led to the classes upstairs and the basement or dungeon below; she wasn't quite sure. Grace gripped the rail as she ascended the flight of stairs. The wooden railing rattled in her hands as if the bolts had not been tightened in decades. Once she reached the second floor, the Aggeloi Princess glanced at the row of windows parallel to the classroom.

Bright lights flashed off and on in the distance. The sound of thunder booming in the dark of night shook the windows. She couldn't quite make out the objects on the school grounds from her vantage point, but from what she could tell, the school seemed utterly peaceful. Despite the weapons of war filling the night with terror miles away, the school grounds appeared ignorant of the trials facing the Aggeloi people.

Four classrooms ran parallel to the row of windows. She could spot rows of desks inside the rooms from the silhouettes cast by the lightning show outside. Grace wasn't sure which classroom Jayden was hiding in. He must have lowered his magical energy signature because she couldn't sense him. They've spent so much time together since they met that she could pick out his energy from a mile away. Usually, it was a massive amount of magical power or barely anything. Right now, it seemed like he had none, which meant he was very weak, or his stealth skills were better than she thought.

Since she couldn't tell which room he was in, she figured it would be wise to let fate decide. Grace took her right index finger and pointed toward the row of classrooms. She grinned as she spun around in place. Her body swayed, and her head felt exceptionally dizzy to the point that she fell to the ground.

When Grace landed on the floor, she chuckled as her head spun. Her left index finger was pointing toward the second door on the left. She jumped back to her feet and smirked at her newly found method of making adult decisions.

Grace pushed open the door and stepped into the classroom. The room was as dark as the night sky, save for the wisps of moonlight piercing through the window. Rows of metallic desks filled the room. She made her way to the nearest row and glanced around the room. Grace couldn't see Jayden anywhere. She half expected him to hop out and scare her. Or he was in one of the other classrooms. She hoped he wasn't because she was feeling a little too lazy to do all of that.

Her ears perked up at the sound of a low growl. She scanned the room, and her eyes landed on a black mass near the window. Grace took a step forward, and the growl grew louder. She reached for her pistol but forgot she left everything downstairs. If this was a monster that had snuck upstairs, she was going to be screwed without her weapons.

Grace breathed a sigh of relief when she realized the growling monster was just an obnoxious boy snoring. *Some security guard*, she thought. The Aggeloi Princess knelt down beside her friend and smiled at him. She had never seen him so tired after all the dangers they had experienced together. She could only imagine what horrors he and Tony had experienced trying to save her.

She went to run her fingers through his hair, and it all went black. Grace blinked her eyes open and winced at the sharp pain shooting up and down her shoulder. Her head was throbbing, and she could feel a bruise forming on her wrist. She tried to get up but couldn't move because of a heavy weight pushing down on her chest and a cold piece of metal pressing into her cheek.

"I'm...I'm sorry," he said meekly.

"Will you get off of me then?" She snarled.

Jayden moved his knee and helped her to sit back up.

"Please don't tell anyone I did that." He said.

Grace glanced at the bruise on her wrist and then looked into his eyes. Even in the dark, she could tell he had bags under his eyes. He must have reacted instinctively to being touched; she knew he would never intentionally hurt her. Jayden has given up a lot to protect others; it would be natural for the battlefield to affect them when bullets aren't flying constantly. Still, this behavior is concerning for Jayden and anyone else, regardless of the reason.

She forced a grin, "You don't need to worry; we can keep this little event all to ourselves. Just remember, the next time I want you to buy me dinner first, you'll have to get me lobster and a dessert."

Jayden laughed, "I guess that will be fine."

"Umm, can I talk with you?" She asked.

Jayden took a deep breath. "I guess so. Why did you come to see me? You should be resting."

"Obviously, I came to see if you were actually running security. But I also wanted to tell you something. Do you remember that night I got shot?"

He nodded, "I'll never forget it."

Grace lifted her necklace over her head and held it out for him. *The Key* jangled against the metallic necklace as it swayed back and forth. Jayden's eyes narrowed on the seemingly unremarkable item that could turn Sarah into a demon-possessed psychopath.

"Do you remember how Sarah started having creepy dreams because of this?" She asked.

He nodded, "I remember her talking to me about it. It would show her things, even though you were wearing it. Now that I think about it, she would transform into that thing and hasn't touched *The Key* since that first time. I've always wondered what the connection was. I mean, it doesn't affect you like that."

Grace cocked her head to the side. "Well, it kind of does. While I don't turn into a Devil Goddess creature like her, I've been having similar dreams. I just haven't told anyone but her. Both Sarah and I think that our dreams are connected. Just like when she transformed, she would just try to go north. It was always north. Well, my dreams are the same. I always see images that are familiar to me, north of here. Is this thing trying to go home or something? I know that sounds weird, but that's not even the worst part."

Jayden scratched his chin and grinned. "What could be worse than having creepy dreams about traveling north? I can't imagine anything being worse than that."

The Aggeloi Princess rolled her eyes. "You are literally the worst. But anyway, Mr. Super Rude, Not Taking Me Seriously, the thing that's worse than those creepy dreams you aren't experiencing is that I think this thing will kill me if I don't take it where it's calling me. I think Sarah feels the same way for herself."

Jayden shrugged. "That sucks. I was planning on marrying one of you two at some point. Now I guess I gotta go with Macy."

She punched him in the chest so hard that he fell backward. "Jayden, you jerk! This is serious! Do you even care about us? Or do you think it's a joke? How can you be so calm about this?"

He coughed as if she had knocked the air out of him. "I'm sorry, you didn't have to hit me that hard. It's just that I'm not shocked you all feel that way, whether it's true or not. I know our luck isn't that great, so I wouldn't be surprised if that were true. But there is a way we can be sure. Macy!"

A dark shadow stepped into the room. Her blonde pigtails had been transformed into one long braid on her right side. The style was similar to how General Floriana would wear her hair sometimes.

"I'm here, sweetie; how may I help you?" Macy asked, without a hint of sarcasm in her voice.

Grace rolled her eyes, "Why do you have to do that to him? You are just going to get his hopes up again. We both know the world is safer with him never marrying anyone. By the way, how long has she been standing in the doorway like a creepy person?"

Jayden swayed back and forth. "It's hard to tell, but she stood there for quite some time. Standing as quiet as a mouse, with no respect for boundaries or social cues."

The Aggeloi Princess nodded in agreement. "Well, that still doesn't explain why you called her, other than she just happened to be the other girl in the room."

"Oh well, that's simple," he replied. "I called her because the Phoenix Monastery is mostly known for teaching spells for combat and healing party members. They also use their fire magic to analyze the impurities within an item, person, or object. That's how she can heal people so well; she can analyze the impurities within a body. My fire magic only lets me sense the type of energy coming from a person or object, but I can't tell you any of the details about the dark energy someone has. I can't sense anything with this key, which is odd because of how much it affects you and Sarah. I thought that I would at least be able to sense some dark energy from it. So, Macy, if you will, could you do your super amazing magic on this? Pretty please?"

Macy shrugged. "I don't know about that. After you said you would only marry me after that magic key kills Sarah and Grace, I don't feel appreciated enough to complete this task."

Jayden shook his head in disbelief. "You were standing in that damn doorway this whole time, then you know for a fact I never said that. It may have been implied but never stated in those exact terms. But if you can forgive me this one time, I won't say such jerky things for the next 24 hours. I promise."

Macy let out an exhaustive sigh. "Well, I guess I could do it. But I am doing it for the Princess and Sarah, not you, loser." She winked at Gracey and cracked her knuckles. "Now let me see this piece of metal that the Daimonia and every power-hungry scumbag is looking for."

Grace extended her hand and slowly dropped her necklace into Macy's palm. The Phoenix Warrior reacted the moment the metal touched her flesh. Her body leaned forward as if the weight of the item was throwing off her balance. While her reaction was nowhere near the level that Sarah had experienced, it was interesting for Grace to witness someone else experience the ancient power of *The Key*.

Macy adjusted herself in her seat so she could hold the item without feeling she would topple forward from the weight of it. Static energy began to fill the room, and an intense heat radiated from her as she channeled her spell. Macy's beautiful irises were morphing into the shape of light blue flame sprites that danced in her eyes. She summoned balls of fire with a white core that formed above her hand and began to orbit the space of *The Key.*

Grace couldn't quite understand the process or how the spell worked, but she could tell it was not a simple task. The Princess was filled with curiosity and concern as Macy examined the object. She noticed how her friend's muscles would tense up, and her veins bulged as her spell scanned the item. What she found interesting was that the hand she used to hold *The Key* was perfectly still. Macy's left hand, however, was shaking uncontrollably from tension. Grace began to feel sick to her stomach as she watched droplets of blood trickling down Macy's nostrils turn into a steady stream of crimson.

"There are two sources!" Macy shouted.

Gracey asked Jayden what sources were. He shrugged and whispered back, "I don't know."

Macy shook her head in frustration as the balls of fire moved faster around *The Key.* "You are absolutely hopeless!" She growled. "Sources are magical signatures; it means that two different sources of magic are attached to this item. To make it simpler for you two to understand, it means that two different people put curses on *The Key.* How did neither of you learn what sources are? Jayden, you literally went to a magic school, and Grace, you were partly raised by witches."

"Well, I was sick on the day they had that class, and Gracey was probably locked up in the basement for having a bad attitude," he replied, feeling a sharp pain in his ribs from the jab that Grace fired at him. "Ouch, that wasn't necessary. Anyway, Macy, is there anything else you can tell us?"

She wiped some of the blood from her nose, leaving a red tint on her skin and scarlet stains across her cheeks. "Well, I can tell the curses were placed on *The Key* within months, or even years of each other. I don't know the exact time, but they weren't placed on the object that far apart. Also, I can tell that the oldest curse is designed to react to similar sources. Apparently, the second source is not the same type and can't interact with the magic of *The Key*. I don't know what it means. The curse from the first source doesn't seem too terrible; the second one scares me. It has what I can only describe as a compass type of curse or something. I think it can draw people to it and make people take it to some place, which would explain why you and Sarah are drawn to go north. It also explains why Daimonia and other people may be drawn to it. I don't fully understand it, but that's not the worst part. There is a death-counter curse attached to *The Key*. Sarah and Grace are right to be afraid of this thing because it can kill you. I can't tell you how or when. I just know this thing is more dangerous than we thought. The Witnesses have no idea what they are dealing with, and the Daimonia are not above sacrificing the world to get what they want."

The flame sprites orbiting *The Key* slowed their pace as the fire in Macy's eyes faded and returned to normal. She placed the cursed item in Gracey's hand and pulled out a napkin to absorb the blood dripping from her nose. For Grace, the blood dripping onto the classroom floor was the price it cost just to understand what they were dealing with, only to find out that the truth was much worse.

"So, if we kill Grace and throw *The Key* in the bottom of the ocean, that should fix the problem, right?" Said a gruff voice coming from just outside the room.

Another dark shadow stepped into the room. Grace didn't need to see his furry tail or the custom .50 caliber revolver spinning in his hand to know that Shane meant what he said. There was no doubt in her mind that her life depended on Macy's answer.

Macy shrugged, "I don't know. If you killed her and even Sarah and then tossed *The Key* into space, it wouldn't do much. This thing draws people to it; that's why it was found during that excavation. It is also possible that more people like

Sarah and Grace can use the power within it. I think there is a reason there isn't much information about *The Key* in our archive or even our Elderian texts. Compared to the other destructive weapons and items from the Great War, we know next to nothing about this. We didn't even know much about it until now. I mean, there aren't many history books that mention it. There must be a reason. I don't think anyone was supposed to find this. I don't think this was supposed to ever end up back in the hands of people. I've never even heard of it being possible to attach curses from two different sources to the same object. You would figure that magic within it would have faded away over time. And the scariest part about it is that if someone took the time to make *The Key* as powerful as it is, can you imagine the power of what it was made to open must be?"

Shane chuckled as he turned his snout toward Jayden. "I'm only going to say this once, but I may have misjudged the decision that your father and the other Rogue Witnesses made in stealing *The Key* from the Eden President. When you consider that Daimonia soldiers were working undercover within the Army this whole time, there was a strong chance that this item would have been used sooner if your dad had done nothing. Our organization should have been more supportive of their mission. That said, I still think your dad was reckless, and Tony's father is still a deadbeat."

Jayden bowed his head in respect. "I will accept that. So, as of right now, we have a death-counter curse affecting both Sarah and Gracey. We also know that only a certain number of people can activate *The Key* or the map that Sarah absorbed, and we know that people can be drawn to this thing without really knowing it. It's obvious that the Daimonia can trace it down somewhat and will look for it regardless of how difficult it is. I think we should use that to our advantage. Shane, would the other members of The Witnesses be willing to help us now?"

The elder statesman spun his pistol in his paw and grinned toothily. "There is a chance, but it is very slim.

Communication with Central has been down ever since Bryce betrayed us. Our organization is so small and spread out, plus the travel limitations due to the war will make getting any help quite difficult. If you are planning to go to do something crazy, then you need to understand that aid is not likely to come. That said, I have a trick or two up my sleeve. So, tell me, what's your plan?"

He smiled, "I don't actually have one. The only thing I can think of is that we have something they want. Now, we can sit and wait for them to come to us. We could also take *The Key* to wherever it leads us. And when they come for it, we give them all we got."

Shane replied, "You do know that is suicide? Clearly, the forces at play here are beyond what anyone could have prepared for. The Daimonia have sown the seeds for war over the years and played the political leaders like puppets. Once the dust settles from the war, the Daimonia will have whatever power *The Key* will grant them. There won't be anyone to stop them; they will ultimately win. We will only have delayed the inevitable. Are you sure you still want to do this? Knowing that victory is not on the table."

Jayden stood up and looked into the eyes of each person in the room. "You know, I've always wondered why my dad listened to me on that fateful day. He could have easily run up into the mountains with Tony and me. Miss Mara and many of the others ended up getting killed anyway. So, what was the point of it all? I've just realized that my dad knew that war would come to him sooner or later. All of them knew that all they had gained was borrowed time. But my dad still stood up and fought, and many others did too, knowing that they wouldn't walk out of that battlefield alive. Mr. Robert did not hesitate to give his life if only it would grant Tony and me just a little more time. I'm sure they would have loved to see Tony and me live up to a ripe old age away from the battlefield. But what if all of their efforts were just delaying the inevitable. Maybe we were always meant to go out like this. But you know what? Because they risked it all for us, there have also been people we have had the opportunity to help. So, my plan is to follow in the footsteps of my father and so many others who gave their lives so that I can be here today, in this moment. In all reality, we all owe someone for being here today. If our sacrifice makes a difference for even just one person, then I think it's a risk worth taking. It is amazing what saving just one life can do for the world."

Chapter 22

Drops of Metallic Rain

The earth shook like it was on the verge of ripping apart. Glass shattered, and shards of wood and brick showered them as they slept. Plaster on the walls of the room melted like ice cream as the desks crashed against each other from the intense pressure. Smoke filled his lungs and his nostrils to the point that he felt as if death was at his doorstep.

His ears rang, and he felt a complete loss of equilibrium as the building teetered back and forth. Soot and dust were embedded in his eyes and nose. Blood trickled from a cut on his forehead, and his knuckles were bruised from the impact of the debris. He jumped as he felt the sensation of gritty fingers interlocking with his.

His body felt weightless momentarily as he was helped back onto his feet. Jayden shivered as a river of ice-cold water was dumped onto his head. As the fresh water flushed the debris in his eyes, specks of morning light came into view. He expected to be blinded by the morning sun, but the light was gentle and subdued. Jayden wiped his eyes and blinked until enough of the debris was gone, and he could actually see.

Jayden, for the first time in his life, was absolutely speechless. Not even with years of therapy would he ever be able to describe this moment. His eyes stared at the light grey clouds and wisps of smoke that obscured the day from the sun's golden light. His toes rested just inches away from the jagged edge of broken tile flooring where a wall and desks used to be.

A gentle breeze blew along the side of the building, and pieces of the roof shifted and fell toward the street below. The remaining pieces of the crumbling wall were turned into dust as ash rained down from the sky. The street below them was virtually destroyed and turned into a large crater. The freeway in the distance looked twisted and bent like a snake from the force of the blast. Strewn across the city were the bodies of soldiers, civilians, and even family pets. There was a crimson hew throughout the city below from the blood that stained the capital's walls like graffiti. For Jayden, the sight of death and destruction was nothing new. However, none of his experiences prepared him to see death and sorrow on a scale like this.

He felt something stringy and coarse against his chin. Macy had propped her head against his shoulder. Her naturally blonde hair was now gray as the ash drifting in the wind. She let out a desperate sob as tears streamed down her face. Blood trickled from her nose and the cuts on her lip. Her lightly tanned skin was bathed in bruises, dust, and soot that covered almost every inch of her body. She must have been the one that pulled him out of the rubble, and while he was grateful for that, part of him wished she would leave him in the dust. His eyes were witnessing more than just a loss of life as he stared into the face of destruction; his mind was replaying over the memories that his heart wouldn't ever let him forget. Jayden had no doubt that as his childhood friend took in the air of death and sorrow, she, too, was reliving the horrors from their stolen childhood.

Even though his mind was filled with anger and despair, part of his adult existence would always be tied to the thought process of a warrior. He didn't want to think about what had happened; the destruction was so immense that it didn't matter. However, his brain was already analyzing what took place on the battlefield. From what he could tell, the spirals of smoke spread sporadically across the city were at least partly caused by the Aggeloi military. Jayden remembered the bombs they had seen in the subway and underground tunnels. They must have triggered them to wipe out some of the Eden ground forces. He still couldn't believe that the Aggeloi would destroy part of their own city just to kill their enemy. Still, the destruction in the distance paled compared to the crater below them.

The school was hit with such a destructive force that it tore the walls off the building, vaporized classrooms, and turned parts of the roof into mountains of dust and ash. The crater below was littered with vehicles shredded into metal shards. Trolleys and commuter buses had been flipped over on their sides and covered in burn marks. Embedded in portions of the concrete were cannonball-sized metal pellets that appeared to have been spread out from a central location. The damage caused by these metal pellets reminded him of a buckshot shell from a shotgun, which, for the poor souls living in this city, was absolutely devastating. This meant the gigantic bomb used was designed to not only cause thermal damage from its initial explosion, but the projectiles from within the bomb would spread out as it detonated, allowing it to hurt people miles away from where it was dropped.

For Jayden, there was no doubt that this crater and the damage that extended outside it was not the result of the Aggeloi's innovative tactics. The culprit was, without a doubt, his own countrymen. The tattered and bloodied military personnel that met their fate on the street below were Aggeloi soldiers. Their bodies were spread out across the crater, along with their civilian counterparts. Outside of the few military vehicles and displaced weapons, he could see from the school this area was clearly not a military holdout to protect civilians. This was a part of the city where no combat was to take place. This meant the Eden military bombed this area, not to weaken their opponent's military but to simply kill people who had no chance of defending themselves. Jayden could only imagine how the Aggeloi military would respond to this afront. He thought they would be tempted to turn all of Eden into a giant crater filled with death. In a way, that response would be almost reasonable; the sheer level of destruction surrounding him was overwhelming to the point that no child born in this country should ever have to forgive the people of Eden.

His ears perked up at what sounded like firecrackers going off quickly. Jayden knew no one was celebrating at this time; the sound he was hearing came from soldiers squeezing the triggers of firearms with souls filled with hate and anger, searching for some form of poetic justice.

Still, the young Dragon Warrior struggled to believe people could still be fighting in an area where bodies littered the sidewalks with no one to bury them. It was such a sad and disturbing sight that Jayden wanted to look away. He was terrified about stumbling across the bodies of his friends lying amongst the rubble. His heart couldn't handle it. In all reality, he would rather not know.

"Ouch!" He cried out as a sharp rock hit his cheek.

Tony shouted. "Hey, Jade! We are down here, you dumbass!"

Jayden glanced down to see his best friend and Gracey picking up more small rocks to throw at him. He wanted to cuss at them but was exceptionally glad to see them alive. Then, his eyes noticed something different about them. The energy surrounding his friends was almost naked to the eye. He could see a film of magical energy covering them like a dome. From what he could tell, the magical shield was almost obvious, except for a few green flashes that moved along the half-spherical dome. Jayden guessed it must have been one of

Shane's shield spells. The spell must have activated the moment the concussive force of the bomb got too close. This reminded him of when Grace had told him about a spell like this the night before. This protection spell was similar to something he had used to protect everyone on the train car he and Priscilla were in. Once the train exploded, his spell was strong enough to protect everyone inside it. Between the explosion on the train and the destructive power of this bomb, there was no doubt in his mind that Shane was exceptionally powerful. They were inexplicably lucky to have him with them, as his friends were blown completely off the side of the building during the explosion.

Jayden and Macy gathered the remaining items that were still intact on the second floor. They both jumped down onto the rubble below. His foot slipped on loose gravel, and he almost fell to the ground but was caught at the last minute by Grace. After his friends laughed at him and Shane's snide comment wounded his soul, they began their trek through the crater.

***

Grace suggested they travel along the upper edge of the crater and circle around to go back into the central part of the city. Oddly enough, Shane agreed that if for no other reason, they had no idea what they might experience walking right through it. Based on the erratic gunfire they were hearing; they were expecting to face pure chaos.

He felt a twinge in his stomach, and his body swayed to the side. There was a high-pitched whistling sound. A mound of dirt and concrete exploded behind him, and he was showered with debris. Shane stepped out from behind a concrete wall to his right before he could even react to what happened. The werefox had his twin revolvers raised and fired off two rounds.

Jayden squinted to see what he actually hit. A dark shadow moved from behind a large boulder and slumped. The

243

Dragon Warrior was utterly shocked as the distance to the target was at least 1000 yards away from their side of the crater. He could not hit that guy with a headshot, which meant that Shane's guns were powerful enough to shoot through boulders. Once again, Jayden was grateful Shane was with them because he knew he would have probably missed if he still had his rifle. Hell, he probably wouldn't have been able to figure out where the shooter was in the first place.

A metal shield appeared out of nowhere, floating to his right. Before he could ask Shane what his problem was, the sound of gunfire ripped through the crater like a freight train. Jayden was hit by the metal fragments bouncing off the shield from a hail of bullets. He rolled over to his right and slid down a slight incline. He concentrated the small amount of magical energy he had into a ball of energy floating above his right palm.

Jayden took a deep breath and shouted, "Heatseeker!"

The ball of energy floating just inches above his hand instantly became engulfed in dark orange flames. The flames stretched and formed a tail like that of a comet. The flaming tail was long enough to reach the center of his palm. He grinned and extended his arm just over the hill. The Fireball rocketed out of his hand. The heat-seeking spell bobbed and weaved amongst the mounds of debris in the crater. Jayden heard a cry out of pain, and the target discontinued shooting their obnoxious machine gun.

Jayden got into a prone position and drew his sword. His muscles expanded, and his eyes narrowed on the potential targets hiding behind shattered concrete walls. He didn't know if they were Aggeloi soldiers, civilians, or even his own countrymen. Hell, they probably didn't even know who they were shooting at. Any combat from within the crater would likely be disjointed. Jayden could imagine that the Eden and Aggeloi forces must have had their communications go down. Usually, there would be military forces searching for survivors or, conversely, a strike team aimed at taking out any survivors from the bombing. None of that was happening, just erratic gunfire and cries for help. The berserk demon within his sword did not care about any of that. It wanted Jayden to destroy anyone that posed a threat. Jayden grinned as the demonic strength of the sword surged through every vein in his body, his muscles bulging like a bodybuilder. His enemies would reap what they have sown.

Chapter 23

Through the Storm

He gently squeezed the trigger, and a brilliantly bright orange flame expelled from the barrel. The bullet moved slowly down the street, making a sharp left turn at the light. It then darted down a few more city streets, followed by another left turn at a light, and slammed into the chest of its target.

Shane chuckled as he reloaded his revolver with some hollow points and homing rounds. He still couldn't believe how much they had to fight just to get out of the crater. Now that they were in the city, it seemed like someone was shooting at them just about every block that they moved. Based on what he could tell, they were mostly fighting the Displacement Corps of the Aggeloi Army. They were a unit designed to root out leftover combatants and were absolutely ruthless. Their main objective was not to take in any prisoners but to eradicate targets splintered off from their main force. They were a formidable and well-trained group. If it weren't for the advantage they had from their magic, they wouldn't have even made it out of the crater.

The werefox stopped reloading when his ears perked up at the sound of swords clashing. His eyes narrowed on a scuffle on the other side of the street. Tony appeared to be engaging an Aggeloi soldier dressed in black and red, equipped with a Gladius and Short-Bearded Axe. Tony was holding his own, but Shane knew he was still recovering from his injuries. He sensed the young man's magical energy was dreadfully low.

The werefox decided to lend a hand or a paw in his case. He reached into his trench coat and pulled out a hunting knife. He flung it toward Tony's combatant, dropping him instantly. The young Dragon Warrior turned toward Shane with a look of disgust on his face that said, I had him. Shane chuckled; you snooze, you lose.

Then he heard a cry for help, piercing through the sounds of gunfire and sword fights. The werefox sprinted down the sidewalk and turned left up the street. Just a few blocks down on the right was an elderly woman stretching out her hand toward the middle of the street. Tears streamed from a child's face that he assumed must be her grandkid, who must have tripped crossing the street, and they got separated. Gunfire erupted from an Eden Soldier poking their head out from behind a skyscraper. The soldier had been switching his line of fire between Tony and a Displacement Core Soldier in a black and red uniform just a few blocks away. The grandmother and her grandchild were stuck in the middle of a gunfight with no one to help them.

The werefox sprinted alongside a skyscraper and jumped high in the air. He shifted his body toward a nearby office building as he gained altitude. Then the werefox placed his rear paws against the side of the dark blue glass of the building and sprinted along it. While he sprinted on the side of the building, he pointed his front right paw in the direction of the little girl and cast a shield spell on her and her grandmother. A clear dome of magical energy with flashes of green light formed a protective bubble around them. He channeled his magical energy to his rear paws and pushed off the building. Shane went into a front flip and, as his body rotated, fired off two rounds and dispatched the Eden soldier.

As the werefox continued to fall toward the cement, he straightened out his body. Then he aimed his pistol to his right side and fired off another round, dropping the Aggeloi soldier. Once his enemy crumpled to the ground, he aimed his descending body toward the young girl. Once he hit the ground, he dropped into a combat roll and quickly grabbed the girl from the street. Then Shane placed her in the grandmother's arms and ushered them down an alleyway just as a squad of Eden soldiers came into view.

The werefox indicated that the others should take cover. He leaned up against the nearest building and checked his ammo. Shane shook his head; this *was stupid*, he thought. Here, they were fighting from block to block just to reach downtown. For him, it felt like they had been fighting for hours and only traveled a mile or so away from the bombed-out crater.

Their idea to stroll through this active warzone was moderately crazy. Grace's plan was for them to track down an old railroad system that was only used by the Royal Family. She stated it was the best way to go north, even though they would likely get shot at. She also believes that only Royals know about the hidden track, which could be true. However, seeing how the Aggeloi Parliament had her family killed and tried to have her murdered, it was also possible that by now, they knew about it. Either way, they were in too deep now to turn back, which wasn't even the worst part.

Shane snarled. He could not stand working with Jayden and Tony. While it was evident they were well-trained and on the verge of becoming combat veterans, they still had a lot to learn. For one, they relied too much on their magic to get them out of trouble. In fact, he noticed that Grace had the same problem. She was exceptionally powerful when her magic was charged. But with the addition of the speed magic she used and her summoning skills, she could be one of the most powerful fighters he had ever known. However once their well of magic ran dry, they were dreadfully average. Another issue was that they knew how to fight quite well as individuals but had no idea how to coordinate anything remotely tactical. That is where Macy was a Godsend because she had training from the Phoenix Monastery and The Witnesses. Unfortunately, he won't be able to teach them on this battlefield. Hopefully, they will learn from the bullets flying in their direction.

Shane sniffed the air, and his mind automatically started to picture the formation of the Eden soldiers heading in their direction. From what he could tell, at least 6 of them were coming his way. They had split into two groups of three, covering both sides of the street. His initial idea was to try his homing bullets, but he was pretty sure they had body armor. Shane had a feeling that whatever decision he made, he would have to be extremely efficient. He either needed to stop them completely or push them back since the rest of his team was currently engaged in fights on a different block.

He gave a toothy grin once he had come to a decision. Shane extended each claw and twisted his large tail like a spring. Once his tail was in a tight coil, he bent his knees and jumped. While elevating himself off the concrete ground, his tail sprung him skyward like a rocket. Quickly, he dug his claws into the concrete sections of the building and drew his revolver with his left paw. Just a few feet away from where he had just been standing, light grey wisps of smoke began to rise. After a few more seconds, the tall wisps of smoke had grown into a giant black cloud of smoke so large that he couldn't even see the sidewalk.

He sniffed the air and realized they must have tossed a smoke grenade because he could taste the gunpowder and white phosphorus. Shane summoned two ceramic bucklers out of thin air. His eyes narrowed on the billowing smoke, waiting for them to make their move. There was a subtle, barely even noticeable change in how the smoke blew in the wind. That's when he sniffed the air again, summoned 4 more ceramic bucklers, and launched them toward his enemies. The shields exploded like grenades when they made contact with two Eden Soldiers; their bodies were knocked out of the cloud of smoke and crumbled to the ground on the other side of the street, never to move again.

A giant green shield appeared out of thin air, just a few inches from his chest, as a third soldier sprung out from the cloud of smoke with his finger on the trigger. The shield flashed from green to yellow as the rifle rounds pounded against it. Shane wanted to move from his spot but knew he would get shredded if he tried. He pointed his pistol directly to his left and spun the cylinder on the revolver. He took a deep breath and squeezed the trigger. The bullet flew on a direct path for about 20 yards, and then it turned and made a downward dive. Then, the bullet turned to the right and sped toward the unsuspecting target. The round hit him in the neck between his vest and helmet. The automatic fire ceased, and his opponent began his eternal slumber.

Before he could celebrate his victory, he realized he needed to take down the other three soldiers and anyone else who may have felt inclined to join the skirmish. The werefox holstered his gun and moved to climb up the side of the building. Once he got close to the highest point of the building, he used his magical energy to propel himself skyward, flipped forward, and landed on top of the roof.

Shane sniffed the air and focused his energy on listening. He caught a whiff of the leather and polymer from the approaching soldiers. His ears picked up the faint sound of shuffling and the soft clicking of the selective firing system of a rifle. Based on their scent and the sound of controlled movement, which were not very close, he could guess they must still be on the main street. With that knowledge, he came up with a devious idea. He conjured up two round metal shields with rubber on the object's edges. Then, he directed them to fly off the roof toward the main street. He snapped two claws and immediately heard the shields bouncing on the sides of buildings like a pinball.

When he heard a soldier cry out in pain and another shout *get down*, he knew exactly where they were. Shane switched to the other side of the roof and sprinted forward. With his pistols in his hands, he jumped over the side of the building. He fired three rounds at two of the soldiers that were directly on the other side of the street. He conjured up a light blue energy shield, which he landed on and jumped off like a spring. While doing an aerial in the air, he turned his guns to a target to his right and fired off a homing round. Then, he curled up into a ball and went into a combat roll before he jumped back up to fire off the remainder of his bullets at a reinforcement squad coming from down the street. Shane channeled his magical energy and summoned his spinning shields to knock down the remaining combatants.

He sniffed the air and relaxed for a second. Shane holstered his pistols and glanced back to see how the others were doing. His eyes couldn't believe what they were seeing. While he was out here fighting and doing arguably the craziest stunts possible. Jayden and Tony stood by a small ice cream shop, hitting on the girls. It wasn't until Jayden noticed he was looking at them that they ran over to him.

Jayden waved at him as he ran up the street. "Shane, that was completely badass!"

Shane barked, "I'm sure you were paying great attention. I'm sorry if I interrupted you boys chatting with Grace and Macy. Do I need to give you all a little more time?"

The girls' faces turned bright red as they approached him. Jayden and Tony, however, continued to wear smug and cocky looks on their faces. It was like they had completely forgotten they were in a warzone and were wanted by both the Eden and Aggeloi governments, not to mention any jerkhole looking for *The Key*.

Jayden grinned, "Of course not. We were just discussing strategy and taking notes on how to be a fighter as great as you are. Isn't the right Tony?

Tony nodded, "Yep. We decided we might take decades to be as good as you. Those Eden soldiers stood no chance."

The werefox snarled, "Whatever morons. Anyway, we must find a better way to get to this Royal Train station. I doubt we can keep getting in the crossfire of these two armies. Plus, we clearly don't look like we live here, making us stand out like a sore thumb."

Grace cocked her head to the side. "Let me think," she said. "Well, we are looking for Platform thirteen, which we can get to by going through the central station. However, if we can get into the subway, we can get there instead of going to Central Station from above ground."

Jayden kicked in a grate on the sidewalk and jumped into it. He shouted from the subway, "Come down here. The water's fine."

***

Shane was reminded once again why he couldn't stand Jayden. He realized this the moment he found himself pressing his body flat up against the walls of a subway. While underground, the train screeched as it passed them at an ungodly speed. This was the first time he had ever almost been hit by a train; in fact, he had never planned on having this experience. Thanks to Jayden's stupid attempt to be helpful, they were stuck in the subway, which was great. However, they landed on a track that was actively being used by the military to transfer civilians. This meant that if trains speeding by didn't kill him, a heart attack just might.

"Clear!" He yelled once the last cart sped by.

They quickly moved further along the winding track like their lives depended on it. Shane had no idea where they were going, and Grace wasn't very helpful once they were in the subway. To keep track of the direction they were going, the werefox made use of his digital compass. From what he could guess, they needed to go westward because, according to the Princess, Platform thirteen was near Central Station.

Shane stopped mid-sprint as they ran up the curving bend once the track split into four directions. The one they had been traveling on seemed to lead in a southeastern direction. The track to his left looked like it curved north, and its corresponding track curved southwest. The track they were currently on had a corresponding track that looked like it went northwest.

He put his paws up for the others to huddle. "Which track do you think we should take?"

Jayden pointed at the one right in front of them. "Obviously, we should take this one, right?"

Tony slapped his friend on the back of the head. "Dude, do you know how crappy our luck is. With our luck, the track will lead us to a part of the subway that's been caved in, or even worse, it takes us to a completely different part of the city."

"You right," he replied. "Well, Shane, you got an enhanced-smelling device on your face. Can you smell which direction we should go?"

Shane shook his head in disappointment. "You know, Jayden, I knew both your father and….mother. They were both brilliant, albeit careless, foolhardy, and a little crazy, but intelligent, nonetheless. You have gained more of their less desirable traits. That said, I can't just smell out which direction to go from here because I have no idea what it should smell like. Now, what I can tell you that the track is directly across from us, and I smell less oil coming from that direction, meaning that it is not being used as much as the other tracks."

Jayden's demeanor changed, "Why did you hesitate when mentioning my mom?"

"No reason," he replied. "My words got stuck in my throat, that's all. So, which way do you all want to go?"

Grace pointed straight. "I think we should go that way. It may seem that if a track leads to Central Station, it will have a stronger smell than any of the other tracks. But it's possible they aren't using it, or something happened to it."

Macy pipped up, "I agree. I think Gracey is on to something. Let's go that way."

As the words left her mouth, his ears perked up to vibrations. The railway signals flashed red and green lights. The tracks in the center of the four-way stop shifted in place. A small white light appeared further down the track to their left. Immediately, he flattened himself against the wall, and others followed suit. Then, a passenger train roared past them with the force of a hurricane. There was nothing like the sensation from the vibrations beneath his paws and the sound of metal screeching as it sped past, knowing he could die any second. The thought that if they leaned forward just a hair, they would be absolute goners was thrilling and could be a great topic to discuss during therapy.

Once the train passed, they reloaded all their weapons and headed toward the northwestern track. As they entered the tunnel, he first noticed how much warmer it was than the previous one they were in. There were mountains of trash, used soda cans, and even canned foods littered the tunnel's floor. Graffiti from street gangs and artists decorated large sections of the tunnel's walls and ceiling. He even noticed military-grade spray paint with numbers and symbols he didn't understand. He assumed they were codes that only Aggeloi military personnel would know.

Based on what he saw, it was clear that this tunnel was used as a main thoroughfare. He also got the sense that, at some point, this tunnel was used as a safe haven for the city's citizens as the war continued. Why they switched to using the other tunnels, he couldn't quite tell. The only conclusion he could make was that the Eden military might have expected them to use Central Station for strategic operations or that the other stations were better for transporting military personnel and civilians. Either way, it was uncomfortable for him to be walking down this empty tunnel. When he considered how many people had tried to kill them in the last few hours, the awkward silence made him more paranoid.

They reached another fork in the road, or a train track in this case. The track split into a Y shape, the tunnel to the left looked like it curved north, and the other track seemed to go southwest. Shane once again turned to the others to see which way they should go. Grace and Macy voted to go to the right. Jayden decided he wouldn't vote until Tony did. Tony then decided to take his happy time to think about which direction to take. At that moment, Shane vowed to never work with these two idiots again.

Jayden pipped up and said, "I think we should go left!"

"You are just saying that to piss me off, aren't you Jayden?" Grace asked with a devilish, I want to choke you to death, smile.

"Yeah, Jayden, what brilliant idea do you have this time?" His best friend asked.

"I appreciate the compliment. I know my ideas aren't typically the best, but in this case, I can see some writing on the wall back there that says Central Station, and it even has an arrow pointing to where you need to go. I am shocked none of you saw that," he said ever so smugly.

Grace rolled her eyes. "Whatever. Just get going."

***

Central Station has historically been viewed as a major component in the kingdom's development. Before airships and gliders were widely used for travel, this was the mecca for transporting goods, construction supplies, and general travel. In the modern era, it still adhered to those roles. However, most of its duties were now for occupational travel and tourism. The war changed all of that. Once again, the Central Station would take on the duty of keeping their country afloat.

The last time Shane had been to Central Station was not too long ago. Macy and Bryce met him here at the train station to go on their most recent mission. When they came here previously, the war had just started. Still, the Eden military had not gotten even close to the capital at that point. Central

Station, at that time, acted like the war was happening a million miles away.

The sheer size of Central Station was immense and awe-inspiring to witness. From what he could recall, it was about the size of a sports field. There were snack shops and vendors as far as the eye could see. You could even get a haircut, shave, and a shoeshine before stepping onto the Main Platform. Now, the Main Platform exemplifies everything associated with the Emerald City, which is all about the glitz and the glam. The Main Platform was always lit with color-changing lights that flickered on and off for all who passed through the doors of the train station. He remembered witnessing how the colors would change based on the seasons or if there was a special holiday going on at that time. Three giant clocks rested at the bottom of the platform, displaying the varying time zones for the rest of the Aggeloi continent.

One of the most intriguing things he liked about Central Station was the overall positive atmosphere that every person who stepped onto the platform possessed. Street performers and bands played music for any soul on their commute. He remembered seeing students dressed in class uniforms, lawyers barking orders to their interns on their cellphones, and even a clown handing out balloons on the train. He still found the clown creepy, but who wouldn't? That wasn't even the best part; sometimes, they would even host a gun show in the train lobby. They had every type of pistol a werefox could ask for; it was like being in heaven.

The Main Platform served as the station's central hub and launching pad for traveling throughout the rest of the country. Steps ran beneath the main platform, leading to the other platforms and vice versa, to get to the other platforms that filled nearly every inch of the station. The subway station was an intricate system normally buzzing with business. The station they had entered today was far from what it once was.

The brilliant lights that would usually greet weary travelers on their journey were just as absent of life as a graveyard. There was now a flat gray tinted color to the normally vibrant station, making it equally uninspiring. There was a heavy film of dust and debris covering each of the platforms and train tracks. The debris and damage from the platforms must have come from the bombings occurring above ground. There were disheveled sleeping bags and a few army tents and cots on the Main Platform. There weren't many, but just enough to make the message clear that people ran to the station to escape the violence on the streets above. They must have left them behind when they moved their operations to transport civilians and the military.

As they explored the Main Platform, Grace stopped by a row of sleeping bags. She bent over and pulled an item from a mossy green sleeping bag. Tears streamed from her eyes as she examined the item in her hand. The Princess held a light brown teddy bear with hearts stitched into the hand. One of the black buttoned eyes was missing with the initials M.E stitched on it. The fabric was relatively worn, and some stuffing was spilling out of the seams. Shane guessed this was probably a teddy bear passed down to the youngest in the family, or maybe it was a special gift given to someone. Either way, the item deserved to be in the arms of the child it belonged to. If it weren't for this damn war, they would have this teddy bear to comfort them.

For a moment, he could not understand why this simple teddy bear was making her cry. Then he realized Grace must have felt some kinship toward the Aggeloi people. That may seem common sense, but she spent most of her teenage years at Southern Convent. Those witches were never her family; she never truly felt at home there. He also got the sense she still wasn't used to all of the violence and maybe felt some guilt for having to hurt her own countrymen. Normally, he would have told her to buck up and keep it moving, but he figured she also had some other concerns on her mind.

Macy squeezed the teddy bear's ears, and tears began to drip from her eyes. "I'm so sick of this. It's like no matter what we do, nothing changes. It always gets worse, and this is proof of it. Shane and I spend so much time fighting to stop these things from happening. What have we even accomplished? We can't truly stop this whole key thing. The Daimonia are pulling the strings in the background, and now we are dangerously close to a full-blown world war. For what? This damn key? Some vendettas we still don't understand. I just hate that people may get hurt because of us."

Jayden approached the girls and asked for the teddy bear. He then placed it in his bag and embraced the both of them. Shane was grateful for his attempt to bring them some level of peace. The werefox knew that he, personally, wasn't the sensitive type and didn't quite know what to say. He had been doing this type of work for decades; it was too late for him to rethink it. However, he couldn't ignore the points she was making.

The Dragon Warrior looked at Macy and Grace in the eyes and embraced them again. Then he said, "I will keep this until we can put our weapons down. This teddy bear is a reminder that people are getting hurt by all that's happening. There is no way we can save everyone; hell, we might not even be able to save ourselves. But we can't forget we are fighting for something bigger than ourselves. Not just for revenge, but to make the world a better place."

Jayden stood taller and more determined after putting that teddy bear in his bag. Even Shane was slightly impressed; it was about time the boy made a decision. The question was how long it would last. The young boy from Eiréné tended to go up and down with his motivations. Watching him jump from platform to platform, looking for number thirteen, was inspiring. Maybe a little foolhardy, but still inspiring.

"I found it!" Jayden shouted from the farthest platform on the left.

Shane ran toward the platform, if you can call it that. The platform was painted in a depressing gray. The number thirteen was painted above a door built flat against the wall. The platform was raised, but there were no tracks; there wasn't even a train. He approached the door and noticed it had no handle or doorknob. The werefox tried to push it, but there was no give. He tried pushing it again, but it felt like he was pressing against a cement wall. Shane stepped back and examined the massive wall connected to Platform thirteen. He closed his eyes and sniffed the air. His nose picked up a hint of vanilla and chocolate, which would typically be an odd smell on an empty train platform. That combination of smells wasn't just tied to dessert; it was the smell of a high concentration of magical energy within an object. This level of magic was more commonly used with powerful magic stones. His ears picked up the electrical buzzing sound of magic flowing within the wall with a greater concentration centering around the door. He didn't quite know why.

He turned toward Grace, who had just climbed onto the platform. Her eyes were wide and glistening with reminiscing tears. For her, this was probably one of the last places she went with her family. She probably never imagined coming back to this place with how horrible the witches of the Southern Convent were. When she placed her hand against the wall, it shimmered and rippled like she was touching water. She ran her fingers along the wall and shifted them to make a figure eight. Her eyes were glowing and fully entranced by the magic of the wall.

The door began to glow the closer she got to it. She placed her hand on the door, which turned dark red. The frame seemed to liquefy and sway like waves against the shore. The waves on the wall began to move more intensely just as the door seemed to fade away. She stepped into the darkness once the door had completely disappeared into nothingness. Shane, along with the others, followed after her. As he crossed the threshold, he instinctively reloaded his pistols with more powerful rounds.

They stepped onto a flat landing at the top of the stairs. Just below him, he could hear the sound of an engine warming up. Then his eyes almost went blind as a bright light flipped on. An orange glow filled the expanse of the station. At the bottom of the staircase was a platform leading to the Aggeloi Royal

Train. Shane knew a little about trains, and from their vantage point, he could already tell that this train was one of a kind.

To describe the Royal Train in a few words, concepts such as luxury and vintage with a hint of magic would come to mind. The train was covered in a cheery oak stain from the driver's cabin to the caboose. A smokestack rose from the top of the driver's cabin. Instead of releasing dark smoke, it was an apple green. Where a coal car would be was a cart filled with what he could only describe as liquid magic. From the strong scent of chocolate and vanilla, he could tell that the magical energy on the train was intense.

He began to walk down the steps to get to the train. As he got closer, he gained an even greater appreciation for the long-distance passenger train. The wheels were painted ruby red and gold. The passenger carts had lightly tinted windows and windowsills emblazoned with gold paint. Each passenger seat was made of red satin fabric, which looked just as comfortable as resting on a cloud. On the roof of the main passenger car was a series of color-changing lights that spelled the word *Regina*. In the old Aggeloi language, that word meant Queen.

He reached the bottom of the steps and placed his paw against the middle car. He felt calm for a moment; all his worries faded. He could feel the hairs on his paws begin to relax and sensed his magical energy restoring and his wounds healing. The stark change from feeling drained to energized due to touching a train car shocked him. He removed his paw from the train, and all his pain and exhaustion swarmed back. He placed his paws back against the train and felt instantly more relaxed. It didn't make sense that the train could do this.

The train's engines roared to life all on their own. He was so shocked by the locomotive coming to life that his body instinctively jumped back from the train car. His heart pounded in his furry chest as the nearest train car door slid open.

Was the train alive? No, it couldn't be that. That would be silly. Of course, just touching the train felt like relaxing at the spa, so anything is possible with this machine.

He glanced over at Jayden and others who were standing right by the door and appeared to be visually nervous about jumping on a train with a mind of its own. Shane went to tell them to stop being scared when his nose flared.

Shane let out a growl and pulled out his pistol. He turned toward them and shouted, "GET ON THE TRAIN AND GO NOW!"

The platform shook with the force of an earthquake. Smoke billowed from an object that had slammed into the station. Magical energy radiated from the being as it stepped out from a cloud of dust and smoke.

Metal clanged against the cement platform as the target approached them. The armored suit was black as the night sky. Metal plates stretched from the base of the foot to the waist. The upper body armor covered the chest and extended to the hands. A bulletproof leather vest protected the exposed stomach area and back. Embedded in the center of the chest plate was a red magic stone shaped like a diamond. A black scabbard with a matching hilt hung from the left side of the suit. The elf had a narrow face with bright red eyes. His hair was silver and slicked back to a spikey point. His pointed ears and ghostly white face matched his razor-sharp canines and nearly bleached teeth.

The train's wheels squealed as they began to rotate and move. Immediately, the elf changed his focus from him to the train. He raised his left arm, and the metallic hand retracted into the wrist and morphed into a forty-inch cannon. The weapon started to channel electrical energy at the tip of the barrel. Shane raised his gun in the blink of an eye and fired at the elf. The cannon exploded from the force of the pistol round. Shane fired two more consecutive rounds. The elf moved with blazing speed to deflect the rounds. It swiped its sword in a horizontal motion and released a purple wave of energy that sped toward the werefox. Shane summoned a blue metal shield to block the attack. The spell exploded when it made contact with his shield. He fired another round at the elf as he was pushed back from the explosion. His enemy deflected it and rushed toward him.

Shane channeled his magical energy as the elf attacked him with lightning-quick slashes. His blue shield grew darker and darker with each strike. He stepped back, avoiding a swipe, then slammed his shield into the elf's chest, which exploded. The elf was knocked backward, and as it rolled on the ground, Shane dashed forward. He used his tail to spring himself high as he jumped over his enemy. He speed-loaded his pistol while flipping in the air and fired downward at the elf. His enemy's purple Auto-Shield intercepted the rounds, and they disintegrated in the magical energy. When the elf jumped back onto its feet, Shane summoned a circular shield with razor blades attached to the edges. He launched it at the elf, slicing it in half at the waist.

He quickly glanced up to gauge how far the train had moved away from the platform. Shane sprinted toward the edge of the platform. While switching to his other pistol, he placed the grappling attachment on the bottom of the barrel. He fired off the grappling dart and attached it to the roof of the caboose. He twirled his tail into a spring and launched himself as high as possible. The werefox summoned a Hover Shield while he was lofted. His rear paws landed on the blue shield and used its forward momentum with the high tensile strength wire attached to the grappling dart. His shield sped him closer to the train as he started to descend. Once close enough, he jumped and twirled forward until he landed on the train.

Shane spun his revolvers on his claws and then holstered them.

"What was it that Jayden called me before? Oh yes, a Badass."

Chapter 24

Intermission

Warm water from the shower cascaded down his brown skin. The scars from his time on the battlefield disappeared from the healing properties infused in the dark blue water. He could sense his magical energy restoring. When he noticed his veins popping up from his forearms, he thought his magical powers had increased. He took a deep breath as he was starting to feel like his normal self again. Jayden couldn't tell if it was because he could shower for the first time in forever or if the train's magic was that powerful.

The pipes squeaked when he turned off the water. Jayden stretched out his arms and found a warm set of new clothes that had been laid out on his bed. There was a pair of black pants, a white undershirt, and a red long-sleeved shirt with matching shoes. He had no idea where they came from, but free was free.

When he returned his towel to the shower room, he found a small glass bottle beside the sink. There was a light green liquid inside it. The young Dragon Warrior placed it up to his nose. It smelled like a nice cologne. He popped the top and put a dab of cologne on his wrist and neck. Then, he put on his Jade necklace, which he had not worn in ages. Jayden checked himself out in the mirror. *Man, I'm looking good*, he thought.

He slid open the red and yellow door of the bathroom. Once he exited his room and began strolling through the train, he passed by rows of compartments. It seemed almost impossible to him to have so many rooms in one train car, but that's magic and enchantment for you. They were like cheat codes if you knew how to use them well enough.

The Dragon Warrior pushed open a door and stepped into the dining car. His senses were greeted by the entrancing scent of blueberry pancakes, sausage, eggs, spaghetti and meatballs, and anything a growing boy would love.

White rectangular tables were set against the dining car's right wall. The tables were big enough to seat six people. He noticed sets of plates and silverware with glasses for toasting to the good times had already been placed on the table. Tony was sitting on the other side of the table beside Macy. Shane was nowhere in sight. The werefox was probably not the eat-with-friends and merriment type. Jayden pulled out his seat and sat across from Tony.

Macy glanced at him and smiled. "You look good and are wearing nice cologne. It's amazing what a shower will do for you."

Jayden grinned, "I do what I can. I put my pants on one leg at a time, just like everyone else. I'm surprised you didn't want to sit beside me because I'm so sharp."

Tony sent a small jolt of electricity at his friend. "Dude, you are such an idiot. You had your chance in grade school. Macy's grown now; she doesn't want to chase someone who ends up in the hospital every five minutes unless she is secretly after your life insurance. Macy, you wouldn't dare!"

She laughed, "I would. My plan this whole time has been to woo one of you over since you both are always one minute away from death. Then it's cha-ching. Grace and I have a bet to see who gets whose life insurance."

Jayden's jaw dropped, "You know what, I'm glad I liked Sarah more during seventh grade and part of fifth."

Macy's lip quivered, and a slow, dramatic tear dropped from her eyes. "How could you be so mean and insensitive."

He cocked his head to the side, "I'm not falling for that. We both know you're half-heartless. That pretty face is a trap that we all fell for."

She laughed, "I tried my best."

Jayden's brow furrowed as he stared at his childhood friends. "Hey, can I ask you all something? Who put the new clothes in my room and cooked all the food? I don't know where the kitchen is, and we all know that Gracey doesn't cook."

Tony and Macy glanced at each other and shrugged. If they didn't know, this was just added to his laundry list of oddities he noticed about this train. He still couldn't figure out how it started driving independently without a conductor.

He noticed something weird on the left side of the car. Grace stepped into the room through a door that wasn't there a minute ago with a huge smile. He felt a sudden cold chill coming over him as she approached him. He heard a loud popping sound. His eyes peered down at his empty plate, which suddenly filled with his favorite foods. Without hesitation, he began to scarf down every piece of food on his plate.

Grace met his gaze with a big smile on her face. "Do you like the food, Jayden?"

"Mmhmm," he muttered while chomping on a chicken nugget.

She asked the other two, "Will you two want seconds?"

In unison, they replied, "Mmhmm."

Grace turned to her left and said, "Would you be willing to take their drink requests?"

Jayden shouted, "I'd like a red ale."

"Sure, we would love to do that! Would you like that in glass or out of the bottle?"

"Can you pour it in…" Jayden stopped mid-sentence, as his brain was immediately confused by the new voice in the room. His eyes slowly looked up at the busty woman floating at the end of the table. She had straight hair that came down to her shoulders and curved bangs covering parts of her eyes. Her youthful smile was gentle and kind despite the cold chills he got from her. The nice lady had light blue skin that was pretty much see-through and had no legs to speak of.

"YOU'RE A GA GA GHOOOSTTT!!!!" He shouted so loud that he tipped his chair backward and crashed onto the ground.

"That's five gold pieces!" Tony shouted.

"Dammit, Jayden," Macy groaned. "You were supposed to make me money, not cost me."

Grace shook her head as she handed him the coins. "I should have gone with my first bet. I changed my mind last minute."

The ghost pulled out five gold coins from her apron and slid them toward Tony. Jayden couldn't believe what he saw, "Did all of you bet on me getting scared of a ghost? And the ghost bet, too?"

Tony laughed, "Of course. We always make bets about you when you aren't paying attention. This is one of the few times I've won."

"Yeah, Jayden," Grace interjected. "I'm not happy with you; you lost me. Plus, this isn't the first time you've seen a ghost. Why would you get scared this time?"

Jayden got up and fixed his chair. "Well, the first time was when I was looking for the Southern Convent to save you from them. You are welcome for that. Truth be told, I was scared then, too."

Grace let out the biggest sigh. "You are the absolute worst."

The spirit's light blue cheeks turned a pink color from embarrassment. "Umm, I'm not a ghost, by the way. I'm a

Pneuma, to be precise. The term might be spirit in your language, but I'm not dead. I'm only twenty-eight. My name is Jennifer, but everyone calls me Jenny. With a Y."

Jayden cocked his head to the side and said, "Okay, Jenny, with a Y. Why are you here?"

She batted her eyes at him, "Well, sweetness, that's easy. I work here. I've been an employee of the Royal Family for years. All of the *Pneuma* on this train are. I've known Lady Grace since she was a little girl. When I was younger, I used to babysit her."

He shook his head, "Wait, there are more of you?"

Jenny smiled back at him. "Of course, sweetie. Who do you think brought you your new clothes? Or made the food or is driving this train. Don't worry, I was the one who dropped off your new clothes for you. I'm glad you wore them."

For a second, Jayden felt mildly violated and confused. He wasn't sure if she was being nice for cultural reasons or hitting on him. Jayden reached across the table and touched her hand. Unlike the Southern Convents ghost, she was corporeal. Her hand was cold, but the longer he held her hand, the warmer it felt. He could sense magical energy coming from her now; she must be able to conceal it for some time.

He pulled his hand back, "So, what have you all been doing since Grace was gone?"

"Well," she muttered. "That is somewhat of a long story. Let me give you all your drinks, and I'll tell you what I can." Jenny snapped her fingers, and drinks appeared in front of them. She lifted up a glass of white wine and offered a toast. "The *Pneuma* clan I am descended from has always played a pivotal role in the Aggeloi government. Some family members serve in the high courts, and I have relatives in Parliament, too. When Grace's parents passed away, we stopped working on the train for the most part. When we were told she was killed, we spent even less time working on the train. Since only a handful of government officials can get through the barrier, most don't even want to bother with it. We still try to maintain it and keep it functional. Our roles have changed to meet the needs of parliament and other government officials. When we heard a rumor that there was a girl in the country fitting Grace's description, we spent more time getting the train ready. We knew that sooner or later; she might come here. Also, we may or may not have had a *Pneuma* following you all once they had that big explosion earlier. We were so elated to know she was alive. My uncles who serve in the Parliament have spent so much time trying to expose the truth of the treachery within the Aggeloi government."

"Well, that's good." Jayden replied. "So, did you all know about that thing that attacked us? How long was it there?"

Jenny shook her head, "No, we didn't. Even our security department didn't know that person was there. We aren't even sure what it was. We were happy to help even if it wasn't a lot."

Tony nodded, "Well, we appreciate all that you did. From what I could see, it looked like a Magi-Knight type of armor."

"Close, but no cigar." Shane barked as he stepped into the car. "That was actually a Light-Armor Magi-Knight kit. They are exceptionally rare. The guy wearing it was a Dark Elf."

Jayden scratched his chin and nodded in agreement. "Ahh, the legendary Dark Elf, only a creature such as that could be so crafty."

Tony shot another bolt of electricity at his friend. "Don't act like you know what that is. We didn't know elves existed until we went to the Water Temple."

Shane flashed his canines as he moved to sit at a table on the far side of the room. "As I suspected, the both of you are still morons. But just so you know, Dark Elves are not that common, just like the armor he used. They typically can only be found on the northern continent, but there is a sect that works a lot with the Daimonia. They aren't officially a part of the Daimonia, but they might as well be, given how often they do missions for them. They often work with the *Lamia* group, the twelfth Daimonia organization."

Jayden examined the werefox cautiously. "Are you serious? Are they working with the group searching for *The Key*?"

The werefox put a slice of pizza between two beef patties on a burger. Then he glanced back at them. "I seriously doubt it. No one wants to work with the *Orias* group. Their methods end up in the news too much. If I could guess, they were waiting for an opportunity. Dark Elves specialize in Dark Energy and Shadow Magic. It is possible they were trailing us and waiting for the right opportunity to strike. They were looking to either take *The Key* for themselves or take back your father's sword."

He looked perplexed, "Why would they want my dad's sword?"

Shane looked Jayden dead in the eye. "I might not be the best person to answer that fully. I'd suggest you ask Raiden for the details. I will say this: the *Lamia* group loves power, especially anything associated with demons. Under no circumstances do you let anyone from their sect get near it."

He had another question before returning to grubbing on some baby-back ribs. "A Dragon Master told us people can die by touching this sword. Would they even be able to use it? She said that's why the *Orias* group didn't take it from my dad."

"Truth be told, I couldn't tell you," Shane replied. I'm not an expert on weapons imbued with demons. I think they have ways of handling and using those types of things. That is why I say again, do not let them close to that weapon."

***

He awoke to the sound of knuckles banging on his door. Jayden couldn't quite understand why they had to bang so loudly. He also couldn't quite understand why they needed to bug him. Even if the train was attacked, he would be fine sleeping through the whole thing. The whole dying in his sleep thing seemed way better than out on the battlefield.

Jayden put on a pair of shorts and a black shirt. He jumped out of bed and made his way to the door. When he slid it open, Grace jumped out at him and shouted *BOO*. Jayden pretended to be frightened so as not to injure her pride. His eyes narrowed as he sensed that there was something different about her. By using his high-quality powers of deduction, he came to one conclusion.

He hugged her and shouted, "You finally lost that last ten pounds you were talking about. Congrats Gracey!"

While in his embrace, she punched him in the rib cage. "No, you jerk. I dyed my hair. Are you saying I'm fat, or I need to lose weight?"

Jayden began to fake a heart attack in the most dramatic fashion possible. She punched him in the ribs again. "I'm not falling for that, you idiot. Do you like it?"

He reached out and ran his fingers through her hair gently. The purple she replaced with a light blue that flowed into her tips of silver. Her perfectly scented hair flowed with the beauty and grace of a waterfall.

"It looks amazing," he said.

Macy came out of nowhere and pushed her out of the way before she could respond. "What do you think about mine?"

Jayden's heart jumped in his throat. He had no idea she was right there. His eyes took a moment to process her new hairdo. It was tough to tell for a second because her blonde hair was in her usual pigtails. This time, she also added silver highlights. It was a subtle change, but just enough to make a positive impact.

He touched one of her pigtails and said, "It looks beautiful, Macy."

She blushed for half a second before Grace pushed her back out of the way. "So that's all you got? My hair is amazing, and hers is beautiful?"

"What?" He replied, looking really confused.

Macy shook her head, "She's right; those weren't super amazing compliments. Tony gave us way better compliments on our new hair. He can watch scary movies with us in the movie theater car, and you can just stay here. Even Shane's compliment was better, and I'm not sure he looked at us."

The girls turned on their heels and walked away. Jayden wasn't quite sure what the hell had just happened. He was tempted to just go back to bed, but he felt he would get accosted for that, too. So, he grabbed a pair of shoes and followed them.

When he stepped into the hall, a spirit waited for him. This one was a male with a round waist to the point he was bursting through his blazer. He had a serving plate in one hand and a bag of popcorn in the other. The spirit bowed when Jayden drew closer and handed him the plate of finger food and the bag of popcorn. Jayden thanked him and made his way toward the dining car.

His hands gripped a gold-plated wheel lock attached to a scarlet-colored door. He applied a little force and turned the wheel. The door slid to the side, and he entered the dining car.

The sound of screams and grunts blared from the canvas screen. Vampires and monsters were on full display as the film rolled. The dining tables and chairs were replaced by folding seats that you would typically find in a movie theater. Macy and Grace sat together in the center row, munching on what could only be described as a preposterously large bowl of popcorn drenched in butter. On the other hand, Tony was sitting in one of the back rows, sharpening his broadsword and occasionally glancing up at the horror flick on screen. Jayden had no idea where Shane was, but he figured the werefox was probably too cool to be watching movies with them and was too busy brooding about their suicide mission and the fate of the planet.

Jayden found a seat in the farthest row in the back. His blue theater seat was pressed close to a window, so it wasn't comfortable. He was willing to deal with the discomfort of staring out at the countryside. Jayden was also exceptionally scared of horror films and did not want the girls to know that.

For a moment, his view of the beautiful Aggeloi countryside had become obscured by a canvas of gray. The train became enveloped by a tunnel made of cement bricks. Blue- and emerald-colored crystals were embedded in the walls, shining gently like a glittering ocean of brick as they sped past.

His forehead burned, and he squinted his eyes as sunlight burst through the glass. He blinked while the train chugged along, leaving the old tunnel behind. Jayden smiled as he was greeted by a cascade of rolling hills. Tall pine trees rose from the sea of green and mint bushes sprinkled along both sides of the track.

A dark shadow flashed across his window, momentarily pausing the wave of sunlight. The young Dragon Warrior smiled as green-colored scales and a ten-foot wingspan appeared. His jaw dropped at the sight of the razor-sharp claws as long as his dagger and a pointed snout with fangs that would give the strongest warrior nightmares.

He felt something bump his shoulder and nearly jumped out of his seat. Jayden turned his head only to realize Macy had moved to sit next to him. Not to spend any time with him, she was enamored by the green dragon gliding over the rolling hills.

"That thing looks scary," she whispered. "Do you know what that is?"

Jayden shook his head. "That's obviously a dragon," he replied.

She scowled at him. "I'm starting to see why Sarah thinks you are an ass."

He grinned, "I don't think she thinks that at all. But seriously, you should watch this part."

Jayden pointed toward a pear tree that stood isolated in a field. The creature slammed into the tree and opened its powerful jaws. It began chowing down on the leaves and fruits hanging from the tree. The dragon moved with the speed and intensity of a chainsaw. Chunks of tree branches splintered into the air as the dragon seized its meal. After a few seconds, the once beautiful and majestic-looking peach tree was nothing more than a fancy thorn bush. The dragon had absolutely demolished nearly every inch of the tree.

Macy's light complexion was now as pale as a ghost. "Umm, that was terrifying. I didn't know they had vegetarian dragons."

"Well, that is what they call a Lime Dragon. They are omnivores, so they can technically eat weirdos like you. We are lucky it went after the tree instead of us," he smirked.

Macy stuck her tongue out at him. "You are such a jerk. What happened to the sweet boy who wanted me to be his Valentine in fourth and sixth grade?"

Jayden crossed his arms in frustration. "He is upset because those letters were supposed to be kept anonymous."

She rolled her eyes, "Every girl in school knew how bad your handwriting was. Even if you didn't write your name on the notes, which you did. I could still tell."

He smiled, "Oh, that makes sense. I thought I was being super sneaky with the ones I wrote for you and Sarah."

His childhood friend raised her left eyebrow, "Don't think I forgot you sent valentines to me and her. I'm still mad you didn't get me one for fifth grade. Either way, you can compensate for being a two-timer by watching scary movies with me and Grace."

Before he could respond, she managed to lift him out of his seat and drag him to watch the movie. Once he was plopped down on a seat next to Grace, a ghost popped out of the closet on the screen, and he let out a small yelp. The girls laughed, and even Tony joked about him being a chicken and that they could turn on a kid's movie if that would make things easier.

***

The hours passed as they laughed and screamed from watching the scariest movies imaginable. Jayden couldn't remember the last time he could sit and do normal kid things. Hell, he couldn't remember the last time he had even watched a movie, maybe at the Dragon Monastery? They had to grow up so fast, and even as adults, they really haven't had a moment to just sit and enjoy life.

A gentle, cool breeze blew through their train car with wisps of light moisture. The walls of the train became translucent as they sped through the countryside. His eyes widened as he could see the beautiful sprawling hills without staring out the window. He grinned as the smell of salt crept in from the outside air and consumed his nostrils. Seagulls and dark blue pelicans flew by majestically over the Northern Ocean. His body felt relaxed from the sound of the waves roaring off in the distance filled the cabin.

The train screeched as it pulled into its stop. Jayden got up and made his way toward his room. Then he reached into the bag Miss Mara gave him and pulled out the black scimitar, pistol, and three magazines. He dug deeper into the bag, which was an uncomfortable feeling because you can put damn near everything you own in it.

He admired the weapon as he ran his finger across the cold metal and satin. Jayden pulled out his martial arts uniform, his red sash, and his lucky Jade necklace from his bag. He quickly put on his old Dragon Warrior uniform, necklace, and father's sword. Immediately, he felt his muscles bulge from the curse attached to the sword. Even his magical power felt fully restored, and he could also sense a substantial increase in his power. He couldn't tell if he was truthfully getting stronger or if it was the magic-enhancing properties of his gear.

Jayden loved the power boost he got from his Dragon Warrior uniform. Even though he didn't wear it all the time. He also didn't mind the physical strength boost and confidence he got from equipping his father's sword. None of the items he wore compared to the magic boost he got from his katana. And unfortunately, his katana was in a thousand pieces and taking up room in his bag. No time to mope. They had too much to do, and he had to try a new trick.

He lifted his bag with his left hand and held it out in front of him at a slight angle. He held his right hand out and summoned a small ball of orange flames. He drew a perfect magic circle with his right index and middle fingers. Jayden chuckled as the circle of fire floated before him, reminding him of the rings of fire that tigers would jump through at the Mirage Circus. This time, instead of a tiger, it would be his enchanted backpack.

Jayden turned his head to look away as he moved his bag toward the center of the circle. He winced once the bag was in the center of the circle, and the orange flames started to shine brighter. Four streams of fire shot out from different points of the magic circle and made a beeline for the bag. Once the line of fire touched the bag, it was immediately engulfed in flames. Then the bag and the magic circle exploded, knocking him back against the wall.

Panic consumed him. "Shit! That was all of my important stuff in that bag. My katana, money, my fake passport that Gracey made me, and beef jerky! It's all gone!"

"Shut up, you idiot!" Said a voice from just outside of his room. "It's supposed to look like that when you try to store your items in another dimension using your element."

Tony extended his right hand, and a small gray cloud appeared above it. Tiny bolts of light splintered across the miniature cloud, and tiny droplets of rain fell to the floor. With his index and middle finger, he drew a perfect magic circle. Then he stuck his hand in the middle of the circle, and his hand completely disappeared for a moment. A second later, he pulled out his backpack from the circle. He placed it back in the center of the circle and snapped his fingers. The magic circle and his bag instantly disappeared.

"See, it's just that easy," his best friend said. "There is a 99% chance you did it right."

"Well, this was the first time I tried to put something that big in another dimension." Jayden said as he got back to his feet. He dusted himself off and shrugged at his buddy. "I also didn't fully learn how to do it when Mariko taught us. I only managed to store things like paper and pens. I burned three different books from her library trying to do it."

Tony heaved the biggest sigh, "I shouldn't be surprised by what you do now. But you always manage to impress me with your stupidity. Your bag is probably burnt to a crisp, and we need to head out. Maybe next time you can try to do CallBack on your wallet?"

Jayden shook his head, "I hate you. Master Mariko forbade me from trying to do CallBack; not even my life depended on it."

***

The train made a screeching sound, and the smokestack blew a high-pitched whistle. Once the luxury vehicle stopped just inches from an auburn-colored stop block, they made their way to the exit. Jayden slid open the car door, took a few steps, and made it onto the landing.

The term landing, by the way, might be a bit of an exaggeration. There was no formal landing or even a platform. He had just landed on a patch of freshly cut grass that he had no choice but to jump on. This was surprising since this area was supposed to be a vacation spot for the Royal Family and dignitaries.

Once they had all gotten off the train, Grace paid a tearful goodbye to the *Pneuma*. Then she led them to this grassy hill that ran parallel to cliffs. Jayden took a deep breath of the cool ocean air, and his spirit immediately felt at peace.

Walking parallel to a grassy cliff, he noticed a bed of yellow and pink daisies. The bed of flowers was both impressive and majestic. The beautiful strip of daisies stretched almost all the way to the top of the hill. There were pale and light blue colored *Pneumas* playing and frolicking in the flowery garden around them. They waved as they passed by, and even a young one brought a small bouquet of daisies for Grace. Jayden didn't quite know if they were hired to maintain the property; he liked to think the Royal Family built this place so the *Pneuma* could have a home of their own.

At the top of the hill stood a rare Green Weeping Cherry Tree that stood tall and strong with the backdrop of the Northern Ocean. The tree stood about thirty feet high and was dressed in a shimmering blanket of emerald-colored leaves with matching cherry blossoms in full bloom. In the center of the tree was a heart that had been carved into the tree.

Grace placed her hand on the tree and ran her index finger over a section in the bottom right of the heart. Jayden tried to better understand what she was doing, and his eyes widened as he saw her name carved in the tree just above her index finger. Then he realized that there were more names engraved on the tree, some inside the heart and the rest scattered in different parts of the tree. Then Jayden realized her parents would have etched their names on this tree. The same parents that were killed fighting the same battles that they were doing today. Even though he didn't quite know the exact purpose of the engravings on this tree, he could tell from the tears streaming down Grace's eyes that this tree was something special.

Jayden helped her to stand back up straight. When he released her, she turned on her heels and began to run off. He glanced to his right and noticed a single-story cottage about fifty yards down the hill to their right. He nodded his head, and Tony and Macy went after her. Jayden took a moment and walked up to the cliff's edge behind the tree.

A giant wall of water slammed into the edge of the continent below him. The waves roared as they crashed and eroded the side of the cliffs. As the ocean made its power and presence known, a teal-colored sea serpent breached the surface. At first, he only noticed the rows of spines moving with the flow of the current. Then the monster lifted its long neck with its viper-like skull equipped with rows of sharp teeth and two gigantic fangs. The creature's size was difficult to tell, as much of the body was submerged under the rushing waves.

He figured running into a snake like that would ruin his day if he was swimming in that water.

Even though he had a healthy fear of the creature, he could not help but admire the beast. He remembered reading books that this sea serpent was an apex predator. He had no doubt in his mind that this animal possessed no fear. The snake could travel the ocean freely, with little to no sense of danger. Jayden initially hoped that becoming a Dragon Warrior, now a Dragon Knight, would give him that same confidence and freedom. Instead, he must worry about being in the middle of a gunfight or being killed by a monster every five minutes. With all the power he could use now, he had to humble himself enough to realize that his destructive magic could not be used in every situation. Jayden had also become painfully aware that even though he was very skilled in combat, there had always been someone stronger or a better fighter than him. He was too arrogant and naïve when he left the Dragon Monastery. Now, he was in too deep to back out of the mess they were in to turn back.

Chapter 25

A Step-Down Memory Lane

Jayden cracked open the door to the cottage. The door creaked
as he eased himself into the building. His feet landed on a
velvet welcome mat. Standing just a few feet before him was
an oval-shaped greeting table. On top of the table were small
stacks of business pamphlets and an agenda from a meeting
from ten years ago. In the center of the table was an ivory cup
filled with ballpoint pens coated in white gold. He ran his hand
along the coffee-colored table. It was perfectly smooth to the
touch.

He could feel a slight buzz of electricity in the air, so he
glanced up from the table, and that's when he sensed that there
must be an enchantment placed on the building. The sections of
the cottage on his left and right were originally walled off
when he stepped inside. To the left of him was a hallway that
stretched as far as he could see, with rows of living quarters on

each side of the hall. The hallway to his right did not extend so far. There were two rooms on each side of the hall, and there appeared to be a large study at the end.

Just behind the oval green table was some light brown wood flooring that led into the kitchen. To get into the kitchen, a small step led up to a room split in half. On the left side of the kitchen was a small glass table with matching chairs, and on the right was the cooking area. A large island with granite tops and a set of candles was in the middle. The countertops were made of white marble with splashes of gray paint encrusted with diamonds. The refrigerator he decided to raid was mostly empty. The only items he saw left in there were a few beers, old slices of cheese, and some mystery meat that smelled like death.

The Dragon Warrior popped the top on the beer and took a sip. The drink's taste was subtle, with a little bitterness and a mild hoppy flavor. There were even small notes of a citrus flavoring he had never had. Jayden was surprised it tasted so good; he had expected it to taste like pure poison.

Jayden dragged his feet, moved toward the back of the kitchen, and gripped the handle for a sliding glass door. He peered through the glass and watched as Macy and Tony gathered around Gracey. She buckled under the weight of her feet and sobbed on the grass in the backyard. For a moment, he thought about stepping outside and joining them. He released his grip on the handle and walked away.

He turned on his heels and made his way toward the study. Before entering the study, he wanted to explore the other rooms down that same hall. Jayden tried to turn the first doorknob he passed in the hall, but it was completely locked. Then he tried another doorknob across the hall, and as he turned it, the knob broke off the door. Oh crap, he thought. Grace is going to kill me if she finds out that I broke a doorknob.

Jayden stuffed the doorknob in his pocket and tried to open the door. He tried to force it open, but the door remained as still as the other one. He was confounded by the difficulty he experienced because the amount of force he used should have torn it off the hinges. There must have been some sort of magic or enchantment attached to this specific door, or that was at least the excuse he would use.

The Dragon Warrior glanced to his left toward the study at the end of the hall. Before he made his way down the hall, he managed to wedge the doorknob back into its slot. It didn't fit exactly as intended, but it was good enough to make Gracey happy.

As he took a few steps toward the study, clouds of dust and dirt were kicked up as his sneakers trudged along the old floor. His nose flared from the musty scent of a wooden desk. The desk was made of three connected pieces, pressed against each side of the wall of the room, save for the doorway.

Jayden crossed the threshold and immediately felt claustrophobic as he crept into the room. The desk was so large that it took up so much wall space that there were only about three feet that he could move in any direction. Old newspapers and books littered the room, making it feel small. Stacks of paper and literature on the desk were as tall as a small child.

Just inches from his right foot were a pile of old dictionaries, a field guide for finding birds in Aggeloi, and a tome for summoning magic. There was perpetual film dust on every corner of the room so thick that pages and covers of books were stained orange. He couldn't imagine how or why the Royal Family would have a room that was this disorganized.

Jayden decided to start sifting through the pile of nonsense. He tried pulling on the metal string under the lampshade, which immediately snapped off. Well, *that's just great*, he thought. The young Dragon Warrior reached for a book sandwiched between piles of trash and old cupcake wrappers. The book was hefty and as thick as an encyclopedia. He wiped away the caked-on dirt from the cover. Beneath the dusty stains, he could recognize its formally immaculate black leather binding. He squinted to read the title because it had almost been completely scratched off. From what he could tell, the book's title was *The Precursors and The Secret History of The Great War*.

He unspun a piece of thread that kept the book locked. The binding cracked a little as he opened its flaps. The pages had a yellowish tint from years of use. Once he peeled open the book, he was greeted by a title emblazoned in a gold print. Beneath the title was a tiny symbol of a hammer and a nail crossing over each other. Jayden touched the symbol and instantly felt a small charge of electric and magical energy shoot through his body. Then, the letters on the title page shifted and moved along the page freely. After about thirty seconds, the letters stopped moving erratically. They turned into some pictographs from a language he had never heard of. He tried flipping through the book, and each page had a similar style of pictographs.

He was stumped momentarily because he did not sense any unique magical properties in the book. Besides the random static energy in the air he felt, nothing special about this book would make it change so quickly. *That is very interesting*, he thought. Maybe the symbol was like a button for a machine. He tried pressing the symbol again, but nothing happened.

Then, he closed the book and reopened it. Immediately, the title page and the lettering reverted to their normal state. The rest of the pages were still littered with pictographs, making this book useless to him. Still, he felt it could be useful to have with them. Jayden made his magic circle of fire and placed the book into the other dimension, filing it under the weird shit he's found section.

He continued his exploration of the ungodly-sized desk. For the most part, there did not seem to be any consistency to the books and newspapers strewn across the wooden furniture. Many of the books were old and almost torn to shreds. The newspapers were from different decades and even centuries. Jayden could not imagine anyone being able to get any work done in this office, let alone a royal.

His eyes landed on a photo from beneath a pile of old newspapers. He attempted to pry it out from beneath a newspaper, and, as luck would have it, the pile teetered over, flooding the carpet with an endless supply of paper and books.

The picture was just a little smaller than his hand, and the film had given the image a reddish-brown tint. He pulled the picture closer because he could not believe what he saw. In the picture, the man on the left had dark caramel skin, thinning, curly black hair, and a growing bald spot. On top of his shoulders, he was carrying a small boy dressed in a lightly colored shirt with a duck on it and a matching pair of soccer shorts. Instantly, his vision became blurry from seeing the bright smiles on their faces. An old wound that he would never forget reopened, and gushing from it was the sorrow he would always carry with him. The face in the photo was one that he, to this day, would long to see just one more time. Just to see in a simple photo, the smile on his father's face filled with happiness and joy made this whole trip and the horrors they had seen absolutely worth it.

A smaller light-skinned was next to his father in the photo. His hair was slicked back, and on his shoulder was a young girl with dark hair. She was wearing a shirt with a picture of a guitarist and a key dangling from her necklace. *Holy crap, that's Gracey*, he thought.

"What the hell?" He shouted. He shook his head and blinked to ensure he wasn't losing his mind.

He felt his heart pounding in his chest. It made sense that his dad would be in a photo with Grace's father. He had no idea he had already met her. His father never mentioned anything about them. Why would he have kept this a secret?

He took a deep breath, and his eyes narrowed on a third adult in the picture with spiked black hair. He held a small caramel-colored child, his hair parted and combed to the side. Jayden realized the young boy dressed in jean shorts was his best friend. This meant that Tony must have met Grace, too, and maybe he remembered this trip.

Jayden placed the photo in his pocket because he knew his friends would want to see it. He knelt down, sifting through a pile of newspapers, and God knows what he had knocked over. The pile of trash was about as thick as the dirty laundry he used to have in his closet at the Dragon Monastery.

He channeled some magical energy and combed through the pile with blazing speed. Jayden triggered his Dragon Sight spell to read through the newspapers and leaflets precisely. From what he could tell, none of the news-related material had anything to do with the Aggeloi people; in fact, they appeared to be perfectly random. This didn't make any sense, other than he knew there may have been some intent to hide something within the piles of documents. The other thought he had was that Grace's dad and the Aggeloi government were nothing but hoarders.

Two photos slid out from between the pages of a wildlife magazine. At first, he thought they must have been prints from the magazine itself. A smile creased his lips when he flipped over the photo closest to him. The print was about the size of the one in his pocket and had developed a yellowish tint from age. In the center of the photo was Grace, who looked to be about 10 or 11. On the right of her was a woman in her thirties with blonde hair. She was wearing some sort of rock band t-shirt with jeans and a belt with spiked studs sticking out. To the right of Grace, Jayden assumed was her father, the King of the Aggeloi. He looked a few years older than the picture in his pocket. They had their arms around each other and stood before a tree. Jayden smiled. It looked like they were a happy family. It was unfortunate how quickly things would turn for the worse.

A lightbulb turned on in this head. He quickly pulled out the picture from his pocket and held it next to the picture of Grace with his family. He could spot a tree standing in the background of the picture with his dad and the others. When he compared it to the other photo, he realized it was the same tree. The tree in both photos was the same one Grace had carved her name into. His heart jumped in his chest; this meant he and Tony had been in this cabin before. This was not the first time they had been to the country of the Aggeloi.

He set those photos aside and reached for the second print that had fallen out of the magazine. This picture was larger than the other two. He had to unfold it like a piece of paper. Approximately thirty people were sitting on chairs in the photo. At the bottom of the photo were the words "The Witnesses Academy Graduating Class" written in bold. The photo itself was black and white but had the first names of each student written in silver beneath their individual pictures.

Jayden's eyes very quickly landed on the image of his father sitting right next to Tony's dad. Written in barely visible lettering were the names Dion and Raiden. They looked to be in their late teens, maybe early twenties. Both seemed filled with joyful spirits, with grins that signified they were the class troublemakers. For Jayden, it was weird to see Tony's dad so happy. He always seemed to have a stern look on his face. Even when they reunited with him at the Water Temple, he seemed perpetually sad and broken.

He continued to scan the photo to see if there were any other familiar faces. In the bottom right-hand corner of the photo, he saw a young Miss Tonya. She did look a little more mature in this photo than his dad, but that made sense because she was older. He didn't quite understand the age ranges for The Witnesses; it might be standard to have a wide range for any graduating year. Jayden also spotted the names of Macy's and Bryce's parents and even spotted Grace's father within the mix. Even a few more names and faces in the photo reminded him of people he knew in Eiréné. He wasn't sure if it was them, but it was too coincidental to not be.

He slowly analyzed this graduating class to see if he could recognize other names. For a moment, his hands became clammy. He could feel his heart pound in his chest, and his legs became weak to the point that he collapsed onto the ground. His wrists twitched, and his eyes began to water. Every ounce of sorrow came bursting forth. He saw a face he thought he would never see again. A smile he would only get to see in his dreams. The name written in silver letters right next to the picture of his old neighbor was Maria. His mother sat in her dark graduation robes with a matching cap on that small chair. Her dark hair with hints of brown and her pale skin, matched with that warm smile, filled his soul with joy.

Jayden could still remember holding her hand until the final moment when the cancer took her. He still remembered watching her struggle through the pain. How he watched the gentle glow of her skin slowly fade away. The one thing she never lost was her laughter and her smile. What he wouldn't give to hear her voice just one more time.

He wiped his eyes and took a deep breath. With his vision blurred from tears, he noticed the letters *CRLNA* on the photo. Jayden shook his head and looked at the name once more. His eyes grew wider as he processed what he was seeing. The name under the individual was Corallina. Her hair appeared to be just as black as his martial arts uniform. It was almost impossible to tell from the picture, but there were barely visible streaks of white in her hair. Jayden knew those streaks would have been visibly blue if this was a modern photo. Her pointed jawline and stern look were unmistakable. In this class photo, the young lady sitting between his mother and Tony's mother, Moriah, was Lady Coral.

***

The wires in his brain were firing off like pistols in the night. He sprinted down the hall and tried to process how small his world had just become. There was no way that three photos could answer so many questions and still create more. He now fully understood how Lady Coral would have known who his father was so well. Jayden assumed she could have been recruited at some point while still a part of the Southern Covenant and later betrayed all of them by joining the Daimonia. It was all a guess, but it explains how she could have known so much about his father's mission to acquire *The Key*. He needed to check on one more thing to confirm if there was any truth to the photos.

Jayden darted out the front door and turned toward the lone tree. Once he reached the top of the hill, he knelt down and began to examine the etchings in the bark. He pulled out the academy graduation photo from his pocket and unfolded it. He used his index finger to trace the etchings of Grace's name. A bright orange bead of flame filled the cracks in the wood, making her name shine like a neon sign. The flames were just an illusion; he figured Grace would most likely kill him if he used a real fire spell.

He tried to trigger his Dragon Eye to examine the tree for names. Unfortunately, there appeared to be some magical protection over the tree because his vision instantly blurred, and he could not focus on anything. He let out a loud groan in frustration. He would have to take his time to see if he could find any of the names from the photo etched into the tree.

The young Dragon Warrior aimed to use the location of Grace's name as a reference point for locating any others. He figured Grace's name would probably have been etched in the tree when the second photo was taken. Even with her name as a reference point, it was starting to be challenging. Many of the etchings close enough to Grace's were hardly legible, and a few were written in symbols he had never seen before. Another challenge he noticed is that, over time, sections of the bark had become worn or damaged from the elements. So, there was a chance that all of his efforts might not amount to anything.

"JAYDEN LONEOAK!"

Jayden was caught off guard so badly that he nearly jumped out of his shoes. His heart jumped in his throat, and he slowly turned his head. Two strong, independent women were stomping toward him, with Tony in tow.

"Why the hell are you burning my tree?" Grace shouted.

Jayden put his hands up in defense. "It's not what it …."

Before he could finish his sentence, Aiko appeared out of nowhere and fired a beam of high-pressured water at the tree and the center of his chest. The air was knocked out of him

287

before he crashed into the ground. His sternum felt like he had been hit by a steel beam. Jayden was sure the bruise he would get from Aiko would be permanent.

Jayden coughed, "What the hell? It was just an illusion. Tony, why didn't you tell her that?"

His best friend laughed, "I'm not going to lie; I really wanted to tell her something, but then I didn't."

He shook his head and muttered, "I hate you." He reached into his pocket, pulled out the picture of Grace with her family, and handed it to her. "This is for you," he said.

She took the picture, and her eyes teared up. Grace kneeled beside him, wrapped her arms around him, and kissed his cheek. Then she whispered in his ear, "Thank you."

His best friend stood over him and looked down on him. "This is what happens when you try and do stuff on your own. Why did you run through the house to look at the tree?"

Jayden attempted to return to his feet but settled for sitting against the tree. He pulled out the first picture he had found from his pocket. Tony took it from him, and instantly, his eyes widened in shock. Even Grace and Macy, who leaned over to look, were equally surprised. This answered the question of whether Grace or Tony remembered meeting each other. Even more so, since there was a chance that Macy had been to this cabin too, it answered if she remembered anything.

He went to speak, but he had to be careful. He didn't want to share information about the panoramic-sized picture yet. Partially because when Aiko blasted him, it was knocked out of his hand, and he didn't see where it landed. The other reason was he did not want to freak Gracey out. He knew that being back at the cabin was an emotional experience for her; he knew that if she learned that Lady Coral had been there before, she might be exceptionally disturbed.

Jayden took a deep breath and said, "I am trying to see if there are any names on this tree that look familiar to any of you. Specifically, names that may be tied to us."

They all nodded and began searching the tree. Jayden stood back up and began to look around the location of Grace's name. His eyes quickly zeroed in on the photo resting just inches from his shoes; he quickly snatched the picture before she noticed it. He moved his gaze toward the lower trunk and saw the letters *DDS*. He used his index finger to highlight those letters with an illusion of fire.

Now, to the untrained eye, those letters would mean nothing. However, if you went to the Eiréné Fair, the Eiréné Autumn Festival, or the Eiréné Winter Carnival, then those letters would strike fear into your mind, for they stood for David, Donna, and Sarah. Her family would always make T-shirts with those initials to compete at the pie eating contests, the three-legged races, and any opportunity to be overly competitive at a festival. One could argue that Sarah and her mom took those contests too seriously and that her dad was an instigator. He would get the crowd, and the girls riled up before any contest. It was a simpler time back then, and he missed seeing them.

"I got one!" Macy shouted. "Wait, no, I found more than one. I have Miss Tonya right here; my parents' names are just above hers, and I found your mom's name. Oh, wait, scratch that, I found three more. I can see my parents' names and Bryce's father's name. Ugh, I hate those people now that I know how much they betrayed everyone."

"What the hell," Tony growled. "Why the hell is my mom's name on this tree?"

"Be cautious about how you speak about your mother," Shane barked. "Even though many of the names that I see on this tree are Rogue Witnesses, at one time, they all served under the traditional umbrella for the organization. If half of what I heard about her was true, then she deserves an ounce of praise and a greater amount of your sympathy."

"You can go screw yourself," Tony snapped as he stormed off with his fists clenched.

Jayden turned to go after his friend when he felt a hard tug on his shirt. He glanced down and realized the Aggeloi Princess was tugging on his shirt. He was instantly alarmed because Grace's lightly tanned complexion was now ghostly white. Her right index finger was shaking as it was directed at something near the tree's base. Jayden dropped to her level to get a better look. The letters that she was pointing at read *Corallina.*

He grimaced and reached into his pocket, pulling out the last photo. "I need you to see this."

Chapter 26

A Lost World

The hardest pills to swallow are the ones that leave you incomplete. There are often situations that will leave you with more questions that will never have an adequate answer. He knew sharing that last photo would open some old wounds that might have been better off closed. Jayden had no idea that examining the tree would trigger so many emotions in each of them. He even sensed that Shane was intrigued by all of the elements at play.

Once the photo was revealed, it was a double-edged sword. For one, it was interesting, to say the least, to see their parents and individuals they looked up to in a different environment. It can be hard to imagine what your parents were like when they were younger, even more so to see them before the most difficult moments in their lives occurred. So, in a way, the photo was like a time capsule that captured an ideal moment. This graduation picture was worth a thousand words, and they weren't all good.

After Tony had stormed off, he spoke in private with Shane. Jade was unsure what was said, but he understood that his best friend had learned more than he had expected. Even the information the werefox was willing to share with all of them about their family connections with Lady Coral seemed heavily redacted. Jayden suspected that Shane either knew more than he was letting on or that there was a large gap of information that he was unaware of. Either way, Shane said it was important for them to learn from these small tidbits of information but not get lost in it because it did not change their current path. Lady Coral was dead, and Tony's mother was God knows where. He did caution them, though. He said that one photo only told part of the story. Many other Witnesses graduated before and after that picture was taken. Many of those same individuals went the Rogue's path and later became members of the Daimonia.

Jayden glanced up as Grace opened the door to the small storage shed if you could call it that. To him, it looked like an old outhouse that was barely big enough for one person. There was a crescent moon engraved near the top of the door. Grace said a tunnel was built beneath the ocean, leading north. She had no proof other than a rather vague dream she had, and that Sarah told her she had nightmares about the tunnel. He still did not know what an outhouse/shed had to do with it.

A bright orange light clicked on when Grace stepped onto the wooden floor. The room was about the size of a small living room. There must have been enchantment placed on the building because the interior was considerably larger than the exterior. Still, it was a rather small fit for all of them. He was basically shoulder-to-shoulder with Gracey and Macy, which he did not mind in the slightest. It was good times for the most part, other than when they were getting annoyed with him bumping into each other. Shane was doing the whole Macy is like my daughter; don't touch her, you bastard thing.

Along the floor was a small rug that took up most of the center of the room. There was a tribal symbol of an eagle in the middle of it. The fabric was a mixture of cream and a faded brown color. In the back left corner of the room was a tan oval-shaped end table with an old ceramic ashtray on top. Just to his right, near the back wall, was a small door that opened to a closet. There was an old broom, a dustpan, and, based on Macy's sudden loud screaming, a decomposing rat or a spider. Either way, he did not want to get closer to that closet.

A full-sized door was on the far-left side of the room, just a few feet from the end table. There was nothing unique or special about it. The door appeared to have been painted black about one hundred years ago and was fading and chipping in spots. He was starting to think that the door matched the aesthetic of the rest of the shed because it was absolutely useless. No matter how hard they tried to pull the door open, it wouldn't budge. Not even Shane, with his mighty werefox grip, could open it. Truth be told, Jayden was half tempted to blast it to pieces with a magic spell.

"So Gracey…" he said before he was completely cut off.

"Don't you say a damn thing, she snarled.

Jayden bowed, "Yes, your highness."

Tony turned to him, "Well, do you have any bright ideas, genius?"

He shrugged, "I have no idea. All I know is that we need to go north without a boat. We don't have a magic carpet or airship to do that."

Shane walked by and lightly smacked Jayden in the back of the head with the cylinder of his revolver. "Grace, I want you to try something. You see that key around your neck; why don't you try and use it."

Jayden was still rubbing the back of his head. "Hey, old man, I mean, Werefox. There isn't a keyhole. Do you want her to just poke the door with the key?"

He barred his razor-sharp teeth and smacked Jayden in the back of the head with his other pistol. Shane bowed his muzzle reassuringly at Grace. "Just trust," he said.

The Aggeloi Princess lifted the necklace over her head. When she gripped the key, its iron body quickly morphed into a key made of silver. She pressed it against the doorknob. The moment the metallic key made contact; a powerful gust of wind blew through the shed. The chilling cold wind sliced through their clothes like a knife and howled with the force of a pack of wolves. Grace's blue and silver hair became very staticky and began to glow. Intense magical power pulsated from every fiber within her being.

Jayden turned to his best friend and shouted, "Not this crap again!"

Once Grace had pulled *The Key* back from the door, it reshaped itself back into its white ivory form. While *The Key* returned to normal, her hair returned to its typical punk rocker state, and the magical energy pulsating from her had ceased. Then, the door disappeared completely, leaving a dark, empty space behind.

Shane grinned, "Crypto…"

Jayden cocked his head to the side, "Curr, what now?"

The werefox sighed deeply as he began to load an explosive round into his pistol. Jayden quickly put his hands up in surrender. "Please, for the love of God, don't shoot me. You already knocked some sense into me."

"Yeah," Tony chimed in. "Jayden is already missing a few brain cells. You probably just took out the rest."

Shane shook his head, "God bless the Masters at the Dragon Monastery for having the patience to deal with you two idiots. Anyway, I said Crypto; it is a type of magic that, in its simplest form, is a magical ability to imbue keys with certain attributes or, in this case, make them change and open doors. It can open magical barriers and dimensions in more advanced forms or keep powerful spirits locked away. Very few teachers of that type of magic are still around, and I doubt your Grace learned it living with the witches. That kind of magic can also be passed down through your genes."

Grace glanced at him sheepishly. "When we fought Lady Coral, she thought there was something special about Sarah and I. Do you think this crypto stuff is why?"

Shane placed his pistol back in its holster. "I believe so."

Jayden turned to him. "How would Lady Coral be able to know that, though?"

The werefox scratched his furry chin as he took the time to think. "If I had to guess, it would have most likely come from her being a witch. Witches tend to be able to sense what magical affinity or type someone uses. For some of them, it's almost instinctual. With that said, I don't think she fully understood how crypto magic works or how it would have helped with *The Key*. It is apparent that Grace interacts somewhat with the object and could even use it to break the barrier on this door. I don't think she even knew what she was doing. However, the magic within her just did it for her. I also see the connection that Sarah has to it is a lot stronger. I remember reading about the Great Cryptologists who could use their abilities beyond what most could do. I guarantee you that Sarah must have descended from the ones who made *The Key*. That is a huge concern, but Grace made me realize that things may have become more dangerous."

"What do you mean?" Gracey asked.

He sighed, "It means *The Key* can open things that it was probably not intended to open. Even you were able to use it with relative ease. This means someone with an affinity for crypto magic could do the same thing. If we survive this ordeal, we must find a way to destroy that thing."

"You are absolutely right," Macy interjected as she pat her superior on the head.

"Now, let's see what's behind door number one." The Aggeloi Princess said with a hint of glee before she leaped, screaming into the darkness.

His head was knocked back by the pressure. The rate at which they were descending was at such a great pace that it made his cheeks jiggle like he was on a roller coaster. He couldn't see his hands in front of him, but based on Macy's screams, he could tell they were sliding through a tunnel. Droplets of water landed on his forehead. The ground beneath him was slick and muddy. He had no idea where they were going. For all he knew, this slip and slide ended at a wall, waiting for them to splat.

He felt his hip slide to the right, his face slamming into a jagged rock wall. Blood trickled down from a cut on his eyebrow and scratches on the side of his cheek and neck. Jayden pressed his hands against the wall, channeled a mild fire-blasting spell, and used it to push himself slightly off the wall. The bright lights dancing on his palms were keeping him inches away from a cracked skull, providing him with just enough visibility to gain an idea of their surroundings.

Jayden tried to process what he could now see, which still wasn't much faster than his eyes and brain could keep up with, making assessing anything harder than any class he took in school. From what he could tell, they were sliding down a muddy chute probably used by giant worms or an army of gophers. There were large tree roots that snaked around the walls of the tunnel. A small forest of mildly luminescent lime-colored moss had attached itself to the ceiling and tunnel walls. He noticed a few large horned beetles and black-striped lemmings scurrying amongst the network of roots and emerald-colored brake ferns.

His body hit a bump, and he was launched into the air. He bumped his head against a sharp root in the ceiling. His body seized. It felt like a thousand ice-cold needles were piercing every inch of his body. His flame was doused the moment he crashed into the roaring underground river. The rushing waves made his body spin in a circle like he was pulled into a whirlpool. His nose burned from the high-pressure water slamming into his face. He felt his body being pulled down into the depths. His lungs were burning like a furnace as he struggled to fight being dragged down any further. Bubbles of air escaped his lips as he frantically tried to breach the surface.

Once he got his head above water, the sound of the roaring waves was absolutely deafening. He let out a wheeze, and as he turned his head, he saw a bright light. *Oh, that's just amazing*, he thought. His body felt weightless, and he could feel a warm breeze against his face. That's when a large lake and brown land mass appeared below him.

"OOO SHIT!!!" He yelled.

Jayden rotated his body forward as he went into freefall. He moved to straighten out his body and made himself as flat as possible. With his hands by his side, he went into a pencil dive. Once he hit the water, he felt a tingling pain in his legs. The lake water became darker as he continued in his dive. His head was throbbing, and his heart was his chest. He needed to find the strength to keep going.

The young Dragon Warrior let out a desperate air bubble. Then he channeled his left-over magical energy into his legs and his arms. Eventually, he could kick his legs and swim toward the surface. As soon as he felt the gentle breeze on his face, he breathed a wheezy sigh of relief. He heard a loud scream while swimming to the shore and glanced up.

***

He blinked his eyes open and was momentarily blinded by a dazzling blue light. Jayden tried to focus and noticed it was shaped like a tiny shield of pure blue light. He felt a cool liquid land on his cheek, and he instantly felt more relaxed. Another droplet landed on his forehead. A smokey green-looking object was floating just a few feet above him. After every couple of seconds, it would release a few droplets of a green liquid. Whenever the droplets landed, he could feel the tension within his body decrease. He almost felt like going back to sleep.

Then he realized the stars were out. He couldn't remember watching the sun set. In fact, he did not remember landing on the ground. All he could recall was diving in a lake and then nothing. His eyes burned again as a bright magenta-colored light appeared just inches above him.

"Oopsies!" The light moved slightly out of view. "Is that better? I didn't mean to blind you."

She moved her glowing hands. Macy's moderately tan face and beautiful smile came into view. Her hands were glowing, and she was chanting in a language he had never heard. It reminded him of the elvish that Sarah would speak when casting certain spells. Usually, those were a type of healing spell. Did he get hurt, he wondered?

A figure stepped out of the darkness and stood at the base of his feet. He glanced up. The eyes that met his appeared to be piercing through to the depths of his soul. Shane spun his pistol and shook his head as he glared down at the Dragon Warrior.

The werefox flashed his razor-sharp teeth. "You are a perfect combination of dumb and lucky."

Jayden couldn't quite decide if he should be offended or not. Before he could respond, Macy motioned for him to be silent. Shane wheeled around and cocked his pistol. The sound of leaves rustling broke the silence blanketed over the clearing. Branches snapped, and the trees swayed back and forth violently. The ground beneath him shook like they were in an earthquake. His ears started ringing as a monster roared into the darkness. The roar was so powerful that the shield above his head disappeared, and Macy's hands stopped glowing. He felt a sudden rush of an unbearable amount of pain in his cheekbones.

Jayden held his cheek in his hand. "Where the hell are we, and what happened to me?"

Grace appeared next to him. Tears were streaming down her face, and she swung her arms around him as she sobbed. He was really confused by her sudden affection and tried to pull away. But she continued to squeeze him.

"I'm, I'm, "I'm so sorry, Jayden. I didn't mean to."
She whimpered.

"What did you do?" He asked.

Shane waved his paw, "I'm going to stop you right
there, Jayden. You have a habit of making things worse when
you talk. So, I'm going to answer that question for her. When
you landed in the lake, you decided to do the classic touristy
move of 'Oohing and Awwing' at the landscape around you
instead of moving out of the way because the rest of us were
speeding after you. Long story short, you looked up at the last
second, and Grace's boot landed in your face. Hopefully, it
knocked some sense into you. Luckily for you, we were able to
conduct an experimental Triad healing spell to fix your face."

Jayden glanced up and turned toward his best friend. "I
thought you didn't know how to do any healing spells. I don't
remember you knowing how to do *Healing Rain*."

Tony shrugged, "Me neither. I guess I am just that good
and talented. I mean, it is a Master Level spell."

"You are such a tool," Jayden replied.

"I can't believe I got so lucky to be stuck on this
mission with you two morons," Shane chided. "To answer your
other question, I am not quite sure where we are, but as you
heard from the monster, we are not alone. We are also not at
the top of the food chain. The magical energy radiating from
the creatures down here is something that I have never
experienced. I guess this is an old nature preserve made by *The
Elders*. I recall from a book I read in the archives that prior to
The Great War, they were beginning to build these nature
preserves. The war sped that along because it was so
destructive to humans and nature. There are enough
enchantments protecting this area to keep it protected. This
means that under no circumstance do we draw any unnecessary
attention to ourselves. We are walking through ancient lands
that deserve our respect.

***

Soft whiskers and a wet nose brushed against his skin. The creature grunted as it investigated the large human that stood in its way. The words Shane mentioned the other night were still resonating within him. So, he did not want to move.

His leg jerked as the creature sniffed his shin. It tickled a little bit. The creature grunted but sounded soft and gentle. Jayden felt a twinge of pain in his chest, which meant the magical power radiating from this creature was something else. He squinted to take a peek at his nemesis.

The creature stood about six inches tall at the shoulder. His eyes widened at its relatively small round ears and bearlike face. The creature had a tiny snout with auburn-colored hair. It licked his face, which was emotionally confusing. In fact, minus the giant magical energy radiating from its relatively small, cute, and cuddly body, the animal seemed sweet, like a wombat or a bear cub. He wasn't scared of it all and decided to sit up.

Immediately, the creature jumped back, and its eyes turned crimson red. Its magical energy spiked dramatically. He looked around their camping area and was the only one there. Jayden glanced at a tree grove and noticed his friends hiding in it.

"Jayden, don't move." Said a voice inside his head.

"Um, who dis?" He replied inside his head.

"Jayden, it's me, Macy," the voice inside his head said. "Tony showed me how to do your Dragon Link spell. I guess it's a Phoenix and Dragon Link spell, in my case. But anyway, that monster is level thirty-nine! Do not touch it!"

Jayden diverted his eyesight from the creature and laid back down. He pretended to be asleep to help the creature relax. "Is level thirty-nine high?"

Macy sent a message into his mind, "Yes, it is very high. According to Tony, you are level twenty-four. So, you are probably going to get beat up by that thing. Don't let it's size fool you."

"That is some bull...," Jayden stopped when he realized he was arguing with a voice in his head. "Tony is telling you a fib. I am not a level twenty-four. I am probably the highest level you have ever seen."

She shook her head, "I am not really sure, to be honest. I am not good at sensing magical and skill energies from humans. Anyway, you need to remain still until it moves on. Shane doesn't want you drawing the attention of the bigger monsters."

Jayden sighed, "Did you guys run up in that tree so I would have to deal with this nonsense."

Ten minutes went by with no response. Macy's silence and having to remain deathly still around this dangerously cute creature made things all too clear for him. He was left behind as bait.

Once the little guy left, he jumped to his feet. For the first time in a while, he felt absolutely perfect. The pain in his cheek was now a far-gone memory. Even his magical energy seemed to be even greater than normal. He felt like when he had the *Jade Blade*. His body must have absorbed some additional magical energies in the air.

His friends rejoined him in the clearing and quickly grabbed their things. Grace indicated they needed to continue to make their way north. While his friend pointed off into the distance, he heard a high-pitched cry from above. Three dark objects moved through the clouds above. He triggered his magical energy to get a better look at them. As his eyes adjusted and zoomed in on the creatures, he couldn't believe what he saw.

The monsters cruising through the sky were like something out of a movie. At first, he thought they were just your run-of-the-mill reptilian birds, but these animals were bigger than any he had ever seen. Their wingspan was at least six feet wide, accompanied by long, razor-sharp talons. Their beaks were about the length of his arm, with rows of pointed teeth. Behind the flying reptiles swung their long-spiked tails. Beyond their intimidating appearance, he could feel the terrifying, magical power emanating from them.

Once the reptilian birds finished flying over, Jayden took point, and they began heading north. He ushered them along a thin trail leading into a thick wooded area. The forest was lush with life and beauty. They were greeted by an array of plants blanketing the forest floor. He noticed dark green ferns and trees covered with moss. There were glowing butterflies as big as his hand gliding along the lush rows of flowers.

He stopped to watch a family of light blue colored salamanders scurrying along a tree log, chasing after some unusually large crickets. He knelt and picked up one of the salamanders. The creature's skin was both damp and smooth. He flipped the tiny animal over and noticed its light blue underbelly changed colors as it moved in his hand. Another thing he noticed was the salamander excreted a clear liquid from its neck. The moment the liquid touched his hand, he felt a little woozy, and his magical power slowly drained. As his magic drained, the salamander grew. He quickly placed the animal back on the log before it grew too big.

Jayden stepped over the log and walked around a wide tree. His foot slipped when he stepped on a mossy root. He leaned forward to catch himself and felt a twinge in the pit of his stomach. Instinctively, he ducked, just narrowly missing a large spike launched toward his head and slammed into the tree behind him.

His jaw almost hit the floor when he realized how big of a projectile he had just dodged. The spike extended from the tree to a spot in the ground four feet behind him. The base of the projectile was about four feet wide and six inches thick; the spike became thinner the closer it got to the pointed end. The spike was dark gray and appeared to be made of some sort of rock he had never seen before. When Jayden touched its bumpy surface, he could feel magical energy pulsating through the object. It was like the spike had its own heartbeat.

He felt another twinge in his stomach and jumped high up. Two more spikes slammed into the tree below him. He landed on top of one of the center spikes as it came down. He flipped forward and landed on a patch of mud. Pulling himself out of the mud, he heard a soft popping sound and a low grunt. Then he swung his sword to deflect a volley of rocks and dirt clods speeding toward him. Jayden jumped back on top of one of the spikes as the fern bushes in front of him shook violently.

Just as he landed, his attacker stepped into view. The animal looked like a humongous brown bear. Four long spines protruded from the back of its neck. The bear's claws appeared to be made of some metal and could extend at will. There was also a white stripe stretching across his chest. His ears perked up as he heard rustling from the bed of flowers on his right. He smiled as three bear cubs jumped out of the bushes and ran toward the big bear trying to kill him. That bear turned out to be their mommy.

The bear nuzzled her young and then disappeared back into the foliage. Once he jumped down from the tree, he breathed a sigh of relief. He leaned to the left to avoid a volley of three-foot-long spikes. Jayden drew his sword and deflected another volley of spikes and rocks. He channeled his fire magic into his legs and jumped high up. When he was high enough, he jabbed his sword into the side of the tree.

Then, the bear sprung out from behind a patch of bushes. The creature extended its metallic claws and slashed through its embedded spikes and tree trunk like butter. As the tree teetered backward, he pressed his feet against the bark and pushed off. He channeled fire energy around his legs, summoned a glide spell, and blasted forward.

He had no idea where he was going as he zagged between the trees. All he knew was that he was aiming north and hopefully drawing enough attention that the bear and other monsters in the forest would focus on him, not his friends. Jayden snapped his fingers, and the flames exploding around him ceased. He tucked and somersaulted forward on his way to the ground.

Jayden landed in a small clearing bordered by redwoods and boxwood shrubs. He stepped forward and stopped when he heard branches breaking and leaves rustling. A black bear stepped out from behind a redwood to his left, and another brown bear jumped out of a bush behind him.

Immediately, he snapped his fingers, and his body instantly morphed into a large floating fireball. Three obsidian and iron spikes burst from the ground, piercing the orange flames. The bears grunted and pawed at the ground. The brown bear sniffed him in his fire sprite form and ran off.

The Dragon Warrior waited for the black bear to leave before reverting to his normal form. Once the bear left, there was a popping sound, and his fiery form began to shimmer. When his shoes touched the forest floor, he doubled over and began to throw up.

"You are such an idiot," a familiar voice said. "You aren't supposed to transform back that quick if you stay in your element that long, or you will get quite dizzy."

Jayden glanced up as his best friend handed him a cloth. He wiped his face and tried to get up to his feet. His head was still spinning, his skin feeling exceptionally warm. He took a deep breath as the reality that he had almost turned into a shish kebab started to set in.

Tony pat him on the back, "You did a great job drawing their attention like that. Shane was able to find a way out of this forest while you were being chased. But that was close, man. Do you think your Flame Shield or Armors could have stopped those attacks?"

He shook his head, "I have no idea. I didn't know the bears could use earth or metal magic like that. They were so powerful, but I couldn't sense any of them."

"Well, according to Macy, sometimes a creature can be so powerful that you can't sense anything. Our brains or magical powers aren't strong enough to sense something like that," Tony replied. "I guess it's like when we used to spar with Mariko or Master Thai. You could sense some of their magic, but we knew it wasn't even close to how much they really had. Even without them trying to hide their magical power, we could never get a good enough read on theirs, but that's neither here nor there. The real thing you need to remember is that this is just a stepping stone. We have a bigger battle to fight soon, and you must be ready for it.

Chapter 27

The Tunnel of Death

Tony led him through a grove of trees that had grown close together. Jayden noticed that the trees were smaller than the ones he had seen thus far, which hopefully meant they were close to the exit. Since arriving in this underground jungle, the air felt cold and damp. However, as they continued to hike through the thick brush, he could feel a change in the air. He could feel the air becoming drier and slightly warmer.

Jayden stepped over a bush, his shoe landing on orange-colored dirt. He took a few more steps out from the tree line. Looking back at the forest, he was taken aback by its size. The forest seemed to stretch for miles, and the trees were still unbelievably tall. He wondered how many other surprises they would have run into if they didn't have to rush through it.

The ground beneath him shook like he was in the middle of an earthquake. Then it shook again, and his ears perked at a low moan above. He turned to his right, and his jaw dropped. Approaching them from the east was a herd of the largest creatures he had ever seen.

They were taller than any dragon he had ever heard of. Their four legs were larger than most of the trees in the forest. They had long necks with equally long tails and relatively small heads. Their skin was made of slightly rough gray scales. They had rows of rounded teeth they must have used to munch on the fruits and leaves near the tops of the trees.

With each lumbering step they took, the ground rumbled. The peaceful giants had a small cadre of little ones and juveniles running alongside their feet. He had no idea how the adults weren't turning them into pancakes, but he guessed they had a system worked out.

He cuffed his ear as a loud roar pierced through the pleasant mood of the plane. Jayden felt his magical energy waiver from the force of the sound. The giant herbivores were now staring daggers in his direction. Instantly, his knees felt weak as two of the largest animals in the herd began moving toward him and his best friend.

Then he heard another guttural roar that shook the ground beneath him. This time, he realized the sound was coming from behind them. Jayden turned, and his knees buckled at the sight. His hands were shaking, and tears streamed from his eyes as he trembled with fear.

He had seen dragons before but had only been physically close to the small ones at the Monastery. The creatures that spooked the peaceful giants were no dragons, although they both possessed similar menacing features and unimaginable power. Three large monsters approached them from the west. In pure height, they stood about twenty-five to thirty feet tall. They had five razor-sharp claws attached to each of their limber arms. Each step they took left an imprint on the ground that would last for eternity. Their eyes were dark

307

as night, with yellow irises resembling the moon. Opening their gigantic maw revealed a row of teeth as long and sharp as a short sword. Their scales were an ugly combination of brown and green, which perfectly mirrored the sense of dread they caused on the plain.

Tony bumped up against him, "What do we do?"

Jayden tried to speak but was still in shock. The last time he recalled being this scared was when his father ran off to save the people of Eiréné. In a twisted way, this was far beyond that; he had no frame of reference for this moment. They were stuck between two groups of powerful creatures that had hardly noticed that he and Tony were even there.

The powerful carnivores let out another earth-shaking roar and sprinted toward their prey. He felt the air around him become icy cold, and goosebumps appeared on his arms. The light that brightened the plains became obstructed like they were experiencing a solar eclipse. Soon, it was as dark as night. The only light he could see was the glowing eyes of the herbivores and the blue ball of energy expanding within their mouths.

"Oh shit," he gasped.

The peaceful giants sent a blast of an unimaginably powerful blue and white energy beam. As the beam passed over them, the temperature around him dropped like the force of a hammer. When the beams slammed into two of their adversaries, the energy exploded, sending shards of ice into the air. The monsters were knocked backward by the force of the blasts and the shockwave from the explosion. The third predator stomped its feet, and mounds of dirt began to form. The coalescing mounds of soil piling on each other reminded him of watching a small wave beginning to breach the surface. There was no doubt in his mind that once this tidal wave of dirt and rock was completely formed, it would absolutely wipe them off the map.

Tony grabbed him by the arm, "Snap out of it. We gotta go!"

His best friend dragged him as the wave of dirt and rocks sped toward them. Tony channeled his lightning magic into his legs. Jayden followed suit with his own magic. Then they sprinted toward a thin line of trees where Shane stood waving them on.

"Don't stop, keep running!" The werefox yelled. "I'll be right behind you. Grace is on the other side. Don't stop running until you see her!"

Jayden took a moment to glance back at the war between the monstrous gods. His eyes could still barely take in the breadth of the moment. This battle was like something out of a movie for the young Dragon Warrior. The sound of their earth-shaking roars and the destructive power of their blasts of magic shook him to his very core. To think that animals like this used to roam in the world above was absolutely frightening. He could only imagine how strong the warriors from the must have had to be just to survive.

His eyes widened as he watched the largest herbivore leap forward just in enough time to absorb the monstrous wave of earth and rock. The creature was knocked back, crashing into a row of trees. The peaceful giant managed to get back to its gigantic feet. The monster was bruised and covered in deep scratches. However, there was no ounce of fear in the herbivore's eyes. There was no doubt in his mind that those predators hunting them would be fighting for their lives.

The Dragon Warrior was humbled by the power that they had displayed. Even the magical power he had experienced from the brown and black bear was something he had never seen. To a degree, he could understand why *The Elders* would want to keep them safe. However, he wondered if the world was safer with them in this preserve.

He took a deep breath, finding his strength and getting over the shock of those monstrous creatures. Jayden channeled more of his magic into his legs. Then he sped through a wooded area and was even able to leave his best friend in the dust. As he continued to speed up, he could feel the air around him become more arid. The trees he was gliding past seemed to look smaller and more depressing. Dried-up twigs and tiny cactuses were coming into view. Then he slowed his pace just enough and burst through a thicket of dried-out bushes. With his legs scrapped from their tiny thorns, he stepped onto the edge of a desert.

The desert sloped and went back up slightly to form a small sandy hill. At the edge of the tiny desert was a wall of red rock covering the edges of the canyon. The entrance to the cave was in the center of this wall of rock and red dirt. Grace and Macy stood outside the cave, showing no signs that they really wanted to enter it.

As he peered into the cave, he sensed the walls were damp and caught glimpses of water dripping from the stalactites on the ceiling. There were dark green puddles of liquid and geysers spewing forth ice-cold water. He watched as a family of large rodents breached the surface of these puddles as they scurried across the rocky floor. His eyes focused on a series of bright yellow lights in the section of the stalactites to his right. He focused and realized the lights he saw were the yellow eyes of a family of Horned Vampire Bats. He remembered reading about them in a zoological book his father gave him. They were supposedly pretty large bats, although it was tough to judge with their wings folded. However, he did recall their sharp fangs could pierce even the toughest cowhides. It would also release a poison that paralyzed its victims. The large horn protruding from their foreheads was both sharp and strong. They were known to use the horn to dig and could even knock down or pierce an opponent if they felt they were in danger. Jayden wasn't quite sure how aggressive they were, but he did not want to find out either. He figured being attacked by bats would probably give him nightmares for life.

The Dragon Warrior took a deep breath and tried taking a begrudging step into the cave, but his body would not move any farther. He shivered as a cold chill went down his spine. Even the hairs on his arms stood on end from a combination of fear and an icy cool breeze.

His best friend was the first to officially step into the cave. He was followed by the werefox, who was now spinning both of his revolvers with his fingers like an old gunslinger. To the untrained eye, it seemed almost juvenile. However, there was a seriousness in Shane's eyes that Jayden had only briefly witnessed. The soldiers for *The Witnesses* took no chances as they took their first steps into the unknown.

Jayden felt a cold, clammy touch on his arm, nearly jumping out of his skin. He took a moment to realize Gracey was clinging to him with no intention of letting go. She seemed to shiver with every step they took, her eyes glancing in all directions frantically. He couldn't tell why she was so frightened; nothing in the cave seemed threatening besides the rats and bats, which was a slight concern. He couldn't sense any magical energy in the cave. Even his Enhanced Reaction spell, which helped him to react to dangerous situations before they occurred, was not reacting to any of the creatures in the cave. This meant that his magical senses found no threats in the cave. So, why was she so scared?

His mind flashed back to climbing the metallic ridge that led up to Lady Coral's creepy house. Even though the magic used for it was dimensional, and he didn't quite understand it, he knew aspects of that climb were based on some level of reality. Jayden began to recall that it wasn't until Lady Coral had reanimated herself on the mountain that he remembered seeing Grace this frightened. The big difference was that she had dealt with the witch before but had never been here, as far as he knew.

He felt a sudden surge of curiosity and wanted to test something. Jayden knew there was something truly off about the Aggeloi Princess. He needed to find out why. So, he reached across his body and tried to reach for *The Key* hanging from her necklace. Immediately, she slapped his hand.

"What the hell are you doing? Are you trying to cop a feel, Jayden?" she shouted.

Everyone else turned around and shot daggers back at him. Shane's right thumb cocked back the hammer and raised his pistol in his direction. Jayden quickly waved his hands in surrender. His best friend and Macy shook their heads in disapproval and turned back around.

Jayden turned to whisper in Gracey's ear. "Hey, chill, lady. I wasn't trying to do anything weird."

She rolled her eyes. "I don't believe it. I know you like my alternative/edgy persona."

He sighed, "I can't stand you sometimes. I just wanted to check out your necklace."

Grace grinned from ear to ear. "Well, all you have to do is ask, and I might say yes."

Jayden shook his head, "Gracey, can I please look at your necklace."

The Aggeloi Princess chuckled as she lifted the necklace slightly off her chest. When his fingers made contact with the metallic chain, he felt a surge of electricity go up his spine. His blood seemed cold, and he felt his magical energy slowly begin to drain as he slid his fingers closer to *The Key*.

Once he grasped *The Key* in his hand, he felt an even stronger surge of electricity shooting through his arm and up his spine. His magical energy seemed to pour into the object with the force of a raging river. Jayden tried to let it go, but his fingers would not release their grip on the metal.

Then, the hairs on his forearms stood on end. He felt goosebumps forming as he held on tighter to *The Key*. Jayden's jaw dropped as his fingers reacted to the sensation of a gentle pulse emanating from the object. The pulsating sensation was rhythmic, like feeling a heartbeat in your hand. There was something odd about how it was beating. It almost felt too real to be a simple spell or a trick of the mind. The heartbeat didn't match his own, increasing the longer he held it. He glanced at Grace when he realized the beating heart within *The Key* was connected to hers.

He forced himself to let go of the object. That was when he realized this was probably the longest interaction he had ever had with the item. At this moment, he vowed to never touch it again. Even though his connection to it was not as strong as hers or Sarah's, he knew he could not carry the burden for them. However, he had an idea of how to make life a little more bearable for her.

Jayden lightly pressed his index finger in the center of her forehead. Then he whispered, "*Thermo Therapeuo.*'

Instantly, Grace loosened her grip on him as her body began to glow. Her muscles seemed to relax, and her shoulders had less tension. The Princess's sarcastic smile returned to her briefly when she nudged against him. The spell he had cast must have relieved some of the physical and emotional drain *The Key* was superimposing on her. The unfortunate part about the spell was that it was designed to provide temporary relief under normal conditions. The condition afflicting her was far from normal.

With a renewed spirit, Grace moved toward the front of the group. He couldn't help but be impressed by her drive to push forward. Jayden couldn't imagine what it must be like to safeguard *The Key* daily since they acquired it. He was sure the item placed some other tortures on its users that were even greater than what he could sense.

The Aggeloi Princess led them through the tunnel with purpose. Her eyes were zeroed in on an unseen goal. She ignored the gigantic mice and rats scurrying along the cave floor. Grace was not even disturbed by the bats or the small cave trolls peering down at them from above. Even if the end result was their deaths, she was determined to discontinue her relationship with that key.

Grace leaned forward, channeling magical energy into her legs, then went into a dead sprint. Jayden's jaw dropped as he watched her transition back and forth between the *Invisibility Speed* and the *Enhanced Speed* techniques. One moment, he could see her, and the next, she would vanish and appear further down the tunnel. She was moving so fast that he was still standing in the same spot.

Shane and Macy had already begun chasing after her. Jayden figured he should probably do the same, so he went to pull up his pants a little higher and stretched his calves. Before he could dash off, he felt a warm liquid dripping down his shoulder. He turned and saw a thick, oatmeal-colored liquid that smelled like rotten eggs and sewage. Jayden snapped his fingers, and a green-colored flame burned away whatever landed on his shoulder. Once it turned into steam, his head started to feel warm. He ran his fingers through his hair and almost threw up as his fingers ran into a liquid that felt like snot. Jayden examined his hands, noticing they were covered in the same goo as his shirt.

He glanced up and moved quickly to his left to avoid a string of that oatmeal-colored liquid. He felt a knot in the pit of his stomach and ducked his head, narrowly missing the edges of a curved blade. Jayden jumped back and let loose an explosive wave of *Sirocco* spell. This sent a scorching wave of concentrated desert wind into the area immediately surrounding him. The spell's impact was as powerful as a shotgun blast, and the sound of the explosive wind reverberated off the cave walls.

His eyes narrowed as a shadowy figure stepped forward. The monster snarled as it approached him. He was staring into the orange-colored eyes of a Snatch Goblin. The creature's skin was as green and dark as the moss on a tree. Rows of razor-sharp teeth matched perfectly with his claws, now clutching a large knife with a curved blade. The goblin had a curved nose and wore a faded red bandana tied along its wrinkly forehead.

The goblin snarled as it drew closer to him. "Our kind and trolls are the masters of this cave. After we slaughter you, we will dine on your friends. That werefox will make quite the meal. Of course, if you gave me all your items, we would be more inclined to let you live and simply eat your friends. The choice is yours."

Jayden stood there in complete shock. He had no idea, nor had he heard, that goblins of many monsters have the ability to talk. In this case, it did make sense. Then Jayden recalled reading about Snatch Goblins, which were said to be among the most intelligent and crafty of the goblin species. If someone were to meet a Snatch Goblin in the wilderness, they were known to rob and steal from travelers. Apparently, in Mirage, they were known to run one of the largest law firms that specialized solely in lawsuits.

He scratched his chin as he considered giving some of his possessions to the goblin because he did not want to be on the menu for the day. Then he drew his pistol and fired off two rounds at the ceiling above him. A loud groan escaped the mouth of a goblin as it fell toward the cavern floor. Jayden then turned and bolted forward. The Snatch Goblin swung its arm with the blade, aiming for Jayden's throat; he quickly somersaulted under it. While he rolled under the swinging monster, he turned his body and squeezed the trigger twice. The bullets slammed into his attacker, and it crumbled to the ground.

Jayden jumped back to his feet and spun his pistol before holstering it. "And that is how the cookie crumbles."

ROAR!!!

The ground beneath his feet shook like he was standing in the center of an earthquake. His ears were ringing as the earth-shattering roar reverberated along the cave walls. He gulped down a gallon worth of fear as the sound of claws scratching against rock drew closer and closer to him. Snarls, an endless wave of animalistic growls, and the smell of rotten eggs seemed almost overwhelming.

Then, just as quickly as the cave came to life, it became deathly silent. The only noise he knew of was his shallow breathing and pounding heartbeat. In his peripheral vision, he became aware of dozens of circular orange lights around him. As quietly as he could move, Jayden quickly removed the magazine from his gun and reloaded it with a new one. Jayden tried to count in his head how many bullets he had left. There were at least eleven left in the magazine he just placed in his pocket and fifteen in the fresh one. The remaining bullets were stored in his bag in the other dimension, and he was not yet skilled enough to pull out any specific items like that from it in the middle of a battle. Even if he could, he knew he might want to save the remaining bullets for whatever comes next.

The Dragon Warrior shook his head. "Why is it always me?"

Jayden jumped when he felt something brush against his back. He spun around as he spotted his best friend staring in the other direction toward a group of goblins that were advancing toward them.

His best friend chuckled. "It's because you are an idiot, and you are slow. But I got your back and am ready whenever you are."

He breathed a sigh of relief. This would be a lot easier now that Tony was with him. Jayden raised his pistol and fired off five rounds into the darkness. He grinned as three goblins crumbled to the floor. Then he holstered his gun once the horde began to rush them. Jayden drew his father's sword.

His muscles bulged, and he felt invigorated and ready to fight. A goblin with an ax jumped from across the room toward him. Jayden stepped to the side and sliced off the goblin's head. Then he glanced to the right as his best friend had transformed his broadsword into a double-bladed weapon to take on the three armored goblins approaching him. Jayden grinned as he stuck out his left hand and shouted, "Flame Whip!"

Cords of fire began to twist together in his hand. The whip extended as he channeled his magic into the scorching flames. He swung the whip furiously in tandem with his sword strikes against the screeching goblins. Jayden snapped the whip, and it wrapped around the wrist of a goblin. The creature howled in pain and dropped its razor-sharp knife. Then Jayden slashed his sword in the direction of the goblin and sent a wave of flames that slammed into the target and exploded.

Jayden ducked under the blade of a great sword. He snapped his whip, and it wrapped around the leg of the attacker. The creature yelped as he yanked on it, and the monster fell to the ground. Tony flipped over him and stabbed his sword downward into the goblin's chest.

His best friend pressed a button on his sword, transforming it into the broadsword form. He channeled electricity into the blade as he spun it above his head. His best friend waited until the goblins drew closer, and then he stabbed his sword into the floor. Then Tony shouted, "May the lightning of the God ignite the sky. Bring forth the power to control the tide of battle. SplinterBolt!"

The ground beneath his feet shook from the aftershock, and thunder roared down the halls of the cave. Tony's Dragon Steel on his sword shone with the sun's brightness as waves of lightning splintered along the floor. The bolts raced toward their targets like a spider building a web for its prey. Once the blue lightning reached the feet of the nearest goblin, the bolts of electricity wrapped around its target's body like a coiling snake. The lightning bolts would bounce from their initial target and then slam into the chest of the Snatch Goblin next to them. Lightning filled nearly every corner of the room as the spell electrocuted target after target.

Jayden turned to give his buddy a high-five when he suddenly felt a burning sensation in his chest. Then he felt his body being forced backward as bolts of blue light crashed into his body.

"WHAT THE HELL!"

His best friend slammed into the rocky wall behind him as he received the last bolt that bounced off a goblin. Tony guarded his face as he bounced off the cave and collapsed onto the ground.

"Oww, that hurts," he groaned. "I think that knocked the air out of me."

Jayden blinked his eyes open and stared at the rocky ceiling above him. His head was spinning, and his lips felt like someone had punched him in the face.

"Well, I think I just peed myself," he replied. "I can't even feel my legs, and my chest is on fire. I hope to God you never use this spell again."

Tony dusted himself off as he got to his feet. "Well, I will try my best not to, but isn't that crazy? We beat all of those goblins in like no time."

Jayden managed to sit back up, and he looked around. Countless bodies of goblins were charred by the power of their spells. Of the few that managed to survive the fight, they had chosen to crawl or hobble away with their heads down. Jayden shrugged and wondered if they overdid it. For a while, the young Dragon Warrior had started considering if they had now become the true monsters? Like the Daimonia, he and Tony have been the harbingers of ruin for others.

His buddy must have sensed what he was thinking and stood beside him. "Don't regret what we had to do. We can look back on moments like this when we are old and gray. Right now, we have to get up and keep moving. Mariko gave us the rank of Dragon Knights to go into battle, which will never be an easy burden."

***

The cave was eerily quiet as they sprinted toward their friends. Small patches of light pierced through the ceiling above, which provided a light brown tint to the dreary appearance of the cave. He felt a twinge in his stomach and began to recognize the presence of a large magical power. The closer they got to the magical presence, the wider the tunnel seemed to become, and the more the light shone down from above.

Jayden took a right and almost stumbled as he slipped on a rock. He couldn't afford to slow down. Beyond the powers he could already recognize, there was a fourth source of magical energy. The magical power was so immense that it pushed away all the heat in the cave the closer they drew to it. The air around them felt as cold as an iceberg. He even noticed his heat magic was being drained, which was a bad sign if they had to fight again.

The amount of energy he could sense was unimaginable. There was only one other time he recognized a magical signature like this. He could remember it like it was yesterday because it happened while he was still living at the Dragon Temple. This happened on a day when he did not want to do his studies and decided to try and go exploring. By exploring, he tried to sneak up to the temple where the Dragon Sage resided. This was absolutely forbidden for trainees or even full-fledged Dragon Warriors. Only a select group of Dragon Masters were typically allowed to go beyond the front lawn of the complex, let alone enter the building.

Jayden, in his search for delinquent behavior, decided to make his way to see the Sage. Tony joined him along the way and decided to try to sneak into the building by hiking to it and circling around to the other side of the mountain. When they were closer to the summit, where the Dragon Warrior resided, a magic barrier stopped their trek. The barrier was invisible, but it kept them from moving forward no matter how hard they tried. One thing he remembered from their failure of a field trip was the unique and massive amount of energy radiating from just the barrier alone. The power he felt coming from the temple was even more impressive. From what he could tell, it wasn't simply that the magical signatures were some overwhelming powers. The magic seemed endless and primordial, as if it had existed from dawn and continued to grow eons later. That is exactly what he was sensing in the cave: old magic with no modern equal, only powers that had existed for thousands of years.

The Dragon Warriors channeled more energy into their legs; they had to reach the others in time. Jayden and his best friend stepped into a wider tunnel that was completely illuminated. This tunnel led to a large open cavern with a dirt floor that had the same consistency as sand. A wall of light blue ice extending to the ceiling stood in the back of the cavern. The ice had a milky color; within the block of ice, there appeared to be a liquid interior that seemed to flow through the glacier like a snake.

Grace was standing inches from the wall of ice. He noticed Macy was standing just to her right, and then his childhood friend turned around. Jayden thought she must have sensed them even though they were still far away. His childhood friend raised her right hand and sent a magenta-colored stream of fire at Shane. The magical blast knocked him to the ground. The flames coiled around him like a snake.

"MACY!" Jayden shouted from down the hall.

He turned back around and rejoined Grace, staring at the ice wall. Jayden and Tony sprinted toward the center of the cavern. There must be something critically wrong. She would never attack Shane. In fact, he had never heard of her attacking another person without a really good reason.

When they got closer, Macy slowly turned and stared at them momentarily. Her irises were as dark as the night sky, and the warm smile she normally carried was completely absent from her expression. The person staring back at them was no longer their childhood friend; they were looking into the eyes of a stone-cold killer. She raised her right hand with that empty expression and launched a blast of magenta-colored flames into the center of Tony's chest. The blast hit him so hard that he was completely knocked out by the time the flames began to coil around him.

Jayden ran right up to her and grabbed her shoulders. "What the hell is wrong with you?"

She stared at him blankly and began to turn back toward the wall of ice. He moved to stand in front of her. Her eyes never moved or locked into his; they were fixed on the blue block of ice behind her. He waved his hand in front of her face, but her eyes never blinked and never even reacted.

The Dragon Warrior switched his gaze toward the Aggeloi Princess just a few feet away. Like Macy, her gaze was fixed on the wall of ice. He walked toward her, noticing *The Key* was glowing as it hung from her necklace. Her eyes were still a normal color; they hadn't changed like Macy's. Her expression was cold, with no ounce of joy or teenage angst. It was almost like Grace had turned into a zombie.

Jayden took a step toward the frozen behemoth. There was something unnatural about the liquid moving within the structure. The liquid in the wall moved like wisps of smoke blowing gently in the wind. The blood in his veins seemed to run cold the closer he was pulled to the wall of ice. He couldn't quite put it in words but could feel strangely drawn to it. Was it the ice? Or was it the liquid moving within it? Or something else? Either way, he couldn't resist the thought pulsing in his mind, and before he knew it, his arm extended forward all on its own.

Once his fingers made contact with the wall, he felt a cold electric charge up the side of his body. His breath became ice cold and felt as thick as smoke from a cigar. He instantly became aware of painful emotions from deep within, beginning to well up on the inside. Jayden's mind slipped back to the day his hometown was destroyed. His mind started to play back when the Dark Prince killed Mr. Robert with his sword. He could feel his muscles bulging from remembering the adrenaline he felt as they ran up into the Dragon Mountain. He recalled the cruel thought he had at the time that he would never see his father alive again. Who knew that the simple request he asked his father to do would open the door for his death?

His vision blurred as tears poured down from his eyes. Jayden took a deep breath as his body became consumed with internal sadness. The truth was that nothing he had done since then had turned out much better. Now, he was stuck in a cave under the ocean with the Aggeloi Princess and a friend who had turned on everyone else in the party. What good has he even accomplished?

Jayden wiped away crusty chunks of ice on a section of the wall just above his head. His eyes widened as he stared at what looked like water with a beautiful turquoise hue beneath the thick layer of ice flowing within the structure. Bubbles of air floated around inside the ice wall. He could even hear the sound of movement within the structure, as if someone or something was swimming within the ice. Jayden pressed his face up against the ice to get a better look.

Boo!

He jumped back as a pearly white skull appeared beneath the ice. He noticed that within the milky tone of the wall were other pieces of human remains and bones traveling along the aquatic routes within the ice. He peered closer at the skull, and as he stared at it, it slowly spun in a circle. Then he felt ice-cold fingers clasp his shoulder. Jayden spun around, but there was no one else around him. The girls were deathly quiet, and even Shane and Tony were completely silent. Her spell must have made it impossible for them to speak.

Retrieve the knife!

Take the stone!

Jayden shook his head; he must be going crazy. He was hearing voices in his head. It must be the lack of oxygen down in the cave. Maybe there were gases. Or all of his friends being on some twisted spell, or maybe because it was kind of creepy down here. He needed to get a grip, so he took a deep breath and tried to concentrate. He had to find a way to break the spell on Macy and Grace.

Retrieve the knife!

Take the stone!

He plugged his ears and took a step back. His foot landed awkwardly on an object, and he slipped and landed on his butt.

Jayden let out a deep sigh. "Dammit, why do I gotta be so clumsy?"

The Dragon Warrior moved his leg to see what he had tripped on. Sitting just inches away from his foot was an old knife. He crawled to it and noticed a magic stone beside the blade. The stone was about the size of a small bowling ball, just big enough to fit in a person's palm but still heavy enough that it would be difficult to carry. Burn marks and deep scratches were all over the stone. Jayden sniffed the air and got a hint of smoke from the object. The fire magic used on the stone was centuries, maybe thousands of years old.

His fingertips glided against the leather grip of the knife, and he felt a twinge in the pit of his stomach. His fingers were completely wrapped around the handle on their own. His left hand turned the blade and pressed it against his right palm. He felt a sharp pain as the blade dragged along the center of his hand. His mind was telling him to stop moving the blade, but his body would not react to his will.

The young Dragon Warrior could sense his left hand releasing its grip on the knife. It clanged as it landed on a flattened rock. He noticed his hand moving to grab the magic stone. He felt his right arm move and then begin to smudge his blood all over the stone. Jayden wanted to wince as he felt the stone dig its rough edges into his flesh. The pain was almost excruciating as he dragged his wound over the edges of the stone, covering the rock with his fresh blood.

He could feel his body bending over to retrieve the knife. Jayden's legs moved independently until he stood beside his childhood friend. He stretched his arm toward Macy. She took the knife from him and then sliced open her right hand. She rubbed her bleeding hand all over the rock. Once the rock was covered in crimson, she turned back toward the wall of ice. Then Macy took a step forward and spread a streak of blood on it. Her body crumbled to the floor, and she lay completely still.

Jayden felt his legs move a few steps forward. He stretched his right hand and slid it against the frigidly cold wall. A burning pain shot through his arm as the ice made contact with his fresh wound. He winced as if a thousand daggers were being pressed into his cut. His hand stopped moving on its own, and his eyes bulged at the sight of the bloody streak he had left on the ice wall. The blood stains dripping from the wall of ice were reminiscent of a murder scene in a slasher film.

The Dragon Warrior's hands started to twitch, dropping the stone. His legs moved backward on their own, taking long strides. His body didn't stop moving in reverse until his right foot landed on a small mound of compacted dirt piled up in the center of the cavern. Then he crumbled onto the floor. His shin hit the compacted dirt, and he felt blood drip from his nose when his face made contact with a conveniently placed rock.

His body ached like he had just been beaten up by the largest school bully. Jayden's nose was bleeding; he was sure he had more than scratches under his chin, and his hand hurt like no one's business. He still had no control over his body, and even his Auto-Healing spell wasn't working. Jayden tried to speak, but control of his vocals seemed stolen, and he had no idea why.

Then he felt a small rock being kicked against his leg. Jayden tried to force his body to move or his head to turn, but still nothing. His ears perked up at the sound of sandals drudging against the dirt floor. A cough and wheeze broke the awkward silence of the cave. A pair of pale-colored sandals, which were mostly covered by a mossy green colored cloth, appeared in the corner of his right eye.

This stranger took a few more labored steps forward and went into a coughing spell. He trudged forward slowly with his cane. Then he stretched out his right hand, and the stone lifted off the ground and hovered in front of him. He slowly turned slightly toward Jayden, still hiding his face in his cloak.

The old man leaned back so his hood slid off just enough to reveal his face. His skin was rather pale and looked weathered from years of a hard life. The old man possessed unique colored eyes that were orange, with a milky white tint to them from age. Although it was significantly faded, Jayden noticed an image of a demon with a sickle tattooed on the frail neck of the old man. At that moment, his heart sunk into the pit of his stomach.

The old man wheezed as he shuffled and turned his whole body to examine Jadyen. "This wall is a barrier between this world and the old. The people who built this powerful feat of magic did so to keep me out. Out of the fear that I would bring to light the truth about *The Elders* and the Great War. The power they built and tossed away out of shame and guilt lies beyond this wall. Thanks to you and your friends, I will now bring about judgment upon them."

Jayden channeled as much magical energy and willpower as possible into his body. He took a deep breath. *MOVE*, he told himself. For a second, he felt a knee slide forward. It may have been just a muscle spasm, but it was at least something. He channeled every bit of magical energy into his extremities again. He moved his elbows just enough to crawl forward a few inches. He collapsed from mental exhaustion.

"Young man, I have been on this planet for quite some time. In those years, I mastered many forms of Magic. However, there are some that I am highly specialized in. One is Spatial Magic. The other, you will only learn if you cross me. The last is Psychological Magic. I possess the ability to make people do as I please. One of the curses within *The Key* is proof of that ability. You are among the few who have demonstrated an ability to resist my spell. Out of respect for the sheer strength of will needed to accomplish that task. I will bring you a few gifts that will make us even."

The old man waved his hand in a circle. Then Jayden heard something pop, smoke billowing around his new foe. Two figures appeared within the cloud of smoke. Immediately, Jayden felt his heart pounding in his chest. The magical power radiating from the two figures in the shadow was off the charts.

A cool breeze blew through the cave, sending wisps of smoke. A girl in a white T-shirt with black shorts appeared. Two short swords hung on her back, and matching twin machine pistols hung from her hips. Her normally dark hair with brilliant highlights was now a blazing red and glowing like the midday sun. Even though her irises were darkened by his mind-control spell, there was no doubt his childhood crush had returned to the fold.

The cloud of smoke continued to waver and dissipate, revealing a second figure. Within the gray smoke, Jayden noticed bits of green and brown cloth. Then he saw strands of brunette hair with streaks of blonde in it. The woman's hands were cuffed with anti-magic bracelets, glowing bright red from struggling to contain her magical power. She slowly inclined her head in his direction. Those beautiful eyes stared deep into his soul, and his heart melted as he witnessed a smile, he thought he would never see again.

The ancient wizard waved away the last wisps of smoke. His fingers shook from years of arthritis as he made the symbol of a cross in front of the magic stone. The old rock started to glow a dark orange color, and the room felt much warmer.

He gave a toothy grin as he stared, "I know these two young ladies require no introductions for you. But I must again congratulate them and, of course, you all. You all are making my dream come true. I will teach you about a type of magic you might not have learned in your studies. This wall was made by sacrificing a thousand souls. Most of the souls embedded in this ice consisted of humans and elves of *The Elder* race. A sacrifice like that is what we call Eternal Magic. Eternal Magic is a type of spell that can never truly be destroyed; it can only change forms. The only way to damage or create that change is with another Eternal Magic spell. So, a challenge presented to me was getting past this wall."

The wizard softly bowed his head, and Sarah raised her right hand and drew her sword. She turned her heels and raised her blade toward Floriana. The curved edges of her sword were pressed lightly against the former General's throat. Tiny beads of blood and sweat dripped from the warrior's neck. The blade was shaking erratically as Sarah gripped the weapon in her hand; she appeared to be struggling to end their friend's life. Then she took a step back and swung her sword.

His heart had jumped into his throat. He could feel sweat and tears streaming down his face. Jayden closed his eyes in just enough time to avoid seeing what his mind was struggling to process. How much more cruelty could his heart take before it would never heal again?

The Dragon Warrior's strength to resist was waning. He couldn't resist the wizard's spell any longer. It was as if the monster planned from the very beginning to stab his heart just one more time. For the wizard, it wasn't just enough to force

326

him and his friends into a trap they couldn't escape. The bastard wanted him to witness his childhood friend kill one of the sweetest people he had ever met.

A bright light pierced through his tightly closed eyes. His vision was blurry from sweat and tears. But through his blurred vision, it looked like two people were still standing next to the old man. Sarah's sword had a small stain on the edge, and a puddle of blood formed at Floriana's feet. Jayden was so shocked that he swore he made his body move forward an inch.

Sarah sheathed her sword and then grabbed the General by the wrists. Then she rubbed Floriana's hands against the ice-cold wall. The blood dripping from her hands was spread along the barrier like a paintbrush. Floriana winced from the pain caused by the rough edges of ice digging into her bleeding flesh. Then Sarah punched Floriana in the lip and stomach with blazing speed and then pushed her on the ground.

The old wizard chuckled, "I am quite impressed, my dear. Even in that Elder form, you still resist my commands with my curse and mind control. I have been around for thousands of years, and I find it amusing that I can still be surprised occasionally." He switched his gaze toward Jayden and narrowed his eyes on him. "My young Dragon Warrior, as I am sure you have already guessed, this Magic Stone uses fire magic. You could say that blood from you and your friend smeared on this barrier is effectively like adding fuel to the fire. However, a challenge with tackling Eternal Magic spells such as this is that they were cast long ago. You need a complementary agent, such as the blood of a Frost Magic user. Alas, they are very rare these days; we were fortunate when the young General came waltzing through our doors. With that said, you and young Macy made an exceptional attempt at recharging this Magic Stone. In fact, the two of you almost brought it back to its former glory. Unfortunately, it is still not enough. We will have to use another natural resource to make my dream, my goal, come true."

He made a circular motion with his hand. Hundreds of cylindrical beams of light appeared in the center of the cavern, and many more went back toward the other side of the tunnel. Jayden was temporarily blinded by the brilliant light show. Once the lights faded, he noticed a set of feet standing just a few inches from his nose. The set of feet was attached to an individual dressed in a black robe. On the left side of this individual was another man dressed in a black robe. He had exceptionally long black hair partially obscured by the large claymore slung across his back. Just inches from Jayden's right shoulder was a third individual. This one had a combat-style bow slung across his back and a quiver with a nearly endless supply of arrows.

The individual in front of him took a few steps forward, and hanging from his right hip was a sword with a platinum hip. Jayden's eyes widened when he realized he was completely paralyzed and was now lying down just inches from his childhood mentor, the killer of his father and a traitor to his own country.

His hope continued diminishing when his ears perked up at a sound coming from the hall. At first, it sounded like thunder, but then he realized it was the sound of an endless number of shoes and boots stomping on the cave's rocky floor. Once his three favorite Daimonia warriors had moved to stand near the wizard, his vision became obscured by the countless enemies now standing between him and his friends. So many Daimonia members packed into the cavern that he could no longer see the great ice wall. Jayden was completely shocked because he was now stuck in a sea of black robes. The Dragon Warrior felt like he was attending a very twisted rock concert or that he was a surprise guest at a cult meeting where they sacrificed virgins.

The wizard wheezed and went into a brief coughing spell. Once he had finished coughing up a lung, the columns of Daimonia soldiers obstructing Jayden's view promptly moved to the side. The Dark Prince and Sarah came back into view and stood to the wizard's right. General Floriana was still crumpled on the ground near his feet. However, a middle-aged woman stood just a few inches to his left. She was dressed in a light blue nightgown with a matching set of anti-magic bracelets. The bracelets were glowing light blue, meaning they were stable and operating efficiently. This aqua-colored glow matched almost perfectly with her sky-blue hair, which was long enough to reach her lower back.

She let out a cackle that pierced the deathly silent ambiance of the cave. The witch tilted her head and directed her gaze toward Jayden. She gave him that cruel smile he wished he would never see again. Her pale skin was covered in scratches and bruises, but she couldn't care less about her worn appearance. In fact, she seemed perfectly content to be in a cave filled with power-hungry murderers and a wizard on his last leg.

The old man gestured toward the Dark Prince. His subordinate picked up the blood-stained knife from the ground. Then he placed it in the hands of Lady Coral. When she took hold of the weapon, he took a few steps backward until he was standing right back next to his leader. Jayden chuckled because he figured even his father's murder was wise enough to know that witch was absolutely deadly under any conditions. The Dark Prince was powerful as they came, but he was no fool. He was not willing to take any chances with her.

"Thank you for that, Jeremiah," his master said with a paternal tone. His fading, orange-colored eyes narrowed on the witch just a few feet away. "Now, my young lady, would you be willing to help an old man in his time of need?"

Lady Coral bowed respectfully, "Of course I would, Arthur. Anything for the Fallen Wizard and the Thirteenth."

The witch rotated the knife in her right hand. She sliced the blade against her left palm with almost surgical precision. She tilted her head slightly and stared at the blood dripping down her wrists with a childlike curiosity. She pressed her bleeding hand against the Magic Stone, now floating just a foot in front of her. The moment her blood made contact with the glowing object; the room temperature skyrocketed to the point he felt like his insides were going to boil. This orange stone was now glowing like the sun at midday. Magical energy bathed the room with static electricity. The stone started to spin on its own.

The wizard gave a cheeky grin and waved his hand as the stone drifted toward him. The elder statesman let go of his cane and stood as erect as possible. He pulled an old magic wand out from beneath his coat. The Fallen Wizard raised his hands toward the sky, his wand glowing in different colors.

His powerful foe glanced back at Jayden and gave him a toothy smile. "My young Dragon Warrior, I want you to witness power you have only read about in your history books. This power will help remove a burden you and your friends have had to carry. The object you have fought so hard to find and protect has been a source of unnecessary hardships for you. You see, the constructors of *The Key* designed it in such a way that it could unlock objects that can give a person nearly limitless power. The curse they placed on it allowed certain individuals and relatives to gain access to such power. The strain this object has placed on both of your friends must be immeasurable. However, once my true powers are restored, I will remove the blight that curse has had on this world. Now, witness the true fire magic you desire in this magic stone. SUPERNOVA!"

Jayden felt the ground beneath him rumble. The hairs on the back of his neck began to rise, and goosebumps formed along his arms. His powers were being drawn to the stone like a magnet. He could feel every ounce of his magical energy being pulled out of him and rushing toward the spinning Magic Stone.

He watched in awe as the rough surface and shape of the stone changed as it spun. The object's physical structure expanded to the size of a tractor tire. Its rocky texture transformed into pure energy.

The energy the powerful magic stone had turned into looked just like a small red sun with a core of white light that was too bright to stare at directly. Puddles of sweat formed beneath him from the intense heat radiating from the spell. The cave now felt like he was sitting on the sun's surface. The brilliant ball of energy slammed into the wall of ice and exploded with the force of a massive rocket. Waves of fire and ash rained down on the cave. Miniature explosions occurred along every inch of the wall, like a line of dynamite demolishing a building. His ears were ringing like they would never stop from the sound of magical energy exploding throughout the cavern.

The fire magic spell continued to roar like a lion in the savannah. As the molten rock from the ball of energy spread across the wall of ice and death, Jayden could no longer see the turquoise hue from the barrier. All his eyes could see was an orange wall of molten rock and an endless wave of fierce embers. For Jayden, the wall looked like a preview of the apocalypse. The lava dripping from the ceiling gave him the sense that it was just as if God had come down and made his judgment upon his people. The only thing they deserved was death.

From the destructive power of the spell, the cavern began to fill with clouds of dust and debris swirling around them. With every new explosion on the wall, Jayden found it harder and harder to see. Dirt and sand were caked to his eyebrows, and the irritation beneath his eyelids was absolutely maddening. The worst part about it was he couldn't wipe it off or do anything about it. The only solace he found in his suffering was he knew that he wasn't alone in these miserable experiences. His friends scattered in different parts of the cavern shared in the same misery.

Jayden had an epiphany about his power amid the scorching heat filling the cave. For the most part, heat or fire magic hardly ever bothered him. Even the heat sensations he felt from lightning spells did not usually hurt him. However, the powerful energy that was torching the nerves in his skin was giving him a new perspective on his own magic. He was beginning to understand what it must be like to be on the receiving end of his fire magic.

His ears picked up on the sound of shoes shuffling against the dirt. That's when he realized the sound of deafening explosions was subsiding. Instead of intense clouds of hot dirt filling the cavern, he felt the cool wind against his skin. He could now see specks of blue light piercing through the blanket of fire and molten rock. The gigantic form of the ancient barrier had not crumbled, not even by an inch.

He sensed he could move his eyelids now and then blinked rapidly to get as much dust out of his vision. Jayden then tried to shift his weight and chuckled when he realized he could move his legs a bit. His fingers regained mobility, and he could now move them just enough to open and close his hands. It took some effort for the young Dragon Warrior, but he could rotate his neck just enough to wipe away some dust caked onto his face. And for the first time, he could sense subtle magical power from both Shane and Tony. This was a good sign, but they had to be cautious about jumping back into action.

Jayden's eyes widened as the Fallen Wizard appeared even more pale as the dust settled. His knees shook, and the veins in his temple almost popped out of his skull. The wand in his hand was now burnt to a crisp, and the Magic Stone had shattered into thousands of ruby-colored pieces at his feet. His body swayed backward, but Cain came quickly to support him.

A series of rocks that were piled against the barrier began to crumble. More and more turquoise-colored light pierced through brown clods of dirt and flame. As the rocks continued to fall and crumble, the room started to feel like the inside of an ice box again. The roar of scorching flames was now a distant memory and had been replaced by the sound of cascading rocks.

After a series of rockslides, the barrier appeared as if it had always been before them. He noticed one major change; the wall now looked like a shattered mirror. Some deep cuts and groves splintered across every inch of the ancient barrier. Jayden spotted something interesting at the center of the barrier; there were now moderately sized holes created by the Supernova. Pieces of ice hung on by a thread from the edges of the gaps. The spell that had nearly killed the wizard had only damaged the wall. The barrier still stood firm despite its wounded state.

The wizard fixed his gaze on the witch. "Mrs. Corallina, would you be willing to add the finishing touches to my painting?"

"I would love to, my Lord," she replied with a bow.

The former member of the Southern Convent took a step toward the cracked wall. She placed her still-bleeding palm against its ice-cold surface. The witch chuckled as she drew a smiley face picture with her blood on the barrier. Jayden's jaw hit the floor as her blood bubbled. He could sense slight heat sources as the witch's blood seemed to boil. His nose flared as he breathed the rusty scent of blood and decaying flesh. He wanted to gag. Just as he was about to throw up, the barrier shattered into a thousand shards of ice and bone.

Then Lady Coral turned toward the army of Daimonia soldiers that filled the cavern. Her eyes scanned the room, drifting toward each of his friends and landing squarely on him. She curled her right index finger over the connecting unit of her restraints. Instantly, her handcuffs became engulfed in a black and blue ball of flame. Then she waved her now free hands in his direction with a smile that chilled him to the bone.

"Jade, I know you and your friends have a million reasons to despise me. In fact, it tickles my heart to feel such hatred radiating from the lot of you. I want you to understand something very important, and young Cain, this applies to you, too. The man standing next to me is the reason for your sorry lot in life. If you wish to exact your revenge on me, you must first survive against him." Lady Coral grinned and gave a flirtatious wink toward the Fallen Wizard. "But don't you worry your poor little heads. I'll give you a little bit of a head start." She pointed bloody index fingers toward the icy remains of the barrier. She shouted, "Bring forth the lost souls of the damned and exact your judgment on the Fallen. FrostFlame Nekron!

Chapter 28

Apokalypsis

Frozen ice blocks and bones began to mold together. Shards of
ice shifted their shapes into blades and shields. The skulls of
the dead attached themselves to shattered blocks of ice from
the barrier. The frosty remains of the wall started to move and
reform into the body of skeletons. Some of them looked like
the bodies of dead humans, while the others had longer
craniums like the elves. Blue flames flickered in the eye
sockets of this frozen army of the damned. It was like watching
an invisible hand put a puzzle of terror and violence together.

A crown of ice and bone appeared on the head of a
Nekron. The monster swung a double-bladed katana over its
newly shaped skull. This creature opened its gaping maw with
rows of teeth as sharp as a razor's edge. He let loose an earth-
shattering roar that sent forth a torrent of shards of ice and a

frosty blast of wind that shook her to her core. The discharged spell of ice rocketed through the columns of unfortunate souls and exploded at the end of the tunnel. The moment shards of ice rained on them marked the very second they would be battling for their lives.

She could still taste the salty sensation of blood on her lips. When the former General rolled to her side, she felt a stabbing pain in her rib cage. She felt a twinge in her stomach and rolled over to the side, narrowly avoiding a frozen foot aimed at crushing her skull.

Floriana had rolled on her back. Her eyes met the gaze of a towering Nekron staring down at her. He drove a frozen spear at her. She raised her arms upward, and the frozen weapon pierced through the central connecting unit of her restraints. Then she grabbed the pole arm just before the spearhead could pierce her heart.

The former General of the Eden Army felt energized from making contact with the Frost Magic imbued in her opponent's weapon. Floriana's magical energy was instantly recharged and boosted significantly. With a renewed sense of power and control, she pushed up on the polearm of the spear, and the base of the shaft slammed into the jaw of her attacker.

Then she rolled back onto her stomach and snapped her fingers. In seconds, her body painfully transformed into a small field mouse. Floriana sped her mousy body past a set of sandals that belonged to an unfortunate soul who was now the next prey of her attacker.

Floriana zigzagged through columns of bad guys, looking for someone she knew. She couldn't sense their individual magical energy signatures; there were too many bodies way too close for that. At first, she thought about helping Grace since she was physically closer to her at the start, but once the barrier broke and all hell broke loose, she lost her in the crowd. She figured Grace might do okay if she was out of the trance. Jayden and Tony, on the other hand, were completely incapacitated and surrounded by Daimonia members.

She moved toward the side where their werefox friend had landed but was nowhere to be found. Floriana moved her tiny feet as fast as she could toward the center of the cavern. She darted through the legs of a group of Daimonia soldiers being pushed back by the Frozen Nekron. Her dark eyes zoomed in on a body lying still on a small mound of dirt. It was Jayden. He was surrounded by enemies.

A balding Daimonia soldier picked up Jayden by his collar. Then he punched him a few times in the face and the gut. Jayden was trying to resist, but his arms and legs were still partially under the spell performed by the Fallen Wizard. The Daimonia warrior tossed Jayden on the ground so he could decapitate an approaching Nekron. Once he dispatched his frozen enemy, his eyes narrowed on Jayden, and grinned.

"The master will reward me if I bring him your head," he snarled.

Floriana quickly transformed into her human form, dressed in her combat armor. She restrained the attacker's left arm from behind and then placed her hand on his face. She snapped his head, breaking his neck. He crumbled to the ground as he gave up the ghost. Floriana drew her rapier from its sheath and quickly launched two spiked ice blocks toward a group of cloaked warriors. She held her rapier upright with both hands as she channeled her magic. She summoned thirty razor-sharp icicles that orbited around her and Jayden, creating a protective circle. The icicles rocketed toward their prospective targets.

Floriana snapped her fingers and summoned a revolver into her left hand. This weapon was known as FireBrand. It was a gift Jayden had given to her. Now, she had a chance to repay him for that. She channeled her ice magic into the weapon, then spun in a circle, firing eight rounds. The gun fired blasted bullets made of ice the size of baseballs. Once the rounds pierced their target, the massive ice bullets would explode against the next opponent, causing them a very intense and temporary hypothermic episode.

She deflected a series of bullets from the right with her sword. Floriana returned the favor with her revolver, firing a series of small shards of sharpened ice. She felt a twinge in her gut and wheeled around. There was an automatic rifle trained on her from the other side of the cavern. Before he could fire off a round, a large metal shield appeared floating in front of her. Once the bullets started firing, the shield blocked and absorbed each round. A red spot appeared in the center of her enemy's forehead, and he was no longer a problem.

Floriana spun around and deflected another series of bullets. The shield remained behind her, absorbing attacks from arrows, bullets, and a few elemental spells. She sensed a group of hooded figures rushing toward her from the left. A massive gust of wind blasted them into the side of the cavern wall. She quickly breathed a sigh of relief, then smiled just as Jayden got to his feet. Her heart pounded in her chest as he placed his arms around her in the middle of the battlefield. He held her so tight that she found it tough to breathe but was appreciative of the moment.

She felt another set of arms wrap around her and Jayden from the other side. Tony held on to them tightly as gunfire and clashing swords echoed in their ears. Floriana couldn't believe she had dropped her guard in the middle of a battlefield. Yet here she was, a warfighter hugging friends she had dearly missed, although she was confused as to why their enemies had not hit them with at least a stray bullet, spell, or even a well-timed rock.

Floriana panned around the room, and it became abundantly clear. The Nekron made a solid dent in the Daimonia ranks while others had already made their way through the barrier. She then realized Tony had summoned a series of small dark clouds throughout the cavern, blasting bolts of lightning, chunks of hail, and gusts of wind at their enemies. Her eyes then zeroed in on a series of small fireballs Jayden must have created that were raining down from the ceiling and slamming into any attacker in a black robe. Lastly, she spotted the werefox, a girl she didn't know, and Grace tearing through groups of attackers on the other side of the cavern.

The boys released their grip on her. They switched their focus to the battlefield and turned off their Auto-Attack spells. Jayden drew a black scimitar from his back and slashed at Daimonia warriors left and right. Tony drew his broad sword and made a vertical slash that sent forth a wave of heated wind energy in a straight line. The spell slammed into a cloaked warrior with enough force that he fell backward into the men behind him. Unfortunately for them, the Frozen Nekron seized this opportunity to end their lives.

Floriana opened her mouth and released a concentrated blast of magical energy and frigid air. Then she conjured a second blasting spell of snow from her rapier. This spell created a snowy path for them to run and reach the others.

She quickly sped through the mounds of snow she summoned. For Jayden and Tony, it was a bit more challenging. The werefox and Grace were providing cover as they raced toward them. Once they reached them, she could relax for a minute because the few Daimonia members still in the cavern had to completely focus on the advancing Nekron. Apparently, the frozen bastards were much harder to kill. Floriana couldn't understand why the Daimonia had such a difficult time with the frozen corpses. The only thing she could think of that made them so much more powerful than the average undead creature was that it might result from a combination of the Eternal Magic plus Lady Coral's spell, which likely made their dead spirits quite durable and strong.

The werefox shook her hand, "Hello there, my name is Shane. I am a Team Leader for the Witnesses. This young lady standing next to me is Macy. She is an honorable member of my team."

Floriana shook his furry hand and then shook hers. "My name is Floriana. I am a General, I mean, I used to be one for the Eden army."

"That is super cool," Macy interjected. "Well, I grew up in Eiréné with these two. In fact, I was Jayden's first crush."

Floriana grinned, "Oh, were you now? I always thought it was Sarah and then me. Are you saying I got third place?"

"Hey, it's better than being fourth," Grace added. "Or fifth unless you liked Tammy before me."

He released an exacerbated sigh, "Macy, I thought we agreed that it was a tie. Plus, can't we just get back to the task at hand? I don't want to spend my last moments talking about my nonexistent love life."

"Honestly, I am cool with the girls continuing to roast you," Tony added. "I think it's best they let it all out."

Floriana laughed, "You two are still the same. Two boys with nothing better to do with their time than bicker. I love it. But anyway, I think we need to chase down their leaders. We gotta stop whatever they are attempting to do. We don't have enough power or personnel to do it."

Shane nodded his head, "I agree. I have contacted a group that may provide us some much-needed backup. I haven't heard from them in a bit, so I don't know if they will arrive in town."

"Where is Sarah?" Macy asked. "And *The Key*?"

"She took it from me. I know she was still under that God-awful mind control spell," Grace replied. "I think she went through the barrier with their leader. We gotta catch up to them in time. If this is how powerful he is without having his true power. I can only imagine how much stronger he will get."

The former General nodded her head. "Okay, that settles it. We need to make our way through the Daimonia and Nekron between here and the barrier as quickly as possible. Once we are on the other side, I think Tony and Jayden, you two need to draw as much of the main force's attention as possible. It's risky, but you two are way stronger now than you were before. The rest of us will have to give it everything we have to stop their leader, get Sarah back, and find a way to destroy *The Key*. Do any of you have any abilities that could help us clear another path through the enemy?"

Shane spun his pistols between his sharp claws. "I have an idea if you can do that blast of snow again. I have a few spells that will help us get there without getting hit. But before we go, do not dishonor yourself again. You are still a General. A leader is a leader no matter the condition or title they possess. A leopard cannot change its spots, and you cannot stop being who you are. Now, be the General that the world needs."

General Floriana grinned as she directed her blade toward a section of the cave where the barrier once stood. Shane's words rang true in her mind; she was still a tactician and would take this time to prove it. Her rapier was aimed at a spot in the cave with a smaller concentration of fighters and Nekron. She took a deep breath and shouted, "Avalanche."

A mountain of snow slammed down on a section of the cavern. The Daimonia were so shocked they couldn't see the bullets Shane had sent flying. He then summoned six large iron shields that spun in the air as they flew. Large spikes and razor blades lined the sides of the shields. The werefox grinned as the shields spun like a top, rocketing the deadly shields toward the hordes of enemies.

The spiked shield spell he summoned was designed so that when the shields struck a target, they would bounce off them to hit the next. This spell was like watching a very grotesque pinball game. The werefox summoned six more shields; three were anti-magic shields, and the other three were designed to absorb large amounts of damage. The protective shields orbited around their group, deflecting bullets and canceling out magic spells coming their way.

Shane took the lead as they made their way toward their makeshift path. Grace was running close behind him while summoning swarms of bees and wasps toward the small mob of Daimonia warriors. The insects weren't as effective against the Nekron. Still, they created a significant enough distraction and frustration for their hooded foes that she did not mind.

Floriana was absolutely impressed by how much power the werefox wielded. His defensive magic was second to none. In fact, she couldn't imagine how he could control both sets of spells at a time and fire rounds from his revolvers, which also used a variety of spells depending on which bullet was in the chamber at the time. The guns he used were very similar to the pistol Jayden gave her; she had to channel specific spells into the weapon. On the other hand, he didn't seem to need to do that or reload, or he at least moved so quickly that she couldn't even tell.

Once her boots landed on the soft snow, everything changed. The energy of the room shifted as they made their escape. Suddenly, there seemed to be endless bullets aimed in their direction. The sound of rifle rounds bouncing off the shields was uncomfortable, to say the least. Her ears were ringing from the roaring Nekron and the expletives from their hooded nemesis. Even the gunfire they were sending back could not compare to the ruckus caused by their enemies.

The General felt a burning sensation against her cheek. She brushed her hand again and felt a twinge of pain as shards of lead and blood fell from her cheek. She felt sick to her stomach for a second and instinctively ducked. She never saw the bullet but heard it whizz by just inches above her head.

Then she pointed her rapier toward the center of the cavern as they ran. General Floriana channeled her magical energy into her blade. The blade became as black as obsidian, and red lightning bolts crackled around its edge. A blue diamond made of ice appeared on the ceiling of the cavern.

Floriana channeled more magical energy into her sword and shouted, "May you all find rest in depths of despair! Black Onyx!"

A popping sound bellowed over the roar of bullets and monsters. The diamond began to spin, and its aqua color turned dark black. Then scarlet lightning bolts flashed across its frame, and large icicles as red as her blood spawned next to the diamond.

The reality was that it didn't take long before she heard the cries of immense pain as her shards of ice rained on her targets. Red lightning bolts singed her enemies. Each crimson icicle that impaled an opponent was accompanied by a scream of absolute terror. She hated using the spell; it would be illegal under most conditions. In this case, they needed an escape to save the world. The last thing they needed was an army of the frozen dead and more cloaked warriors following them. *May they rest in peace*, she thought.

Floriana forced her mind to block out the screams of the damned. She was so zoned out that the sound of winter crunching beneath her feet brought her back into focus. The General sensed her balance was off as her shoes pressed against uneven ground. Normally, the snow magic she would conjure was either soft or hardpacked, but this felt like shards of ice were beneath her feet. That was when they reached the part of the cave where the wall of ice once stood. And just after a few more steps, her shoes made a hollow sound as they landed on the hard, rocky surface of the cave.

The surface floor on the other side of the wall was relatively flat. In fact, compared to the rest of the cave, it was obvious that, at some point, this tunnel was very active. The path they were led to was smooth and had slight bends like a snake. There was no one else in this part of the cave. The army of hooded warriors must have moved farther rather quickly.

Floriana did not quite understand why they would leave their comrades behind. As a General and a warrior on the battlefield, she could never turn her back on her team like they did. In fact, for her, it would have made more sense for them to wait around and destroy the Frost Nekron, especially since once the spell was cast, Lady Coral disappeared into a column of fire. They must either be worried that she was still around, or the Fallen Wizard was on a timeline.

They made a left around a curve, and she glanced backward. There were no enemies in pursuit. She couldn't imagine the Frost Nekron or the remaining hooded warriors being completely defeated. Her spell and the intense combat back there were immense, but she could imagine they had all fallen by the sword. Still, even though she couldn't see anyone chasing them, it didn't mean they weren't being pursued. At least they still seemed to be in the clear for the moment. This tunnel they were sprinting down was a little too quiet; if you listened hard enough, you could probably hear a pin drop.

She signaled to Shane for them to stop, "This is too easy. There is no way they would just let us follow them like this."

The werefox glanced toward a section of the tunnel that seemed to split off from their current one. He sniffed the air, his brow furrowing. "For the most part, I would agree. The path they took splinters off from this trail. I can tell they are not much farther away. It seems like they have stopped moving forward. I think I lost the old wizard's scent, which can't be good. If any of you thought that what we just went through was bad, I don't think it will compare to what is coming next for us and the entire world. His sect of the Daimonia seem poised to follow him to the bitter end."

Floriana nodded her head in agreement. "You mentioned that we might have backup?"

Shane grinned toothily, "I did. Her name is Priscilla, and she is a Dragon Warrior. Unlike these two worthless idiots, she is actually useful. One person may not seem like much, but it is still something. I am hoping she found a way into the tunnel." He stopped talking for a moment and stared daggers into Jayden. "I know you have been very worried about her. I have intentionally been very coy about what happened back on the train. You get too distracted by other people and your feelings and forget the task at hand. Stick to your purpose; we are beyond a life-and-death situation. You both need to take this seriously."

That was harsh, she thought. However, from the short time she had spent with Jayden and Tony before, there was no doubt they were a bunch of goofballs. She also knew they were extremely powerful when they wanted to be or exceptionally weak when they took their eyes off the prize. She learned on the battlefield that sometimes using your best weapons for last was good, but sometimes it was one of the worst mistakes you could make.

Her eyes locked in on Jayden; his nod to her was all she needed. They might have a chance if he and Tony were in it to win it. Hell, who was she kidding? They were completely outnumbered. Even if this Priscilla was as strong as he claimed, they were still outmanned and outgunned. However, with those two boys by her side, she knew there was always a chance. They were the best at throwing a wrench into the plans of others

Chapter 29

The White Rose

There was a buzz in the air that she could not quite describe. Her mind was swimming in a pool of shock and wonder. With every step forward that she took, it seemed like she was traveling back into a different era. A time of war, magic, and hate. In truth, the reality seemed poetic, as it was not vastly different than their current state of existence.

The sound of canvas flapping in the wind was an uncomfortable sound deep within a cave. She felt a chill going up and down her spine as her eyes trained on the object of her fear. Her eyes could barely process the angelic wings stretched out alongside the ship with the grace and elegance of an eagle. Next to the gorgeous wings stood a column of pure pearly white sails swaying in tandem with the gentle breeze. Three tall wooden masts stood regally in their prospective positions like pillars sculpted by the gods. The rudder moved with the slow-moving waves as the boat rested at the dock, patiently waiting for its next journey.

A mighty warrior appeared near the back of the ship. He wore a dark cloak with a long sword hanging from his hip. The weapon's hilt was a decadent platinum, matching the large jewel-encrusted book in his arms. He paced around the expertly designed ship's balcony. The rails were made of solid white gold with specks of silver. Even the lantern hanging from the ship's rear still shined as if its flame had never been quenched.

The ship's wheel was as regal as the white gold that aligned the rails on the ship's side. There was no captain, but its ivory frame was the very height of elegance. The jib sail and its boom stretched from the front of the ship as if reaching for the next port. And the icing on the cake was an intricately hand painted red rose that covered the side of the ship. Soft hints of white paint were dusted along the rose petals. Stenciled in gold near the rudder was the name *White Rose*.

There were two reflective devices on the forecastle deck. They looked like large mirrors made with very thick glass. In the back of the mirrors were metal attachments that protruded from the center of the glass. A compartment housed emerald-colored magic stones at the end of these metal attachments. The odd part wasn't simply their design or that there were more of these mirrorlike devices throughout the ship. Floriana found it peculiar because if she glanced at the objects at a slightly different angle or closed her eyes, the objects would completely disappear from sight. She couldn't tell if it was due to the light coming from the cave ceiling or if it was something more.

Placed near the front of the ship and the rear were offensive weapons. The primary offensive weapons were four magic cannons. Each of these was designed with dual barrels that sat on top of each other. The barrel placed on top was thicker and designed for extensive ordinances and spells. Their frames were made of white ceramic material with lines of gold swirling on the weapon's surface. Near the ship's bow were two openings for what she assumed were rockets or torpedoes. Just like with the mirrorlike devices, they would completely disappear if she glanced away for a moment.

Floriana handed her binoculars to Jayden to get a better look. She was really confused by everything. The frame of the airship appeared to be quite sturdy. Back in its day, this vessel would have been quite formidable in combat. In fact, she couldn't imagine the last time this ship would have fired any ordinances. The barrels themselves had no burn marks or any deposits of gunpowder. It was possible that *The Elders* used a different type of gunpowder that she had never seen, but not likely. The question mulling over in her mind as she examined the war machine was that she could not quite understand why the Daimonia would want this ship in the first place.

While in the military, she specialized in aerial combat; most of her work focused on clandestine missions. The airships and gliders she used in the military were far more advanced than the Galleon ship floating on a dock. Plus, the color of the ship would stand out under most circumstances. The one advantage she could guess was that the weapons systems on the ship would be hard to see, and a spotter might never know this was a military vessel.

Their plan of attack, in her mind, seemed pretty straightforward. However, she had not prepared for the terrain and structure of this underground wet dock. I mean, who would have guessed that an airship that should belong in a museum would be floating comfortably inside a cave.

The path they had been traveling on had been pretty straightforward thus far. This expanded cavern presented a unique problem. The airship was on a small lake and tethered to a dock. The entrance to the dock was rather simple; all they had to do was run straight down their current path. Then, they would have to move up a steep incline to reach the plank. Considering the challenges they've experienced thus far; it was a nice change of pace.

Their real challenge was that the area right outside the ship had only one guard. Most of the hooded figures were posted on the left and right sides of the lake. A smaller contingent of fighters stood at the base of the hill. The trail they were on split into three directions, which meant the larger forces would converge on them if they made a move. An opening leading to the surface was on the farthest end of the cavern. A wash of sunlight poured through at the end of the cave, and a few seagulls managed to fly in and out. She had no idea how an exit to the surface could exist down here. If they ever survived this, she was going to find out.

She jumped at the sensation of a set of fingers interlocking with hers. Floriana turned her head to see Grace, who was now holding her hand. The Aggeloi Princess's eyes were fixated on the enemies mingling farther down their path. Floriana sensed some of her magic was being transferred to Grace through touch. It wasn't the same sensation of a magic-draining spell, but Grace seemed to be borrowing some of her energy.

Grace's hair became staticky, her magical aura increasing. A ball of light blue energy appeared next to her. The ball of energy spun with an intensity that matched her power. This ball began to expand and reshape. After a couple of seconds, the ball of energy morphed into the shape of a dragon. The creature had blue and white scales reflecting the light cascading into the cave. Her eyes widened as two large horns with rounded tips formed on top of the creature's head and a tail made of scales with rows of icicles pierced through them. The monster's claws were as sharp as her knife, and its eyes were as blue as the sea.

Gracey gave it a gentle pat on the head once it had completed its transformation. The Dragon nuzzled her back and let out a contented snort. With each breath the dragon took, tiny snowflakes were expelled from its massive jaws. The Dragon's claws were a dark blue, which complemented its eyes.

Grace whispered, "Aiko, it's time to send forth your minions."

As the Aggeloi Princess spoke those words, her creation started to glow. Then, smaller balls of energy appeared on all sides of the animal. The balls of light quickly shapeshifted into similar-looking Dragons, half the size of Aiko. Even though they were smaller, their magical energies were formidable.

Grace pointed at an area of dirt in front of her and said, "Snow Tigladon."

Instantly, four pools of milky liquid appeared in the spot Grace had been pointing toward. The puddles bubbled as they reformed and changed shape. These pools were rapidly changing into the forms of four huge animals. It didn't take long for their six-foot frames and spiked tails to appear beside her. The Tigladons had a mixture of white, blue, and faded gray stripes. Their massive jaws were layered with shards of ice. Their muscular shoulders and massive claws were poised for destruction.

Grace's fingers became untangled from hers. Floriana moved with blinding speed to catch the Aggeloi Princess as she almost fainted. The General figured her friend might overdo it by summoning creatures of this caliber. Floriana was still shocked at what she saw; she had never seen a summoner be able to do what she just did.

As she steadied her friend, she caught a glimpse of Shane loading explosive rounds into his revolver. He summoned five spiked shields and three more shields that were spinning wheels made of fire. His eyes were intense and ready.

Then Floriana glanced toward her left at the sound of gunfire. She didn't notice it while Grace was doing her magic show, but Tony and Jayden had already gone toward the paths that splintered off. They were already engaging the enemy to give them a chance to make it to the ship.

Floriana grinned as she drew her rapier and clutched her revolver. Macy took a step forward to stand beside her. The young lady was radiating with an intense heat. Wings made of a magenta-colored fire protruded from her shoulder blades. This powerful woman loaded a shell into her gunblade. She was ready. It was now or never.

J. Edwards

***

Suicide missions were a part of the game, she was once told. Her commander explained that sometimes, the end goal is not achievable. He used to say that there would be moments where the concepts of wrong or right will never truly come into play. It was just alive or dead. Her Uncle Robert, a General, then emphasized that sometimes you simply put your life on the line with no chance of victory. The suicide mission should never be your first option, but on occasion, it may be the only one.

Once the first Tigladon took down a Daimonia member by surprise, she knew this battle would be one for the ages. A handful of people versus an army with an end goal they still did not quite know. The war being fought in the world above was, in a twisted way, being reenacted in the world below. Only this time, there will be no records of their heroism. If their names were to ever be mentioned, they would be described as traitors, violent criminals, and runaways. No one will celebrate their attempts to protect the world above from the devils below.

Despite the overwhelming odds, she was extremely grateful for the Aggeloi Princess fighting beside her. She was impressed by the thrashing her unique summons gave the enemy. Each of the tiny dragons she had summoned rained some of the strongest frost magic on their hooded nemeses. Their glacial scales were as tough as an iceberg, and any Daimonia bullet that struck them might as well have been a pebble. They were lightning-quick and could easily use the *Invisibility Speed* technique. The Daimonia were shocked every time the creatures appeared to disappear and reappear behind them with rows of sharpened teeth. Even the few Daimonia wizards that could use fire magic could barely land a meaningful hit on the frost dragons. One of their fire magic's few downsides is that their spells take a while to charge and are not designed for fast-moving targets. So, at the moment, their enemies were completely outclassed due to the presence of the dragons alone.

350

The Tigladons, like the dragons, were equally as destructive toward their enemy's ranks. They moved along the rough and rocky battlefield with the efficiency of a special forces team. If one of the animals was spotted by their cloaked enemies, they would destroy them in a matter of seconds with a bite to the neck by another monster that would attack the Daimonia from the blindside. In stalking their prey, they could send explosive magical blasts of ice-cold energy at long ranges. This meant that Daimonia members lined up closer to the ship and the cave exit had to be on their guard.

Aiko, however, chose to fly relatively low next to Grace as they traversed the battlefield. The Dragon would summon a thick ice shield to intercept any bullets or offensive magic spells from their enemies hiding amongst the rocks. Then Aiko would speed toward them and send them promptly to their maker. Even with the friendly Dragon by their side, Grace chose to summon some insects onto the battlefield. Despite almost fainting in the process, she conjured a small army of poisoned scorpions that appeared at the feet of large groups of cloaked warriors that were farther down the trail. Unfortunately, they didn't realize their danger until the scorpions began climbing into their combat boots.

Grace channeled her magic to summon clouds of bees, wasps, and locusts to utterly annoy their enemy. What really impressed Floriana about her friend's battle prowess was that she could sense that the Princess had not even remotely used all of her magic power. There was still an ocean of deadly magic within Grace that the enemy would come to fear.

She felt a twinge in her stomach and pushed Grace to the side. Floriana raised her rapier and her pistol just in time to do a cross block to resist the strikes from twin cutlasses with the edge of her blade and the base of her gun. She then pressed upwards with all her strength, just enough so that her attacker was off balance. She quickly took a step back, then fired three frost bullets into his chest. Instantly, he crumbled like a sack of potatoes. The General rotated her body to the right and pointed her swords at three large boulders resting on an incline. She channeled her magical energy into her sword, and before she could cast the spell, a leather shield appeared in front of her weapon. The shield absorbed a hail of bullets, and she grinned. That damn werefox was something else.

Then she shouted, "Frostslide!"

As her words left her lips, her rapier released a light blue blast of energy. This energy blast sent a beam of magic toward a spot on the hill about twenty feet above the row of boulders. Large blocks of ice the size of small cars appeared above the rocky formation. The ice blocks then rolled toward the unfortunate souls hiding on the other side. Once they had been pelted to kingdom come, the remaining blocks of ice sped toward a group of Daimonia soldiers trying to flank Jayden on the other side of the cavern. The blocks of ice completely obligated their targets. Jayden glanced in her general direction (pun not intended) and gave her a thumbs up.

"Get Down!" Shane shouted as he pulled her down behind a large rock.

A second later, machine gunfire erupted around them. A rocket exploded near a patch of dirt behind her. Floriana's ears were ringing, and her head was spinning. The Dragon conjured ice shields to protect them, but they were quickly whittled down. Aiko curled up next to Grace as her shields absorbed the brunt of the machine-gun bullets and rocket fire.

Then, a voice from above shouted, "Flames of Doubt!"

Floriana glanced up as a magenta-colored flame slammed into the twin machinegun nests. Immediately, their attackers picked up their machine guns and turned them on each other.

The student of the Phoenix Monastery flying above them aimed her gunblade toward a contingent of moving fighters attacking Tony. Then she shouted, "Technical Boom!"

The world around them flashed with an impossibly bright white light for a second. Then, it flashed completely black. Just as quickly as their world went dark, the cave returned to normal, and they were once again surrounded by a cavern that was bathed in a brown and gloomy shade. Floriana was confused because it was like someone turned the lights on and off.

The area where Macy had fired exploded into a cloud of dust. Dozens of cloaked warriors were knocked into the air and crashed to the ground. Then she heard someone croak *Ribbit*. This socially unacceptable sound was followed by more *Ribbits* occurring almost in unison. The General glanced at her two comrades, who both had confused looks.

Floriana's curiosity overwhelmed her battlefield sense, so she poked her head out from around the boulder. She spotted a dark cloak lying across a large, flattened rock. The empty hood began to move back and forth sporadically. Then, a bright green frog jumped out from under the cloth. Floriana laughed; she never imagined having to fight frogs on the battlefield. Unfortunately, she left her fishing net at her old military post.

The Eden General was beginning to understand the value of Macy's magical abilities. She had met a few soldiers trained at the Phoenix Monastery. Most only learned how to use hand-to-hand combat or weapons skills. She had never seen their magical abilities before. Macy's fire magic could cause physical damage and status ailments. On the battlefield, it was beneficial, especially when she got the Daimonia machine gunners to turn on their own people. The truth was Jayden's childhood friend was an absolute game-changer for them. Like Grace, Macy's training made their small team appear much larger and deadlier.

The contingent of cloaked enemies posted at the bottom of the hill closest to the ship had become razor-thin. She couldn't believe how many of their soldiers had either perished or were too wounded to fight, thanks to all of the magic expelled by Grace and Macy from a distance. The rest of their squad must have fanned toward the eastern and western sides of the cavern. It looked like they must have been heading to the section of the cavern where Tony and Jayden were fighting individually. The two boys were so outnumbered that it tore at her heart. Floriana wanted to go to them, but they were so spread out that she would only be able to help one.

The werefox stood up, tapping her shoulder, "I know what you are thinking. I also know your relationship with those two boys can cloud your judgment. As a General, I am sure, better yet, I know that you have to make tough calls that probably still keep you up at night even to this day. We make tough calls for a reason and need to stand by them. Right now, our two most important assets are Sarah and Grace. Those two are the only people we know who can interact at any level with *The Key*. Right now, we only have access to one of those, and the other is even more important. Those boys have done a fine job. I would never tell them that, but they have. We need to honor them by completing ours. The last thing they would want is for the world to crumble just to save them. They have already experienced that hell. Their hearts don't deserve to be broken a second time."

Chapter 30

My Humanity

The large rock next to him exploded. His eyes closed as he was pelted with shards of rock. Blood started to drip onto his shirt from the cuts forming on his face. The pain from the exploding rock and ringing in his ears paled in comparison to the bullet wound he had wrapped on his left shoulder.

He wasn't used to burning sensations anymore. When the rifle round pierced his skin, Jayden became all too familiar with it. His Auto-Shield and Internal Body Heat spells managed to melt most of the round before it could really do him in.

Still, shards of the bullet managed to do some damage. They must have been using a magic-resistant coating. Ammo like that was rare and expensive, which meant the Daimonia were planning for something big and terrible.

He moved his head to the left as another bullet pierced through the rock he was hiding behind. The Dragon Warrior loaded another magazine, leaving him only one left. Jayden was truthfully grateful for the help that both Grace and Floriana sent his way. He only hoped they didn't notice his bandage when he gave them a thumbs up. The last thing he wanted was for them to interfere.

A pile of rocks and pebbles slid down a slope to his left. Jayden quickly backed away and crouched under a small overhanging boulder. The sounds of gunfire filled the air, and tracer rounds appeared sporadically in his vision. He took a deep breath to remain calm. Jayden closed his eyes and focused on more elusive sounds. His ears perked up at what he thought were boots and shoes, softly pressing down gravel and sticks. A wall of black cloth appeared, coming up from a hill of rocks ten feet in front of him.

Jayden made himself as flat as he could to fit in the shadow caused by the overhanging rock. From what seemed like a blanket of sackcloth, he could spot pairs of leather gloves and automatic rifles. He channeled his magical energy and summoned three fireballs with metal cores that appeared thirty feet to their left. The meteors slammed into his intended targets and exploded. Jayden managed to incapacitate four out of the five of their unit. The fifth was dazed and covered in burn marks and blood. His cloaked nemesis turned toward where the attack came from and fired off his weapon. But, of course, Jayden wasn't there.

All of a sudden, more rocks spilled down from the incline to his left. Five more cloaked warriors appeared in front of him. They appeared to be checking in on their wounded friend. The cloaked Warrior, wiping blood from the injured one's face, shoved a dagger into his chest. The poor man hit the ground before he even knew he had been betrayed.

Jayden was instantly filled with rage. How could they kill one of their own? He raised his weapon and emptied the whole magazine into the row of enemies. Then, he used his left hand to send a blast of red flames to those who didn't catch a bullet.

He slowly crawled out from under the rock. He channeled his magic but couldn't sense other hooded enemies trying to get closer. He decided to approach the pile of bodies he had created. Next to the man who had perished with a knife to his chest was the one who stabbed him. The stabber was still alive, but barely. His consciousness was fading in and out as he choked on his own blood.

The young Dragon Warrior felt nothing but rage toward this person, this creature. He could not understand the idea of turning on his own people. It just didn't make sense to him. Jayden wanted to know what would make someone do that. To go through all of the violence that he was sure was required to join any of the Daimonia sects. He couldn't understand their continued devotion during the current state. They were being used as bullet sponges or food for the Nekron. Were their lives so worthless that they would give them up for some sort of power?

At this point, he had an idea why the Fallen Wizard, the Dark Prince, and even Cain wanted true power. In a way, he could understand why their underlings might be searching for the same thing. But how much power would they really get in the end? Or were they just simply evil people? Did they really need a reason to cheat, lie, and kill?

Jayden hated having to take lives. He was used to it now, but it always destroyed him on the inside. The nightmares never stopped. However, the individual he was standing over he wanted to utterly destroy or watch him choke to death on his own blood. If he did that, he would be no different than the hooded warriors that destroyed his hometown.

He shook his head and decided to give this unworthy man an ounce of mercy. He wasn't going to let him suffer until he met his maker. Jayden channeled his magic, then held out his right forearm. He closed his eyes and said a prayer. Then he snapped his fingers, and an invisible flame scorched the warrior's heart, killing him instantly. In most cases, that spell was absolutely forbidden. Jayden figured that bestowing mercy on a dying man was worthy enough.

The Dragon Warrior felt a twinge in his gut when he sensed the soldier passing by. While he felt a smidge of guilt, he knew he had to return to his feet. Jayden could sense attackers coming from below him and others from higher on the hill. Jayden knew he might have a better chance if he could draw them closer to the lake.

Jayden could still feel his rage was not satisfied. He could not afford to hold back anymore. If they were willing to kill their own people for power, what weren't they willing to do? The world will never be safe with people like that who are willing to hurt others for some pocket change.

He glanced toward the cave ceiling and shouted, "Blue Scorching Speed Armor On!"

Instantly, the air around him became unbearably hot. The twigs and weeds around him burst into flame. Even the droplets of water dispersed across the field of rocks surrounding him turned to steam. Yellow and blue colored flames began to swirl around his body like a tornado. The blade of his sheathed sword had become hot enough to scorch bare skin with just a simple touch. Magical power radiated from within him to the point that his attackers had completely stopped their forward advance.

Jayden bent his knees, then launched skyward, leaving a trail of fire in his wake. As he accelerated into the air, he turned his body toward the cloaked warriors coming down from the lake. They aimed their weapons in his direction and fired. The scorching hot blue flames completely melted any rounds that came his way. Even their magic spells were completely canceled out on a molecular level by the extreme temperatures his body released.

He shouted, "Rapid Shot."

The Dragon Warrior punched the air as quickly as possible toward his targets. Blue and yellow flames rocketed from each punch he threw. The yellow flames were the quickest and struck their targets before they were hit. The light blue-colored flames would put them out of commission.

Jayden channeled more fire to encircle him. He felt a twinge in his gut, then darted to the right and sped toward a squad of cloaked warriors climbing up the rocks toward him. He used the *Invisibility Speed* technique once his feet touched the ground. His body disappeared, then reappeared right next to a target standing on a flat rock. Then he shoved his sword into the enemy's side while firing four rounds from his pistol at approaching targets.

He spun his sword above his head, using the power of the scorching wind he was creating to move the weapon. The air around him became even hotter, and burn marks appeared on the scorched rocks within any radius of him. Once his spell had finished charging, he grabbed the handle of his spinning sword. Then he stabbed the blade into hardpacked dirt, and it pierced it like it was made of butter.

Jayden shouted, "Wall of Fire!"

A shockwave of magical energy spread from his body. Every cell within him pulsated from the magical energy he produced. The air around him began to buzz with energy as his body became encircled by a yellow and blue flame wall. While the wall of flames grew skyward, the barrier of the flames started to expand and push away from him. Any enemies caught in its wake were either completely incinerated or never wanted to fight the boy from Eiréné ever again.

He channeled his fire magic into his legs and rocketed back into the air. Then, he flattened out his body and directed it toward a spot to the far left side of the lake where absolutely no enemies were. He blasted himself forward into a glide.

As he soared above the sea of rocks and boulders, the flames propelling him forward began to completely disappear. His magical energy plummeted faster than his grades and dating opportunities in the sixth grade. Before he knew it, his body was descending and flipping forwards uncontrollably.

He slammed into a set of boulders that were stacked upon each other. He managed to hear something crack or pop.

This sound was followed by an intense sensation of unimaginable pain. His head was throbbing, and he fell on his left arm, which was the appendage that had recently been shot. His unfortunate fall from grace helped him to figure out where the cracking and popping sound came from.

Jayden adjusted himself up against the ginormous rock so he could sit up. Then he popped his dislocated shoulder back into place. This action was harrowing, and he was angry about how actors and movies make it seem easier. He brushed his hand against the back of his head and found some dampness in his curly hair. Jayden pulled his hand back and saw that his hand was now scarlet red. This helped him to solve the mystery of his splitting headache and possibly permanent dizziness.

Jayden felt a twinge in his stomach. Part of him hoped that feeling was the sheer embarrassment of failing to do a glide properly during a rather important battle. He was sure his friends and enemies probably didn't miss seeing a yellow fireball in the sky. He let out an exhaustive sigh as he lifted his right arm and fired off the remaining bullets in his magazine in the direction, he knew his enemies were coming from.

Jayden took a strained, deep breath as he holstered his weapon and pointed his right index upward. Then he shouted, "Heatseeker!"

A small dark cloud formed in the space above him. This cloud was as dark as night and about the size of a pillow. It began to glow for a second, then unleashed a maelstrom of orange balls of fire that rained down on his pursuers. Any enemy with warm blood flowing within their veins was an instant target of his rage.

His right arm slumped to the ground.

"That's about all I got left, guys."

***

A cool mist filled the air. He could feel his consciousness coming in and out. His mind appeared to be playing tricks on him as a small pool of water started to form next to him. He touched the water. It was ice cold.

That's odd, he thought; he was still a significant enough distance from the lake. He didn't notice any water trickling down through the rocks and boulders. Jayden touched the water again. When his fingers breached the surface, he could hear the sound of rushing waves. He quickly pulled his hand away, but he still felt cool moisture in the air. It was like standing outside on an overcast day at the beach.

The sound of waves crashing against rock grew ever closer. Then he noticed that he could hear the sound of water in the lake raging like they were in a storm. As he listened, he could spot the distinct sound of people screaming for help as the waves continued to break. Jayden slid to his right and pressed his back against a hill to force himself into an awkwardly standing position. He turned his head to get a glimpse at what was going on.

A swirling vacuum of dark water was on the far left side of the lake. The waves were spiraling around like they were in a tornado. Each of the waves that were created by this massive vortex slammed into the airship with extreme force. The Daimonia members standing too close to the lake were sucked in by a gigantic tidal wave.

Jayden sat back and stared in horror as they fought to resist the pounding waves. His heart sank as a cloaked warrior clung onto a triangular rock for dear life. Tears were streaming from her eyes as she stared back into his. Her blonde hair was blowing violently in the torrential wind. Her fingers desperately clung to rock after each wave slammed against her and her colleagues. There was true fear and desperation in her eyes. He saw something in her that he had not seen in the other cloaked warrior. This was not the face of a killer but the look of a lost soul crying for help.

He took a deep breath and channeled his life energy. He used the *Invisibility Speed* technique to quickly get to her, then grabbed her by the wrist. He pulled her away in less than a second, just as a gigantic wave came crashing down.

Jayden laid her against the rock next to the one he had been resting against. He sensed blood trickling from his nose and scratches on his temple. The cost of using his life energy always involved taking a few steps closer to death. He figured saving an enemy wouldn't be the worst way to go. Maybe it would help him from losing his humanity.

He switched his gaze to the girl sitting next to him. Jayden could tell that all the color had drained from her face. Her eyes were still filled with fear and shock. There was nothing like the feeling of impending doom. He also sensed that she never envisioned herself being in this position. She probably imagined being on the airship with the real Daimonia members.

Jayden gently nudged against her, "My name is Jayden LoneOak. I think you are pretty much safe now."

She glanced at him wearily. There was still a sense of pure hatred in her eyes, but then her look softened. "You can call me Kel. Just call me Samantha Kelly. It won't matter anyway. You are just going to kill me in the end. Just go ahead and do it."

"That's the most unique way of saying thank you I have ever heard," he replied.

His eyes shifted back to the large mound of rocks and dirt in front of him. It was so high that he couldn't see anything beyond it. He didn't need visual confirmation to know that their end was coming. The sound of boots crushing gravel and rounds being racked into rifles grew louder than the crashing waves behind them. Jayden knew there was nowhere left to run. So, he placed his left arm across the front of Samantha to protect her. He would use his last breath to save her.

"Look," he said with a shallow breath. "I won't be able to protect you much longer. You need to run; they will kill you as easily as they will me. You don't have to die here. Just go!"

Samantha Kelly shrugged at his weak attempt to protect a complete stranger. He hoped she would comply or make a run for it, but who was he kidding. She probably would get killed by one of her people minutes after they got to him. There was also a chance one of his friends would take her out. He figured she probably thought it was better if she died comfortably sitting down instead of running for no reason. As a fellow lazy person, he respected her choice. But still, he hoped she could have a chance at resetting her life. Despite the fighting and bloodshed, he was glad it might have made a difference in someone else's life.

The waves raging just a few yards behind them seemed to change. Each splash from the rising tide became more intense. Every roar from the waves grew louder and appeared to get closer. He could hear rocks split by the raging water and gravel dragged toward the depths.

Then, a bubble popped up next to them. Samantha jumped in her seat at the sound. Her eyes grew wide, and she scooted beside him out of fear. He followed her gaze to figure out what scared her. The puddle of water they were sitting next to started to bubble. Each of the large bubbles popped at different times. The bubbles of water began to stack on top of each other. A human form became visible once the stack of bubbles grew to over five feet tall.

As he stared at the human-sized blob of water, he felt a drop on his cheek. He turned his head and looked up, his jaw almost hitting the floor. There was a one-hundred-foot-tall tidal wave standing above them. He closed his eyes for a second, expecting to be drenched, drowned, or dead.

Jayden jumped at the next drop of water that landed on the back of his neck. He peered up again, but the gigantic wave had not crashed. In fact, it seemed to be frozen in animation. He felt Samantha patting his arm; he turned to her, super annoyed. His eyes could not believe what they were seeing; the gigantic blob of water was now turning into the body of a human. He heard the sound of thunder, and then lightning struck the humanoid-shaped puddle of water.

He quickly turned away at the blind flash of light. His vision became blurred and filled with spots. Jayden's nose flared at the scent of ocean water. Then he felt ice-cold fingers gently combing through his hair. He felt saltwater dripping down his face, the pain in the back of his head decreasing.

When his eyes could fully open, he noticed strands of sky-blue hair. He spotted a pair of Jian-styled swords with a golden hilt and red tassels attached to the base of the handle. The weapons were sheathed beneath a black sash wrapped around a gray martial arts uniform. Her sky-blue hair parted in front of her face, revealing intense, deadly eyes and a warm smile.

The young woman flicked him on the nose before she stood fully erect. She turned her body in the direction they were facing. Figures draped in dark cloth appeared on the hill just above them. They were armed to the teeth, like the warriors that destroyed his hometown all those years ago. Their hooded adversaries did not say a word; they hardly even acknowledged their existence. All he remembered was a series of bright flashes.

His hand went numb from the tight grip that Samantha had on it. He had closed his eyes briefly; he couldn't stand to watch his killers have their day. Jayden was completely shocked to be still breathing. His heart was pounding in his chest like it was trying to jump out of his rib cage.

He squinted wearily in the direction of his would-be killers. They were still standing on the hill with their fingers pressed against their triggers. His eyes tried to focus on the bullets. That's when he noticed the solution to their survival. Once it left the barrel, each round would have to pass through a barely visible veil of clear water. Once they entered the wall of magic, they instantly turned into tiny water droplets.

Mariko slowly drew one of her swords with her right hand and pointed it toward the Daimonia. Her eyes flicked back at him, "Your Master made you a warrior, and I turned you into a Knight. Was your plan to save this woman only to die in disgrace?" She asked as bullets rained down upon them.

He didn't know what to say back to her. She knew he placed himself in this position because he was careless. Once again, he punished himself by holding back in another life-or-death situation. He would be dead now if it weren't for the Dragon Master.

"I thought as much. I want you to know that I am very proud of you. You have passed my test by saving this young woman, your enemy, with your life energy. I want you to know that this will be the last time that I will remind you of the power that you possess within. Because, my young pupil, I need you to find your strength, the last bit of bravery you possess. Under no circumstance are you to besmirch the name of a Dragon Knight and the path of the Warrior. You may only greet death upon completing your life's mission; failure is unacceptable." The Dragon Warrior said with fervor. She trained her eyes and fury toward their advancing enemy. "Your teachers had led you all down a road that leads only to death and misery. I will be your personal guide to your destination. Treat this not as a threat or a soft promise, for a Master of Dragons has spoken."

Chapter 31

Gigas and Aegis

The slow sense of impending doom creased the brows of the cloaked army of lost souls. Their faces appeared to get darker from the enormous shadow of water. Droplets of ice-cold lake water pierced the pores of their skin, filling them with fear and regret. There was not a word, scream, or shout from the victims of their own sin. They each greeted the bringer of death with a somber grin while the wall of water washed them away as if they had never existed in the first place.

For a moment, friend and foe mutually respected the power of magic and nature. The lake's waters sliced through rock with ease, creating rivers across the dirt and sandy landscape of the cave. Many of the cloaked warriors fought against the rushing water, only to be defeated by the power of a Master of Dragons.

The dark river of water began to produce large bubbles. These bubbles coalesced and formed into humanoid-shaped creatures. Thunder erupted within the quiet and calm cave. Bolts of white and blue lightning struck these humanoid bubbles of water. In an instant, there were hordes of warriors dressed in gray martial arts uniforms. They let out the battle cry of the Dragons and commenced their fight for humanity.

Master Mariko drew her second sword from its sheath as the water she had summoned disappeared. A small contingent of Daimonia Warriors appeared above them. They raged angrily, their cloaks dripping with mud from the saturated ground. The Master of Dragons made a cross-slashing motion across her body. Waves of crystal-clear water launched from her weapons, slicing cleanly through their midsections.

She appeared to turn invisible as a second wave of attackers appeared. Her body then reappeared in front of an unfortunate soul. Her left blade pierced his chest while she swung the sword in her right hand over her head. A wave of water appeared above her and crashed into the rest of the attackers. They were knocked out cold when their bodies slammed into nearby rocks and boulders.

She signaled for them to get up and move back toward the lake. Jayden drew his father's sword and helped Samantha to her feet. He then climbed over the rocks behind them. Once they reached the top, he could see the lake and a corner on their far left that was relatively dark and secluded. He instructed Samantha to run and hide there until the battle was over.

As she sprinted toward a small semblance of safety, a blast of black flames was directed toward her. Jayden used the Invisibility Speed technique to intercept the attack. He channeled his Fire Magic Shield and used his sword to block the attack long enough for her to escape.

His shoes dragged against the ground as he was pressed backward. The spell exploded and knocked him backward.

Jayden's back slammed against the wall of the cave. His forearms were singed, but he forced himself back to his feet.

Mariko sent a blast of water toward his attacker. Their cloaked nemesis drew a long claymore to block her attack briefly. While he braced himself to block the spell, he adjusted his stance. He used the *Invisibility Technique* to move himself completely out of the way of the spell. The blast continued to go forward and slammed into a rock.

The cloaked warrior flipped his long hair backward and widened his stance. He formed a ball of dark flame energy. Once the spell had been channeled, he launched four black fireballs with Zirconium cores.

Mariko quickly turned into her watery human form. She let the spells pass through her and explode against two unfortunate cloaked warriors behind her. Jayden fired back with two white holy fireballs with silver cores. The two spells collided and sent ultra-heated metal shards into the air, instantly igniting the dried roots hiding amongst the rocks.

"That is the magic of the traitors," Mariko shouted, with a stare that would put fear in even the bravest warriors. She adjusted her posture and stood up straight, lowering her weapons. "Take note, Jayden, that black flame is just like the *Yūrei* ghost flame. They are strictly forbidden. Yours, however, has a saving grace. His is rooted in pure evil and hate. You may not know this, but he is not using any arbitrary fire magic. You know of our three schools of Dragon Magic, but there is, in fact, a fourth. And that, my young man, is where he learned to kill."

Jayden took a relaxing breath. Then he said calmly, "Well, in that case, will you give me the honor of taking the life of my childhood friend."

***

An arrow narrowly missed his ear. His right arm was still dripping from the one he couldn't dodge. He quickly snapped the arrow and pulled it through.

Blood dripped down his right arm with no intention of stopping. Still, he maintained his grip on his broadsword. He sent a dust devil toward the former Sergeant of the Eden Army.

His arm moved seemingly on its own to deflect a downward strike from his former classmate. Tony adjusted his weight and pushed up against Bryce's blade. With his enemy off balance, he summoned a series of hailstones and rocketed them toward his enemy's stomach. Bryce grunted as he reeled backward and fired off three bullets from his semi-automatic pistol.

Tony easily deflected rounds and sent one in the direction of Jason. This singed the side of his bicep. The army soldier responded by launching an arrow with a red tip. Tony snatched the arrow in flight, then it beeped twice. The Dragon Warrior summoned a shield of electricity just as the arrow exploded.

He was flung backward and flailed in the air. Tony flipped his legs backward to control his fall. When his knees landed, he slammed his fist into the dirt. Then, super-heated gusts of wind blasted his two cloaked enemies.

Tony got back to his feet and sprinted toward the weapon he dropped. He snatched his sword up and slashed at Bryce. Their weapons clanged as they fought fiercely. Bryce aimed to slash downward at Tony. He caught the attack and held his own from Bryce's overwhelming strength.

Bryce gave a cheeky grin as his blade began to glow. Tony pushed up higher, and then his blade flew out of his hand out of nowhere. He managed to sidestep Bryce's blade at the last second. He grabbed him by the wrist and summoned lightning bolts around his knuckles. As he held Bryce out of balance, he punched him repeatedly in the ribs.

Tony pushed him away and ducked as another arrow came from Sergeant Jason. He flipped backward three times to put some distance between them. He quickly summoned a gust of wind to lift his sword back off the ground and launched it at him. He caught the weapon and then defended himself against a barrage of mini-arrows.

There were blotches of red stains appearing all over his clothing. He spit out blood and lost his footing for a moment. Then he channeled his magic to push the arrows he couldn't block out his body. He pressed a button on his sword, and it shifted to double-blade mode. His body felt drained, but he had every intention of defeating them. If for no other reason than to rub it in Jayden's face.

Jason sent another barrage of mini-arrows at him. Before Jason attacked, the Dragon Warrior was already spinning his weapon in front of him, channeling as much magic as he could. He released a powerful blast of wind that kicked up scores of rocks and clumps of dirt. The wind was so intense that it pushed back the incoming mini-arrows, dispersing them in different directions.

Both of his enemies had to retreat to avoid the debris caused by his counterattack. They must have been frightened because they did not return fire or hide well. Tony took a deep breath. Judging by the crimson stains left behind where his enemies stood, he knew they must have taken a solid hit.

Just when Tony could take a second breather, Bryce was back on his feet. The former resident of Eiréné's black clothes were in tatters. Blood dripped down Bryce's face, with pure anger and hate in his eyes.

Tony launched and summoned a mini-cloud in the area where Jason would have landed. The cloud launched lightning blasts toward the former Sergeant every time he moved. That would keep him busy and turn this into a one-on-one fight.

The Dragon Warrior stepped back to avoid Bryce's reckless strike. He quickly kicked him in the ribs as he dodged the attack. Bryce winced, and Tony swung his blade toward his neck. His enemy ducked and slashed Tony across his chest. The cut wasn't deep, but he could feel blood trickling down his body.

Tony blocked the next series of attacks. Even though his enemy was a complete jerk and a womanizer, he couldn't help but be impressed by how fast and strong he was. Bryce may not be his favorite person in the world, but he is also not a person anyone should take lightly.

Bryce grinned again as he ducked a slash from Tony. The Dragon Warrior quickly swung with the other side of the blade before his enemy could respond with an attack. Bryce's sword glowed again as he blocked Tony's attack. Instantly, the tips of his blades bent, and the connecting piece that kept the double-bladed sword together shattered.

The moment the connector exploded; he was caught off balance. He felt a twinge in his stomach and ducked as an arrow narrowly missed his spiky hair. Tony morphed his body into a gust of wind and moved farther away from both enemies.

He landed just behind a large boulder. He felt an ice-cold hand on his shoulder. He glanced up as the silhouette of a woman dressed in a gray martial arts uniform appeared.

The young woman made a blue circle of magical energy. He caught a soft scent of salt water and felt like he could hear ocean waves crashing in the background. She stuck her hand in the center of the magic circle and slowly pulled out a Jian-styled sword. The blade was crystal and had a greenish-blue tint to it.

Priscilla flipped over the rock he was hiding behind. Then she slammed her sword into the dirt. Two large waves of water shot out of the ground and sped toward his two enemies. Bryce managed to duck behind a large mound of dirt. On the other hand, Jason was slammed against a sharpened rock and laid still for a moment.

Tony returned to his feet and channeled magic into his Auto-Healing spell. Then he examined his bent swords and tried to meld them back into one. They wouldn't combine back into the broadsword form, which was disappointing.

Bryce shouted, "Not this bitch again. I don't like fighting women. I hoped I'd get to kill Jayden, but you will do, for now."

He sprinted toward her with his sword out. She managed to dodge each of his strikes easily. She did a quick stab toward his stomach. He managed to step back before she could fully pierce him through. But the red stain on his cloak revealed her blade had touched flesh.

She shrugged in his direction. "Who are you again?" Priscilla replied as she adjusted into a fighting stance, holding the blade over her head. "Regardless, I want to be abundantly clear. I will be the one to run Jayden through."

Bryce spit on the ground and used the *Invisibility Speed* technique to close the distance. Priscilla ducked under his lightning-quick strike. She blocked the next slash as his blade began to glow. Her weapon was ripped completely out of her hands, skidding across the rocky floor.

Priscilla managed to dodge his next few strikes. She channeled her magical energy and created a sword made of rushing water. Bryce's weapon glowed again as its metallic edge made contact with the concentrated liquid. His widened when his spell did nothing. Her weapon remained in her hand. Then she pushed up on his blade and then blasted him with pressured ocean water.

Tony assumed that Priscilla's last attack must have broken a rib because Bryce struggled to get back to his feet. Another series of arrows sped his way, but Priscilla created a nearly invisible veil of clear ocean water. Once the bolts pierced the veil, the arrows' molecular structure changed into that of water. The transformed arrows turned around and sped back toward their sender.

Jason was caught off guard when the arrows splashed against him. Blood started to drench the areas of his uniform where the attacks landed. He flipped his hood back and ran his bloody hand through his hair.

"You are quite the opponent. The both of you are, in fact. That spell you cast was something extraordinary. To have the ability to convert an attack into your own magical ability and reflect it back is something very unique." He let out an exhaustive sigh. "Both of you have earned my genuine respect. Therefore, I will grant you a warrior's death."

Sergeant Jason drew from his quiver a black arrow. The arrow's feathers were dark gray with a single light green thread.

He notched the arrow, but before he could get a lock on them, Tony stretched out his right arm and rocketed a bolt of red lightning toward him. Thunder cracked above them as his spell struck Jason hard in the chest. He doubled over and began to throw up blood.

Tony breathed a sigh of relief, then felt his knees go weak. His knees seemed to get weaker, forcing him to the ground. He glanced up, seeing Priscilla also losing control of her body, crumbling to the ground.

Then he sensed it, unimaginable power pulsating from the white airship. He fixed his gaze on an individual in black clothes descending the ship's steps. The old man moved very slowly, with his cane guiding his movement. Sarah was moving like a puppet behind him.

Tony redirected his eyes toward Jason, who got back to his feet. His enemy moved over to Bryce and wrapped an arm around him. Then he fired an arrow from his crossbow with a long rope attached to it. The arrow embedded itself into the ship's railing and pulled them toward it.

The Dragon Warrior channeled all his magic to resist the wizard's spell. He managed to move his right index finger. Then he pressed it into the dirt in front of him. A gust of pressurized sand, dirt, and rocks blasted toward his escaping enemies. The blast knocked Jason and Bryce into the side of the ship before they could get on. They lost their grip and fell into the lake. The rope still hung over the side so they would be forced to climb. Tony might not have been able to stop them, but he was at least happy to make their day a little worse.

***

The wizard descended the ramp like a conquering king. Power radiated from every inch of his frame. His dark green cloak flapped in the wind like the wings of the angel of death.

Sarah followed behind him without a thought of her own. She was carrying across her arms a violet-colored pillow. On top of this pillow were two bracelets made of pure gold.

373

Once they reached the bottom of the ramp. Sarah placed the pillow in the hands of the cloaked warrior standing beside them. She lifted a necklace off her shoulders, and hanging from it was *The Key*. She placed the key in a hole on the left bracelet and turned it. There was a snapping sound, and the top of the bracelet became unlocked. Then she moved toward the right bracelet, following the same procedure, and unlocked it.

Floriana's jaw just about hit the floor, or it would have been if she had any control over her body. Unfortunately for her, the wizard had cast one of his Psychological spells and had lost complete control of their bodies. They were now prostrate on the ground, watching an episode of destroy the world theater.

The reason she was so shocked was that nothing happened. Once Sarah unlocked the bracelets, she expected the world to blow up. But there was nothing. She couldn't sense any additional magical energy in the air. In fact, she was highly disappointed.

The Dark Wizard shuffled toward his subject. He dropped his cane as he raised both his arms. The top part of the bracelet split apart. He placed his wrists inside each of the bracelets. The top part of the bracelets reconnected.

Floriana felt sick to her stomach as the ground beneath her rumbled. The Fallen Wizard turned his body toward her and her team. Then he gave a toothy grin as his loose and frail skin became smooth and firm like that of a man in his thirties. His posture became more erect, and lean muscles sprouted all over his body. The dark green hood was pulled back as his face reshaped into that of a much younger man. On top of his bald head was a black wreath tattooed shaped like a crown.

What scared her the most about his sudden transformation wasn't that it happened. What scared her was that she could no longer sense his magical power. At least in a way she could truly process. His strength now was so overwhelming; it was like the sensation of the buzzing energy of the morning dawn. It was like experiencing the thunderous power of a nightly storm.

"I greatly appreciate all of you in your efforts to be here." He said with a slight grin. "I must say I think fate played a role in each of you being here now." The Fallen Wizard turned toward Sarah, still standing in her Elder Form. "Even after my transformation, do you still resist me? Well, no worry there, you have served your purpose well. I have canceled the limitations that your ancestors placed on *The Key*. Now, all with the blood and talent of the Cryptos will be able to use it. Therefore, out of gratitude, I will return you to your fold."

He snapped his fingers, and Sarah reverted to her normal form. He made her crumble to her knees and writhe in mental pain. His smile grew as her eyes filled with tears from every fiber in her body, screaming like she was on fire, but she could not speak. He made her mute just like they were now.

Then he turned toward Floriana. "My lady, would you care to do me a favor?"

She found her voice and replied, "Hell no!"

He chuckled, "I figured you might resist. I will sweeten the deal if you can kill me. My subjects will leave you all in peace. My request is for you to skewer me with your icicles."

Floriana's strength immediately returned. She got back to her feet and pointed her rapier toward him. She fired three icicles with sharpened edges. The projectiles pierced through his skin like butter. Blood spurted from him, and he coughed up droplets of crimson.

He smiled as the icicles faded away, revealing fresh wounds. The torn skin and bloody wounds closed up, and the material of his cloak rethreaded itself all on its own. There was no longer any ounce of blood stains on his body.

Then he pointed toward the werefox, "You, sir, must be a member of *The Witnesses*. I doubt they told you the true power and opportunities *The Key* would provide me. Now, I regrettably have a request of you. Could you honor an old man and use your hand cannons to dispatch me?"

Shane jumped to his feet in a flash and spun his pistol, firing off a round. The Fallen Wizard's head exploded like a grape. He holstered his weapon and shrugged like it was nothing.

The Wizard's headless body still remained standing. In seconds, his head had completely reformed and returned to normal. The Wizard snapped his fingers, and Sarah was back on her feet.

"You specialize in explosive magic if I recall. Could you destroy my whole body with one of your strongest spells?" He asked ever so sweetly.

Sarah summoned a ball of dark blue energy. She said with a strained void, "Dark Implosion."

She tossed the magic spell and it landed at his feet. Instantly it exploded and sucked his body into the ball of energy. Leaving behind the two bracelets that landed in the dirt. Sarah turned toward Floriana and gave her a thumbs up.

The bracelets lifted off the ground and floated in the air. His body then rephased back into existence. The Fallen Wizard came back into existence out of literal nothingness, as if he had been standing there the whole time.

He cracked his neck, "Well, I appreciate you immensely for participating in my small experiment. All of you are worthy of such praise. Now, I have one more request. I need to be sure of the extent of my powers. I want you to all attack me like your life depends on it."

Shane let loose a barrage of bullets the moment those words left his lips. The bullets pierced the wizard's skin, but his wounds healed almost instantaneously. Then the werefox doubled over in pain from some unseen force.

Sarah and Macy went in for a combined attack. Sarah threw countless Thermal Grenades, and Macy fired off magenta-colored fireballs from her gunblade. The area around the wizard was completely torched from their attacks. There was a boiling pool of blood in the epicenter of the explosions.

The Wizard's body reformed back to the way it was. He teleported out of view and appeared right next to Macy. He touched her right arm, and she crumbled to the ground in pain. She gripped her arm as if it was fractured. As Macy cried out, he disappeared in a cloud of smoke. He then appeared in front of Sarah. Before she could react, he pressed his thumb into her forehead. Tears streamed from her eyes, her lips quivering. Her body became completely rigid, and she seemed lost in her mind, reexperiencing traumas that have long since passed.

Floriana pointed her rapier at the all-powerful wizard. A giant block of clear ice melded into his body. Then Grace instructed Aiko to attack. The Dragon let loose a breath attack of frigid ice. The block of ice shattered into a thousand pieces. In a matter of seconds, the shattered blocks of ice reassembled into the body of the Fallen Wizard.

He grinned, and then his eyes shifted to the left. A magenta-colored flame appeared in his line of sight and quickly wrapped around him before he could react. Macy stood holding on to the other end of the rope of fire and yanked on it. She managed to pull the powerful wizard in her direction. Then, a tiny silver-colored shield of pure magical energy appeared just an inch above his forearms. Blood began to spurt through his sleeves once the shields sliced through the green fabric.

For a moment, the leader of the Daimonia appeared shocked. Then, he raised his arms and disappeared in a cloud of smoke. The Fallen Wizard reappeared at the base of the ship's ramp. With his arms fully repaired, the leader of the Daimonia snapped his fingers, and all of them lost their ability to move. His fingers pressed against a section of his forearm, where the shield had sliced through. On the tip of his finger were crimson stains from the wound that had not completely closed. The Wizard held out his fingers as they dripped blood with a childlike curiosity. He directed his attention toward the werefox.

"That was quite interesting," he said. "I can tell you have surpassed some of the training that the average member of your organization receives. You stand at the very threshold of power and technique that your superiors tend to keep for themselves. This is why I must thank you for your skill and the tremendous efforts you have put into your craft. Even after living on this planet for more than I can remember, you have taught me something today, and I will honor that."

The Fallen Wizard fixed his gaze on all the unfortunate souls currently under his control. Save for the Dragon Master, who he managed to briefly slow down and was still running laps around his men. Which was extremely impressive on all accounts. Now that his powers were wholly restored, he managed to bestow control of almost everyone within the cave.

He bowed respectfully toward them. Then, his orange eyes became cold. A dark, hazy mist expelled from his body. He lifted his arm in a smooth motion. "I recall having mentioned to you all about some of the magic that I am quite proficient in. However, there is one that I chose not to mention to you, and that is the power of Death. I want you all to take note and share what you see with the world."

Then he pointed his index finger at Shane and said, "Think of Death."

A blast of white light struck the werefox in the chest. Then he fell backward, and his body convulsed in insurmountable pain. The Wizard snapped his fingers, and Aiko disappeared. "I have one more trick up my sleeve that you truly must see." He shifted his gaze toward a single Dragon Warrior locked in combat.

Chapter 32

The Reaper

For what seemed like a lifetime, their world was consumed with slashes of blades, the expulsion of lead, and sparks of magic. He felt a mild rage from every hit he took and countered with his own power. His mind was focused unlike ever before. There was no Red Eye to power the rage. This battle was unequivocally him.

The Dragon Warrior side-stepped a stab from his opponent. At close range, a mere inches from his opponent's face, Jayden let loose a volley of fireballs at the man he considered his big brother. Cain summoned a shield of black flames at the last second to protect himself. The shield managed to block some attacks, but the flames that snuck by exploded against his skin. Blood dripped from his chin, and scratches appeared on his childhood friend's face. He knew the battle was just beginning and that no quarter would be given.

Cain took a step back and raised his claymore above his head. He whispered under his breath, and waves of magical energy were drawn to his blade. Black began to snake around its metal frame. His friend grinned and slashed the sword downward.

Jayden flipped backward, avoiding the first wave of black flames. He quickly channeled white flames around his sword. Then he slashed his sword at an angle to intercept the second black wave heading his way. His muscles bulged when the wave of magic slammed into his sword. The wave pressed against him with the force of a freight train. It took every ounce of strength in his body to keep his footing. His vision became obscured as the black and white flames merged into a canvas of amazing light and smoke. He noticed his friend wink and snap his fingers through the haze of light and smoke.

In an instant, the spell exploded, and his sword was flung from his hand while he was pushed backward. He could feel blood trickling down from the back of his head onto his neck. Jayden mustered enough strength to return to his feet in just enough time to be disappointed again. He placed his arms across his body and closed his eyes as a wave of black flames slammed into him.

As the spell propelled him skyward, he forced his body to flip backward in the air. As he descended, he channeled a whip of white flames into his right hand. Once he landed on the ground, the white flames extended to where his sword had landed and wrapped around it like a vine. With a quick yank on the magical whip, his sword was back in his hands. As he pointed his blade at his friend speeding toward him, light, magical energy started to glow at the tip of his blade.

"White Death," he said in a hushed tone.

A gigantic blast of white plasma burst from his sword. The light beam sped toward his childhood friend like an angel of light. Cain tried to block it but was consumed by the holy light, which exploded against his flesh. His friend crashed onto the ground as white flames danced across his chest, exploding whenever his body would move.

Jayden took a moment to catch his breath. The Dragon Warrior could sense the heart beneath his chest was banging like a bass drum. He could still feel blood dripping down his neck from an injury to the back of his head. His chest was burning, and beads of sweat and blood trickled down his forehead. He could feel intense pain in his ribs. Every step he took required energy that he didn't quite have. With his adrenaline decreasing, he was finally able to notice an endless stream of blood flowing down from the bullet wound in his shoulder he had sustained earlier. The hope he had of victory now seemed null and void.

His mind jumped back into focus as he ducked under a slash from the freshly recovered Cain. He felt his body being knocked back from a backblast of heated wind created by his opponent's strike. He sent off a blast of fire at his opponent. A shield of black flames intercepted the spell. Cain returned fire with a series of small fireballs sent his way.

The Dragon Warrior attempted to dodge them. His chest burned when the spell made contact with his charred shirt. Jayden slashed downward with his sword, sending an orange-curved wave of energy at his childhood friend. Cain quickly did an aerial to avoid the wave of energy which exploded behind him.

The Daimonia soldier spit up some blood when he landed on his feet. He took a moment to pull a flask from beneath his coat and took a swig of whiskey. Cain then pulled back his hood and sheathed his sword. "Jayden, you can't beat me. My magic is too strong for you. You should just go. I don't want to have to kill you or Tony."

"What about Sarah and Macy?" Jayden asked.

Cain shrugged, "I don't know about that now. Truthfully, I forgot they were here. If I had to pick, I'd probably say both will have to meet their maker because Sarah has been pretty mean lately. I haven't seen Macy since I left at thirteen. You and Tony can make it out of this fine if you agree. Maybe a few bumps and bruises, but that's not a bad price to pay. Look at how many of our guys you have killed."

Jayden sheathed his sword, "I'm okay with that."

"We heard that!" shouted an uproar from within the cave. He quickly glanced around to see where they had shouted from. He figured he was still probably safe from the wrath of his former classmates.

"Can I ask you a question?"

"Sure," Cain replied.

"Why'd you do it? Why turn on everyone?"

Cain pulled out the bottle of whiskey again from under his cloak. He drained the remaining contents of it. "I will give you the short version. I knew the grandparents who raised me weren't telling me the truth. I never met my father or my mother. They would never tell me about them, nor did they have any pictures of them anywhere. Then, one day, the men you know as the Dark Prince and Sergeant Jason came to me. This happened when we were all still pretty young. They told me they were my half-brothers and that I had a full brother who was older than me. A year later, I left and joined the Daimonia at thirteen. I learned why I didn't grow up with my brothers when I joined them and why I never knew anything about my family. The only reason I grew up without knowing anything and living in the Town of Peace was because of your Father. For that alone, I was more than happy to destroy that town."

Jayden nodded his head, "I guess that makes sense. I mean, if my grandparents withheld information from me, I'd probably come back as an adult and kill a bunch of people. I mean, it would only be fair."

Cain fired a blast of black flames that struck Jayden in the stomach, and he doubled over. "I didn't expect you to understand. You still haven't let the world break you enough."

"You are correct about that. I still think most things in life are simply funny," Jayden replied as he coughed up blood. "Maybe you can help me learn."

His old friend disappeared and reappeared in front of him. Black flames swirled around his knuckles. Then he punched Jayden so fast his hands were like a blur. Before he knew it, he was back on the ground.

Cain kicked Jayden in the ribs, and he rolled over, completely consumed with pain. "How about now? Do you feel like you learned a little more? Or do I need to beat you down like when we were kids? Your big brother will set you right."

The Dragon Warrior looked at him, "I know it was you. I've always known."

His friend stopped kicking him for a second, "What did you say?"

Jayden coughed up more blood and let out a wheeze, "I said that I knew it was you. You didn't sit on the sidelines when my hometown was destroyed."

Cain grabbed Jayden by the shoulders and lifted him to his feet. "If you know, then why won't you just kill me?"

Jayden channeled holy flames into his fist. Then he punched Cain with all of his strength. His childhood friend was knocked backward and crashed onto a pile of sharp rocks. He summoned a large white fireball and threw it at him. The fireball exploded, and Cain writhed in pain.

"The night that my dad died, he showed me what happened in a dream. For the longest time, I had no idea why he would show the last moments of his life. Those memories have haunted me every day since then." Jayden fought back tears as those images filled his mind. "But I realized he didn't want me to hate. The tears you shed as that spear pierced my dad's chest were genuine. I don't care what you believe right now about yourself. Or that you smell like a cheap ass bar. You can't hide who you really are. I know that your heart broke that day the same as mine. Unfortunately, you have helped the Wizard and your brothers done some very awful things. And I can no longer allow you to do that. I will educate you with the kind of magic a tortured soul like yourself can only dream of."

Cain managed to get back to his feet. He darted toward Jayden. The Dragon Warrior sidestepped a downward slash from his sword. While he avoided the slash, Jayden punched Cain twice in his face and then once in his ribs. He pushed him to the ground and fired multiple fireballs into his friend's side as he fell.

Jayden jabbed his sword into the ground. A wall of holy flames encircled Cain. The column of fire rotated as it spun around him. Cain jumped out at the last second as the wall closed in on him. The wall exploded, knocking him to the ground.

The Dragon Warrior smiled as small whisps of gray-colored flames swirled around him. Blood began to drip from his nose and lips as he channeled his life energy. The temperature around his body rose significantly while pure white flames mixed in with the *Yūrei* flames. The gray and white flames swirled around him like a tornado surrounding him.

"Holy Ghost Armor on!" He shouted.

He launched himself toward his childhood friend. Jayden swung his sword with blazing speed at his opponent. Their blades clashed, sending multicolored embers into the air. Blades of grass ignited into miniature fires spreading across the battlefield. Large boulders were transformed into molted rock piles, creating rivers of liquid death. It was like fighting in the pits of hell.

Cain let loose a breath attack that sent forth a massive blast of fire magic. Jayden gathered his ghost and holy flames into a shield. The blast pushed him back against a rocky wall. The sharpened pieces of rock pierced his back and arms, blistering from the intense combined heat. Jayden could feel the wall behind him give way as he was blasted through it. The spell exploded, and he was covered in rocks and soot.

The man he considered an older brother laughed, "With all those theatrics, you still lost. You just got blasted through a wall. If I were you, I would stay..."

Cain stopped midsentence as the pile of rocks began to glow. In a moment, the pile of rubble burst into shards of scorched rock. Jayden emerged from the cavity they created. His armor of ghost and holy fire whirled around him intensely. His muscles bulged, and his eyes were set intently on his adversary.

Jayden channeled his life and magical energy and shouted, "Fear the power of the unknown. Rise and face thine enemy. Bring forth the Seraph!"

Cain pulled out another bottle of whiskey. He took a giant swig of the brown liquid, then took a precautionary step back. His liquored-up eyes glanced wearily in all directions in anticipation of an attack.

The ground beneath their feet started to rumble. Then tiny flickers of light appeared on the right and left sides of the cloaked warrior. The tiny flickers began to elongate and grow. Their physical forms grew slowly into gigantic snakes made of fire. The seraph on the left was covered in the *Yūrei Flames*, and the one to the right was draped in the holy fire.

Jayden snapped his fingers, and both snakes let out a hiss that chilled even the caster to the bone. They both released blasts of scorching heat from their mouths. Cain summoned two shields of black flames, but they were utterly destroyed by the force of the attacks. The energies from both spells exploded, and he crumbled into a heap. The powerful Seraphs then slithered toward Cain with the force and speed of a locomotive. When their fire-filled bodies slammed into each other, they exploded, sending a giant fireball of gray and white flames into the air.

Once the smoke cleared, the spot where Cain stood was now a giant, deep crater. His eyes locked on to three barely noticeable fingers holding on to the edge of the newly made cliff. Jayden rushed toward the crater. He glanced down, and his heart sank. Cain, his older brother, was clinging on for dear life. His robes were tattered. His skin was charred, and blood streamed from nearly every pore. There was a small hint of fear and regret in his expression.

Jayden took an exhaustive breath, extended his hand, and lifted his friend from the crater. Once he got Cain upright, he tried to help him escape from the crater. His cloaked friend pushed him away and sent him flying. Cain redrew his sword and channeled his rage and magical energy.

"Why didn't you just let me die?" shouted.

"Well, I…." Jayden stopped midsentence. He quickly turned his head just as a gigantic Phoenix appeared beside him out of thin air. The curved blade of the sickle sliced through the bird of fire. The Phoenix cried out in pain, and then its body seemed to shimmer and change. A moment later, the bird that saved his life had turned back into the body of another childhood friend.

Macy lay across his arms, her skin turning pale as a ghost. Her warm blood streamed down his arms as he held her. She brushed aside a curl in his hair.

"I love you," she whispered.

Then his heart broke for a second time, just as the ground beneath him shattered.

***

The Dragon Warrior looked on in horror as his friend fell into the nothingness below. A single tear dripped down his cheek. Then, his right eye turned dark red.

"You will all taste death," Tony said as he raised his arm toward the sky. Clouds as scarlet as the blood in his veins formed in the cavern above him. Then bolts of crimson lightning rained down on the cave like a God issuing his final judgment.

Chapter 33

The Seeds of Our Destruction

His cane made a dull sound on the marble floor. He shuffled his feet toward the crystal-clear glass wall. The sky was as blue as the ocean below. His eyes tried to take in the breadth of the view as the ship made its way to its final destination.

"My Lord, may I ask you a question?" The Dark Prince asked as he moved to stand beside him.

"Of course, Jeremiah. It would be an honor," The Fallen Wizard replied.

"Why did you choose to leave so many of our adversaries alive?

The Wizard let out a wheeze and a cough. "Your curiosity has always been your greatest gift. Honestly, I never would have imagined our foes would have defeated so many of our brothers and sisters. To think that young man could conjure the Scarlet Clouds of the Death Storm was quite a sight. I can honestly say I have not seen that spell cast in many a year. To answer your question, any plan's truest essence is reaching the goal. The plan itself will invariably always contain a flaw, an overlooked scenario. As I have bestowed upon you respect for the way of the warrior, I, too, must live out that ethic. In this case, they deserved to continue on. I want the world to see the scars that are left upon them. Controlling the masses does not simply come from a sense of control. No, it comes from providing them with the understanding of what they should truly fear."

The Dark Prince bowed, "Then why bring so many of our men to the cave? Was the loss worth what we have gained?"

His facial features relaxed, patting the young man on the shoulder. "My young man, you have grown so much over the years. You are starting to ask the right questions. The first thing to always remember is to never underestimate the power of your enemy. Desperation can draw out latent abilities even in the weakest of combatants. Now, my young Jeremiah, remember that we possess many powerful souls within our ranks. Unlike most of the other sects of the Daimonia, we need not worry too much about our number of personnel. The challenge is never forgetting that soldiers are sometimes like pieces on a chess board. Each piece has a unique value, but its value might not be used the same in all scenarios. Our brothers and sisters served their purpose. The ones who survived the battle can join the rest of us on our journey. They are more hardened and will be better prepared for our next battle. That said, I still cannot underscore how impressed I am by our foes' strength. The power that was released during our escape was very intense. Had it not been for this ship's well-designed defenses, we might have crashed on our way out. Was your intelligence on our enemy flawed?"

Sergeant Jason stepped into the room as those words left his lips. "My Lord, I apologize for entering this conversation unannounced, but I must take responsibility for that. I believe I may have underestimated their abilities. I take full responsibility for our casualties. I am concerned that I may not have gathered enough information for our final destination."

The Wizard slowly turned around to greet him. "Young sir, you fought valiantly. You must tend to your wounds and check on your youngest brother. You need not blame yourself; conflicts come with risk. We cannot be surprised when we meet substantial resistance. You also need not worry about *The Elders*. With my magic, they will pose no threat. They will be subdued and as docile as a puppy. The few who may resist will meet the end they so deserve."

The Sergeant bowed, "Well, my master, I appreciate your wisdom. We have reached what we believe to be the island. Will you accompany me to the upper deck?"

***

The clouds above were as pure as a newborn child. A cool chill filled the air as they broke through the *Nimbus Barrier*. Their eyes were greeted by sights of rolling green hills, lush with trees and animals running free. The land and people that had forsaken him would now learn the error of their ways.

Airships and gliders from the Eden and Aggeloi forces flanked the White Rose. Their forces were prepared to subdue any resistance his magic could not quell. He felt a subtle sense of glee as they rose higher toward the Sky Castle. The capital of the Elders was to crumble in his hands without lifting a finger.

***

He shuffled across the stage with a sense of eternal purpose. His mossy-colored cloak flowed beside him as he made his entrance. His cane would no longer be viewed as an instrument of the infirm but as a symbol of his strength.

The court members stood in utter silence as he approached the microphone. He stared out into the crowd, entirely under his control, with pride and joy. His heart was full because he was finally home.

"I have returned, The Destroyer that you sent away. Now that I have returned to forgive your sins, you must rejoice. Your sons and daughters, your homes and fields of grain, even your very life belongs to me now. The Reign of King Arthur the Fallen Wizard has begun!"

First Draft Previews

Baptized by Magic

The Witches Pendent

Genre-Crime/Young Adult Fantasy

Chapter 6

My First Investigation

The gentle sound of someone knocking ever so loudly at his front door was just the music he wanted to hear in the morning. He hoped that if he continued to ignore them, they would eventually get the hint that he was trying to sleep or dead. Apparently, after what he assumed was either five- or ten-minutes worth of knocking, the subtle hint he was giving was not enough.

He groaned as he forced himself to open his eyes and sit up. His neck and back ached so much; he thought maybe someone had suplexed him in his sleep. He reached into his bag and grabbed shorts and a black shirt. Once he got up, he looked at his wannabe army cot bed. He decided that he would get himself a moderately more comfortable bed before the day was over.

The ladder creaked as he pulled the release and descended the stairs. His feet dragged as he made his way to the door. He probably should have grabbed his gun before he answered, but it was probably better that he didn't. Since he was already half tempted to shoot whoever was banging on his door in the leg for waking him up.

He opened the door. The sky above was just as gloomy as he felt. Standing in the doorway was a beautiful blonde detective with red streaks in her hair and an annoyed look on her face. She grabbed the cell phone attached to her belt and pointed at it.

"Do you know what this is?" she asked in a snarky tone.

Johnny scratched his chin, "I'm not quite sure, Detective. I'm sure you are resourceful enough to figure it out."

"I have been trying to call you all morning. Your phone is supposed to be on 24/7. We have a crime scene to investigate. Don't you want to help us local cops?" she grinned.

He scratched his head, "I'm not going to lie; I have no idea how to turn on that communicator."

"Oh, that's an easy fix." She replied as she pushed past him to enter the building. "Now, where is your communicator and your badge?"

He pointed toward his desk. She quickly walked over and grabbed the black oval-shaped communicator. She picked up his gold-colored badge with her left hand and held it just above the communicator. A bright light flashed from the communicator, and a white digital screen appeared on the oval-shaped phone. She held the phone toward him; in red letters, it said Welcome Agent Silver on the screen.

Johnny's jaw dropped as he tried to process what had just happened. Not because turning on a phone was a big deal, but because he had spent two hours the previous night trying to figure out how to turn the damn thing on.

She pretended to hand him the phone and then pulled it back. "Before I give this back to you. Tell me, why couldn't you do this on your own?"

He looked down and said, "Well, I suck at magic, and I assumed I needed to use it to charge the crystals in the phone."

"Wow," she said, "A fed who can't use magic or read instructions. Come on, noobie, let's go."

Rachel led him to her police cruiser, parked just in front of the floral shop. This car was different from what she drove the other day. The vehicle he stepped into was covered in matte black paint. When she turned the keys, the engine roared to life with the veracity of the line. Behind the steering wheel was a set of paddle shifters, and he could even spot a white tachometer. The back seats and the cage were more compact than a typical police car. You would feel scrunched like a sardine in a can if you were six feet or taller.

When she hit the gas, the car launched forward like a rocket. Then she pulled on the e-brake and made the car drift a U-turn. Her foot was glued to the pedal as they sped by the boarded-up shops that made up his neighborhood.

"Can I safely assume this is one of the new Takashi Blackhawks modified for police use?" He asked as she weaved through traffic like a maniac.

"More or less. I actually bought this myself, and when I started working out here, I had one of the mechanics add the cage for me. Since it's my own vehicle, they will give me a bit of a tax break at the end of the year. So that's a win for me." Rachel replied as she drifted around a right corner.

"Well, I hope they aren't paying for your insurance. I do have a question for you. Can you tell me how you got my phone to work when even I couldn't follow their vague instructions?" he asked.

Her demeanor changed as she thought about how to respond. She sat straighter in her car, and her shoulders flexed from an inner tension. Her gaze narrowed with almost a violent intensity, and her lip quivered as if struggling to formulate the right words to say. Then, just as quickly as the rage built within her, she relaxed again.

She gave him a quick fake smile and said, "Oh, it's nothing. I read about that trick in a magazine. Honestly, I didn't think it would work. We're here, by the way."

"Wait, what?" he exclaimed as she drifted the car into a parallel parking spot. "You do know that there is a thing called a speed limit?"

She ignored him as they got out of the car. They stopped in front of the building on the northwest side of town. This jewelry shop looked like a palace. The store was covered in pearl white paint, and six cement pillars held up the triangular roof. A beautiful green field served as a backdrop for the one-story building. Steps made of granite led up to the building.

Once they made it up the steps, they were greeted by hosts who were dressed in tuxedos. They carried silver platters with triangular sandwiches and what he assumed were expensive chocolates. A maroon-colored, satin carpet guided them to a six-foot-tall white door with a handle made of pure crystal. There was a sign above the door that read Giovanni Gioilleria.

Rachel turned the handle, and before stepping across the threshold, he was greeted by the wonderful sound of EDM blasting through the speakers. If that wasn't enough, he just walked into what was probably the most extravagant jewelry store he had ever been in. On the ceiling were three chandeliers made of platinum. The room had six glass cases filled with jewelry that cost more than his and Rachel's cars combined. Heated marble flooring blanketed the ground they walked on.

Johnny Silver sniffed the air and was blown away by the sweet smell of blueberry pancakes. His stomach began to growl, and Rachel shot him a look, saying she had heard it too. Now, he was hungry and regretting not grabbing a protein bar.

"Ciao, Ciao!" shouted a man approaching them dressed in a gray suit. "My name is Cassius, and I am the assistant manager. I would like to welcome you to Giovanni's Gioilleria. We are the best jewelry store in the whole country. We specialize in high-quality products and items for your everyday consumer. May I interest you two in a set of wedding bands?"

Rachel's lightly tanned face turned bright red for a second. Then she replied, "No, we are here because you reported a robbery. Why didn't you just call 911?"

He chuckled, "Forgive me if I'm being too forward. I almost completely forgot that I was a salesman first. I didn't want to make a big ruckus; we have a reputation to uphold. If there was a line of police cars outside, Mr. Giovanni would lose his mind. I hoped we could keep this between us and the Detective's Office for now."

Cassius beckoned for them to follow. He guided them past the semi-circle of glass jewelry cases to a section in the back. Rachel pulled out her kit to test for fingerprints, and she followed closely behind him. Cassius stopped before a black jewelry case whose litter shell looked made of obsidian. He flipped a switch under the case, and an LED light illuminated the box's contents.

There were rings made of platinum and jade throughout this jewelry case. Necklaces made of white and yellow gold hung from the necks of mannequins inside the case. The diamond-encrusted watches shined so bright it was overwhelming. He couldn't tell what could be missing with the high-quality jewelry in this case alone.

When he looked to his right, he felt an increased level of concern. A series of blue, red, and green crystals were resting on a velvet cloth. Yellow and silver lights swirled about in the center of a few crystals. These would appear to be simple trinkets or even your average magic crystal to the untrained eye. The way the lights swirled around in some of the crystals, like galaxies, implied that they could have some powerful spells or charms.

Johnny looked up from the case, "Excuse me, Mr. Cassius, but do you have a permit to sell magic crystals? Also, I'm concerned by the spells that may be in some of them. I'm going to need a list of them before we leave.

"We have a permit to sell up to Level 2 Magic crystals with spells. I know the lovely Ms. Rachel Elise, but I'll need to see some identification from you if you want that spell list." he replied. Johnny flashed his FCSI badge for him. Seeing his Federal I.D. seemed to put a smile on the jeweler's face. "Oh, you must be our new special agent then. The last one we had was quite an interesting man. Well, I hope you are enjoying our little slice of paradise so far, and I hope you are keeping our Detective out of trouble."

The Detective rolled her eyes, "Can you just tell us why you think there was a robbery?"

Cassius grinned and lifted the top of the jewelry case. Then pointed toward a small indentation next to a row of platinum rings. "We have had ring a missing from here for about a week now. I just noticed it last week and talked to Mr. Giovanni about it. He instructed me to not worry and just to keep looking for it. So I did, and I've checked our inventory. According to that, no one has purchased the ring. I'm not sure if that helps."

Rachel took down his account of the days before the ring went missing. Then, she took out a small brush and began dusting for prints. Once she got an indicator for a print, she placed a small, clear piece of paper on it. Then she snapped her fingers, and a green image of a print was transferred into the clear piece of paper. Rachel did this three more times in the area around the ring.

She placed her kit back in a pouch on her belt. "Agent Silver is unaware of this, but we investigated another item having gone missing a few weeks before this one did. Could you give him a rundown about what happened with the necklace?"

"I would love to, darling. Follow me, Mr. Silver." Cassius replied with a smile bright enough to make you feel uncomfortable.

They were directed toward a jewelry container near the front of the store. The items, in this case, were almost in Johnny's budget range. There were rows of silver rings and necklaces made of steel. In the bottom right-hand corner was a pair of cubic zirconium earrings and a black watch made of hard plastic. Johnny wasn't a jewelry expert by any means, but from what he could tell, there would be nothing in this case worth stealing.

"We had a beautiful silver necklace with a wannabe emerald pendant stolen three weeks before the ring was taken. Mr. Giovanni....wouldn't let me report it until two weeks afterward. The necklace itself isn't as special as some other items in the store. What made it unique was that within the pendant was a small magic crystal. Most people looking at the fake emerald stone couldn't tell it was there." Cassius said.

Johnny scratched his chin as he thought. He walked around the case to see if there was any indication that it had been broken. None of the hinges looked bent, and he saw no damage from someone trying to cut into the jewelry case. The more he looked at it, the more he realized he wouldn't find anything. Clearly, these objects were taken by someone with easy access. The thing he needed to know was why.

"Cassius, can I safely assume that the ring taken also had a magic crystal attached?" Johnny asked. Cassius nodded. "I have one more question: Have any other items gone missing in the last month or two?"

The middle-aged jeweler piped up and exclaimed, "Yes, in fact, one more item was taken. It was a small wooden charm given to the shop decades ago by a witch. Supposedly, it was worth a lot. Honestly, it was the ugliest thing in the store. We don't usually keep hippy trinkets like that. Mr. Giovanni Sr was the one that got the item, and I guess his son has kept it the whole time."

"Why didn't you report that being stolen?" Rachel asked."

"It's not worth anything; our insurance won't even cover that insignificant piece of firewood. Since I was transferred to this location, I can think of only once that a person has even given that item a second glance: Miss. Valkyrie. If she really wanted it, she needed to ask, and we would gift it to her for free." he replied.

"Why would you do that for her?" Johnny asked.

Cassius pat him on the head, "You really are from out of town. The Valkyries own this town. If they want something, they get it, no questions asked. The Valkyries were the original investors in Giovanni Sr's company."

The Detective jotted down more notes and took pictures of the jewelry display cases. Then she approached the jeweler and gave him her card. She reached the door, turned around, and said, "Well, thank you for your time, Cassius. We will need you to send the information about the magic crystals. I will be taking over the investigation of the first robbery. We will contact you or Mr. Giovanni if we have any more questions."

Johnny followed after her as he tried to piece together his first case. Before he could get his seat buckled, Rachel put the pedal to the metal. He wanted to ask her questions about what had just happened. Still, she seemed preoccupied with her thoughts or focused on not speeding into other people, so he wasn't sure.

The ride back to his office was uncomfortably silent. He didn't quite understand it. Maybe it was because he was a fed and she was a local cop. Truth be told, he didn't quite understand the role he was to play working with the local police department. He didn't want to overstep his bounds because, at this point, there wasn't a federal crime committed. On the other hand, it would make him look good and possibly get him transferred to one of the big cities.

Rachel slammed on the brakes when she arrived in front of his office. She quickly jumped out of the car and stomped to the door like she owned the place. When he finally exited the car, she was tapping her feet impatiently. Johnny took his time unlocking the door, and once the latch clicked, she barged right past him and sat down at the first desk.

"So, newbie, what do you think after all that?" she asked.

"Well, dusting for prints after the fact was probably wasting our time. The time that it took them to report it is concerning. The only person who seems to be taking a mild interest in this supposed robbery is Cassius. So that leaves us with not much to go on. I am concerned that magical crystals are missing, and I don't think they realize how serious that can be." Johnny replied.

She leaned back in her chair and said, "You are a pretty sharp newbie; even though you suck at magic, at least you are smart. I completely agree; they assigned me to deal with this case because they knew something terrible might happen. Since you have all of these fancy federal computers, I think you could do a fair amount of research about Giovanni's overpriced jewelry store."

A light bulb went off in his head, and he instantly frowned. "So that's why you brought me along. You were just using me for my assets."

She made finger guns with both hands and replied, "See, I told you you were smart. Now, be a sweetie and do your computer magic. If you're quick enough, I'll let you buy an ice cream cone.

Before he could move a muscle, he heard knocks at the door. He made his way to the front office, turned the handle, and standing in front of him was Chloe. She was dressed in the same outfit from the other day; her mascara was running from her tear-stained eyes, and her hands were shaking as she clutched onto a used tissue.

A tear rolled down her left cheek, "My Aunt died."

My Journey Through Hell

The Prison Within

Genre-Fantasy/Horror/Psychological Thriller

Chapter 1

Help Us

He felt a cool breeze as he walked along the river. The gentle touch of the wind brought his mind back into focus. Jordan held his coat tighter as his footsteps echoed along the stone path.

The night was as black as he had ever seen. If it weren't for the few specks of moonlight piercing through the clouds above, he would be walking in complete and utter darkness.

Fishtails clapped against the gently rolling river. A family of coypu scurried across the path in front of him and jumped into the water. They looked like an ugly step-cousin of the good old American beaver. In Prato, Italy these creatures could be found cruising along the waterways without a care in the world. Even though they weren't the most attractive animals, it was a pleasant sight on this peaceful night.

Besides the sound of the small waves on the river, the city of Prato was deathly quiet. There wasn't another soul walking along the river. It wasn't a bad thing to have this peace and quiet. However, it also wasn't a good thing. Evil spirits thrived on destroying any ounce of peace and quiet.

Jordan tucked in his cross as he walked up a set of steps. The metallic necklace felt cold against his skin. His father gave him his necklace when he was baptized at age thirteen. It wasn't like a Catholic Rosary or anything special. He just knew that it kept him safe when all Hell breaks loose.

Another cool breeze blew across his path. He shivered again as he walked through the park parallel to the river. The grass his Black Nikes trampled on was soft and damp. A cool mist descended upon this quiet neighborhood, and the world around him became even more eerie.

He looked up and saw a sign that said, "Viale Roma." Jordan approached the street, and an Italian gentleman was on the other side of the crosswalk. His name was Sergio. He was a retired minister of the Church. Sergio was only in his fifties, but he decided to retire from direct church service because, and, I quote, he was "tired of all the *pazzi.*"

Jordan thought that was complete bull crap because Sergio had become the Italian liaison for the Daimonia Hunter Organization, which meant he dealt with real *pazzi.*

Sergio embraced him and said, "Ciao, Signore, come stai?"

Jordan released him, "Bene grazie."

The old Italian grinned, "Prego Jordan. Are you done with your stroll through the park?"

"You know me, I always have to get a little exercise before I exorcise a demon."

Sergio shook his head and turned up the street. Jordan took a deep breath and followed after the Italian man. Even though Sergio was getting older, he walked with the pace of a younger man. Honestly, the young demon slayer didn't want to catch up with him.

Before every exorcism, Jordan always got this deep sense of dread. The reason is that he never knew what to expect and was always afraid of the outcome. Evil always seemed to have the upper hand when dealing with pure evil. Sometimes, the exorcisms went on without a hitch, and other times, they've gone to hell at the speed of light. Demons and evil spirits have no problem with hurting or even killing their hosts.

Sergio led him to a series of large apartment complexes three stories high. Technically, they were four stories tall, as the lobby was often the first floor in Italian apartments. Jordan hated climbing stairs, so it helped him to think that he didn't have to walk as much as he really had to.

They stopped in front of one of the buildings. A woman stood outside and greeted them with a kiss on each cheek. She was a beautiful Italian woman with pale skin and an average build. Her eyes were brown, and her hair was put in a bun.

From what he could tell, she was in her late thirties, maybe early forties. Her name was Sofia Rossa, and she looked just like her younger sister, whom he had met a couple of months ago. See, members of her family over the last year and a half had been victimized by the forces of Hell. It all started with one of her nephews in Napoli becoming possessed by a spirit. When that issue was solved, a few of her cousins were possessed by demons. After every successful exorcism, another person in her family would be attacked.

Sofia looked tired, and he couldn't blame her. She had been dealing with a lot over the last year and a half. When your family members become possessed, it isn't just a spiritual problem. People must take off work, which can become an expensive issue over time.

She ran her hands through her hair and looked at him up and down. "Are you the one that has been helping out mi famigilia?"

"Si," Jordan replied. "I have been one of the individuals who has helped with a few of your family's cases."

Sergio translated what he said to her. Then she looked at him again in a way that meant she still wasn't convinced. She scrunched her nose and said, "Where is your robe? Are you not a priest?"

He shook his head no, "I'm not Catholic if that's what you're asking."

She shook her head in disbelief. "Then how are you going help mi bambino?". Sofia continued to barrage him with questions in Italian. Her face turned red as her fear and doubt consumed her.

Jordan tried to listen to her, but he became distracted by a faint tapping noise. He gazed up at the building as he searched for the sound. His eyes landed on a window on the third floor.

A dim light was barely visible through the windowpane. Glass from the other side of the window began to splinter as if something was cutting into the window. Jagged lines and indentations slowly appeared on the glass.

The letter L was traced into the glass. As more letters slowly appeared in the window. A chill went down his spine as he realized that it didn't make a sound when letters were cut into glass.

"Capito Signore?" Sofia shouted.

Jordan glanced briefly away from the window. "Wha what?"

"She said, do you understand?" Sergio said.

"I got that part," Jordan replied. "But what does she want me to understand?"

Sergio shook his head in disappointment. "You know it's rude to not pay attention when an Italian woman is talking to you. She asked if you understand that she is going to trust that you can do this, even though you're not Catholic. Also, there are other spirits in the house besides just the demon you need to worry about. You capito now?"

Jordan nodded his head, but his eyes were back on the window. The word LEAVE had been engraved into the glass. What made his spine tingle as he stared up at the building wasn't the fact that the glass didn't make a sound as it was cut. What scared him was that he didn't see a person or even a shadow on the other side of the window.

Sofia took a few steps toward the door, and the two men followed. As she turned the knob on the front door, the hairs on the back of his neck stood up. He felt a cold chill go down his body, and fear filled his soul.

When she pushed open the door, she shrieked. The window above them shattered. Red liquid dripped from the ceiling onto Sofia's white blouse. She turned back toward them.

Then cocked her head with a wild look in her eye. Sofia gave a toothy grin. "Benvenuto Signore."

The Depths of My Soul

Book One:

The Forgotten

**Genre-Science Fiction/Young Adult
Fantasy/Horror**

Chapter 1

A bright light flashed, coaxing him from his mildly restful sleep. He stretched out his arm and felt a pop as he knocked over everything on the nightstand.

"Shit." He groaned.

His hand rummaged along the floor, looking for that accursed light. Then, his fingers brushed against a slick piece of metal. He knew it was what he was looking for as he strained to keep his eyes closed. For in truth, he wanted to hold onto his last remnants of sleep. His mind wished to remain in the world of dreams, but alas, his landlord would not let him pay his rent in the currency of hopes and dreams.

Theodoro raised the square block of metal, and some plastic from God knows what planet. His eyes squinted as he was greeted by a light bright enough to compete with a red dwarf star.

The light brown skin on his hand trembled as he tried to type in his password. After the second attempt, he realized he probably needed to be hungover less often. Or maybe he was still drunk from the night before; he wasn't quite sure.

An icon appeared on the illuminated screen. The object was shaped like an envelope, flashing obnoxiously in his face. If it weren't for the fact that he needed rent and staying alive money, he would toss his DigiCom out of the window.

He pressed down on the envelope. The screen shifted, and the document filled every inch of the screen. The insignia of a sailboat was in the left-hand corner of the digital letter. Beneath it was the name of his least favorite travel agency, Sail the Stars Inc. He didn't hate them because they didn't pay him well. He despised them because he normally had to guide and protect pompous rich people to dangerous locations throughout the galaxy. And unfortunately, they would always stipulate in his contract that they would have to come back alive and with most of their limbs.

He would have thought this was a scam letter if he didn't know any better. He thought his eyes were playing tricks on him as he scanned the letter because it was written in such a bizarre fashion. The first odd thing about the letter was that the introductory paragraph started with the words, "We greatly appreciate you and all the work that you do." Normally, they tend to be more condescending when they send him contract introductory letters. The language in their letters is usually summed up, as we know you need the money and will do whatever we ask. This was true, but he didn't like it implied in a company letterhead contract proposal.

He used his index finger to scroll the letter. Then he let out an exhaustive groan. The letter told him nothing about the client nor where they were going. The letter basically said thank you for helping us with our previous customers. If you agree to this contract blindly, we will pay you a lot, but only after you agree and sign on the dotted line will you be provided with additional information.

Now, in truth, letters this vague weren't completely unusual. Sometimes, they were written like this to hide the identities of elite tourists, or at least that's what he had heard at the Mercenaries Guild on Earth. The wealthy clients he would usually get were either spoiled college kids or real estate agents who wanted a little adventure to deflect from their failing marriages or massive amounts of debt.

He sighed briefly; this would probably be a bad idea, but he was tired of eating frozen waffles and desperately needed a payday. So he placed his finger in the middle of his DigiCom. The device scanned his finger, and the contract screen turned bright green, and then a robotic-sounding voice shouted from his phone, Contract Approved. Best of luck to you, Theo.

A smile creased his lips as the screen shifted. He was looking forward to finding out what part of the Universe he would have to take these poor souls to. Then his jaw hit the floor along with the device with the words, "Meet at the Plutonian Space Station for more instructions," emblazoned across the screen.

He groaned, "You bastards, now I really feel like a son of a bitch."

***

He shut off the valves to his shower. The pipes screeched like a banshee as the water flow stopped. He reached for his anime-themed towel and dried off his caramel-colored skin.

Once he was dry enough, he looked at himself in the mirror, his eyes zeroing in on the X-shaped scar above his left eye. He could still feel the intense pain from the Cyber Sword that gave him the wound.

He shrugged; despite his origins, some scars won't heal. And not just the ones that appear for the world to see.

Theo stepped out of the shower. Once he was dry, he made his way to the closet in his room. The closet door was made of glass and shined under the glow of light in his ceiling. A square-shaped digital pad right next to the door rested against the wall. He pressed the number one and took a step back.

A whirring sound filled the room, the door sliding back in the blink of an eye. A light shone inside the closet, revealing rows of shoes and clothes. He grabbed a red shirt and a black leather jacket with matching pants and shoes.

Once he got ready, he pushed the number one again. The closet door immediately closed. He pressed three more numbers on the pad, 619.

A motor whirred, and the door slid open again. A red light clicked on, revealing gun racks on both sides of the closet. In the center of the closet was a dresser made of white oak. On top of the dresser was a stand with three katanas.

Theo stepped forward and pushed a round green button on the dresser. He heard a clicking sound, and the top drawer slowly unlatched and opened.

The drawer had black felt bedding, and a series of pistols and two CyberSwords handles were resting on it. He reached in, grabbed a silver blaster pistol, and tucked it into his shoulder holster. Then he grabbed a compact black .45 caliber kinetic pistol. He quickly tucked it in his hip holster, grabbed one of the CyberSword handles, and latched it onto his belt.

Then he stepped back out of the closet. Once he pushed the button on the digital pad, the glass doors closed instantly. He took a moment to examine his mildly 5'8 imposing frame. The youngish mercenary grinned as he pushed a button on his belt buckle. Then, in a snap, all the weapons hanging from his hip disappeared, leaving behind just a normal black leather belt. The last thing he needed his clients to do when they met him was to ask some dumbass questions.

Chapter 2

The City of New San Diego on Venus was alive and well. His ears perked up at flying cars and interplanetary ships roaring across the sky. He glanced up and down the Gas Lamp Quarter, watching souls passing by on their way to work or hailing rides to head to the nearby airport. Even though it was still early in the day, patrons were already filling in the breweries' chairs that lined the streets. He guessed that it must have been five o'clock somewhere.

As its name might imply, the Gas Lamp Quarter was on the ritzier side of town, mirroring its Earthborn cousin in Southern California. While it may be shocking that a Space Merc would be able to live on the more expensive and posh side of town, he found it was the best place for someone of his pedigree to live. No one would notice him, and that's the way he wanted to keep it.

Those Who Lived by the Sword

Book Three

The Lie of Tranquility

Chapter 1

A Flicker

A Dragon glided through the dark clouds like a phantom spirit. Her windbreaker flapped in the wind as they sped toward the target. She shivered from the thick, misty clouds. Her companions flew beside her like a military escort.

Her squadron soared across the sky in perfect harmony. Their dark scales blended with the gloomy night sky, making them nearly invisible. They were like owls in the night, poised to strike their unlucky prey.

Strands of purple hair blew in her face. The Princess frowned as she moved her hair aside for the thousandth time. Her body rocked forward from their squadron, beginning their descent.

The quiet night became enveloped by the resounding chorus of car horns and voices filling the night sky. Her eyes were attracted to the blue and pink colors blanketing the land below. The city's neon lights were the most glamorous and regal buildings she had ever seen.

Her Dragon let out a soft grunt. Then she felt knots in her stomach. Singular lights were flying above the city, heading in their direction. The formation of the shadow dragon split off into different directions. Grace snapped her fingers, and the squadron opened their jaws. White beads of energy formed around their mouths as they gathered energy. Then, they released dark purple beams of magical energy.
The sky lit up with explosions. An air raid horn blared over the sounds of the busy city. Gliders for the Anti-Resistant Squadron took to the skies. Their eyes were focused on the Princess and her stealthy squad of Shadow Dragons.

Aiko adjusted her flight angle and went skyward. Sparkly silver stars released from their wings as they gained altitude. The anti-air missiles they were pursuing exploded when they made contact with her magic stars.

Once the Dragon reached a significant height, she leveled out. Then Grace gave her oldest friend an affectionate squeeze. When she released her friend, Grace attempted to stand on top of the back of the Dragon. Her balance was slightly off because the wind blew, and she was clumsier than most princesses.

She closed her eyes for half a second and took a deep breath. Then the Aggeloi jumped over the side, diving toward the ground like a rocket.
Her cheeks flapped from the air and wind pressure as she descended. She found it tough to breathe, but she had to fight through it.

Grace pulled the cord on her backpack. A mini-parachute unfurled itself from her bag. She guided her descent toward a skyscraper covered in darkness. She pressed a button on her bag once she was low enough. The parachute retracted into the bag. Then she flipped forward to control her fall.

When her feet landed on the ground, she drew her pistol and scanned the area on the roof. The coast was clear. She holstered the weapon that Jayden gave her. Then she snapped her fingers. The Dragons were serving as her distraction and fighting valiantly against the enemy. Their bodies began to shimmer. One by one, they disappeared, leaving behind a glittery residue of magical energy.

In the past, she would have normally let her summons fight until the end. Since she continued her training at the Dragon Temple, she changed her mind on that. Master Mariko helped her to understand her powers more. Any summon she can keep from phasing out during combat will get stronger after every battle they survive. So now her mini army of dragons was more powerful than ever before.

Grace moved toward a door that led into the building. The door was locked, and she couldn't force it open with her shoulder. She drew the Elder Dagger from her sheets. She sliced an X shape into the door. The Aggeloi Princess grinned as pieces of the door fell backward. Then she kicked the remainder of its standing frame. The door crumpled apart, and she stepped over the threshold.
Her feet landed at the top of a metal staircase. It was only down one floor, and then she stopped at another door. She sprinted down the flight of steps and then slashed the next door.

Grace stepped into a high-rise office. There were rows of desks with computers laid across them. She noticed pictures of family members, frames with degrees, and awards hanging from the walls of the cubicles. On a few of the desks were pink flowers and bonsai trees.

She found each one interesting as she ran past the rows of desks. With most of her memories, she could not think of a time when she had been in an office like this. Part of her wondered if life had panned out differently, would she have worked a regular job in a place like this? Grace enjoyed traveling, and she's been allowed to do so, but it would be nice to know what a normal job life was like.

The Princess ran up to a row of windows. She peered through to see what was happening out on the street. From what she could tell, the area below was pretty quiet. The business district was pretty much a ghost town on a Friday night. Everyone else in the city had flocked toward the casinos and the neon lights, which was perfect; all she needed to do was reach the sewer.

Grace took a few steps toward the elevator when she noticed a light in the upper right-hand corner of the wall. The white light flashed on and off and melded into a bright red frame. There was a stencil on the frame that said alarm. She expected it to make a noise, but it was as silent as a mouse.

The doors she destroyed must have a sensor, she thought. This was a silent alarm. She had no idea how soon it would be before the authorities arrived at the building. She figured that would give her some breathing room because they were probably preparing for a second attack from *The Resistance*...

Magic Spell

List

Absolute Zero- Anti-Object spell cannot be used on living beings. This ice magic spell is the ultimate version of Flash Freeze. Absolute Zero will turn any object into pure and destructible objects. Requires Master Level Training.

Absorb- a technique typically used by elemental magic users. This ability allows the caster to absorb the energy of an attack spell. The energy absorbed can sometimes heal injuries and restore or temporarily increase magical power. Caution should be given when absorbing more powerful spells, as the energy increase can damage the human body.

Anti-Magic Shield- A green shield is conjured by the user. This shield can meld with the individual's skin or equipment and become invisible to the eye. This spell makes the individual resistant to magical spells or enchantments. This spell can also mask the caster's magical and life energy from their opponents. Advanced versions of this spell can even mask scent and thermal scanners. A master-level version of this spell can allow the user to cast it on 4 or more people at any given time.

Arrow Magic- This was once a very popular school of magic before firearms and artillery were invented. The Arrow Magic School is still favored by assassins and some officers in the military. Partially because it takes great skill to master and due to its innate unpredictability. Just like gun magic, techniques are similar to other magical styles, where a specific spell is not always required to produce the magical results that the user requires. This makes it very appetizing for training archers as the time and dedication to learn the basic methods are not lengthy. The basic approach involves the user channeling their magical energy into their bow, crossbow, arrows, or combination. Once enough magic is infused into the weapon or projectile, they can use their magic to change the elemental properties of the weapon. They can even allow the user to attach a homing enchantment to the projectiles. Advanced users of this technique can increase the number of arrows they carry using their magic alone, without carrying large amounts of arrows on their person. Additionally, the users can even develop the ability to change the density and length of the arrows or even adjust the size of their bow with their magic. Master Level practitioners of this style of magic are said to be able to even control the arrows fired from another person.

Auto-Heal (Fast Acting) is a simple healing spell that only activates after mild to severe bodily injury. The healing magic in this technique is intended to keep the user alive. It cannot fully heal broken bones nor seal up open wounds. Once this spell activates, the user should seek medical attention.

Auto-Shield- A basic technique for summoning a protective or defensive spell to absorb or repel kinetic or magic-based attacks. Advanced versions of this technique can be used to combat more powerful spells. The master-level version of this technique can even defend against large explosions. Caution should be considered when using this spell as it does not automatically defend against all attacks.

Avalanche- A magical spell that causes an intense blast of snow. If the user is trained well enough, they can summon ice blocks along with the snow.

Berserk (Enchanted/Imbued)-This is a technique similar to *Rage*; the user will experience an increased sense of agitation and increased muscle growth and strength. This occurs when an item is enchanted with the berserk spell or imbued with a being cursed with the berserk status. Caution should be considered when using items with this spell attached to them as it can lead to extreme aggression, and an individual could become hyper-reliant. Additionally, extended use of items with Berserk magic attached to them can also drain an individual's life force to the point that it could kill them.

BioFlame- Green flames are a rarity amongst fire users. This spell uses a green fire to immobilize opponents, making them extremely sick. BioFlame is intended to be a non-lethal spell and is a Master Level technique.

Black Onyx- This is a Master Level Magic spell and is intended only to be used to kill multiple targets. Black Onyx is considered a Fusion Class spell that employs aspects of dual cast and combined elements. The spell involves connecting techniques from Frost Magic and Storm Magic. The Black Onyx begins by channeling large amounts of magical energy and summoning a diamond brimming with power. This will be accompanied by lightning bolts swirling around the diamond and bursting forth from the object to strike down opponents. Then, icicles are conjured from within the diamond and launched toward targets in a specific area. The colors of the lightning bolts and icicles will determine how powerful each strike is, with crimson and black being the colors that will guarantee the death of any given target. Caution should be considered when using this spell as once it is cast, it is nearly impossible to control, and the spell will last as long as targets remain, even if the user runs out of magic. Few magical practitioners have ever gotten the spell to stop or cancel out. Multiple governmental agencies and magical schools forbid this spell from being used.

BlueBomb- A blue ball of explosive energy is channeled by the user. When the ball of energy is tossed or launched at a target, it will strike them with tremendous force. The target will feel like they got hit by a heavy iron block. This spell is then followed by a small explosion. This technique emphasizes knocking out an opponent from the initial contact with the ball of energy, and the explosion is intended to ensure that they cannot recover quickly. More advanced versions of this technique can allow the user to throw the ball of energy through a bunker or an armored vehicle.

Blue Scorching Speed Armor- A highly advanced Fire Dragon technique. Like other fire armors, this spell boosts the individual's physical and magical abilities. Additionally, just as in other armors, this is intended to make them more resistant to magical spells. This spell, in particular, is a hybrid between the Blue Flame armor, often considered the Ultimate Fire Armor. The Blue Flame/Ultimate Armor is designated the title because it possesses some of the highest temperatures of all the Fire Armors and can boost all of an individual's abilities in a balanced manner. This is unique as some armors are designed to boost one specific stat or ability over the others, which can create a significant imbalance. The Scorching Speed Armor is the other technique combined for this spell. The Scorching Speed Armor is intended to boost someone's physical and magically based movements dramatically. This spell is accompanied by yellow flames that will encircle the individual. A glaring weakness of this spell is that it is one of the least resistant armors and increases the individual's vulnerability to physical and magical attacks. In this hybrid form, the individual will be surrounded by blue and yellow flames. A challenge in this technique is trying to balance the overall boosts of the Blue Flame armor and the extreme speed boost caused by the Scorching Flame Armor. A perfect balance is achieved when the same amount of both colors of flames is visible. If one color is more visible than the other, then that more prominent color will be the major attribute increased, and the other will experience a stark drop in increased ability or protection. Caution should be considered when using this spell as it requires extreme concentration and significantly drains the user's magical abilities.

CLOUD- In its most basic form, the user summons a plain old cloud. Sometimes, this can serve the purpose of creating shade and is often one of the first Storm Magic spells a user might learn. Once summoned, the cloud can be altered for size or converted into a cumulonimbus cloud. An adept user of this spell can use the cloud as a land marker or even track people. Master Level users of this spell can meld their bodies into the cloud.

While melded into the cloud, their magical energy is nearly impossible to detect.

Combined Element- This is a technique that involves the transfer of powers between at least two spell casters or summoners. Once enough magic is shared between the participants, a new spell or ability can be created that combines the powers of both individuals. Individuals who use elemental magic can create spells that have the qualities of both individuals' elements. The casters can also combine the same element to increase their power. A summoner can also take on the powers of their counterpart and imbue their summon with the other individual's element or magical ability.

Control- A Telekinesis spell that allows the user to control the body movements of another human being, creature, or object. This technique is very difficult, as it requires a wellspring of magical power and an adept opponent who can resist this spell. Control is a Master Level Magic spell.

Cyclone Blade- This sword magic spell causes a user to spin in the air or on the ground while swinging a weapon. Cyclone blades can create speeds of up to 65 mph. This is a hazardous technique, as it requires the ability to adjust at high speeds.

Crypto Magic- This is a rare style of magic used by the *Precursors* and *The Elders*. In its basic form, Crypto Magic is intended to lock, unlock, or create limited access to whatever the user desires. In combat, a Crypto Magic user could cast a spell to lock an enemy's ability to use a certain spell or even to move a body part. Enchantments are often used to limit access to treasure chests and to seal parchments or books that contain powerful spells. Crypto Magic users can also use their skills to limit someone's access to a Dimensional Zone. Master Level users of this style of magic have been known to stop the blood flow in an enemy. Sage Level users of this technique can lock and unlock Ultimate Magic Spells or Enchantments and imbue them into an item. Caution should be considered when studying this style of magic because it requires a wealth of knowledge.

Depending on the systems a person wants outsiders to have limited access to, it may even require the sacrifice of life. In modern times, techniques from this school are taught in other magical disciplines. However, certain techniques and abilities are passed down through hereditary means.

Dark Flame- A Master Level technique. This spell conjures a dark fireball or wave of fire. Dark Flame is a lethal spell that can be used efficiently against fire users and is moderately effective on water magic casters.

Dark Implosion- An anti-material and anti-personnel Explosive Magic spell. This spell involves channeling dark energy with murderous intent. Once the ball of dark magic is complete, it is tossed at an enemy, enemies, or an object. The spell will activate and draw in the very essence of the enemy or object and destroy it with the energy of the spell. Part of the individual or object's cellular will contribute to its destruction as those parts of its existence will implode once its physical and spiritual essence is absorbed by the Dark Implosion spell.

Deathscythe- An ultimate spell from the School of Death Magic. This spell requires the conjurer to summon an executioner from the other side of existence. Once an executioner is summoned, they will seek out their intended target or targets. Once their target is struck by their weapon or energy spell of death, the individual will die on contact or over time. Depending on the type of executioner that is summoned will determine the length of the spell and how instant the death the unfortunate victim will experience. Some executioners will kill the target immediately or cause them to slowly bleed out or can also bestow upon them a curse that makes the target sickly and die at a predetermined time. This type of magic is challenging to counter. **The counter to this type of magic will be unlocked in Book 3.**

Death Storm- An ultimate Storm Magic spell taught only to select Storm Magic wielders at the Dragon Monastery. This spell typically comes in two main versions, the Scarlet Cloud or the

Dark Cloud versions. There are hybrid versions of the clouds, but those are usually the result of an imperfect casting of this spell or murderous intentions on a grand scale. The Scarlet Cloud version is the easiest one to learn. This version is intended to cause immense pain and burns on targets before they expire. The Scarlet Clouds will be accompanied by steaming hot rain that scorches their targets, and then the clouds will hit them with the Crimson Bolt. The Dark Cloud version is accompanied by Black Clouds that will rain down dark droplets of rain. The rain droplets are intended to fill the target with immense fear and muscle pain, making running away impossible. The Dark Clouds will release Black Onyx lightning bolts that instantly kill on contact. This spell is forbidden to be used by Dragon Masters 99.9% of the time. The reason is simple: this is a Disaster Level spell intended only to kill as many people as possible. This spell also ravages any community or biosystem in which it is conjured. The bolts of violent lightning may reappear randomly in the area where the spell is cast for years or even decades. Additionally, if friendly targets are near the spell, they are at great risk of being killed by lightning bolts if the caster does not have absolute control of the storm.

Defensive Magic- A school of Magic that focuses on defense. Most combat magic users will be taught defensive magic basics, typically involving the Auto-Shield technique. However, that training is not at the level in which individuals in this school are educated. In its basic form, it allows the user to approach combat from a defensive mindset, which includes hyper-awareness of attackers, the intentions of others, and even using their magic to give their physical body greater resistance toward damage that can break the skin. More advanced versions of this technique can allow them to bolster the resiliency of clothing or armor with their magic. Additionally, they can create physical or energy-based shields at will. Some of these shields can be optimized for defense or offense.

Deflection- A technique made to deflect and rebound projectiles. Originally, it was intended to combat arrow and high-speed magic attacks. Deflection is a spell that can be combined with Enhanced Reaction to deflect bullets. Requires a mild amount of magic to use.

Dimension (Enchantment)- Powerful magic that was created by The Elders. Magic of this type is designed to protect locations or property by creating a dimension for storing them. Magic of this type requires physical objects to serve as a boundary for the item or location.

Disarm- A technique used by Sword Magic and Martial Arts Magic practitioners. This technique requires the individual to summon magical energy or a weapon into their body. Once their energy level is high enough, the user must make contact with their opponent's weapon or magical tool. Upon contact, the individual's physical weapon will be flung out of their hand; if it is magically conjured, it will dissipate. Caution should be considered when using this technique as it does not always work. The stronger and/or quicker an opponent is, the chances it works successfully decrease. Advanced versions of this spell allow the user to hit the individual with a blast of magical energy from a distance that will disarm them and send them flying.

Dragon Sense- A technique invented by the Dragon Monastery. This skill is difficult to learn as it increases users' ability to smell and hear things they would not normally sense. This power should be used sparingly as it can overwhelm the caster, and they can risk rupturing their eardrum or damaging their ability to smell.

Dragon Sight- A technique invented by the Dragon Monastery. This is a difficult skill because it enhances the user's ability to see and survey the details of the land around them. This increase in sight ability can cause strain on the eyes and shouldn't be used for an extended period.

Dual-Cast - A technique where a magic user casts two spells simultaneously. While very similar to Combined Element, this technique is not a spell in and of itself. This technique is intended to use two spells in tandem. For example, a user might use a physical speed increase spell in conjunction with a gliding technique to temporarily fly.

Eagle Eye- This spell is similar to Dragon Sight but intends to be used for an extended time. Eagle Eye is a technique used with Arrow and Firearm magic. This allows the caster to see long distances without straining the eyes. Caution should be used when using this type of magic, as there is a delay in adjusting back to normal vision.

Elemental Arrow- A magical technique used by bowmen or wizards. If using a bow, the user must have an arrow designed for the magical element the individual intends to use. A wizard can summon and use this technique without a bow by summoning the arrow, using magical energy. Caution should be used with this technique, as the greater distance between the caster and their opponent will lessen the spell's potency.

Elemental Counter-This spell is an advanced technique that is not in many schools of magic. The basic intent of this spell is to absorb an incoming attack, whether kinetic or magical energy-based, then convert that attack and reflect it back on their enemy. For example, bullets are deflected by a sword, converted into that user's element of choice, and launched back at their target. Caution should be used when considering this technique as it does not work 100% of the time. Additionally, this technique can drain an individual's magical reserves rather quickly.

Enhanced Jump- This spell gives the caster increased jumping ability and allows them to land safely when jumping from a great height. The greater power the magic user has, the higher the jumping ability they will have.

Enhanced Movement- Similar to Enhanced Jump, Speed Magic users created this spell. Enhanced Movement, if channeled properly, can allow the user to dodge arrows and bullets. There is no guarantee that you will dodge them; it simply gives the user the ability to do so. Users can even move so quickly that it appears they have gone invisible and teleported to another location. That technique is sometimes called Invisibility Speed.

Enhanced Reaction- A technique that comes out of Speed Magic. This spell was originally intended to be used with Enhanced Movement. The user can react to rapidly moving targets and stimuli with this spell. When coupled with Deflection, a talented caster can deflect some bullets. Caution should be taken, as this spell drains a lot of magic and causes incredible strain on the human body.

Ensnare- A blue energy blast that can effectively trap and ensnare living creatures and the undead. Once the energy blast has wrapped around the target, the user can make the energy beams constrict and choke the target.

Esplosione- The most basic explosive spell. Creates a yellow ball of energy, and it explodes on contact. Esplosione can be charged to create a ball of energy as large or as small as the caster requires. This spell is not intended to be lethal and is better used for crowd control. An adept user of this spell can also imbue an object or a weapon with explosive energy. Once a significant amount of energy is imbued in the object, the object can cause an explosion on the target. Depending on the density of the object that is infused with the spell, the object may explode in the process. This means caution should be considered if there is a risk of shrapnel. Additionally, the lethality of this spell increases dramatically depending on the objects or weapons infused with this spell.

Eternal Magic- A type of spell that can never truly be destroyed; it can only change forms. Eternal magic can be imbued into a weapon, enchanting an object or even an area of land. This magic tends to be relatively old, and the concepts of any eternal magic spell are often passed down orally. The conditions to create eternal magic tend to require some sort of sacrifice. If the requirements of the sacrifice are not met, the spell will not work. Often, it will require a blood sacrifice or an individual's life. When a life is required for the sacrifice, it is more often than not going to require multiple souls, and they do not need to be voluntary. The greater the sacrifice, the greater the spell's strength and durability. Even once destroyed, the magic will still exist in the air and can only be reformed or changed once certain conditions are met.

Exact Copy- This is a Master-level technique that is popular among summoners. The caster can summon an object or creature that is an exact copy of another to be indistinguishable from the original. A Sage Level version of this technique can allow the caster to copy the enchantments and skills attached to the original object or creature. Caution should be considered when using this technique as the copied objects or summons tend to not last as often as normal summons. Only summoners with the ability to *Create* can extend the life of an Exact Copy.

Expanding Object (Enchantment)- An enchantment that allows an object, such as a bag, to expand. The expansion volume will be determined by the enchantment's power and the expanded item's material.

Expanding Object (Spell)- A spell that allows the spell caster to expand the size of a spell, a summon, or an object, such as a fire spell, a dragon, or even a bag to expand. The expansion volume will be determined by the enchantment's power and the expanded item's material. This spell is not as permanent as the enchantment version. The items only remain expanded when the spell is being used.

Familiar (Summon)-An advanced spell from the school summoning. This spell allows the caster to summon or create a creature or an item from their imagination or another plane of existence. Additionally, this spell allows the user to summon the creature or item repeatedly. With creatures, the user can gain a personal relationship with them, and the creature will retain its memories of the summoner. Recreated items can grow stronger and even be modified for the user. Additional stipulations for this technique **will be unlocked when Book Three is released.**

Fire Armor- A master-level spell that surrounds the caster in fire. The powerful magic causes the fire to spiral around the user, creating a barrier of protection. Fire armor toughens the user's skin, amplifies their speed, and intensifies any fire magic spell they possess. The downside of this spell is that it requires a massive amount of magical energy, and the user can typically only maintain it for a short period.

Fireball (Basic)- One of the earliest combat spells a fire user will learn. A ball of fire is created in the hand of the user, and it can be thrown to cause a modest amount of damage. This is a non-lethal spell and should be used as a deterrent.

Fireball (Advanced)- This intermediate spell requires more concentration than a normal fireball. The Advanced Fireball allows the user to create multiple projectiles of varying sizes. The temperature and color of the fireballs can be adjusted based on the user's needs. If the temperature and size of the fireballs are significant enough, they can be lethal. Fireball (Advanced) only permits use by Dragon Warriors prepping to complete their trials. There is a variant of this spell called Heatseeker. This spell version allows the user to summon a ball of fire that will lock on to a specific target or a series of targets. The Heatseeker is ideally used when hiding in a covered position or to be used if an enemy is hiding behind an obstacle. This spell can be deadly if enough fire magic is conjured but can also risk reducing its speed, giving the target a greater opportunity to block it.

FireBlast- This intermediate spell combines traditional heat, plasma energy, and fire magic. The user will channel their magical energy into a central location, such as their hands, weapon, or instrument. Once the energy level is adequate, the user can blast their target with this spell. Depending on the user's skill level and preference, this technique can appear as mostly energy blasts if the user emphasizes the plasma form of this combination spell. Additionally, if the user emphasizes the heat magic side of this spell, they can harm the user long before the blast gets there by the heated energy it will send out first. Now, if the user emphasizes the fire element in this spell, the technique can allow the blast to stick to the person and cause burns to the skin. However, the fire-emphasized version of this spell has a more limited range and tends to have a reduced speed compared to the others.

Fire Buddy- A small Sprite that is created using a minimal amount of magical energy. For a young Dragon Warrior who chooses the path of fire, this is the first fire spell they will learn. The Sprite can be conjured to reflect any personality or color the caster desires. If threatened or commanded by the fire user, the Sprite will explode, causing burns on the aggressor.

Fire Snake- Similar to Fire Buddy, the Fire Snake is conjured by the young Dragon Warrior. Fire Snake is usually the second or third fire spell a Dragon Warrior in training. For the caster to learn Fireball, they must master this spell. Fire Snake is considered a summoning spell, so the user must concentrate on creating its likeness and functionality. The creature can create irritation on an opponent's skin by having it crawl along an attacker. The snake can also explode, which can cause first-degree burns in extreme cases.

Firestorm- This is a Master Level Dual Element spell. The Firestorm requires combining high-level Fire Magic and Storm Magic. The caster will typically begin the spell by summoning dark clouds. The clouds will often be filled with bolts of lightning that slam down on opponents and are accompanied by balls of fire descending from the sky. Firestorm is a Disaster Level spell only intended for large-scale destruction. Variations of this spell can allow the user to create different storms as desired, such as blizzards, tornados, or even hurricanes. Some have been able to create Desert Storms infused with fire. An Ultimate Version of this spell can create a storm lasting for years or even decades. This spell is forbidden under most circumstances. Once summoned, it can quickly become uncontrollable and strengthen based on the weather conditions.

FireWhip- The caster summons a fire spell that attaches itself to an object. The object develops the qualities of a whip, giving the user great mobility in a combat scenario.

Fire Wall or Wall of Fire- A powerful spell that requires intense concentration to be used successfully. The fire user channels their energy and can create a protective and destructive barrier. The shape and size of the barrier are at the user's discretion.

FireWave- The user's arms become engulfed in red and yellow flames. The user must make a swiping motion across their body, and then a wave of flames is launched at their target. This technique is a non-lethal spell intended for groups of enemies.

FlameBolt (Normal Version)- This is a dual-element spell taught at the Dragon Monastery. This is an advanced technique that combines fire magic and lightning magic. The user summons a fireball with red and yellow flames. This ball of fire will become encircled by red bolts of lightning. Once this spell makes contact with an object, the fireball's heat and lightning's electricity can completely vaporize a target. This spell is absolutely lethal and is not intended to be used against most humans. The Flamebolt is useful against water-based creatures or intercepting water-based magic spells. This spell can only be used in a life-or-death situation against a water magic user who can liquify themselves. **More advanced versions of this Spell will be unlocked in Book 3.**

Flamethrower- This basic fire spell is intended to be used in close to mid-range quarters. The user summons a stream of fire intended to ward off or moderately injure a target. In advanced versions of this spell, the user can conjure this technique through an object, like a sword or wand, for increased accuracy. It can also increase the velocity and temperature of the spell.

Flame Ward- The spell caster conjures a small purple or red sprite. The sprite is designed to protect the user when they are in a vulnerable state, i.e., sleeping or injured. If someone breaches the established territory of the flame ward, the sprite will slam and explode against the invader. Advanced versions of this spell allow multiple sprites to be created. Master-level versions of this allow the sprite to reform after an explosion and continue to attack the transgressors.

Flashback- A spell that comes out of the school of Psychological Magic. This spell activates parts of the brain associated with long-term and short-term memory. The spell caster can then choose to amplify the emotions attached to those memories and twist the way the events in that memory took place. The receiver of this spell can re-experience the images of the memory in real-time. Caution should be taken when using this spell, as it can cause permanent brain damage and can cause suicidality. An even crueler version of this spell exists called the *Torture Type.* In this version, the individual can recall physical pain or even imagine in their mind pain they have never experienced, with or without visual stimulus to accompany it. The individual this spell is cast on can also experience pain so severe, that their body can start bleeding from open pores in the skin, which also leads to bursting blood vessels. Master-level practitioners of this technique have even made this spell cause ongoing effects on their target where nightmares or physical pain sensations from this spell are experienced repeatedly, long after the spell has been cast. Some individuals have experienced the residual effects of this spell decades after being cast by a master. The Sage-level casters of this version of this spell have made the individuals they cast a spell on lose their minds, and some have even experienced enough mental pain from the spell that they have gone into cardiac arrest.

FlashBang- The magic user creates a bright white or yellow light. The ball of energy can explode on contact or have a delayed detonation. If done correctly, FlashBang will cause temporary blindness and deafness on the intended target. The spell can rebound and affect the caster if incorrectly done.

Flash Freeze- An anti-object spell. Flash Freeze creates a temporary ice area that lasts five to ten minutes. This spell requires a moderate level of magic to cast and should be used sparingly.

Freeze Flame- This is a hybrid spell originally created by a wizard from the Southern Convent. Freeze Flame combines the traits of fire and ice magic. A blue or white flame is created. The opponent will feel a burning sensation similar to what one would experience from jumping into a frozen lake. Freeze Flame is a powerful spell that kills a fire or heat magic user.

Frost Bullet- An intermediate frost magic spell. This spell involves conjuring a shard of ice launched at the speed of a bullet at a target. The Frost Bullet spell can be summoned through an individual's skin and imbued into a weapon like a gun or a magical tool. This spell can create lethal or non-lethal Frost Bullets. Additionally, an individual can customize the bullets to fit their needs. Master Level practitioners of Frost Magic can even curve the Frost Bullets midflight.

FrostFlame Nekron- This is often considered a Fusion spell, as it requires understanding Dual-Cast and Combined Element principles. The FrostFlame Nekron begins by casting the Nekron spell, which involves bringing the dead to life. Typically, the conjurer will summon skeletal warriors from the ground around them. Using a staff or a wand can amplify the power of this spell. The Nekron are infused with the FreezeFlame spell, which imbues them with the power of frost and fire. Once cast, the Nekron will have all their abilities enhanced and possess the ability to use magic, and their vulnerabilities are greatly reduced. This spell, once cast, will remain in effect until the Nekron are completely destroyed; the spell will not fade away once magical energy is reduced or even if the caster is killed.

Frostslide - A spell from the school of Frost magic and is the icy cousin of RockSlide. The Frostslide spell involves the user summoning large blocks of ice intended to be dropped upon and crush targets. This spell requires the user to launch a beam of magical energy that makes contact with a piece of land or can be directed toward a spot in the air above the ground. Once these conditions are met, the ice blocks will begin to speed toward the intended target as they descend. However, if the angles of descent are inadequate or the ground is too flat, the spell will cancel itself out.

Geyser- An intermediate water spell that combines water magic with heat magic. The caster will typically stab a weapon or staff into the ground. Then, a puddle or a hole will appear beneath the target or series of targets. Once enough magical power has been channeled, a super-heated blast of water will burst skyward from beneath the target or targets. This technique should be used cautiously as the spell is tough to contain once the water bursts. Additionally, the water in this spell can be lethal from the pressure alone and the heated liquid.

Glide- This is a technique that is taught in many schools of magic. The user conjures their magical power to propel them in the desired direction. This typically requires the user to jump from a lofted position. In advanced versions of this technique, the user can go into a glide without jumping from an elevated position and can do so from a standstill. A Master of this spell can convert a glide into the Flight Spell, allowing them to ascend and descend as desired. However, the distance they can cover is greatly reduced compared to the actual Flight Spell technique.

Gun Magic- This style of Magic is commonly taught to select soldiers in the various militaries worldwide. The Gun Magic techniques are similar to other magical styles, where a specific spell is not always required to produce the magical results that the user requires. This makes it very appetizing for training soldiers as the dedication to learn the basic methods is not lengthy. The basic approach involves the user channeling their magical energy into their firearm, bullets, or a combination. Once enough magic is infused into the weapon or projectile, they can use their magic to change the elemental properties of the weapon. They can even allow the user to attach a homing enchantment to the projectiles. Advanced users of this technique can increase the number of bullets they carry using their magic alone, without carrying boxes of bullets on their person.

Additionally, the users can even develop the ability to change the density of the bullets or the length of a gun barrel with their magic. Master Level practitioners of this style of magic are said to be able to even control bullets fired from another person or firearm. Some are even rumored to be able to control the trajectory of rockets or artillery rounds.

Grenade- A spell that comes from the school of Explosive Magic. The spell caster summons a ball of yellow energy, and the object explodes on contact. Depending on the skill of the magic user, the explosions can be delayed or amplified. This spell can be used in a lethal or non-lethal capacity.

Hail Storm- A deadly storm typically conjured by using a staff or other magical weapons. Hailstorm is a potent spell that creates intense gusts of wind, dark clouds, sheets of rain, and hail that can get as large as a soccer ball. Like most storm magic, this spell is difficult to control and can last longer than the magic user intends. Dragon Warriors who are taught this spell are forbidden to use it within cities or large communities.

Healing Drip/Rain- An intermediate healing spell taught to Storm Magic users. This spell involves summoning a green-colored cloud that drips green liquid or rains down droplets on a target or targets. The spell is intended for moderate to severe injuries and is especially helpful in treating head wounds. Depending on the severity of the injury, the individual will need to rest under the droplets of water for anywhere from 30 minutes to a couple of hours. The Healing Drip specializes in reducing inflammation from an injury and can assist in blocking pain receptors. The spell can also be used in emergency situations to create dramatic healing.

Heavy Fog- This spell creates a blanket of fog. The user can set the amount of fog that is produced. However, weather conditions at the time can impact how much total fog can be produced. Advanced versions of this spell can even disrupt radar instruments and drain the magic produced by any spell that enters the fog. The Sage Level version of this spell can even create a permanent haze of fog in fixed areas. The Sage version of this spell is banned under most circumstances.

Holy Flame Armor- White flames form around the caster when channeling this spell. This magic increases the user's resistance to piercing weapons, holy magic, and minor fire spells. Holy Flame Armor, like all armor spells taught at the Dragon Monastery, will increase the user's speed, agility, and reaction time. This spell will automatically switch the user's normal fire magic spells into holy magic spells. With this change in spell properties, this armor makes it an effective tool against the undead and dark magic users. Holy Flame Armor is resistant to dark and death magic to a point. If too much negative energy is absorbed by the armor, it will likely dissipate or change to what is called Tainted Flame Armor.

Holy Fire- A fire magic spell that uses holy and positive magical properties. Holy Fire is effective against dark magic users and the undead. This type of spell can also be mildly effective against water magic spells.

Holy/Fire Armor Hybrid- A highly volatile master-level spell. This armor spell combines the properties of fire and holy armor spells. This hybrid technique can double and even triple the user's movement speed. In addition to that, the user's magical spells have an increased potency. This armor benefits fire users by hiding moderately increased resistance to water and intense ice magic spells. However, caution should be used when attempting this spell as it drains the individual's magic quickly. It can burn up and kill the spell caster.

Holy Ghost Armor/ Ἅγιος *Yūrei* Armor- A Master Level Armor spell. This spell combines the Holy Fire Armor and the Ghost Flame Armor. The user will begin this spell by channeling the holy and ghost flames around them. This spell allows the user to reap the benefit of holy magic, making them more resistant against dark or black flame magic. The *Yūrei*/Ghost Flame Armor will grant the user resistance to all fire magic and can make them more lethal against all fire magic users.

Combining these two techniques is unique, as the Ghost Flames will draw from the individual's life force, and the Holy Flames will draw from their magic reserves. This combination of magical techniques is a challenge, as the color of the flames must be perfectly balanced to reap equal benefits from both techniques. However, if the individual is critically low on magical energy, the Holy Flames can be fully fueled by the individual's life force to extend that power. Extreme caution should be considered when using this technique because even when the spell is perfectly balanced, or even if the holy flames represent the majority in the individual's conjuring of this technique, they could still run the risk of running out of life energy and being killed by their own spell. Additionally, a caster is at great risk of death even while learning and practicing this technique.

Holy Seraph- A hybrid spell that combines fire and holy magic. This master-level spell creates a large, powerful snake covered in white holy flames. The snake smashes into its target. If the target isn't powerful enough, it will be vaporized.

Lightning Blast- This spell is popular amongst lightning and storm magic users. The caster summons a series of lightning bolts at a target in its most basic form. For storm magic users, this spell by itself is weaker as their lightning attacks are stronger when caused by an actual storm. Lightning magic users have greater versatility with this spell. They can modify the range of the lightning at will and can summon multiple bolts.

Icicle- A lethal shard of ice between three to ten feet is summoned by a magic user. The edges of the icicles are sharp enough to cut through metal. More devious and advanced ice magic users can even cause the icicles to splinter and spread shards within the flesh of their intended victim.

Instant Duststorm- With a flick of the wrist, the magic user conjures a Dust storm. Unlike most storm spells, this one does not have a delay in summoning. Due to the quick nature of this spell, the caster needs to have complete awareness of their target and the magical energy to summon it.

Intuition- A spell that allows the user to examine the thoughts or feelings of another person. More advanced versions of this spell can give the user greater insight and/or accuracy related to what another person might think. A master of this technique would be able to know exactly what that person was thinking, to the point that they could write down verbatim the inner workings of another individual.

Inner Turmoil- A spell that comes from the field of Psychological Magic. This spell was invented near the end of the Great War by The Elders. Inner Turmoil allows the caster to aggravate an individual's insecurities and twist their morals. This spell can functionally control a person's actions and mind if used as intended. Inner Turmoil is a rare spell requiring a wealth of magic and concentration. The caster is at risk of splitting their own mind while trying to control their target. Inner Turmoil is a banned spell worldwide, even amongst the Witch Covenants; it's considered a spell of pure evil. The spell of Inner Turmoil is similar to *Control*. However, the prime difference between the two is that this technique uses the target's pain to gain compliance. This technique can also be *Dual-Cast* with the *Control* spell, to gain greater power over the individual.

Lightning Magic/Lightning Manipulation- A favorite spell and technique used by storm and lightning magic users. In its basic form, this spell allows a caster to summon lightning for whatever their intended purpose. This technique allows the caster to use lightning as they will without having to cast a specific lightning spell. Advanced versions of this spell can allow the caster to somewhat manipulate lightning and electric currents in the air. The Master Level version of this spell can allow them to manipulate the flow of lightning from a massive storm and increase the intensity of each lightning strike. The Sage Level version of this technique is rumored to be able to conjure lightning from other planets.

Limiter (Enchantment)- An enchantment designed to limit the maximum amount of magic an individual can use. This enchantment can be imbued into objects and even placed on the skin. More enhanced versions of this enchantment can limit specific spells and even magic-enhanced physical abilities. The Limiter enchantment is very hard to fight against. However, it is not a perfect solution for limiting the power or magic of another person.

Magenta Flame (General)- A series of fire magic techniques created by the Phoenix Monastery. As determined by the caster, the magenta-colored flames can be adjusted to their size and lethality. Instead of relying on particular spells, the caster can adjust the magic output using this technique to fit their needs. Additionally, one of the unique differences between the magenta fire-related spells is that in addition to causing burn damage to a target, they can also cause status ailments. So, a caster can infuse a spell to make a person sick to their stomach or experience hot flashes in addition to experiencing burns from the fire spell. Even if a target has an affinity for fire magic, they can still be injured by the kinetic energy of the spell and still be afflicted with status ailments. Adept users of the Magenta flame can also use it to heal a target from an illness or an injury. Depending on the severity of the injury, contiguous chanting will be required in the Ancient Languages of *The Elders* or *Precursors*. The Master Level technique of this technique can even cause permanent status ailments on a target.

Melodic- A beautiful sound enters the intended target's ear, and they feel calm. More advanced versions can create delusions and deep sleep. Melodic is a spell created by an individual's vocal cords or through an instrument. This spell was originally developed to address high anxiety and individuals who have night terrors.

Mental Text- This is an advanced technique from the school of Bonding Magic. The Mental Text spell is intended to communicate with one or more parties. In its basic form, an individual can communicate the basic premise or idea they are thinking about to another person. An adept user of this spell can actually transfer a series of thoughts from one person to another. A Master level user of this spell can even send mental images of words directly into another individual's line of sight. This spell is similar to telepathy spells, but this spell is much more limited and is harder for other magical users to intercept.

Metallo Thermotata- A simple heat magic spell that can warm up metallic objects. Metallo Thermotata is a spell capable of melting metal if the user can channel enough magic power.

Meteor (Basic)- A spell created by the first Dragon Sage. Only the best-trained and self-controlled Dragon Warriors are taught this spell. Meteor is a spell that is conjured by thought or by vocalization. A medium to large-sized fireball is created in the hand of the spell caster. An iron core is created in the center of the fireball and then launched toward an adversary. This spell can only be used as a last resort and is one of the few lethal fire spells taught to Dragon Warriors.

Meteor (Advanced)- This is one of the most powerful fire spells taught to Dragon Masters. When the magic user summons this spell, a large fireball is created with a core made of iron. In its advanced form, the user can control the meteors with their mind and can even conjure them at a distance. A true master of this technique can summon multiple meteors at a time. Caution should be used when attempting this spell, as it can drain a lot of magical energy.

Monsoon- Storm magic spell that creates a powerful monsoon. This is like most weather control spells, requiring conditions in the area of effect to be favorable for this type of storm. If conditions are in the area where the spell is conjured, magical energy can be drawn from a person's life force.

Nekron- A powerful spell that brings the dead to life. Typically, the conjurer will summon skeletal warriors from the ground around them. More advanced versions of this spell allow flesh to form on the skeletal bodies. Using a staff or a wand can amplify the power of this spell. A caster using this type of magic should be cautious, as the Nekron are vulnerable to fire and holy magic.

Oceanic Thunderstorm- This is an advanced Storm Magic technique. The user can cast a thunderstorm over a body of salt water. The spell will be followed by intense gusts of wind, lightning, and thunder. Additionally, the storm can create massive tidal waves from the wind. Once cast, this spell is difficult to control, if not impossible. This spell can endure as long as the weather conditions support it. Even if the user is completely out of magic.

Pain Blocker Shield- The caster summons a light blue shield. Once enough magic is infused into the shield, the individual or individuals will experience a reduction in pain they have received from an injury or illness. Advanced versions of this spell can significantly reduce pain sensations from broken bones in different body parts. It can also be cast on multiple people, including animals or monsters. The more individuals this is cast on at a time, the less effective the spell will be. Master Level users of this spell can completely block an individual's pain receptor like an opioid drug can. Caution should be used when using this spell as it is only intended to block pain; it is not designed to heal injuries and only mildly reduces inflammation. Additionally, individuals who receive a large dose of this spell can find their nerves more sensitive to pain once the spell is lifted, and receiving this spell can become habit-forming.

Quick Change- A transformation spell that allows the caster to change their outer garments in the blink of an eye. For this spell to work, the caster must be able to imagine whatever garments they intend to wear.

QuickDry- A Heat Magic spell that can dry skin and other materials. Caution should be used when attempting this spell, as it can cause skin burns and combustion if used on clothing.

QuickFreeze- An anti-human/anti-monster ice spell. The target becomes encased in ice and becomes immobilized. QuickFreeze is a non-lethal ice spell, and its effects are temporary. This spell is ineffective against most fire or heat magic users and can sometimes be effective against water magic conjurers.

Rage (Uncontrolled)- This spell is almost as old as magic. When Rage is activated, the user's eyes turn bright red. Usually, the rage is activated by intense pain or anger. The caster's magical and physical abilities are doubled or quadrupled in this form. Due to the amount of energy expelled when the spell is activated, the rage cannot last more than ten or thirty minutes. Caution should be used when activating this spell, as the magic caster loses all sense of control. When the spell is over, the user is extremely vulnerable. Intense depression, anxiety, and psychosis can occur after the spell is cast.

Rage (Semi-Controlled)- Ancient magic created during the Great War, also known as the Red Eye. In this iteration, the user has semi-control over their rage. The individual's base magic and physical abilities can be doubled or tripled. With the added control, the user can take fuller advantage of the power increase. Caution should be used when attempting this spell, as it takes years to hone. In addition to that, since it is semi-controlled, the rage does not last as long, and it is very easy for the user to lose control of their rage.

❖ Rage (Right Eye)- A subset of the Semi-Controlled Rage. In this case, instead of both eyes turning bright red, just the right eye will change colors. In this iteration, the individual will gain a steep boost in their magical abilities that are on par with the original Rage form. However, the time the power boost will last is significantly lower than both Semi-Controlled and Uncontrolled versions. Additionally, this form can put the individual at a greater risk of entering Uncontrolled Rage than the Semi-Controlled and Left Eye only Rage.

❖ Rage (Left Eye)-A subset of the Semi-Controlled Rage. In this version, the left eye is the only one that changes color. This version is accompanied by a moderate increase in physical and magical abilities. The Left Eye version, while not as powerful as the other Rage forms. has the greatest potential longevity for its power boost. Since it drains significantly less magic than the other versions, the user can sustain its power for much longer. Some Masters of this specific technique have been rumored to be able to do it indefinitely. Caution should be considered when using this version because the longer a person remains in its boosted form, the greater the risk of falling into the Uncontrolled Rage. The reason is they may feel a temptation for more combat power or underestimate the impact their emotions are having on their state of being.

Rapid Shot-An advanced version of the fireball spell. This spell involves releasing a series of fireballs from the knuckles or the palms. The fireballs are released toward a target as the user does a series of punches or palm strikes. Adept users of this spell can customize the color, size, and speed of the fireballs released. Additionally, an adept user can pull from the fire magic type of armor used at the time to give the rapid shot an even greater magical boost and tactical use. Master Level users of this spell can also combine principles of the HeatSeeker technique with this spell to greater effect. Caution should be considered when using this spell as the Rapid Shot can only be conjured for a limited amount of time, and it is tough to track and aim each shot properly.

Rebound- This is a defensive magic skill capable of bouncing any spell back against an enemy. Rebound is an advanced magic spell and requires an extreme amount of concentration to work. The user must understand how an oncoming spell is intended to work. With that understanding in mind, the caster can say, "rebound," and the spell will strike back at the enemy.

Depending on the caster's power, Rebound can also amplify the magic in the spell. Caution should be used when trying this spell, as there is a 50% chance of failure.

Repel- A blue ball of energy is expelled from the caster. Repel can affect both living and non-living beings. This is a type of defensive magic and requires a minimal amount of energy. Caution should be used when activating this spell against powerful magic users because it can be deflected and canceled out.

SandWall- A powerful earth magic spell. The user conjures a wall of earth that becomes impenetrable. Sandwall requires objects to create the wall. If the dirt or sand products are buried beneath concrete, the magic user must be strong enough to pull some dirt to the surface.

Scarlet Bolt- This is a duel element spell. The practitioner summons scarlet-colored bolts of electricity. The user infuses those bolts of lightning with heat magic and plasma. Once a target is struck by this spell, the lightning bolts will slowly wrap around the target. Then, the spell will explode, leaving the target covered in smoke. This spell is similar to the crimson bolt technique of storm magic practitioners. A major difference is that this spell's deadliness is delayed until the spell explodes. Therefore, this spell is not ideal for most combat situations. Another difference is that if the practitioner is skilled enough, it can assist someone whose heart has stopped.

Seraph- This master-level spell creates a large, powerful snake covered in orange or red flames. The snake smashes into a target, and if the target isn't powerful enough, they will be vaporized. Hybrid-specific versions of this spell, such as the Holy Seraph, can be conjured in specifics as the caster needs. However, a unique ability of the general Seraph spell is that the flames of the snake can become whatever fire armor the individual is in at the time. Instead of conjuring a magically draining hybrid spell, they can simply pull from their armor's magic.

soZo- One of the most powerful healing spells taught by individuals of elven descent. This magical ability requires the user to chant an elven parable. The spell is powerful enough to stop internal bleeding, heal some bone fractures, and moderate organ damage. Due to the amount of energy required, a healer best conducts this spell.

Spirit Flame- The caster summons a light blue crown of fire. This spell is an advanced fire magic healing spell taught by the Phoenix Monastery. This spell is intended to help treat head wounds. Specifically concussions, brain bleeds, and some traumatic brain injuries. Caution should be considered when using this spell on moderate or severe head injuries. This spell is no substitute for medical intervention in most severe cases. Additionally, this spell needs to be administered soon after an injury is acquired. If not administered quick enough, this spell will have no healing effect.

Split Arrow- An ability that is traditionally used by qualified bowmen and magic users who summon elemental arrows. When an arrow is fired or summoned by the user, when the projectile is launched, it gains the ability to split into multiple objects. An adept user can adjust the size of the projectiles when they are split. Master-level bowmen and wizards can even combine this spell with elemental magic to amplify the accuracy of the arrows.

SplinterBolt- An Advanced Storm Magic spell that is intended for multiple targets. This spell involves channeling one's magical energy into their body, weapon, or magic tool and then infusing it into a desired location or object. Users often press their hands or weapons against the ground, a wall, or a tree. Once contact is made, bolts of lighting will disseminate from the location it has been infused with and will actively pursue any targets in the vicinity. Caution should be considered when using this spell because it cannot be controlled once cast, and the user is at risk of being struck by the spell.

StarBlast- This is a spell from the school of Galactic Magic and a technique used by monsters. A bright yellow light shaped like a star is conjured. This spell can then strike an enemy, typically followed by an explosion. More advanced techniques can be applied to this spell, such as adding a specific element or metallic core. One should be cautious when using this spell because it is very destructive and can cause unintended implosions on targets such as *Blackholes.*

Storm Barrier (Base)- This spell creates a cage around an intended target. The storm barrier begins with clouds being summoned slightly above the target or targets. The size of the clouds summoned, and their overall thickness will determine the size of the cage. A target caught in this cage will be struck by yellow lightning bolts. The yellow lightning bolts are intended to paralyze the target.

Storm Barrier (Azul Bolt Version)- This is an advanced version of the Storm Barrier. This technique is designed to create a cage around a moderately strong target or group of targets. The storm barrier begins with clouds being summoned slightly above the target or targets. The size of the clouds summoned, and their overall thickness will determine the size of the cage. Yellow and blue lightning bolts will strike a target in this cage. The yellow lightning bolts are intended to paralyze the target. The blue lightning bolts are intended to cause immense pain to the target and can even create permanent scarring if exposed to the lightning for too long.

Storm Barrier (Crimson Azul Bolt Version)- A master-level version of the Storm Barrier Family of spells. This technique is designed to create a cage around an exceptionally strong target or group of targets. The storm barrier begins with clouds being summoned slightly above the target or targets. The size of the clouds summoned, and their overall thickness will determine the size of the cage. A target caught in this cage will be struck by crimson and blue lightning bolts. Crimson lightning is intended to paralyze the target and inflame nerves throughout the individual's body. The blue lightning bolts are intended to cause immense pain to the target and can even create permanent scarring if exposed to the lightning for too long. Caution should be used when considering this barrier because extended exposure to crimson lightning bolts will kill the target.

Summoning Spells- This magical technique allows the caster to conjure monsters or objects to do their bidding. Intense concentration is required to summon creatures and control them. Most summons will last only a few minutes. A rare skill within summoning magic is the ability to summon familiars. A familiar is a specific summoned creature or item that can be conjured up repeatedly. For example, a creature that is a familiar will remember its summoner. With a more advanced version of this technique, a user can create living beings that exist in another dimension or from their imagination. They can also store weapons in another dimension. Creatures brought into this world from another dimension that are created can gain strength and familiarity with their summoner over time. Weapons and items stored in another dimension and summoned will require a magic circle and/or a summoning circle to bring into this dimension. Enchantments can be placed on items and or weapons so that they will eventually return to the aforementioned dimension if they are ever lost. The skill to bring items back is known as **CallBack.**

SUPERNOVA- An absolute terror of a fire spell. This spell is one of a handful of fire spells that can destroy whole land masses. The SUPERNOVA is a spell known by a few fire magic users for that reason. Once cast, the spell will vaporize any target and destroy any competing magical energy signatures in its path. The SUPERNOVA also has an Eternal Magic version often imbued into magic stones. Once the spell is used from the magic stone, it will not be useable again without the sacrifice of the blood of a skilled fire magic user. **Caution should be considered if a person ever uses this spell, as it is challenging to destroy, and the caster is more likely to be killed before the spell fully manifests itself.**

Technical Boom- This is a spell that is taught to magical practitioners who are highly skilled in the area of status ailments. The Technical Boom can be conjured with or without a magical channeling tool. This spell requires the caster to say the name of the spell for it to come to fruition. This spell cannot be wordlessly cast. Once the words exit the user's mouth, the world around them and any enemies around them will begin with a blindly bright white flash followed by a flash of black light. Once these flashes subside, witnesses of the spell will regain their normal perception of the world around them. However, the intended targets of that spell will begin ailing from whatever status ailment they receive. This spell draws from every status ailment a person can experience; this includes burns, confusion, fear of sleep, and even being turned into a frog. A Master-level user of this spell can channel their magic into the spell, potentially letting them influence which status ailments a specific target receives instead of making it random.

Teleport (Enchantment)- Similar to its spell form, teleportation via enchantment requires extreme concentration by the caster initiating it. An enchantment that uses teleportation magic can only transport the individual to a corresponding location. Depending on the enchantment placed on the object, an individual can recover from injuries while teleporting.

Teleport (Spell/Element Transport)- Teleportation is very difficult to use in spell form. Teleport is a technique that requires extreme concentration. The caster must have an exact picture of the location they are going to in their mind for the spell to work. Teleportation is only instant if the traveler is going fifty miles. Any distances exceeding fifty miles may take an hour or a day to arrive. Teleportation is a technique usually taught to masters and dark magic users. Like the basic spell version, a caster can teleport to and through their elemental spells or formations of their element in nature. A caster who uses fire magic can transport a fire to where it is burning naturally. They can also transform into the element and reappear elsewhere. For example, a caster could transform into a puddle of water and reappear as a puddle in another location.

Thermal Grenade- The user forms an orange and yellow ball of energy. This is one of the most powerful grenade spells. Thermal Grenade combines the energy of a normal explosive spell with fire magic's heat and burning damage. Caution should be used when attempting this spell. The fire energy in this spell is lethal and destructive.

Thermo Therapeuo- The user channels their magic to be bestowed on another person or persons. This spell can relieve some physical pain but is more intended to assist in relaxing muscle tension, mild-moderate anxiety, or depression. The spell was invented by the Dragon Monastery for individuals in combat or disaster zones. Still, it can also be used in sports medicine and psychiatry. The relief from this spell is most often temporary. Advanced users of this spell can set it to reoccur throughout the day for the target. Master Level users of this spell can set it at the same potency as anti-depressant/ anti-anxiety medications. They even can be on par with muscle relaxers. Caution should be used when considering this spell, as some individuals may become overwhelmed by the sensations and reliant on it.

Think of Death- A perfect marrying of magical properties of Psychological Magic and Death Magic. The user can conjure either white or black magical energy. This energy will be launched toward a target or series of targets. Upon contact, the user will feel pain so severe that they will think they are dying. This spell often comes with auditory, olfactory, and visual hallucinations. If the energy conjured is white, the individual will mostly feel the psychological effects of the spell. If the energy is black, the individual will feel the mental and psychological effects of the spell briefly and then will go into a death-like coma. The coma is mentally triggered. So, if the individual wakes up from the spell, they might not view the physical present as actual reality. They may view it as a moment after death and interpret the real world as the afterlife. The unfortunate souls who experience the effects of this spell might only have to live with them for a few minutes or a lifetime.

Thunderbolt- This spell appears similar to most lightning attacks. However, this technique is slightly different. In its basic form, the user conjures a yellow lightning bolt that slams down onto a target from above. This spell is intended to create temporary paralysis on a target and cause moderate damage to an enemy. A spell like this can be amplified by the conditions in the atmosphere that can be conducive to creating powerful thunderstorms.

Transformation- A rare skill for any magic user to have. This type of magic is usually passed down hereditarily, but aspects of it can be taught. Transformation in its basic form can allow a person to transform a limb or an item into whatever the caster desires. The more drastic the change, the more magic is required. Transformation in its more advanced forms allows users to transform their whole body and clothing. Caution should be used when attempting any transformation magic. If the user is off by a fraction, they can experience severe physical injury and even a permanent transformation.

Water Manipulate/Wave Control- A spell often used by storm or water magic users. This spell allows the user to manipulate water magic as needed without conjuring a specific water-based spell. This technique can also allow the practitioner to gain control over bodies of water to some degree. A more advanced version of this spell can allow the user to control waves somewhat. Some practitioners summon with specific properties, such as bogs or swamps. Highly trained practitioners can summon water from hot springs without combining a water spell with Heat magic. Master-level users of this spell can have greater control of bodies of water and can control more waves at a given time. Caution should be used to conjure this spell as the user's control is still limited, and it can cause unintended chain reactions.

Water Sense- This technique is unique among water and some storm magic users. In its simplest form, the user can sense some objects or creatures in small to medium-sized bodies of water. The more advanced versions of this spell could be used to sense creatures and objects in larger bodies of water such as seas or lakes. The Master's Level of this technique can allow a user to sense individual creatures and objects within a large body of water with moderate accuracy.

White Death- A Master Level hybrid fire spell. This technique combines the Holy Flame spell, FireBlast, and the Flame Ward technique. The spell begins with the user channeling holy fire magic into the person or magical tool they choose. Once enough magic is channeled, the user will release a large blast of plasma energy toward their target. When the target or targets are struck, the spell will explode. White Flame Wards will be produced as the target is consumed by the explosion. The Flame Wards will then spread across the target's body, making them appear to have caught fire. The target will be burned by the Flame Wards on top of them. The Flame Wards will explode randomly if the target moves even an inch. This spell is absolutely devastating to Dark Magic users and Dark Creatures. The louder the individual says the spell's name and the longer they give the spell to charge, the more powerful it will become. Caution should be used when considering this spell as it takes time to conjure and is not instant like other magical techniques. Additionally, the user must keep their mind focused while using this spell. If their thoughts fall into the darkness, the spell will be converted into its cousin, the **Dark Flames of Death Blast.**

Wind Gust- A basic storm spell that conjures a gust of wind. Formally trained storm magic users and mature practitioners can acquire this spell. An adept spell caster can use this spell to intensify the wind's speed and power. More advanced users can use the wind gust to launch forward and even glide in the air. Some have reported that master-level users can use this spell to fly for short periods.

Yūrei- A technique often called the ghost flame. This technique is recognized by the gray flames produced by the technique. The **_Yūrei_** flames are intended to be used in environments where fire magic cannot be adequately summoned or to be used against someone who may possess some immunity against fire magic. In addition, the **_Yūrei_** will immediately increase the individual's speed, strength, and the intensity of their fire-based spells. Caution should be used when considering activating this technique. Some of the negative symptoms of this spell include harsh breathing and blood dripping from pours, open wounds, and even old injuries. This spell draws from the individual's life force, and extended use of this technique will cause the user to bleed out and perish. The more blood the individual releases from the body and the harsher their breathing becomes, the greater their power will be while using this technique. This spell is a Master-level technique and is forbidden in most circumstances.

Tony

Sarah

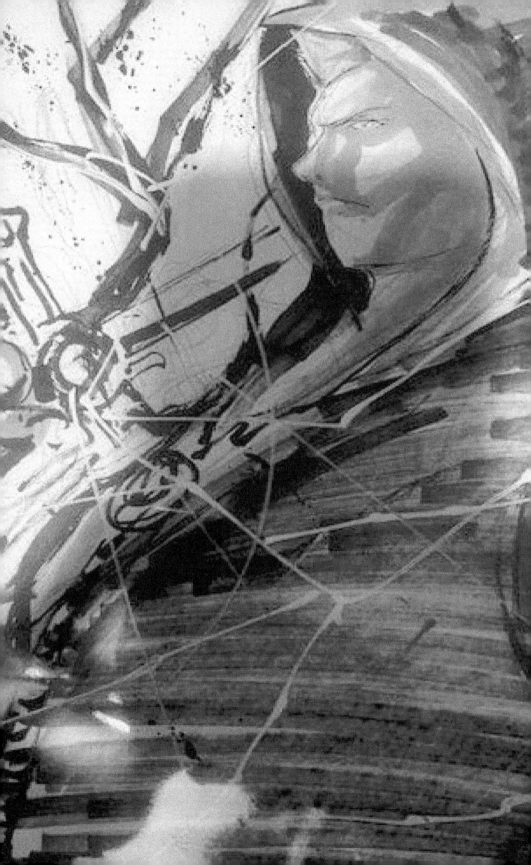